TALLIS'
THIRD TUNE

MIDWINTER SONATA
BOOK 1

ELLEN L. EKSTROM

Whyte Rose & Violet, Scribes

Tallis' Third Tune
ISBN: 978-0692024201
Published in the United States of America
Tallis' Third Tune is a work of fiction. Names,
characters, places, and incidents either are the
product of the author's imagination or are
used fictitiously, and any resemblance to
actual persons, living or dead, business
establishments, events, or locales is
entirely coincidental.

Cover design: Whyte Rose & Violet Artists
Images courtesy of deepblue4u, AdobeStock, and
Susan Stewart, iStockPhoto.com by Getty Images

Whyte Rose & Violet, Scribes
www.whyteroseandviolet.net

To the Quinns and Donovans of Life, and Especially the Alices....

TALLIS'
THIRD TUNE

CHAPTER 1

MY STORY BEGAN much in the same way as any other, say, for example, David Copperfield.

I was born.

Where it concerns this story, however, it was a different kind of birth, one that began with death.

I heard the conversation, and they called it around twelve oh-two in the morning—at precisely the same time as my birth, strangely enough. Even so, I'd like to respectfully disagree with those who assumed things they should not: that I died.

I did not die; I am not dead. Not yet, at least.

At least, I hope not.

Oh, wait…

I didn't remember the exact moment of my demise, nor did I remember pain. I remembered *minutia*, like ordering breakfast, or waiting for transit, or falling to sleep clearly as if it were a second ago—but then, I knew somehow that I existed in *kairos* rather than *kronos*. A second in *kairos* is a thousand years on Earth.

Objects and places, people, appeared out of the ether like rainbows—there wasn't a bright light to herald comings and goings, but soft flows of color became shapes, then objects, then people, and places. For example, when I wrote this, I was sitting in what looked like a See's Candy Store, the one at the convergence of Market, Sutter, and Sansome in San Francisco. Still, it was set in a picturesque English village, perhaps somewhere in the

Cotswolds or Dorset, somewhere in Thomas Hardy's imagination—or mine. There were yellow daffodils and freesias in vases on every counter; the display case wasn't stocked with caramels or almond bark or Bordeaux creams but with books. Little leather volumes with straps across the front cover—like a child's diary, the one you had to open with a key that usually hung around your neck along with a skate key, keeping one's secrets safe from a brother's or parents' inquiring eyes.

Small casks of parquetry wood were on the shelves where heart-shaped boxes of nut chews and creams usually sat. There was a coffee bar with an espresso machine and a display case full of cheesecakes of every variety: classic, berry, and chocolate. There were round café tables with heart-backed, cushioned chairs to match and yellow gingham curtains on the mullioned windows. It was as if I had entered one of those faux Victorian shops at Disneyland.

Over the counter was a medieval sign with the word "CURIOS?" in great purple letters—curious in English. I called my home away from home, my way station on the way to wherever I was going, "The Curiosity Shop," or just "The Shop."

Yet I was the only one in The Shop who was curious.

No one seemed to mind that I was sitting in the corner farthest from the door with my laptop. My Starbucks coffee travel mug, the one with the strawberries on it, was never drained of its cappuccino: small, skim milk, no cinnamon. I had a bottle of Diet Pepsi, too, and that was always cold, never lost its fizz. A messenger bag crammed with notebooks was slung over the back of the chair with a Prada bag.

People came and went quietly. Many were strangers to me; most were historical people I studied, wrote about, and idolized. A few approached The Proprietress, a stern, beautiful woman who resembled Helen Mirren, but Mirren as she portrayed Queen Elizabeth II. Her hair was coiffed in a 1950s bob, and around her neck was an opera-length strand of exquisite pearls. She wore an ill-fitting, severe blue suit and carried a Princess Grace-style handbag in the crook of her arm. I looked down at her feet and nodded in approval; at least she wore Vivien Westwood pumps: Anglomania—Lady Dragon, to be precise.

Customers' needs were met efficiently and with an economy of motion and conversation. Once in a while, a cask came down from the shelf. Sometimes the book in burgundy leather with gold-tooled arabesques came out of the case, sometimes the vermillion with silver findings, but never the book in lapis lazuli suede with silver clasp and decoration. I wanted more than anything to see what was in that book and gaze down at the mysterious trinkets in casks that were unlocked, opened, and locked up quickly and replaced on a shelf.

One thing was sure: I must have been dreaming.

Or…*I really was dead.*

For I looked up from my writing one day, and standing out on the sidewalk looking in was my brother Dennis, who died at the age of thirty-one. When our eyes met, I felt the breath go out of me, then a surge of adrenalin coursed through me like an electrical current. He smiled, every dimple increasing, and turned away, walking into a hat shop across the street.

This occurred several times, perhaps seven in as many days until I couldn't stand it. "Dennis!" I shouted after him. "Denny!"

I was out the door and in the high street dodged the traffic, though when a taxi came at me, I froze and waited for my imminent demise—*which didn't happen.* The cab went through me and sped around the corner to the bridge. Yes, it was one of those cinematic moments when all I could do was stare at my hands and torso while other vehicles and people collided with me, and yet nothing happened to them or me, and nothing had changed. I didn't look transparent or ethereal or wear gossamer or wings. I looked the same as I did.

When I was sixteen!

I had been fifty-seven when I fell asleep, or the last time I remembered falling asleep.

After these moments of revelation, I bolted after Dennis into the hat shop.

The doorbell rang sweetly when I pushed the latch and entered a nineteenth-century establishment. No one seemed to pay attention to me, certainly not The Proprietress—again, the woman resembling Helen Mirren in a severe blue suit. Customers were trying on hats and whispering as if it were a library or they were in the middle of a church service. In fact, over the door was a placard demanding "SILENCE, PLEASE!"

A shop assistant in a Regency gown thrust a cloche at me: pale blue with white, mauve, and yellow roses tucked into the crown band. It went well with the Laura Ashley dress I found myself suddenly wearing. When I turned to admire myself in the full-length mirror behind me, I was face to face with Dennis.

"Hello, Alice." He kissed my cheek, and it felt like the sun warming me after storm clouds parted. "You've always had a face for hats."

"Hello," I managed to whisper. Dennis smiled gently and nodded as if to cue my thoughts, and I asked timidly, "Am I asleep?"

Now Dennis's smile was more sympathetic, and he shrugged indifferently.

"Oh! *Ohhh*…geez, well, in that case, I suppose this will be where you tell me an angel named Clarence or Phillip will visit and tell me I have three tasks to accomplish before I can meet Saint Peter at the gate."

Dennis raised his brows to mock me or get a better answer. "Phillip?"

He waved a hand at the costume jewelry laid out on a velvet-covered countertop. Fingering a string of creamy ivory pearls, he shook his head. "You know me better than anyone, Alice. When did I ever fall for the Kapra way? Yes, I think the pearls—or do you prefer the silver cross with garnets? The cross it is. It's medieval, and it's you. What do you think?"

I wore a heavy Byzantine cross set with garnets on a silver filigree chain around my neck. "It's gorgeous, but I think the pearls go better with this Laura Ashley country frock—*what the hell?!?*"

I was wearing a pale blue-gray dress of soft wool now, and the hat changed with it, matching color and fabric.

"Perfect! A perfect faery princess," Dennis murmured.

"Denny, I'm not understanding anything right now."

"Well, that's the way it's supposed to be. Takes some getting used to, though."

"When did I die?" I asked.

"August of 1978."

"What?"

"August 1978. I think you know what I'm talking about."

"I got married, had a child! I didn't die!"

"Didn't you?"

"Oh hell, I'm supposed to figure this out, aren't I?"

"Alice, you're not expected to do anything like save kittens up in trees or go back home and save the town from bankruptcy. Angels won't earn their wings by anything you do now. No bells or *Buffalo Gals*. You're expected to do what *you* want."

"But…"

"There are caveats and conditions, however. You get do-overs if you want. It's entirely up to you. And the situation, of course."

"Do-overs? Like jacks or hopscotch?"

"Certain things must be played through—you'll figure

it out."

"But…!"

"Oh, and it's more about changing *you* than anything or anyone else. That was a hard one to catch."

Another kiss was planted on my cheek, and I caught the scent of Number Six as he waved and went on his way. Though, what his way was, I didn't know.

Not yet, at least.

CHAPTER 2

THE PROPRIETRESS AT The Curiosity Shop nodded when I appeared at my table. I didn't remember returning to The Shop; I didn't remember sleeping or having a place to sleep, but I felt rested, and my stomach was full as if I had a breakfast of sausages waffles with a Starbucks cappuccino on the side.

"You'll want to choose now," The Proprietress suddenly announced.

I looked up from my typing. "Pardon?" I asked.

"Your book — you'll want to choose. Come along!"

I glanced about; no one else was in The Shop, so I pushed my chair back and went to the display cases. The lapis book held my attention.

"That one."

After a moment, while The Proprietress scrutinized my face down to the last freckle on the bridge of my nose, the book came out of the case and was set before me on a brocaded cushion.

It was magnificent. Between the latticed vines decorating the leather suede cover were stars tooled in silver gilt. The clasp was a sapphire set in a silver finding. I ran my fingers over the book, tracing the outlines of vines and stars, my hands trembling. I had to have this book. I wanted to tuck it into my faux Prada bag and let it stay there forever…

"Some people think they know what they want before understanding why they want it!" The Proprietress sniffed.

I ignored the comment and fumbled with the clasp on

the book. I didn't see a key attached to the book or dangling somewhere in the case. "Is there some way…?" I muttered, and The Proprietress snatched the book away to be locked up again.

"*Some* people seem to think!" she hissed.

"Well, that was rude…."

"Take one!"

The Proprietress was pointing at a rack behind me, one of those carousels holding postcards—no postcards of a quaint English village here, but what looked like train timetables. Unfolding one, I discovered it was a timeline of my life. Turning it over in my hands, a name stood out among the others placed neatly under tick marks.

Quinn Radcliffe.

"The train station is down the road. You don't have much time," The Proprietress ordered.

My messenger bag and laptop were thrust at me, the Prada bag slung over a shoulder. I peeked inside, hoping…

"*Nooo*, Alice! The book isn't there."

"Can I just…?"

The Proprietress pointed out the door and to the north. She stamped her Westwood pump and roundly gestured to the street.

"Well, goodbye then," I said, trying to be friendly. "I get it now. You're God."

The Proprietress glared over the rim of her cat-eye glasses, my mother's glasses. "Oh please, dear child! I'm much too busy for that! Hurry! It all must be done in a week!"

"A week?"

Colors flowed and bled into one another like a '60s light show, and paisley patterns swirled around me until I stood amid Union Station. It was not the boutique-infested strip mall interrupted by Amtrak trains, life-size cutouts of the president and vice president, and racks of souvenir key chains shaped like the White House or the Capitol, but the station as it should be: a living organism of people and machinery, of purpose. Before me were the boarding gates. A sign flashed arrivals and departures. It didn't surprise me that a non-stop train for Berkeley, California, was ready to depart. I knew that was my destination, and I sprinted for the train, amazed at my energy and the lack of pain in my back and knees.

But then, I was sixteen again, wasn't I?

There was one empty compartment on the train, and I slid in, throwing my bags on one bench and myself on the other. The train eased out of the station, Washington's famous and familiar buildings starting to disappear. I closed my eyes for a moment, and when I opened them, a man was smiling at me: Jack Lemmon, I thought at once. He wore an Amtrak uniform and held a ticket punch in his right hand.

"Good afternoon, Alice. Your ticket?"

"Geez!"

I hadn't purchased a ticket!

"The outside pocket of the book bag, Miss," he said in a friendly, comforting voice.

Reaching into the messenger bag as instructed and never diverting my glance from his, I pulled out a book of tickets: rectangles of brightly colored stock paper like the old ticket books for rides at Disneyland. Each ticket had a letter printed on its face, A to E. I thumbed through the book and asked, "Which ride is this?"

"This would be an 'A' ride, Miss."

"Ah."

"You sound disappointed."

"The 'A' rides are the least exciting. I don't suppose we're going to Sleeping Beauty's Castle?"

The ticket was punched. "See you in a while, Miss. The café car is the next one over—to your left as you go out," he said. "Do you want me to close this?"

I nodded, and he closed the compartment door as he

went, humming *A Time for Us*.

Curiosity compelled me after a few moments to go out into the corridor. The smell of a roast turkey dinner was even more compelling. I turned right and found myself in the café car of the Orient Express circa 1910, surrounded by the most eclectic of passengers: Albert Einstein, Richard the Third, and Thomas Cranmer were engaged in a spirited debate about Archbishop of Canterbury William Temple's legacy while Boadicea and C. S. Lewis were sharing tea and scones; the astronauts from the Challenger Space Shuttle were playing poker with Thomas Hardy, Marilyn Monroe, President Kennedy, and Joan of Arc. Eleanor of Aquitaine was trying to show George Eliot how to knit. At the same time, Jane Austen scribbled furiously in a notebook, and Agatha Christie kept slapping her hand and growling, "Mind how you write, Girl! Mind how you write!" Off at a table by himself was a seventeen-year-old boy faced with a bacon double cheeseburger and fries.

My stomach lurched, and I broke into a sweat and then trembled.

Quinn…

Jack Lemmon approached, this time dressed in an impeccably tailored tuxedo. He offered a menu and extended a hand. "I suppose you'll want to sit with him?" he asked, jerking his chin towards the boy. I wanted a table near the door to eavesdrop on the Einstein-Ricardian-Cranmer conversation, but the tables were suddenly full of more historical personalities. The only spare seat was at the table in the corner.

"You have a guest, sir—dinner for two," Jack Lemmon announced as he seated me opposite the boy.

It made sense, looking at him. If I appeared as I did at sixteen, it only stood to reason that he would be the same age as when we went on our first date. He struggled to fit the cheeseburger into his mouth when he noticed me.

"Hello!" The exclamation was of genuine delight. He

put down the burger and poured a glass of Diet Pepsi, shoving it toward me.

"Thanks! You remembered. So…I guess you're…"

"Glad to see you? What do you think?"

"I honestly don't know," I murmured, looking around.

"Going to Berkeley?"

"I don't know…"

He reached out and brushed the hair out of my eyes. "There. I like to look at your eyes — the smile's not bad, either. Mighty fine, Miss Alice!"

After a few bites, Quinn started in on the burger, looked up, smiled—that knee-disintegrating smile I remembered from years past—and said, "You're not hungry?"

I saw a plate of fish and chips before me, a bottle of malt vinegar close at hand. "Wow! I was just thinking…I guess I shouldn't be surprised, should I?"

"Remember our dinners out?"

"We didn't go out much—a movie once in a while."

"I didn't have an allowance, remember? I just liked being with you. You were the only girl who really listened, Alice, like you were interested. You were patient and kind, especially loving."

"And you."

"We had some pretty interesting conversations, didn't we?"

"Let's see . . . there were books—*Lord of the Rings*, music—Ralph Vaughan Williams and Jimi Hendrix."

"There was love." Quinn again brushed the hair out of my eyes, which I closed, sensing that his face was near, and waited for his kiss. When I opened them, I was no longer on the train but sitting on the swing in the backyard of the house where I lived with my brother, Dennis.

I spun around, unbelieving at first. Calm set in as something deep within me told me it must be. It would be.

It was a particularly warm day. From the color of the

grass and the blown roses, it must have been August, sometime in the early evening. Music drifted out of the house, *Are You Sitting Comfortably*, a favorite song of mine, as did the sound of dishes being taken from the cupboard and meat sizzling on a grill.

"Alice! Supper!"

Dennis's voice didn't surprise me at all. I shoved myself off the swing, climbed up the stairs to the back room of our Mediterranean-Style house, and walked through to the kitchen where Dennis was scooping mashed potatoes onto plates and Harry, his college friend, was spearing steaks off the range for delivery to the table.

"Uh oh…" Harry hummed and winked.

"No drama tonight, okay?" Dennis demanded, leveling the spoon in my direction so that globs of mashed potato fell onto the floor to be lapped up by my Pomeranian puppy, Sammie.

"What?" My response was a bit forced and too high in pitch.

"You've got that look. You're not still moping over that jar-headed jock of a boyfriend, are you? It's been months," Dennis grumbled. "C'mon, eat. It takes food to mend a broken heart."

I dug into the mashed potatoes after spooning a bit of margarine on top of them. A bite and then another, and I said, "Will Parmenter was ages ago. And if you must know, I was thinking about someone else."

"Great! More drama!" Harry chuckled.

"Not funny," I sniped.

The telephone in the living room rang, and Dennis glared at me, saying, "Dinner hour is for dinner, socializing is for after, with martinis—or in your case, a Shirley Temple," before he got up to answer it. He returned a moment later and took up where he left off with the meal. "You know, I have to give Louie a call. These are the best steaks he's had in The Shop in a long while. What do you think, Alice? Should we get our Thanksgiving turkey from Louie's Butcher Shop this year? That was Quinn on the phone, by the way…".

"*Dennis!*"

"…and I told him you were eating and that you'd call him back. Okay?"

The meal was consumed in the quickest time possible and made me wonder if I'd expired from a heart attack. As I got up from the table, Dennis took my hand gently and pulled me onto his lap.

"I didn't say when you'd call him back," Dennis continued. "Haven't you used up your phone allowance for the week?"

"C'mon!" I whined. "Those were calls about the winter play and costume parades and fittings!"

"You've been using the phone way too much, and the phone bill's been too high. We can't afford that while I'm trying to get the business off the ground and make some money."

"Five minutes—c'mon, Denny! It's been all summer."

"If he's interested, he'll wait until tomorrow."

"Why don't you get me my own phone for Christmas?" I hinted.

"Why don't you learn to be patient?"

"You're a stinker," I grumbled, sliding off his lap and heading toward the door. "I'm going to finish the costumes for act two."

"Dennis, you really have to stop doing that to the poor girl," I heard Harry say as I left.

Once out of the kitchen, I darted as quietly as possible through the dining room that now served as Dennis' office/studio, skirting past the stacks of books, portfolios, sketchbooks, and art supplies both on the floor and on the table, almost knocking over our mother's dressmaking dummy that now wore one of his suits and a tie. I set it back and stepped respectfully around my mother's neglected sewing machine cabinet that had been idle for a year now, the pieces to a dress she was making for me still stacked neatly on the platform where she'd left them. Drawing tightly the lengths of tapestry fabric that divided the office and the spacious mission revival living room, I carefully lifted the phone out of its box inside the roll-top desk, cradled the phone in my arms, and gently pulled on the length of cord, letting it snake behind the sofa and end table, allowing it to trail behind me as I went out into the enclosed porch and eased the door shut, but not before grabbing a pillow off the sofa and throwing it into a corner by the potted palm. I sat knees drawn up to my chest with the phone balanced on my stomach. Reaching for my purse on the coat rack, it took some time to find a slip of paper tucked away in an inside pocket. I unfolded it carefully as if it was an archeological find and studied the neat, architectural handwriting. Moments passed before I picked up the phone receiver and started to dial. It was odd, watching the rotary disc spin around as each number was selected in turn, no less strange to me than the anticipation I was feeling, the dread and excitement, even though I'd dialed that number almost a thousand times…

I stretched out and held my breath, waiting for someone to pick up.

"Uh, hi! Hello, this is Alice, Alice Martin. May I speak with Quinn?" Moments passed—dreadful, painful moments—until I heard the receiver click.

"Okay, Dad, you can hang up now!" Quinn was shouting, then, into the receiver, "Alice, hi!"

"Hi! Welcome home," I greeted.

"Just got back a couple of hours ago—Dad! Damn it, hang up the phone!"

I stifled a laugh.

"You okay?" he asked.

"No, I'm fine. A piece of celery in my throat, from dinner, you know, the threads."

"Wow, you should be careful…"

"How are you, Quinn? It's been a while."

"Fine, fine. At least now…so, what did you do this summer?"

"Not much of anything really, just hung around the house—oh, I've been designing more costumes—they asked me to do the winter play!"

"Wow! How many does that make, three, four? What's the drama club doing?"

"A Scottish play."

"Which one?"

"The one with three witches. You're not supposed to say the name—bad luck."

"Too bad it's not Romeo and Juliet. You know your Italian Renaissance stuff."

"Well, technically, that's medieval, the original story, that is."

Quinn laughed. "Okay, you won that round. Still, everyone says you're a great costume designer."

"Everyone, huh?"

"That would include me. Are you thinking about making a career of it? There are schools back east, and there's New York, Broadway."

"I want to teach history at the college level—but I guess I could design on the side. My brother's got connections."

Tappa-tap-tap-tap-tappa.

Tappa-tap-tap-tap-tappa.

I listened, trying to figure out if there was a hidden meaning in the cadence. "Quinn? Are you alright?"

"Huh? Oh yeah, yeah. Hey, I finished *Lord of the Rings*."

"The whole trilogy???"

"Wasn't much to do most nights . . . lockdowns after the auditions and concerts, and there wasn't anyone to hang out with, so…y'know, when I got to the *Return of the*

King, I kept thinking of you. As Eowyn."

"'I am no man!'" I quoted from the battle of the Pelennor Fields.

"Exactly! Yeah! Yeah, great book…"

"I cried at the end."

"You *cried?*" Quinn was incredulous.

I put my feet up on the door, wondering what my legs would look like in chain mail. "Well, it was romantic and so moving. I should get some chain mail. What do you think?" I said aloud and regretted it until he spoke up.

"Uhh…yeah! With a mini skirt! You'd look great with those legs, and, shit, that was really stupid. I don't know why…"

"No worries! Okay, didn't you think it was beautiful and moving? How Frodo and Sam saved Middle Earth? And how Aragorn and Arwen were meant to be together?"

"Well, yeah, but how many endings does a book need?"

"If I had written it, one."

We laughed and were silent, though I could hear him on the other end of the receiver.

Tikka-tap, tikka-tap, tikka-tikka-tikka…it was a pencil being tapped on a surface like a drumstick.

He was on the end of the line — that's all that mattered.

"I was wondering — do you want to go to a movie or something?" He asked all of a sudden.

"Uh, sure! When?"

"Tonight, maybe?"

"Yeah! Okay. Do you want to meet downtown or…?"

"I'll pick you up."

He was silent for another long, torturous moment and then, "Okay, well, I'll see you in an hour?"

"Okay…I'm looking forward to it, Quinn."

Another pause. Why?

"Yeah, well, okay! See you soon."

I slammed down the receiver and did a happy dance that was interrupted by Dennis.

"Gotcha!" he said, yanking the phone from me. "We can't afford another fifty-dollar phone bill, Alice!"

"I'll work extra hours at the dress shop, and I'll take on some students for tutoring," I giggled, dancing past him to the stairs, and he played along, doing the Frug and the Chicken behind me up the stairs and down the hallway to my bedroom. "I've got a date tonight!"

"Who's your latest victim?"

"Quinn Radcliffe!" I pushed Denny back out into the hallway. "I'll make it up to you—I always do, don't I? Now go. I have to get ready."

"Nothing sexy!" Dennis called over his shoulder as I slammed the bedroom door.

The closet was full of dresses. My one weakness was clothes, yet I frowned at everything taken out and inspected. My favorite, a sleeveless red velvet mini-dress with a high waist and gold brocaded bodice, was bought with three months' allowance. Olivia Hussey wore a red velvet dress in *Romeo & Juliet*, and I'd seen stills from the film in a *Scholastic* magazine feature earlier that year. I didn't care that it was too hot for velvet and slipped it over my head anyway, adjusting the bodice around the strapless bra I'd chosen to wear — the pink lace number I'd bought with lunch money, the one Dennis said I couldn't have. I momentarily looked at the budding cleavage and then at the tissue box. No. Boys could tell the difference. Next, I scuffed my feet into a pair of gold sandals. The dirty-dishwater blonde hair was unraveled from its perpetual braid and brushed out so that it was all waves and curls like a Pre-Raphaelite Madonna or angel. I sprayed a bit of Yardley's O! De London on my neck for added measure.

"There!" I sighed, glancing into the mirror.

Still, the girl looking back wasn't what I wanted.

The eyes were too large and far apart; the hair could

never make up its mind to be blonde or brown and settled mostly for taupe unless I was out in the sun, and then it went to the shade of dirty dishwater; the mouth was thin and wide. Someday I hoped I would develop more curves. At least I'd gone up a bra size over the summer, though no one would notice, not even in my low-cut red velvet dress. I looked back at the tissue box and sighed. No. It would be too obvious. There was one saving grace to my adolescence: I'd been spared zits. Dennis said I was enchanting and pretty, but he lied. What did he know about girls, especially when all he seemed to attract were pretty boys? I wanted to be stunning, exotic in beauty, the kind that made boys and men walk into telephone poles or trees when I passed by with an air of confidence…

The doorbell buzzed.

"I'll get it!" I shouted in a most unladylike manner and practically threw myself downstairs to get the door before Dennis or Harry.

I was too late. Dennis was at the door and was chatting amiably with Quinn.

"Here she is," Dennis announced and did a double-take in my direction. "My! Look at *you!*"

"Alice! Oh wow, my favorite dress!" Quinn blurted out and then recovered with a "Hi!" that sounded too boisterous.

"Hi! You look great yourself," I greeted.

"I thought I was too dressed up, but seeing you…"

I was glad of my choice of outfits, for Quinn was dressed in a linen sports coat, pair of slacks, shirt, and Sperry Topsiders. He was a "Hill Kid" from a family of wealth and privilege and always dressed like he came out of a prep school or *Esquire* magazine ad. I was uncomfortable under their smiles and gave Dennis a sideway glance that meant 'Go away now,' but he snapped his fingers and said, "Can't wait for the prom! You're taking her to the prom this year, aren't you?" Dennis crowed at a clearly embarrassed Quinn. "Let me get the camera!"

"Shall we go?" I pleaded, desperate to make a getaway.

"Behave!" Harry called as I slammed the screen door in his face, and Quinn and I scrambled down the stairs to the street.

"I like Dennis," Quinn laughed as we turned left up Rose Street and walked to Oxford.

"He's annoying," I grumbled.

"He's your brother—aren't brothers supposed to be annoying? My mother did the same thing when I left the house. Sometimes I wish I had a brother — at least you can sucker punch a brother."

"Didn't you say your father's musical instruments have their own room?"

"Yes."

"Well, think of them as brothers and sisters."

"So my guitar and cello would be their nephew and niece?"

"I guess," I said, "and that would definitely make your family as strange as mine—maybe stranger."

We both laughed at this as we followed the perimeter of the university en route to the movie theater on Addison and talked about his "family" of musical instruments and the acoustic guitar his mother had given him for his birthday, the auditions for orchestra chairs and how he spent part of the summer with his grandmother in York, England. From there, we discussed the costume designs I was working on, the collection of short stories I was writing, and what classes we would take in the fall.

The noise of a crowd made us stop short when we stopped at Oxford and Center.

A cadre of National Guardsmen had arrived in Jeeps and took up position near the entrance to the stadium. A band of protesters taunted them, waving anti-war signs. Someone was burning a flag. Police sirens started to wail as the Guardsmen moved into formation.

"Oh wow," I sighed. "The last time this happened, I almost wound up in the hospital."

"Why?" Quinn's voice had a sharp edge to it.

"The tear gas. I was walking home from school, and I was in the wrong place at the wrong time. A few of us were going to the library to study, but we saw the protesters and wanted to join them. The Guardsmen threw canisters just as we walked past, and the fumes burned my eyes and throat. I thought Dennis and my mother were going to kill me."

"Why? It wasn't your fault . . . maybe this wasn't such a good idea—damn, tear gas! C'mon," Quinn grabbed my hand, and we took a sharp right towards Kittredge, pushing against the crowd coming at us from downtown to join the protest. "We can go over to the U.A. Theatre. It's playing there," he said, quickening the pace. A handkerchief came out of his pocket, and he thrust it toward me. "Just in case—I don't want our first date to be in the emergency room."

I glanced up at Quinn, and he winked.

We skirted by J.C. Penney's, Hink's, and the public library, and as we approached the box office, he relaxed the death grip on my hand but didn't let go.

"Thanks," I said, handing back the handkerchief. I craned to look up, hoping for a smile. Quinn had grown a foot taller over the summer. He looked older, and the grim set of his jaw and eyes made him look formidable, though it was hard to believe a boy as gentle as Quinn Radcliffe was someone to be reckoned with.

"Don't they know it won't do any good? They just keep sending people over there to die," he muttered, shoving the handkerchief back in his pocket.

"Sorry?"

"Nothing."

"I hope you don't get drafted."

"That makes two of us." Quinn glanced down and smiled. "That really is my favorite dress."

"Is it? Thanks."

"You know what movie we're seeing, don't you?"

A line was forming at the box office, so I saved our places in line while Quinn went across the street to Edy's Ice Cream Parlor. He came back breathlessly and handed off a strawberry cone. "My favorite!" I gushed.

"Yeah, the school cafeteria — you always seem to go for the strawberries," he remarked.

"I thought you ate lunch in the band room with the orchestra kids."

"Part of the time, but I mostly sit in the back of the cafeteria and work on compositions. The noise actually helps. It's called white noise—like a TV when the station signs off, and you get that static-like noise? It blocks out everything and helps me concentrate."

"You watch me go for strawberries, huh?"

"I'm not a Peeping Tom or following you around or anything like that, if that's what you're thinking," Quinn blurted out nervously. "I hope you don't think—"

"I'm teasing you, Quinn!" I laughed. "It's okay if I tease you? I'm the type of girl that if I don't tease or try to make you laugh, you better worry."

"You're the only interesting girl in the school. That's why I noticed you at first. Other guys did, too. I heard them talking. You don't draw attention to yourself. There's something about you, well,"

"Thank you," I whispered, touching his arm and smiling at him.

"And then there's the smile," he said now.

There wasn't much more I could say. I brushed the hair off my face and glanced at Quinn occasionally as we moved slowly in the long queue that had snaked down Shattuck to Kittredge and around the corner, with more people arriving as the showtimes approached for this, the most talked-about movie of the year.

"Hey, is that…?"

I looked where Quinn was gesturing with his chin.

It was!

My ex-boyfriend Will had joined the line with his latest conquest, my best friend—actually my *ex*-best friend—Amber Lynne Smollers, the sister of Quinn's rival in just about everything. I looked away but not soon enough. Will hailed me with a wave, a stupid grin.

"Don't mind me," Quinn murmured and planted a kiss on my brow, another on my neck, pulled me closer, and shot Will a smile that could be interpreted as smug or victorious. I didn't mind that at all, especially when his arm stayed around my waist and I was close enough to inhale the scent he wore. The next day I went to Bill's Drugs and bought a bottle of that same cologne; I kept it hidden in my vanity, taking it out now and then to partake of what I thought was a guilty pleasure: to remember how he smelled and wished that he was beside me at night…

"It must be strange coming back here after spending so much time in England," I commented.

"We have better food," Quinn answered. "Truth be told, I didn't want to go this year, but my grandmother expects me to, and after she closes up The Shop at six, there's nothing to do. I don't know anyone. And I actually looked forward to music camp."

"How was it?" I asked as we finally walked inside, and Quinn passed our tickets to the kid at the door.

The kid glanced at me slack-mouthed, eyes darting up and down, and exclaimed, "Wow, didn't know it was you, Alice!" He sat behind me in Social Studies and bore holes into the back of my skull with watery blue eyes when he wasn't trying to get my attention or blow on my neck. Now he looked up at Quinn, looking down quickly when Quinn glared.

"Enjoy the show—they die in the end!"

Quinn spun about, glaring once more, and then recovered. "What was that all about?"

"He has a crush on me or something."

"He should have moved faster," Quinn said with a wink and held me back, saying, "There's Will and Amber Lynne. Let's go this way." We stepped in line behind a group of sophomores from the high school and followed them in, pausing just inside the threshold. "Wait a minute, my eyes haven't adjusted to the dark—don't want to trip and make a fool in front of you while I'm trying to be so cool and suave," he quipped, but I saw that he was making careful note of where Will and Amber Lynne was going, and he steered me in the opposite direction.

"Do you want to sit up close, or…" Quinn had paused near a back row.

"Back here."

We took seats in the back row away from other Berkeley High kids coming in. No sooner had Quinn settled in than he got up and handed me his coat, saying, "Don't go anywhere," and moments later returned with a bag of popcorn and two drinks. He looked perturbed and glanced around before taking his seat.

"Something wrong?" I hinted.

"What? Oh, nothing. Ran into Will."

"Lucky you!"

"I told him I was, if you get my meaning."

I did.

With the bag of popcorn between us, Quinn started to eat, and I stole sideways glances at him. He was classically handsome, dark, with large, expressive, sloe eyes and a dazzling smile that dimpled. Did I mention that it was knee-disintegrating? His father was English, and his mother was of English and Italian parentage from an ancient family in Siena. His father taught music at the university and was head of the music department when he wasn't singing the second lead with the San Francisco

Opera. His mother stopped traffic on Shattuck Avenue when she glided into Hink's Department Store, a tall, thin woman with the glamorous dark beauty of an Ava Gardner or Vivien Leigh and Quinn, I thought, inherited all of their best qualities.

"You were asking about music camp," Quinn murmured when the house lights dimmed.

"Yeah, was it the same as last year?"

"Same as always — same kids, same music, same fleas, and mosquitoes," Quinn said, laughing nervously. "Some of them had a search and destroy mission for me—the fleas and mosquitoes, that is, some of the kids . . ."

"I wish I could have gone to the chorus week at camp, but with everything that happened in April, Dennis and I couldn't afford it."

"Are you okay?"

"I guess," I nervously shoved the hair behind my right ear and then the left. "I guess I'll get used to Mom not being around."

"I tried to call you back when it happened—I wasn't home, you see. My dad took me to New York for an audition and then to England."

"You did?" I asked, looking up at Quinn. His dimples increased when he smiled gently, sincerely, and I looked down at my lap, brushing the crumbs and kernels of popcorn off the velvet.

"Mother called when she read the obituary in the Chronicle, so I tried to call—man, I just said that, didn't I? I thought maybe you'd want to hear from a friend."

"That was thoughtful. I didn't see you around, and I didn't know what to think . . . everyone else pretty much stayed away, and I thought, well, it doesn't matter now, does it?"

"You got the card and flowers, right?"

"Yeah, I did. It surprised me because, well, you know, like I said, I hadn't seen you around, and then I heard you'd gone out of town. So it meant a lot that someone like you would go to the trouble."

I didn't add that I had saved the card and pressed one of the flowers he'd sent.

"Someone like me?" he wondered, shifting to his right to look at me. I was glad the theater was dark — he wouldn't have been able to see my blushes as he smiled at me.

"Everyone looks at you and smiles when you're walking down the halls, and the girls practically melt — damn! I said that out loud."

Quinn gently laughed, saying, "I don't think my sex appeal is what they're gossiping about. I'm just a freak to most of them."

"How can you say that, Quinn? You're talented, funny, good-looking,"

"I like that. The way you said my name," he replied softly. "If you want to know, I think you're my only friend at school, and I sent the flowers and card because I couldn't talk to you when your mom died, and honestly, I couldn't imagine what you were going through."

"I don't think I properly thanked you."

"Consider tonight payment in full—the date, that is. I don't mean to say — shit! I'm doing it again…"

"Quinn, you can relax," I giggled, patting his shoulder.

He casually draped an arm around the back of my chair; his hand brushed against my neck and shoulder, sending a delightful shiver through me. Quinn offered his jacket, thinking I was cold, and I took it because it smelled like him and held his warmth. I was so happy that I started to feel tears in my eyes and a lump in my throat. He glanced over, concerned, and offered the handkerchief from his pocket. I was still holding that little square of fine linen when we left the theater two hours later and retraced our steps along Oxford.

"Sorry," I said, blowing my nose. "I cry at everything!

Good thing I didn't put on mascara."

"I like you without makeup. Good thing they haven't made a movie of *Lord of the Rings*."

My response was a loud honk. I was ready to give him back the handkerchief embroidered with a 'Q' but thought better and shoved it into my purse. Quinn laughed and playfully slung his arm around me and pulled me close. When he'd realized what he'd done, he moved away quickly, as if I was made of fire.

"No worries," I whispered as we paused on the sidewalk. Quinn gently brushed the hair out of my eyes and let his fingers glide along my cheek.

"I think," he sighed, "I think you're beautiful."

As on the train, I sensed that he would kiss me, and I closed my eyes, waiting. When I opened them again, I was kneeling in my bedroom before a cardboard box of baby clothes. I was holding the handkerchief.

"What's there?"

I was startled, more surprised that I was in our brownstone in Providence, where we'd gone to live after the wedding, than the sound of his voice. He was crouched beside me, his chin on my shoulder, the two-day-old beard scratching and irritating.

"Something from my mother's funeral," I lied. "My heart nearly broke. All that crying. I never thought…"

"You weep? I don't think I've ever seen you shed a tear."

"I've learned that crying doesn't solve problems or find answers." He watched me twist the fine linen square into knots.

"Don't suppose they do, Angel."

"No worries," I replied, tucking the handkerchief into my sweater pocket.

"Do you need to keep it?" he asked as he headed out. "Look at all the stuff you've kept. Best to get rid of most of it. There's no room, and it won't change anything—

doorbell!" he shouted on his way to the kitchen.

"Why don't you get it?" I called back. I went to the door, nevertheless.

A postal carrier was on the doorstep. He smiled and handed off a square parcel that could not have fit in the box. I set it aside, not recognizing the hand in the address. Later that night, as I was washing the dishes and settling down for a night of research and writing, I glanced at the parcel and carefully unwrapped an album, an LP of Ralph Vaughan Williams' music.

Fantasia on a Theme by Thomas Tallis.

My heart stopped.

CHAPTER 3

"GREAT! THAT'S ALL we need—more stuff."

Again he was looking over my shoulder. He reached for the album, but I held it close and waited until he was gone before I pulled the record from its paper sleeve and cradled it as if it was a holy relic. Keeping it to the light, I studied the grooves and found it: a hairline scratch going the diameter of the disc. We had no record player; he got rid of my old RCA portable when we started collecting CDs. I ran a fingernail over each groove, hearing in my mind the lush, evocative strains begun by a single violin and then the cellos as I kept moving my finger along the perimeter.

The opening measures of this piece, my favorite, were playing over a sound system when, as the light reflected off the vinyl, I looked up and found myself in The Shop. The Proprietress was scowling in my direction. That did not surprise me in the least.

"Well, at least you're punctual!"

"If that's the least of your concerns," I muttered, looking around, hoping to see something different, perhaps a clue as to why I was there. "What do I do now?" I demanded, my voice as steel-edged as hers. That made her happy, for she tried not to smile and pointed to the corner table while she made a notation in a ledger.

"What were you doing before, Alice?" she wanted to know, in a sing-song, academic tone, but not raising her eyes to look at me. I already knew that would have been too easy, too nice, for her.

"Alrighty then!" I sighed and went to my place. Sitting down, I flipped open the laptop and watched the screen as I took sips from the Starbucks mug. The coffee was still piping hot.

"Have you decided, then?"

"Pardon?"

Tap-tap-tap, tap-tappa-tap-tap…Tap-tap-tap, tap-tappa-tap-tap…

A perfectly manicured nail was striking the cover of the lapis book while The Proprietress glared. "You'll want to make a decision."

"Don't I have all the time in the world? Is this not *kairos* rather than *kronos?*"

She didn't appreciate my jest or my laugh. "Come then! A decision, Alice."

I took another sip from my travel mug and approached the counter. She was still tapping on the book cover. She snatched it away as I reached for the book, locking it in the display case.

"Well, how am I supposed…?"

The Proprietress snapped her fingers and pointed roundly at the literature rack. Sighing and not taking my eyes from her, I whacked the wire stand, letting it spin. Without glancing, I snatched a brochure and held it up defiantly, my brows raised, waiting for her next barb.

"Well, indeed!" The Proprietress sniffed. She actually smiled!

I looked down and saw it was about Thomas Tallis, an English composer of hymns during the Tudor dynasty. Curious, I unfolded the brochure and held it up like a road map. When I brought it down to ask The Proprietress a question, I was in Quinn's study, holding an album sleeve.

"Sorry, didn't mean to startle you!" Quinn laughed, thinking I'd jumped when he banged open the stairwell door. He came in with a tray laden with tumblers full of ice, cans of Diet Pepsi, a bowl of popcorn, and a plate of little sandwiches and set it on the coffee table. "Since we didn't grab dinner after the movie, Mother thought you might be hungry."

"I am," I admitted, waiting for him to sit beside me before reaching for a sandwich. I took a bite of chicken salad and offered the sandwich to him. Quinn devoured it in one bite.

"Next time, I'll bring more cash. Eat! *Mangia!*" he laughed. "She says you're too skinny. Though she should talk!"

"She does? She is the most beautiful woman I've ever seen. She's a model, isn't she?"

"No. Psychiatrist. And she just told me that you were enchanting and sweet." He fed me some popcorn.

"And you said I was beautiful."

"I did — and I meant it, even when you spit popcorn all over my favorite dress."

"I do that because I am a lady," I quipped.

"A *beautiful* lady."

We were tossing kernels up in the air and trying to catch them in our mouths.

"Thank you. No one's ever said—well, someone I wasn't related to. Relatives have to say nice things, don't they?"

"Wait 'til you've been around my family a bit."

"Or my brother," I sighed.

"I like your brother," Quinn said, feeding more popcorn. "He doesn't seem to care what others think."

"He cares what people think of me, of us."

"Us?" Quinn stopped shooting popcorn and looked at me, the popcorn scattering on the sofa. His brows were raised, hopefully. "There's an 'us'?"

"I meant what people think of Dennis and me. Of us being alone now."

"Oh."

He sounded so disappointed that I reached out and touched his face. His hand, long and slender, tanned and muscular, trembled as he took mine.

"Of course, if we wanted, there could be an 'us,'" I whispered.

"I should be so lucky! Damn! Not what I meant to say. I mean, if you wanted it...to be an 'us'...okay, I'm going to stop talking now." He took a sandwich and ate, and handed me another. "Actually, I'm not done. Can I ask you something?"

"Sure."

He slipped off the sofa and rummaged through a record cabinet under the stereo to our right. "Why did you go out with Will? I mean, he's the football team's captain, and I never thought someone like you would fall for someone like him. You're smart, funny, interesting," Quinn said. "Where is. . .ah, you have it."

"Beautiful?" I teased.

"That, too. Can I have the record?"

I took the record album out of its sleeve and passed it along. "I thought he liked me. I wouldn't have gone with him if I'd known he was trying to get to my former best friend. Can we talk about something else now?"

"Sure. Do you like Thomas Tallis?"

I picked up the album sleeve. "Yes, and I love Vaughan Williams' interpretation of his Third Tune, oh, and his version of *Greensleeves*. Whenever I hear his *Fantasia*, it's hard not to think of the English countryside. It's like a musical Thomas Hardy novel."

"Here, listen—this is my favorite part."

He turned up the stereo. The Royal Philharmonic introduced the main theme. I would later sing it with the Cornell University Choir: Thomas Tallis' Third Tune, *Why Fum'th in Fight*. Quinn sat beside me on the sofa, and we listened with rapt attention. "A musical Thomas Hardy novel, huh?" Quinn murmured with a chuckle.

"Doesn't it bring pictures to mind?" I asked. "Like, a meadow, or a moor at sunrise, or walking across the moors, standing on a cliff, looking out to sea. A village of stone cottages with a bridge over a stream, gardens full of bright flowers like bluebells, hollyhocks, roses, a Romanesque church near the village square."

"If it did, you'd be in that picture," Quinn whispered, gently pulling the album sleeve from me to take my hands. He held them for a moment and then released me, reached up to raise my chin ever so gently, and we looked at one another.

I smiled and looked down, daring myself to look up again. He was still looking at me. Quinn leaned back against the sofa cushions and held out his hand. I tentatively moved closer, feeling the soft velvet brocade pattern under my hand as I edged nearer.

Our hands locked, and I could feel his strength and warmth, the softness of his palms against mine. My heart and breath were racing, and I took some comfort knowing that, looking at Quinn in the soft, dim lamplight, I knew he was as uncertain as I was. When our lips finally met, we instinctively embraced and held each other for the longest time. I was afraid to let go for fear that when I released him, I would be propelled away from Quinn, jettisoned to yet another compartment in my life, sent to view my past, present, or future accompanied by one of Marley's ghosts.

Yet it did not happen.

I moved away first, and Quinn reached for me again, but we didn't kiss; he held me by the shoulders. "Do you know how long I've dreamt of this?" he whispered.

"I couldn't guess—I've never thought—I mean, had I known that you wanted me of all people and to kiss me, that is," I stammered nervously.

"If you want to test that statement, I won't object."

"Let's see."

I kissed him, which led to a delightful, eager exchange

that ended as the music swelled. A pact unspoken was now sealed.

I nestled in his arms, happier than I'd ever been. One hand held mine; another caressed my hair. Slipping off my sandals, I curled up, quite comfortable and happy to just sit with him, and was glad he was of like mind.

"I wait at my locker before second period hoping you'll walk by. Just to see you," I murmured.

"I always hope you'll be there. I go that way to Chemistry."

"Is that where you're going? The labs are on the third floor. Isn't that out of the way?"

"Well, it's worth the extra miles."

We laughed, and he squeezed me in a gentle embrace. I closed my eyes as we listened to Vaughn Williams' masterpiece. In my mind, we were walking along the cliffs at Scarborough and in a desolate expanse of the North Yorkshire Moors, places I had seen in National Geographic and atlases but would not see in reality until ten years had passed. I could feel Quinn's body relax beside mine, the gentle rise and fall of his breathing, and it lulled me to sleep.

When I woke, the record was skipping on the turntable, and someone had thrown an afghan over us. I saw Quinn's mother tidying the study, tiptoeing around in an impeccable Chanel suit and string of pearls, a pair of Ferragamo slingbacks crooked in an index finger.

"I'm sorry. You two looked so sweet, I couldn't resist tucking you in, and I didn't want to wake you," Mrs. Radcliffe said.

"Here, let me help you," I offered, sliding out of Quinn's arms and kneeling before the record cabinet where she was slipping records back into their sleeves.

"So you're Alice," Mrs. Radcliffe said, smiling. She was stunning in her beauty. The smile I knew was genuine— the eyes were Quinn's. For once, an adult didn't take a disapproving measure of me, that dismissive flicker of eyes up and down, passing judgment, and she nodded at my dress. "The color suits you."

"Thank you," I whispered, smoothing back my hair and glancing nervously toward Quinn, who was snoring.

"Quinn's favorite color."

She winked and picked up the tray, raising perfectly arched brows and narrow chin toward the stairs. I followed her downstairs to the kitchen. I expected to find a bistro where famous personages were dining and drinking, perhaps with Beethoven leading a nightclub band in a Rumba tried out on a dance floor by Queen Elizabeth II and Henry VII. At the same time, Julius Caesar and Boadicea would share a Camel cigarette, a Grey Goose martini.

Or worse, be expelled from this house as dear to me as mine.

No, it was the same bright kitchen with yellow walls and yellow gingham curtains, spotless white countertops dotted with decorated Italian majolica tiles; the stainless-steel kitchen table with a faux marble Formica top upon which sat ceramic salt and pepper shakers in the shape of an apple and pear, the perfectly folded napkins in the wicker holder. It was a place that invited one to sit and share a cup of coffee.

Mrs. Radcliffe set about to wash dishes, and I took a towel from the rack on the wall and stood next to her, waiting for the first dish.

"Well, this seems natural," she commented, winking as she placed a dish in the drainer.

"I always helped my mom," I said, taking the warm plate and swiping the towel around it several times. Her brows arched when I opened a cupboard and set the plate on top of others just like it.

Damn! I did that out of habit. I should not have done that!

I knew where the dishes went on the shelf; this had

been my second home for almost four years, and after my mother's death, this gentle, quiet woman filled a void.

"What was the cause of death?" Mrs. Radcliffe wanted to know. "The obituary didn't say."

"Stroke—a cerebral hemorrhage is what they called it. It wasn't enough that she had cancer."

"But she was so young!" Mrs. Radcliffe turned to look at me, and I avoided her gaze, paying more attention than warranted to a green glass tumbler. "And your father?"

"Left when I was five—that's what I was told. He was an architectural engineer and worked in London after the war. Reconstruction and all that, restoring Victorian houses and buildings. We lived there for a bit. He didn't come home one night."

"Quinn said you have a brother named Dennis, who's now your guardian?"

"Yes."

"Wasn't he at school?"

"Came home from Dartmouth. I didn't want him—I didn't expect him to give up school."

I paused and carefully placed the tumbler on the shelf beside its mate, turned away so she wouldn't and couldn't see the tears I was struggling to keep in. I didn't cry. I wouldn't cry.

"Oh dear, I shouldn't have—are you okay?" She turned me to face her, and our eyes met. I usually looked away out of shyness, but I wanted to be held by those large, dark eyes that reminded me so much of Quinn and, strangely enough, of my mother. I wanted her to comfort me as if I were her daughter.

"Who's not okay?"

Quinn had entered the kitchen, yawning and rubbing his eyes. He grabbed a coffee mug from the shelf and, in doing so, kissed the top of my head lightly. I blushed when I saw Mrs. Radcliffe watching. She offered a wink. Spinning about to smile at Quinn, I was now face-to-face with Dennis in our Berkeley living room.

"Dennis, I think I'm in love," I blurted out.

"Quinn? Yesterday's news. I like boys," he responded.

"I know," I said.

"You knew?"

I followed him back into the dining room, dumping the carton of art supplies and sewing patterns I carried onto the floor.

"Of course. You played with my dolls, and all your friends were guys who were good dressers and who liked musicals. I don't know any guy that likes musicals, not even Quinn, and his musical tastes are interesting and scary at the same time. Denny, what is all this stuff?"

"Today's news, Faery Princess. I'm not going back to school."

"Dennis!" I exclaimed. "I thought you said you were transferring to Berkeley so we could stay together!"

"I'll go back in two years. I can reapply or something. You'll be out of the house and off to school in two years. Right now, you need someone to keep an eye on you."

"I behave—unfortunately—and I'm not a juvenile delinquent. I can take care of myself. I take care of this house and try to cook, don't I?"

"Not what I meant, Alice. I don't like the idea of you living with relatives we don't know or care about us enough to come to a funeral."

"What are we going to do for money?" I asked as we knelt to sort out sketchbooks. "Mom's lawyer says we can't touch the trust money until we turn twenty-five. For you, that's two years from now. The social security money I get isn't enough to get by. At least we could get by on your student loan and my after-school job."

He waved his hands. "Look around you."

The dining room table my mother had crafted in a carpentry class was cluttered with even more sketchbooks, sewing patterns, fashion magazines, and piles of fabric swatches. The cover on Mother's sewing machine had been opened. There were silk ties where the pieces of a prom dress had once been stacked on the pull-out shelf. The colors were vibrant, the fabric unconventional for men's ties—calicos and Liberty of London prints, bold geometrics devised by patching different fabric pieces together, the designs daring.

"You're going to design men's clothes?" I asked when it finally hit me.

Dennis picked up a sketchbook. "And theatrical costumes for the local companies as soon as I get my union card. You make it look so easy, Alice, and you can help with the history and authenticity!"

I nodded approvingly of the drawing: a medieval prince, and from over the top of the book, I saw the first floor of the high school, the hallway outside my locker. Quinn was coming out of a classroom down the hall from where I sat in a corner with my sketchbook and pencil. A boy from the jazz ensemble came dashing out of the classroom and spun Quinn around, blocking his path.

Anthony Smollers.

Tweedy, conceited, competitive Anthony Smollers who wouldn't let anyone stand in his way or succeed if it meant his coming in second place. His goal in life was to crush his opponents and always be on top of whatever heap it happened to be on a particular day.

"What now? Don't you listen?" Quinn was saying and trying to get away.

"Yeah, well, you're going to have to do some explaining," Smollers sniped, trying to grab his arm. Quinn shoved him off.

"I'm done with the whole scene!" Quinn shouted.

"Don't think this is the end of it, Radcliffe!"

"It's not worth the aggravation. Get yourself another fucking bass player!"

The outburst was uncharacteristic and shocking.

Students and teachers stared, and a few glanced sympathetically in my direction. I started drawing again and pretended to ignore them, refusing to acknowledge them or offer an explanation because I would have none. Life went back to usual when Quinn joined me in my corner.

"I guess things aren't working out as a math tutor," I murmured.

"Don't have the interest or the time. Did you have lunch?"

"No. Are you buying?" I held up the sketchbook and asked, "What do you think? A costume for Romeo for the spring play."

"That's pretty good—hey! Is that me?" Quinn laughed.

"What do you think?" I giggled.

"I think you're damn good in so many ways. Come for a walk with me."

He helped me up, and we headed towards the music room, where Quinn muttered greetings at fellow orchestra and jazz ensemble members, tactfully ignoring the stares a few boys were burning into me as we went past them to a maze of corridors and practice rooms, not to mention the whistles and solicitations a few offered.

"I'm not supposed to be in here," I protested as we went into the "Boy's Band Room" at the end of a twisting corridor.

Without switching on the lights, Quinn went to his locker and spun the dial on the combination lock. He shoved the band uniform and musical instrument cases back into the locker when they started spilling out and then pulled out a gift-wrapped package, which he held up with one hand, beckoning me out of the doorway with the other.

"Collins is in the teacher's lounge for another twenty minutes, and he wouldn't say anything if he caught us.

C'mere," he said.

"Are you sure this is okay?"

"Yes. Now, c'mon, Alice! I've got a present for you, and you won't be able to see if you don't come a little closer."

"What is it?"

"Open it and find out."

While I opened the package, Quinn stood close, a hand on my shoulder. "I wanted to give you a ring or a pin, something more traditional, but I thought this would do."

"Vaughan Williams!" I exclaimed at the sight of two record albums. "The *Fantasia*—oh my God! The music soundtrack from *Romeo and Juliet!!*"

"In honor of our first date, Alice," he said softly. "That's when I knew."

"Tell me," I implored, moving closer and placing a hand on his broad chest that he took.

"That I wanted you for a girlfriend. I'm asking if you'll go steady. When I get some money, I'll buy you a ring or something."

"I was hoping you'd ask so I could tell you yes," I whispered.

When Quinn moved in for a kiss, I felt my heart pounding and more alive than I thought possible. The disappointment was palpable when I opened my eyes and saw The Proprietress and not Quinn after feeling his lips on mine.

"It's time!"

"Time for what?" I demanded.

"Don't think you have it in abundance — it's a great disappointment when you find out."

The man's voice startled me. Turning about, I faced him. He was familiar: slate gray eyes, tall and thin (boney would be a better word), dressed in late fifteenth-century garb and fidgeting with rings on his fingers. He was handsome with fine features. The portraits didn't do him justice. King Richard the Third of England smiled back as I gaped at him.

"Stop looking, Alice," he quipped with a wink.
"Looking for what?"

"The hump."

"I wasn't!"

"That was an invention — and a cruel one."

"Indeed so," sighed a nun in twelfth-century garb. She had skin as porcelain and pure as her habit and wimple, the veil covering her hair falling in precise folds around her beautiful face. I knew this woman, too. Hildegard von Bingen patted my cheek as she passed by on her way to the flower boxes.

Richard the Third pulled out a chair at the table beside mine, reaching behind him for a mug of coffee. He unfolded a copy of *The New York Times* and sighed, turning to the crossword puzzle. I heard him mutter, "A five-letter word for equine . . . a horse, a horse…"

Hildegard von Bingen was putting fresh freesias into the cut glass vases. As I passed by on my way to where The Proprietress stood behind the counter, Hildegard handed me a bouquet and said, "He's been working on that puzzle for centuries!"

I was breathing in the fragrance of the flowers when the lapis book was placed on the glass countertop. The Proprietress looked at me and then at the book, again, at me.

"Well?" she hissed. From around her neck, she took a key.

"So that's where it's been," I murmured.

"All you needed to do was ask, Alice!"

My hands trembled as I fumbled for the lock, and as the key turned smoothly, I felt ethereal, joyous.

As I opened the volume, my left hand took up a pen, and I noticed the heavy wedding ring on the third finger, weighed down by emeralds paired with an engagement ring, just as significant. I glanced up, hopefully, and saw my husband. A moment of uncertainty and nervousness passed just as quickly as it arrived, and I signed my name next to his on the certificate and then in a register. The priest entered his name beside ours and returned my bridal bouquet of yellow and white roses with calla lilies.

"Congratulations!" Dennis called as we left The Cloisters and ducked as rice showered down upon us. I stopped when I heard him and threw myself into his arms, allowing my precious wedding dress to be crushed in his embrace. "I hope you'll be as happy as Harry and I have been!" my brother whispered tearfully.

A limousine waited for us in the street. We were in New York, and my husband's family gathered as he helped me into the car. I caught a reflection of myself and saw the heavy lace dress cut in the line of a fourteenth-century gown with a train, tight-fitting sleeves with bell-shaped cuffs, and a simple veil with a coronet on my hair. I had designed this dress when I was nineteen, anticipating a wedding in my future, but here I was, twenty-six, and I had indeed been married.

Once my dress and train had been gathered and taking up most of the limousine's back seat, the doors slammed shut, and I suddenly felt trapped. People were taking photos and waving, shouting wishes of good fortune.

I noticed him as we pulled away and started into traffic.

I gasped, and my husband laughed softly. "Did I bite you?" he murmured into my neck. "You do look good enough to eat!"

How could I tell my husband of less than an hour that I had seen Quinn Radcliffe on the edge of the crowd?

CHAPTER 4

"BACK TO THE Shop, I suppose?"

The Proprietress was looking in the rear-view mirror at me.

The limousine was driving slowly through a landscape that changed from the crowded, busy streets of Manhattan to a quaint and picturesque New England village to a cemetery in California, the scenery melting as if the sun was scorching it, colors blending and bleeding together, swirling in all directions, like a psychedelic light show from the '60s.

"No," I murmured and wiped condensation from the limousine window to get a better look at a funeral party.

"Not yet? Very well!" The Proprietress snapped and sped up. She suddenly slammed on the brakes, and I knew then that this was how I had died, or this would be the moment of my death: I was killed in an auto accident, propelled from the back seat of a limousine and through a windshield.

The horrible pain and shattering of glass didn't come. But there was a blinding, painful light, and instinctively I threw my hands up to my face.

Familiar sounds and scents came to me now: the smell of floor wax and woolen fabric, the sound of classes changing and the slam of a door, the echoes of feet on the raked wooden floor of the school auditorium stage. I opened my eyes to see the dark stage upon which a single spotlight shone, and sitting in the middle of that white circle was Quinn, in rehearsal with the high school chamber orchestra and the music director, Mr. Collins. He was playing Bach's *Wachet Auf, Ruft uns die Stemme*—in English, *Sleepers Awake.* Sitting in the front row of the balcony, I wasn't close enough to see the gently furrowed brow as Quinn concentrated and paid close attention to instructions and encouragement. I'd seen him rehearse more than a dozen times and knew how it would be. The light threw dark and frightening shadows on his face, and his curling hair danced and fell across his forehead as the bow was drawn back and forth in precise strokes and flourishes, making exquisite music. When the last note drifted into silence, Quinn leaned back in his chair, all his energy sapped, emotionally and physically drained. I wanted to stand up and applaud, but slow, deliberate clapping came from backstage. I couldn't see who it was, but Quinn shot up and looked, as did everyone else, waiting.

"Now, let's hear it done *right!*"

Andrew Radcliffe, M.A., Ph.D., came on stage and stood over his son.

"On the contrary, that's the best I've heard a student play in years," Mr. Collins said. He leaned forward and patted Quinn's shoulder, saying, "Good job, Radcliffe."

"Quinn isn't just a student. He's got a future in the performing arts," the Professor said. "Half-assed isn't a ticket to first chair or concertmaster. Or Conductor."

"Dad, please," Quinn sighed. "I hit every note, didn't miss a beat."

"Did you now? Let's hear it again."

I didn't want to be there, and clearly the orchestra students didn't want to be there either, for they started moving off-stage. I slid down in my seat, hoping no one could see me.

"Again!" the Professor shouted.

"Look, I'm not going to..." Mr. Collins protested.

"You don't have to. I'll accompany him."

Mr. Collins hesitated and said, "Excellent rehearsal, ladies and gentlemen. We'll leave Professor Radcliffe and Quinn. Quinn, see you tomorrow?"

"Right. Thanks," Quinn muttered, ignoring the stares as the rest of the students filed out quietly with Collins behind them. The door slammed and echoed. "Dad, what happened to our agreement?" Quinn started when they thought they were alone, his voice on edge. "You said you weren't going to come to rehearsals. You promised Mom. You promised me. I don't need this!"

"The Royal Philharmonic wants to see you again," the Professor said. "Are we going to pass that up because you don't want a dressing down in front of your friends and inferiors?"

"It isn't that. I'll see you at home." Quinn pushed himself out of his chair.

"SIT DOWN!" the Professor bellowed, his voice reverberating through the auditorium.

From up in the lightbox above the balcony, I could hear the sniggering and remarks from the stage crew, two boys who were lower on the social scale and high school food chain than Quinn but found amusement in teasing him none-too-softly.

"*Tarquin…Tarquin, whatsa matter? Can't stand up to Daddy?*"

"*Maybe you should go cry on Alice's shoulder.*"

"*Maybe you should try to get in Alice's pants instead of going down on those guys in biology class!*"

"*He probably wouldn't know what to do with a girl if he got her alone in the back seat of Daddy's big limo.*"

"*Hell, if it was that Martin chick that everybody says he's doing or trying to do, I'd be more than happy to give him some pointers! She's one stone fox, that Alice! Get it? Pointers?*"

"*Like you're not still a virgin, Frank!*"

"*Give me a half-hour with her…*"

"*I thought Tarquin was more your type.*"

It took all my willpower to keep from jumping up and taking the stairs by twos to storm the lightbox and rip the balls off those idiots. However, Quinn didn't need any more embarrassment, and I sunk even lower down into my chair, compelled to stay for Quinn's sake.

The Professor sat at the piano, started to play pick-up notes that he counted out, and waved his hand at Quinn, who resolutely started precisely on the count. This time there seemed to be no joy or passion in the execution. It was too much; I slipped away, ensuring the light crew saw my smile as they came out of the box.

Several hours later, when I returned to the auditorium and found it empty, I knew I would find Quinn in the band room, putting the cello away. The latches clicked with a hollow echo, and he shoved the cello into his locker, holding the door ajar as he studied the worn leather and canvas case. He stood silently over it, his shoulders sagging. He moved his foot back, and for a moment, I thought he would kick the case. It was the door that received the brunt of his anger.

"It was beautiful the first time," I said, crossing the threshold.

"Hey!" Quinn greeted softly, and his smile was assurance that he survived this skirmish with the Professor unharmed.

"Do you want to go for a walk?" I hinted.

Quinn turned away from me and switched off the light, putting us in late afternoon shadows. I playfully followed as he went further into the recesses of the locker room, hoping that he'd lure me into a dark corner for a quick cuddle. As I skipped around to face him, I saw the bruise. My shock was apparent as he tried to hide the purplish welt and ring around his right eye and down his cheek.

"It's nothing," Quinn muttered before I could demand an explanation. "A difference of opinion."

"With a fist?" I exclaimed.

"Just a guy, that's all."

"Not Smollers again!"

"No, another asshole. A matter of honor."

"Yours?"

"No," Quinn softly said as he kissed my forehead. "Yours."

He put on a pair of expensive sunglasses as we left the high school and headed up Center Street past the construction of the new subway. We walked hand in hand silently across the university campus to the Graduate Theological Union, where we settled under a gnarled olive tree and sat on the grass despite the cold and dampness of the winter day.

"Were you there the whole time?" he wanted to know. The tone was almost accusatory.

"No. I left after Mister Collins and the rest. You *are* good, Quinn. Why can't your father see it and hear it?"

"Good isn't great. Being good isn't what gets you into an orchestra. Being great does. Being good doesn't get you concert dates. Being good doesn't get you compared to Pablo Casals. It's all about being great," Quinn said matter-of-factly.

"What if it ruins your spirit? Your passion for music?" I asked. "What if it ruins your life or breaks your heart?"

Something I had not asked in the winter of 1969. I knew it!

"I won't let him get to me." Quinn pulled me close, and I rested my head on his shoulder. "D'you know, all the while, as I went over and over that piece, I was thinking of what you said when we listened to the Tallis *Fantasia* that night."

"What was that?" I asked, snuggling closer when a breeze cut through our coats and shook the tree boughs.

"How the music evoked images of moors, a sea, a meadow, standing and looking at a sunset. And you were there in a long, white dress made of lace. It made the session with my father bearable."

"Thanks." A kiss landed on his cheek, and I marveled at the stubble of beard against his smooth skin, something I'd not noticed before, but it was exciting to notice something mature and manly about this beautiful boy. Quinn turned when he noticed my preoccupation.

"What's the matter?" he laughed softly.

"A long white dress? Of lace?"

"Yeah, I don't know why. Maybe it's all the medieval stuff you like."

"Am I beautiful in it?"

"What do you think?"

"Quinn . . ."

"Yeah?"

"Do you want to become a concert musician? Deep in your soul, is this what you want?"

"Yes—and you. If I have these two things, I have everything."

His whisper was restorative. I opened my eyes after we kissed and found myself staring at the laptop screen in The Curiosity Shop.

"But there was something more…" I murmured.

"What was that?"

The Proprietress noisily locked a display case and soon was tapping her fingernails on its glass top.

"He wanted something more," I spoke up and started typing.

"How long will it take you to finish that book? You've been working on it forever."

"I'm working on two books—one on Joan of Arc, the other on a history of the Fourth Crusade if you want to know."

"I don't. Drink your tea, child, and stop wondering what people want!" The Proprietress sniffed.

"I haven't got . . . oh."

A Wedgewood cup and saucer were before me, and

the fragrance of Constant Comment was enticing, but I ignored it and continued my work.

The doorbell jangled.

"Ah, *Mademoiselle Jeanne! Vous êtes bien ces jours? Comment passer les guerres?*" The Proprietress greeted.

I glanced over the laptop screen and raised my brows at the sight of a girl in her late teens walking through The Shop to my corner. The ash blonde hair was bobbed, and she wore brilliant, white silver armor. She was pretty, and her round face tanned from a life outdoors on campaigns; her dark brown eyes were expressive, and she had a wide but full, rosy mouth. The bobbed hair couldn't decide whether to curl or not. What surprised me most of all was how diminutive Joan of Arc was.

Joan paused by Richard the Third's table and studied the crossword, murmuring, "A seven-letter word for misfortune...hmm, begins with 't.' Ah . . . that would be your life, Your Grace!"

"Pardon?" Richard demanded.

"Tragedy, sir. Tragedy!"

"Really, Joan!" The Proprietress chuckled.

Now my favorite saint sat across from me at the table, smiling and pushing the cup of tea in my direction.

"Quinn wanted you to love him," Joan said. "And he wanted very much to love you, but as with all love stories, there were insurmountable circumstances, weren't there?"

"I suppose..."

"Of course he did," quipped Richard, who reached for a PopTart from a vintage toaster that had yet to pop. "He's an adolescent boy, and what is the one thing boys want from a girl? Well?"

"A deep subject, Your Grace." A bearded gentleman in a nineteenth-century morning suit and top hat spoke up. The close-cropped beard and accent gave him away. Sigmund Freud winked at me as he entered The Shop with another man in tow: the actor Tyrone Power by his smoldering good looks. They headed for the coffee bar.

"It all depends on the boy, doesn't it?" Tyrone asked. "Some know right away what they want and expect and receive. Some, like Quinn Radcliffe, have extenuating circumstances, and what should be easy enough to say and do isn't."

"Must I spell it out?" Richard demanded. "Oh, bloody hell, really!"

"Watch your language, young man!" Hildegard von Bingen snapped, pointing at him with a pair of pruning shears.

"*Ohhh!*" Joan and I murmured in unison. Joan blushed, and I could feel my cheeks burning. The Proprietress rolled her eyes with dramatic effect.

"Not only *that*. He wanted respect and understanding." Tyrone said.

"Do you think that's all men care about?" Richard demanded of us.

"Yes," Sigmund answered. "But here we have an interesting young man whose emotions run very deep. As Mr. Power stated, Quinn wanted respect and understanding, and here I suggest the physical act of love."

"Which she gave to him…" The Proprietress chimed in. "And yet she still doesn't get it. Alice! Drink your tea!"

Doing what I was told, I took a sip and immediately began to feel warm and cozy, drowsy even, something I had not felt in a while. Colors swirled around me, and I remembered the light shows: the paisleys and splashes of bright hues, and how happy I felt when watching them…

Richard the Third had finally succeeded in claiming the PopTart and now sat down to work on the crossword puzzle.

"What's a five-letter word for love, Alice?" the king muttered.

Screwing up my brow, I put a lot of thought into the question. It helped that Sigmund Freud slipped me a note upon which one word was written: *Quinn*.

"No helping!" Richard spoke up. "Joan! What did I just say?"

Joan of Arc had been drawing something in one of my sketchbooks and held up her work. It was a drawing of the *Jesu et Marie* banner she carried into battle, which began to ripple and dance as if a breeze were within its folds—or it might have been the operation of the tea making me think that. Still, the banner continued to wave, and the figure of Mary slowly morphed into my silhouette cast onto the bed sheet I was now pinning to a wall in my basement hideaway, the place Dennis and Harry were forbidden to enter.

I had taken an ample, cluttered space and made it my own with throw rugs and tapestries from Cost Plus, a day bed that Dennis and Harry refinished as a birthday present and set on a carved wooden platform decorated with gothic trefoils in lozenges and strewn with overstuffed pillows that were covered in medieval and renaissance patterned brocades. Gauze curtains decorated with stars surrounded and separated the bed from a work area consisting of a drafting table, stool, workbench, and my father's old recliner and bookshelves. The walls were covered in trompe l'oeil skies that went from sunset to dawn on three of the walls, complete with clouds, planets and stars, the sun, and the moon. On the fourth wall, Dennis set three mirrors into gold-leafed panels like a triptych and placed them beside a five-panel screen decorated with medieval ladies based on the illumination from The Duke of Berry's *Tres Riche Hours*. The screen gave me privacy from the open stairwell up to the kitchen.

"Wow!"

Quinn stood at the door leading into the backyard, an overhead projector in his arms. He set it on the drafting table and looked around as if he were in another world. "You're sure this is okay?" he wanted to know.

"My brother is all for artistic expression," I said. "We can use this old sheet as a screen for the light show. You can use the drafting table for the projector and your stuff—it's the right height."

"Is this your room?" Quinn now asked, glancing at the day bed in the corner and my feminine, romantic interior decorations, which were attempts to make it a medieval lady's bower.

"No—it's my refuge. I won't let Dennis and Harry come down here, and they know better not to—one of our agreements. Sometimes I work late on homework, or my own writing, my costume designs, and just crash on the bed. Dennis wishes I hadn't chosen this room because the water heater and furnace are behind the wall. If something were to burst…"

"I'm with Dennis," Quinn stated, helping me down. I slid into his arms for a kiss. "Thanks for letting me work here," he whispered. "My dad just won't listen."

"I guess I should count my blessings because Dennis doesn't care what I listen to as long as it isn't too loud after ten o'clock."

"If it's not opera or classical music, it must be shit," Quinn muttered as he took the box I lifted from the doorstep.

"Is this what I think it is? Are you designing a light show?" I asked, peeking into the box at the clock crystals, stage light gels, and bottles of food coloring and paint.

"Yes. You put the liquid in the crystal, set it on the projector, and move it in time to the music. Here's the music." He handed me a record album.

"I've got the record player — oh, great choice!" I purred.

Soon Quinn was moving the projector in time to the song *Are You Sitting Comfortably* so that the room was filled with dancing hues of purples, oranges, greens and blues, reds, and golds.

"Now, let's make it interesting," he said and took a light gel and placed it in front of the lens so that the background was a vivid purple. He exchanged crystals quickly, and bright pastels now swirled and flooded the screen. Another gel was placed before the lens: a black-and-white rendition of a knight and his lady from a Victorian fairy tale book. Quinn exchanged the crystals rapidly until the song faded into the next.

"Wow!" I exclaimed, breathless. "That was amazing. You're good, Quinn!"

"Really?"

"I think it's good enough for Winterland or the Fillmore," I said when Quinn switched off the projector.

"It has to be great," he sighed. "If I get this gig, it will lead to others, and with the money the band's bringing in, I can save for my own car, get my own bass, so I don't have to keep borrowing Andy's."

"Does your father know about the band?"

He grinned and shook his head. "Just imagine the screaming when I tell him about the gig at the Keystone. He'll hit a high C."

"Keystone…? Quinn!" I giggled. "You're not twenty-one!"

"Andy's brother made these. What do you think?"

He pulled an ID card from his wallet.

"It says you're twenty-one! Wicked! Oh, I wish I could come with you."

"Why not? A bit of makeup, do something up with the hair, and the right clothes, you could pass for twenty-one."

"You'd like that, wouldn't you?" I laughed.

"It might help to have such a fine-looking woman admiring Blackthorne Rose from the front row—and while all the other guys are looking and wondering, I'll know she's coming home with me."

"Blackthorne Rose?"

"Names like The Rolling Stones and The Beatles were

already taken. So, are you up for it?"

"Sure!"

I turned to look in the mirrors and saw myself with an up-do, a glittering A-line sheath of blush pink in a metallic double knit, silver tights, and a pair of knee-high boots in silver leather. I was applying a last coat of mascara and touching up the eye shadow when there was a knock on my bedroom door.

"Wow! Look at the go-go queen!" Dennis greeted.

"Trying a new look."

"Looks…sexy."

"I guess that's a good thing, but coming from my brother…"

Dennis handed me the silver handbag on the bed, and I carefully dropped in a tube of lipstick, a handkerchief, and my allowance money. Turning away from my brother's inquiring eyes, I opened the nightstand and slipped a condom packet into the bag, hoping he didn't see or know I kept a few, just in case. If I were forced to tell the truth under pain of torture or, worse, a week's restriction, I would easily fold and say, honestly, no, I was still a virgin. What I was going to do that winter night was, at the time, for myself to know. I knew, in hindsight, it was a bad idea.

Dennis pointed to the bed as I grabbed a pale blush shawl of angora and mohair.

"Sit."

"I'm meeting Jenny and Rachael in ten minutes. Quinn's taking us to a party at Connie's—you know, the Air Force brat who lives near the high school?"

"We haven't had The Talk."

"Do we need to?"

Dennis tugged at the hem crawling up my thighs so that the garter tabs weren't so apparent.

"I wish Mom were here because I know what needs to be said. I just don't know how to say it."

His face was pale, and his eyes were the darkest and

most serious I'd seen them since our mother's funeral. "Sweetie," he continued, "if Quinn is putting on the pressure or making threats to break up—"

"No!" I squealed. "He's never pressured me, and he's never made a threat. What could he possibly say?"

"Things like, 'If you loved me, we'd go all the way, or it's how a girl shows her love,' and dumb shit like that."

"Oh, and you're an expert on this," I said, trying not to laugh.

Dennis sat next to me and took my hands. "Believe it or not, before I admitted to myself that I was homosexual, I dated quite a few girls in high school and my first year of college and did some heavy experimentation."

"I can't imagine you at a frat house beer bust making the moves."

"I hosted a lot of those parties. Trust me, I used all the lines and made all the right moves. Broke a few hearts."

"Do you expect Quinn to be like you? Or like you?"

"He's a guy, and we all think with our—guy."

"Sorry! Quinn's not like that. We've talked about it, Denny."

"And how did that go?"

I slid off the bed and went to the vanity to check my appearance. "This is something I don't want to share with my big brother."

"Well, Mom and Dad aren't here, and I think you'd have an easier time with me."

"You think so?"

"I wouldn't do anything to hurt you, but Alice, I do worry."

"When have I ever broken curfew, or drank, or did drugs? Have you ever gotten a call from the police?"

"No, and I count my blessings about that."

"Then don't worry about this."

"Do you love him?"

"Yes."

"How do you know?" Dennis asked. "How do you know it's not just hormones?"

"There isn't a moment of the day when I'm not thinking about him," I said softly. "If I hear something or see something that would interest him or has something to do with a conversation we had or a book or music we shared, I think, 'I can't wait to tell Quinn.' I love how he smiles and looks at me as he approaches in the corridor or the way he says 'hello' on the telephone. He can't keep his eyes off me when we're in the same room. And if I could just sit and stare at him all day—yes, I do know, and I know I'm in love."

"That will make it all the more difficult to wait."

"I don't know if I want to. Say no, that is."

"Alice, if something happens,"

"Dennis, don't worry! I won't let Quinn hurt me. I think it would be impossible for him, anyway. I promise!"

Blowing a kiss, I was out the door before he could continue the interrogation, running into The Proprietress, who was walking Sammie out on the sidewalk.

"Did you really believe that?" she asked, following as I hurried to my rendezvous spot with Quinn.

"Yes!"

"Lying to your brother. Now that won't win you any gold stars!"

"I couldn't tell him what I was doing tonight!" I sniped. "At least I was honest about Quinn and me. Surely there are stars for that?"

"Play it through, Alice," she sighed as I jumped into the front seat when Quinn pulled up.

The Keystone Club was in downtown Berkeley on University Avenue, where it cut off Shattuck. We met the rest of the band and got in through the stage door. No one seemed to care as I slipped in on Quinn's arm. The club manager gave me the up-down with bagged and bloodshot eyes and took the cigarette out of his mouth, jabbing it in my direction. "Singer?" he asked Quinn.

"Girlfriend."

"Umph," the manager grunted, shrugging. "*She'd* bring in crowds." Quinn threw an arm around me protectively when I received another appreciative once-over.

"What's your angle?" I spoke up, and Quinn frowned, eyes darting at me.

"Do you sing?"

"I've got a voice."

"Forty bucks. At least three songs in the set, and the band gets ten extra apiece."

"For real?" Quinn demanded. The band members had gathered around when they heard the offer.

"Only if she sings. *She* gets the forty." The manager walked off after smiling and winking.

The band looked at Quinn now, who turned to me and asked, "Do you know *White Rabbit?*"

I knew it, and what surprised me then and now was how effortless it was to belt out such a legendary song from my youth in a room hazy with the smoke of cigarettes and pot and full of strangers, with my boyfriend thumping the bass line on a guitar behind me. I smiled nervously and bowed very ladylike at the raucous applause and catcalls that followed my performance—and slipped off stage only to be met by Dennis and Harry.

"Well, there's a talent we didn't know about!" Harry greeted.

"It was my idea," Quinn blurted out when he dashed over to join us.

"Do you know you could get this place shut down?" Dennis said quietly.

"I wasn't here to sing," I began.

"The club manager asked if she could sing and—"

"Save it, Prince Charming!" Dennis snapped at Quinn and then looked me straight in the eyes. "You're coming with us, Alice Rose."

The next thing I knew, I was home, wrapped in a bathrobe and seated on the sofa, freshly bathed and scrubbed, feeling all of my sixteen-and-a-half years as Dennis paced the carpet. Harry prudently went into hiding.

"I almost wish I'd caught you in bed with Quinn!" Dennis began in a low, angry voice.

"What?"

"I could deal with that! But this? Do you know what you did tonight could get you taken away from me? Underage, in a place that sells liquor and the drugs being passed around! The social worker is coming by Monday afternoon for her monthly visit! How am I going to explain this?" he growled.

"You don't have to say a word."

"Some of our neighbors were at the club, Alice! My God, what were you thinking?"

"I'm sorry, but the club manager thought I was the singer, and he offered some money. I wanted to help the band. Quinn wants to buy a car and have his own bass! His parents won't give him spending money and treat him like a baby."

"So it wasn't Quinn's idea?"

"No! Honestly, it wasn't!"

He was ready to say something but closed his mouth and ran his hands through his hair. "You've got one hell of a guy there to take a rap like this," Dennis sighed. Then, while he again ran his fingers through his hair, he said, "Alice, your living with me is conditional."

"Why? Why is it conditional? You told me our relatives had to think about it, and they didn't want me."

"I didn't tell you the truth. The County wanted you to live with our relatives in the Bronx rather than stay with me. I convinced them I was old enough to do this, that it would work, and there'd be no problems."

I started to cry, and Dennis lit a cigarette—something he rarely did unless deeply troubled.

"I'll tell her everything, Dennis! I'll ask her to go easy on you. It was my fault. She can't blame you for my being stupid. I'm sixteen, for God's sake! I'm supposed to do stupid, dumb, scary stuff, aren't I?"

"Let me think about that. For now, you're on a month's restriction."

"*A month??*"

"You come home straight after school, music lessons, and drama club. No stopping by Quinn's."

"But…!"

"I could make it worse. I could call his parents—and from what you've told me about them, it would be a damn sight worse for Quinn."

"No!"

"A month, Alice."

I took my punishment. I was in The Curiosity Shop when I walked back upstairs and opened my bedroom door. Running a paper-tape calculator, The Proprietress didn't miss a click or a beat as she handed off a bottle of Diet Pepsi as I passed by.

I looked around at the patrons, who ignored me. Dennis was seated at a table near the door, enjoying a slice, or rather, a chunk of cheesecake. He motioned with the fork to an empty chair, pulling it out and patting the seat. I chose to stand over him and glare.

"It was for your own good," he said between bites.

"You're supposed to say that!" I grumbled.

"True, but it was."

"Like you never did anything to piss off Mom and Dad."

"I'm just sorry I wasn't around later to prevent you from making more stupid mistakes. But I guess we all play the stupid card to figure out life as an adult."

Joan of Arc looked up from her *New York Times Book Review* and frowned, a hand resting lightly on the hilt of her sword. "True love is never stupid!" she countered.

"It makes us do stupid things," Dennis defended himself. "There she goes! Off to write it all down," he said as I brushed past him to my table and made a lot of angry noise, opening the laptop and settling in.

"What if love demands things of us beyond our control?" Joan hissed. "Or do we love someone so much that we hurt ourselves in order to prevent others from being hurt? Or, and more to the point here, what if we are too young to understand what actions love takes—and we do not understand those actions until it is too late, or we have matured?"

"A good argument, that," Richard the Third spoke up. He raised his coffee cup in tribute.

"How many of us have an opportunity to make things right after an accounting's made, or want to?" Tyrone Power chimed in.

Everyone in The Shop turned and stared at me, including two new patrons: Marie Antoinette, who had live birds in her powdered wig and wore a pink striped gown with panniers that made her look like a walking peppermint stick, and the Goddess Athena, carrying a great snowy owl that seemed bored by his surroundings, for it immediately fell asleep. After rudely staring at every person in The Shop, from Saint to Monarch to Goddess and Shrink, to Matinee Idol, I ignored everyone and kept typing at a furious pace.

"Does anyone know what she's typing?" Richard queried, glancing around.

"Worried about the bad press?" Joan teased him.

"No, but doesn't anyone else notice that Alice is always typing on that thing when she is here?"

"She's writing a history of the Fourth Crusade," Athena said. "Now *that* is one of the best examples of men's stupidity, don't you think, Alice?"

"Only one of the best?" I quipped.

"Oh dear," Richard murmured, his eyes sliding to the

door. The Doge of Venice, Dandolo, who instigated the sack of Constantinople that was the legacy of the Fourth Crusade, had entered The Shop and departed just as quickly when he saw me.

I looked up over my reading glasses and hissed at the people still staring, "Haven't you all better things to do?"

The Proprietress started to speak and then thought better of it, for she took out a cloth and started dusting the immaculate countertops and shelves. I noticed workmen in a corner struggling with wall sconces and lights. After a short while, they stepped back to admire their work, and one of them flipped a wall switch. The most exquisite light patterns were thrown on the walls and floors, a gigantic pattern of rich colors I now admired through a kaleidoscope I was playing with as I sat in Quinn's upstairs study.

"This thing is a hundred years old?" I asked, turning the barrel.

"Nearly," Quinn answered, throwing himself on the sofa with his head on my lap. "Ellie found it at an antique fair in Whitby. Do you like it?"

"Love it! Thank you!"

"Love *you*," Quinn murmured, reaching up to kiss me.

"What did the guy at the Fillmore say?" I asked, turning the wooden barrel to marvel at a purple butterfly of colored glass and light.

"Wasn't interested," Quinn muttered, picking up an issue of *Rolling Stone* from the coffee table and flipping through it, pages slapping angrily one against the other.

"Impossible! That was some of the best artwork they've had in a long time!" I protested.

"Seems like everyone had the same idea—using The Moody Blues with medieval themes."

"Did Anthony Smollers have a show?"

"Yeah, it was pretty good. He got the gig."

"They don't know good when they see it!"

"You're my girlfriend. You have to say that."

His comment wounded me; I felt a dull ache in my chest, hearing the words as if a weight had been dropped on it and the air forced out of me.

"You don't think I know good artwork?" I demanded quietly.

He jerked his chin at my history textbook, the brown grocery bag cover decorated with my paisley patterns and castles, roses, and medieval ladies in profile.

"Paisley patterns and castles are for coloring books."

"That wasn't kind! What's gotten into you, Quinn?"

"I'm not in a mood to discuss what is and isn't art, Alice. Let it go."

"So you think I know nothing about art and music? Of light shows?"

"You listen to Mary Hopkins!" he chuckled.

"Well," I sighed, "maybe when you play the Fillmore *you* can sing and get paid forty dollars. Do that enough times, and you won't have to worry about a light show, money for a car, or guitar—or a girlfriend who knows nothing about art!"

"Alice!"

I grabbed the history book and my purse and fled, not in the least interested that I'd pushed Quinn off the sofa, and the thump heard going down the stairs was his head hitting the coffee table.

CHAPTER 5

"ALICE, PLEASE! WAIT!"

I ran down the stairs, though it surprised me how many stairs there were. As I ran, the photographs and paintings on the wall came to life in paisley, kaleidoscope, and Spirograph patterns in bright colors that swirled and spun as I passed by. Family members long dead were standing on the sidelines as if it was a race, calling my name and trying to take hold of me. The Proprietress was at the foot of the stairs. I was ready to collide with her when she snapped her fingers, pointing behind me.

I stopped.

Quinn had a hold of me now. "I didn't mean it!"

We slid onto the stairs, and I didn't struggle when he wrapped me in his arms. It was some time before I spoke or responded to his whispered apologies and words of love.

"When two people care for one another, they're honest about their feelings and thoughts, as you were, but they don't belittle the other or their interests," I said, sniffing back a runny nose and wiping away tears. "I expected the same from you, not more, but the same."

The statement was direct, quiet, and far from argumentative. As quickly as I had felt the pain, it was replaced by elation and lightness. In the spring of 1970 that that had *not* been my response.

"I didn't mean it! You don't have to be angry, okay?" he sighed.

"Don't assume to know my mind."

He leaned in, his face close, and I began to tremble,

anticipating one of his kisses that made me weak all over.

"What about your heart?" he whispered huskily.

He pulled me back upstairs, and I gave no resistance as we tumbled onto the sofa, letting our kisses and exploration go farther than we'd ever had in the year we'd been going steady.

"I don't hear anything! Hope I don't see anything!"

Quinn's father was on the stairs. We both moved away and rearranged our clothes as the footsteps stopped. There was a pause and a knock, and Professor Radcliffe poked his head around the door. "There's the faery princess herself!" he teased in an over-the-top Yorkshire accent, leaning over to bestow a kiss on my brow. "What an angel she is, too!"

"Hi, Professor," I mumbled self-consciously.

"Don't mind me, children, just looking—ah! The concertos."

The Brandenberg Concertos recorded by the New York Philharmonic were removed from the record cabinet. The Professor struggled to his feet and winked at his son. "We're going out if you two want to come along—a matinee at the Opera House. New Italian tenor with an extraordinary voice. *Gianni Schicchi*, Quinn, one of your favorites."

"A comic opera by Puccini," Quinn said, noticing my raised brows. "You'd like it. It takes place in thirteenth-century Florence."

I nodded like a dumb bunny, holding my blouse closed and keeping my eyes on the Professor, who was staring at the lace brassiere down around my waist and my breasts undoubtedly showing through the gauze peasant blouse I wore.

He looked at us, one and then the other, expectantly. "No? Maybe another time when you're not so engrossed in each other's charms—no pot or drugs, I hope?"

"Dad," Quinn sighed. "We've had this conversation

before."

"Yes, we have, haven't we? Well, see you this evening." The Professor started out and then turned. "Be a gentleman, Quinn. At least lock the door if you're going to have a right good snog!"

"*Dad!*"

"Be a gentleman to this perfect lady. Bye, Children!"

When he was gone, we sat staring at the door, bewildered, and burst into laughter.

"Damn! I almost forgot!" Quinn swore softly and scrambled off the sofa, heading towards his bedroom. "Don't go anywhere!" he called over his shoulder. No sooner had the bedroom door slammed than I heard a crash—what sounded like books and pottery falling as if a shelf had gone.

"*Ow!* Shit! I'm bleeding!"

"Are you okay?" I called. "Quinn?"

"Don't worry! I didn't break anything!"

"Quinn!"

It was quiet momentarily, and then Quinn reappeared with a package. As he passed the stairwell, he kicked the door shut and locked it.

"Your forehead!" I moaned, noticing the cut and the trickle of blood starting at his hairline. I took a tissue from my purse and pressed it to his scalp.

"Dictionary dropped on my head, that's all," Quinn said dismissively.

"Grammar can be heavy."

"Ha, ha." Quinn knelt before the sofa, holding out the package. "I brought this back from England. It was for your birthday—it *is* for your birthday. I know we missed it with my being away during Easter Vacation."

"You didn't have to," I purred with delight. "'Eloise Radcliffe's Antiques and Curiosities. York,'" I read aloud from the gold foil label with black lettering and then exclaimed, "From your grandmother's shop!"

"She picked it out herself."

"She doesn't even know me," I murmured, smiling, as I ran my hands over the tissue paper decorated with gold starbursts and roses.

"But I know you, and I told her what I was looking for. Open it!" Quinn demanded and put on a record, *Never Comes the Day*. He sat close with an arm around me as I carefully lifted the tape on the paper and uncovered a cardboard box that held a snow globe and a jeweler's case. The snow globe caught my fancy immediately: a knight on horseback in the globe, the base encircled by a castle. Opening the case, I discovered the *rosa alba*, the White Rose of York, crafted of silver and suspended on a thin silver rope.

"Look at this," Quinn said as he flipped the globe upside down and turned a key. It was a music box. We stared at the globe while the song *Greensleeves* tinkled from a clockwork mechanism, expecting something more than snow and glitter to fall after the song wound down. "I hope," he said, slipping the rose around my neck, "you'll correct me if I'm wrong, but ladies used to wear their lovers' favors, so I hope you'll always wear this."

I tugged at the ribbon holding my hair back in a braid, a length of iridescent purple silk. Then I wrapped it several times around his wrist and tied it. I leaned over to kiss him in thanks and ignited a fire. Quinn became more daring, more passionate, and despite my fear, I allowed him the freedom to do what he wanted.

"Do you want to go into the bedroom?" he whispered.

"Quinn …"

"I'd never hurt you—I won't hurt you. I just want to be with you. Do you want to? Do you want to be with me?"

"What about protection? I could get pregnant. I didn't bring anything."

"We can stop—I can. I know I can. I can get

something out of Dad's bathroom. Understand, please, that I don't want to hurt you, Alice, but I love you. Sometimes I wake up in the middle of the night and wish you were there," he said, brushing the hair out of my eyes and holding my face in his hands. "I feel this emptiness because you're not with me, and I think of you, wondering if you're feeling the same."

His kiss was gentle, as were his eyes when he lifted my chin and met my gaze.

"I do!" I whispered. "I think about you before I fall asleep at night, every night, and wonder what it would be like."

"We can find out together then."

"But it's important to a girl," I began, between petal-soft kisses. "I mean, I don't want a reputation."

"I wouldn't let that happen. You know I don't talk, and it's no one's business but ours."

"But," I paused. "There are things…"

"Tell me?"

"I'm trying to say that I'm confused because I am in love with you, and I've thought about it, but I've always thought it would be my husband the very first time because that's how it's supposed to be, isn't it?"

"I can imagine us being married. In fact, I dream about it. I love you, Alice!"

"Do you?"

He smiled, nodded, and then, kissing my neck, whispered, "Let me show you."

"Wait here," I said, slipping out of his arms.

I padded over to his bedroom and, before closing the door, winked at Quinn and blew a kiss. I undressed and slid under the covers of his unmade bed, pushing aside the *Rolling Stone* magazines and the sheet music. I was trembling from excitement, fear, and anticipation. The bed linens smelled of Quinn's cologne and Quinn and were smooth against my naked skin. I wondered how his skin would feel next to mine.

There was a knock on the door, and I called in a hoarse whisper, "Come in!" And then, in a somewhat louder voice, "Quinn?"

The door opened.

"*Finally!*"

The Proprietress woke me out of a nap. I lifted my head from the table in The Curiosity Shop, and my eyes darted around suspiciously.

"Come along, Alice!"

Yawning—wait! *I yawned? I was tired?*

That hadn't happened in so many hours, days, weeks!

And yet, I felt more alive than I'd been in years. The Proprietress placed the lapis book in front of me and handed over the key when I stood before the counter. I could open the book without trouble but was disappointed by what I found: empty pages.

The first page was empty until The Proprietress placed a tiny gold star on the page and wrote the date.

"It's a start," she sniffed.

"I don't understand," I murmured as the book disappeared.

"What did Dennis tell you? It's not about understanding but doing."

I went to my usual table in the corner, opened the laptop, took a sip from my coffee mug, and looked out at The Village.

It was a picturesque place with neat rows of houses and shops, a cluster of medieval and Tudor architecture divided by a stone bridge across a river that flowed somewhere, a village taken from a postcard, or as I mused, a Thomas Hardy novel or my imagination, and placed here. Wherever here was.

People came and went, exchanged greetings and conversations, entered automobiles, and drove away. Buses lumbered down the high street every hour or so, but where they came from or where they were going, I couldn't figure. And the people weren't just villagers but historical figures. Some were characters from my favorite novels, even a few from my stories. It didn't seem strange that Richard the Third was hailing a taxi or that Phoebe of Cenchrae was trying on hats at the haberdashery across the street.

No, what was strange was seeing Quinn across the street—looking as he had when he was twenty-six.

Without thinking, I darted up and knocked the laptop and the coffee mug to the floor in my haste to go out into the street. By the time I had pressed through a crowd that suddenly appeared in The Shop, Quinn was walking away. I called his name, but no sound came out of my throat. Once again, automobiles and people came at me, and nothing happened.

But the pain was unbearable.

It began to rain, or what I thought was rain. I was weeping like the girl Alice when she'd gone down the rabbit hole and found herself too large, her tears flooding the narrow corridor; now, however, I was standing in the living room of my Berkeley apartment in March of 1978. Rain was lashing the windows as if someone was throwing buckets of water on them or hosing them down, making the lamp-lit reflection of myself distorted, frightening— what I was feeling at the time. I looked the same as I had when sixteen, only a bit older, more sophisticated, and more unhappy.

My arms were folded defensively. The Tallis *Fantasia* was playing in the distance.

"Would you turn that music off? It's depressing, and I can't hear you."

Donovan's comment made me turn and stare as if I was seeing him for the first time. With dark, smoldering Mediterranean looks, height (though Quinn was taller by at least two inches), and an athlete's body, he was a mirror image of Quinn. Quinn's older brother, to be precise, down to the pedigree of talent, charm, and privileged birth. His eyes, however, were cold and calculating.

"Sorry?"

"You're not listening, Angel!" he continued in the condescending, professorial voice he used on students and those he thought inferior, which was anyone in the room. "Why don't you turn off the music so you can hear me?"

"Leave it!" I ordered quietly. "And stop calling me Angel!"

"Well, I can't hear you, and I most definitely can't read your mind, Alice, so if you've got a definite opinion about the wedding plans, now's the time to say something."

"Not that you'd listen to me."

Donovan slid off the sofa, his notes and books sliding to the floor and landing on my Pomeranian, Sammie, who yelped and scampered out of the room, wondering what he'd done wrong.

"I don't listen to you, Angel?" Again the voice was condescending, and there was a tinge of amusement.

"No."

"You don't want to get married?"

"I don't want the wedding in New York."

"You don't want the wedding in New York."

"Is there an echo in here? My family and my life are here, and most of my friends and family can't afford to go to New York for a wedding. They can't afford the airfare and lodging. Dennis and Harry will have to take out a loan if they want to come."

"We can have a reception here in Berkeley when we return from the honeymoon. Something at the Fairmont or the Mark Hopkins?"

"Again, Dennis and I can't afford that. Your mother and her husband, the rest of her family, your dad, his girlfriend, your grandparents, your friends—they can afford to come to California."

"My father's schedule couldn't be changed, what with the election coming up, and Mother was only able to get the caterers, the priest, the band—"

"Wait, wait! Is your mother getting married, or are we? I thought I was the bride!"

"You agreed to accept her help, didn't you? You said you didn't have the time or interest."

"True, but,"

"And let's face it, a big wedding is what's expected of my family, and we know you can't afford everything that goes with it."

"I can afford a dress!"

"I didn't suggest—"

"You did in so many words! Is this the right thing, Donovan? All we've been doing is arguing since we got engaged. What if we were to go to city hall some afternoon when we're both in the same city and have nothing going on?"

He took me by the shoulders like a small child, setting me on the sofa. "No. Because I know that isn't what you really want, and I can't do anything other than what we've planned, and you know it. Listen to me, Alice. I owe everything to my parents, the chair at Brown, the dig, everything."

"The senator has that much clout at Brown, does he? Pretty good for a carpetbagger from New York!"

"I need to make concessions. I've already had to do some serious damage control with the family over my choices in life and my bride."

"Oh, thank you very much! Make me feel like Cinderella or Eliza Doolittle again!"

"Sorry, that wasn't what I meant."

"I'm too sure!"

"This may be the twentieth century, but rich New England families still arrange marriages to keep everything convenient in the family and the bank. I meant to say that

I need to make concessions if I want to keep my life as it is."

"Not our life, Donovan?" I asked quietly. "Are those apron strings tied in a knot?"

"It will be worth it, I promise. Besides, Mother's managed to book The Cloisters."

"The Cloisters? Oh my God, you didn't!"

"She's friends with the Curator and was owed a favor. The Cloisters, Alice! I knew you'd love it. You can't say no to that."

"She's taking advantage of me," I started and shoved off the sofa, going back to the window. I was torn between rage and elation.

Donovan waited for what he had hoped would be a happy, tearful acceptance of his surprise plans and, when he got nothing, knelt to retrieve his papers and books and shove them into a briefcase. Whenever we quarreled, he used it to beat a retreat.

"The choice of dress and flowers are still mine, I hope?" I said after a long, painful passage of time, punctuated by his sighing and the rustle of papers.

"Of course! I hope Dennis is designing it?"

"Actually, I did. Something medieval in theme—I suppose appropriate for The Cloisters?"

Donovan pulled me down for a kiss. "Can't wait to see it on you and slide it off you!" he purred.

"I have an idea," I said, slipping out of his arms to finish gathering his things. "What if we had a ceremony here in Berkeley and the one in New York? That way, my friends can attend, and Dennis will have a hand in planning the wedding. We could have a civil service in New York and the religious service with a blessing of the marriage here in Berkeley at my parish church."

"That's not a bad idea at all."

"Or, even better, and a gesture of peace towards your mother, I could ask my friends at the cathedral, maybe something in the Chapel of Grace? I know the Dean."

"A cathedral is what Mother is used to."

It would have been a little joke if anyone else had made that comment. But it was Donovan, and he was serious.

"Now that we've sorted one predicament, I wonder if you have time to look at houses tomorrow before your flight. There's a house not far from my brother's place on Rose Street."

"Ah, that reminds me! Remember that little cottage in Newport we stayed in last year?"

"The mini-Breakers on your mother's estate? What about it?"

I wouldn't say I liked the way he was smiling. He'd done something . . .

"It's ours—a wedding present from Mom. She saw how you loved it, and I thought, why not make it a weekend getaway or give it to Dennis and Harry so they can be close?"

"Oh no, you didn't say anything about living in Newport!" I sighed, trying to pull away.

"Think of it! A beautiful setting in which to write, and your brother nearby, sailing whenever we want—"

"—I get seasick in a bathtub. Your mother a heartbeat away? No. I'm not living in your mother's backyard."

Donovan sighed and then pulled me roughly towards him. His kiss tasted of garlic and mint gum, and he was angry.

"Are you willing to give up that?" he whispered, releasing me.

"Yes."

I was as surprised as he was by that response. When he looked as if he would strike me—he pulled back his hand—I refused to waiver and stared head-on, waiting for the blow, a bruise to mar my face for a week, something that would make me dig into the depths of creativity for a plausible explanation. Instead, I closed my eyes. Still waiting, I felt a tap on my shoulder and a playful brush against my cheek. Spinning around, I was inches away from Quinn.

"Fancy meeting you here, Alice!"

I was standing in a living room on Durant Street in the spring of '75; the room fogged in with the smoke of pot and cigarettes, filled with the sickening sweet pong of incense.

A party was at the height of its progress around me. My date deserted me when we arrived, and until that moment, I had been alone except for the ice melting in an empty glass.

Quinn hadn't changed: the hair was longer, and the five o'clock shadow was roguishly sexy. He was wearing glasses, though, and removed the stylish wire rims self-consciously. Mine were safely tucked away in my bag.

"Hello!" I exclaimed, feeling my cheeks burn with color. I suddenly felt like I did in the winter of 1969 when we first became friends: tongue-tied and bashful, stuttering and stammering as if I'd lost control of my speech. Quinn just smiled down at me and nodded.

"If I'd known fine-looking women were coming to this shindig, I would have cleaned up a bit," he teased, smoothing back his tangle of curls.

"You're fine. No worries! You look great," I gushed.

"Do I? I feel like I'm overdressed for this crowd. You know, the super-intelligent," he chuckled.

"Welcome to my strange little world!" I laughed. "I've always hung out with history and philosophy types, but I never thought you did!"

"There are some music types here. Me, for one." He looked around and added, "Christ, guess I am the only one!"

"Good to you see you, Quinn. You look great—I just said that, damn, I just said that…."

"So do you. Your birthday was last week. Here, let's celebrate twenty-two." He pointed at my glass. "What was that?"

"Gin and ginger on the rocks. I think." I took a sip and nodded. "Yeah."

Quinn looked around and patted my shoulder, saying, "Don't go anywhere!" Then he was back with two drinks. He handed one off and then raised his, saying, "To the most beautiful girl I know."

I looked around at the girls in the room. "You once said I was beautiful—but that was before we both needed glasses, so you're either crazy or drunk!" I laughed.

"Crazy glad to see a friend and such a beautiful friend after being gone so long."

"Almost three years, right? When did you get back?"

"Last week."

I felt a stab of remembrance, of some unpleasant memory…the exact words coming from his mouth.

He drew me outside to the front yard, where we sat on the porch and faced each other while resting against the support beams. "How've you been, Alice Rose? Everything okay in your charmed world?" Quinn asked softly and thoughtfully.

"Yes. As a matter of fact, I just got back from Florence, if you want to know."

"I do."

"It's where all the faery princesses go to escape it all."

"And what would you need to run from?"

"Strange that you, of all people, would ask."

We stared at one another, waiting. Quinn blinked first and looked away. "I deserved that," he murmured and took a very long pull from his glass and set it down, moving to my side of the porch. "How was it?"

"Italy, or the afterlife, or life after?"

"Italy."

"Beautiful, just as I imagined it would be."

"The perfect place for a perfect faery princess," he said, tapping my nose playfully. "How did you get that nickname? I remember kids calling you the faery princess and, of course, Denny."

"My mother bought me a tutu and tiara one year for Halloween, and I refused to take them off after she had me try them on at Freed's. I must have been maybe three or four. I rode on the London underground in that ensemble—walked home with her on the coldest afternoon in October wearing a short-sleeved leotard, tutu, and ballet slippers. I didn't care that I was cold. I thought I looked like a faery princess. My brother started calling me faery princess to tease me, but I ruined his fun by taking on this new persona. Now it's become a term of endearment, I guess."

"You've always looked like you belonged to or were in another world. My father used to say it would be like finding the Holy Grail to get inside your head or your heart."

"Did he?" It was my turn to take a very long pull from my drink. "Why he should care, I don't know."

"You don't? Remember, I managed to unlock your heart."

And break it!

I watched him from the corner of my eye as he gave me a surreptitious up-down. Maybe he noticed that I had filled out, and though I still looked the same, there was a difference brought by life's hard lessons. I hoped he saw that, too.

"I bet he's glad he finally got you all to himself. Those devious machinations must have worked," I muttered.

"What?"

"How's the Royal Philharmonic?" I asked, offering my drink when the ice clattered to the bottom of his empty glass.

"That," he took a sip and expelled a painful sigh,

"didn't work out as I'd hoped. Being arrogant and talented works for English guys here in America, but they think you're an arrogant bastard with talent when you're American. Well, it doesn't work so well across the pond. I've got some auditions coming up, but until I've locked up a chair, I'm teaching guitar and piano at the night school, and here's the worst part. I'm back living at home for a while. Mother didn't like the idea of me starving in a garret somewhere."

"And the idea of having a consumptive girlfriend wasn't too appealing, I guess."

"Ugh. I hate that opera."

"I saw your father in it. The Chronicle said it was the best *La Boheme* in decades."

"Yeah, well . . ." Quinn paused and then glanced over. "Your health has always been excellent," he quipped, then added, "You got a degree in History, I bet."

"Aces straight up, Mr. Radcliffe."

"Are you teaching?"

"Not yet. I'm taking some time off before grad school. Dennis can't afford to pay for it, so I've put in scores of loan applications. I'm an appraiser and doing book restoration for an antiquarian bookseller on Post Street in the city. I do costumes and sets for local companies when I get offers. I'd rather be teaching or doing serious scholarship."

"Emphasis on serious, I think," Quinn commented, raising my glass to his lips and then mine. The movement was loving and sensual. I couldn't help but notice that his eyes never strayed from my face, and I loved it; it made me feel alive and happy.

"There's nothing I can do with a History degree except write until I have my doctorate," I continued as the glass passed back and forth. "Your passion is music, and mine has always been history. I want to go to England and hunker down in some serious research on the Italian merchants and bankers in London and Bruges who pretty much bankrolled the English monarchy before and during the Wars of the Roses, then work on a history of the women of the conflict—the banker and merchant wives, the nobility. I know I can write popular histories like Barbara Tuchman, or at least try. And then there's the Norman Conquest, or what happened after the Bastard invaded. Do you know he really was a Bastard? Shit, your eyes just glazed over—a bit much? I'm sorry. I forget that not everyone likes history."

"Wow, ambitious…I thought maybe you'd get a gig with the Starship or Fleetwood Mac."

"Thank God you didn't mention ABBA."

"They called and left a message—loved your rendition of *White Rabbit*."

We laughed easily. How many years had it been since our last date, our last kiss? Our last anything? Circumstances and obligations had made decisions for us.

"My mother wishes you would come by the house, not be a stranger."

"My life's been complicated, and you know, given the history, I didn't think she'd want to see me." I paused. "Or you'd want to see me. I would have. If you'd called."

Not what I had initially said; I was sure of it!

It was too painful, you see, to pretend that nothing had happened.

"I'm ready to make amends. All I need is your absolution."

Quinn had reached out and drew me close, our lips ready to touch. I felt dizzy, and my heart was pounding. *He was trembling…*

"Who's the friend, Tarquin? Am I interrupting?"

A tall, striking brunette was standing over us, glaring.

I moved away, self-conscious, brushing back my hair as I always did when nervous, but now I was in my tiny apartment a few blocks away, facing a mirror and brushing

my hair slowly, nervously, as if waiting, and I knew I was
waiting.

I was also hoping...

The familiar knock on the door.

I set aside the brush and switched off the bathroom
light, padded barefoot to the living room to turn off the
overhead and switch on a lamp so that the light was soft
and diffused, and then glanced at my appearance in the
mirror one last time before opening the door and smiling
up at Quinn.

"Hello!" he greeted, holding up cartons of Chinese
takeaway. "I'm not drunk, just hungry."

"Chicken chow mein and cashew beef, mmmm! You
remembered," I said, recognizing the scents.

"Nice place," Quinn said, following me into the
kitchen and setting the cartons on the dinette table, gently
shoving the fashion magazines, sketchbooks, watercolors,
and pencils to one side. "Hey! I remember this sketch.
Wasn't this for the Scottish Play?"

I turned to see what had caught his attention and
smiled, for he was tapping a design for *Hamlet*.

"This is for the Danish Play. It's a new rendition of
something I had in mind then."

"You were always drawing."

"This is for a repertory theater," I explained, and
shuffling through a stack of watercolor sketches, held up a
few more. "These are for a ballet troupe."

"Good to know some things haven't changed," Quinn
remarked and closed the sketchbook reverently; using the
same care with a pencil case and bundle of paintbrushes he
moved to make space on the table.

"Let's eat in there," I suggested, pointing with a
serving spoon towards the living room. "That way, I don't
have to move my work, and you don't spill Coca-Cola on a
drawing."

"You remember that!" Quinn laughed.

"It was an interesting lesson in *chiaroscuro*—I used the stain to make a shadow on the figure."

Everything was set on the coffee table, and Quinn pulled out one of the bean bag chairs and plopped himself down, watching intently as I served up portions, as if late-night suppers together were a weekly event.

"Does your girlfriend know you're here?" I quipped, half-seriously, sitting on the carpet beside him.

"Girlfriend? Oh, her. Her dad sings with mine in the opera. She was in town visiting from school, so my father...."

He didn't need to finish the sentence.

"I guess there's somebody?" Quinn hinted.

I shook my head. "Not anymore."

"Funny, I thought that in Italy . . ." his voice trailed off. He looked at me as if I was deliberately keeping something back or lying. We both ended the awkward moment by looking away.

"Well—*mangia!*" I said.

Quinn handed off a fork while he took the chopsticks, and we both dug into the carton of chow mein simultaneously. "It's been so long," he murmured, digging.

"Since you had dinner with a beautiful girl?" I jested.

"Well, that and being with a friend."

"From what I heard, you weren't wasting any time making friends."

"Depends on what you mean by 'friends.'"

"The Pink Section of the Chronicle had some pretty interesting stories about your dating models and actresses and driving the company directors crazy with your coming in late and hungover or not showing up at all—real diva stuff. Local boy makes good and goes really, really bad sort of storyline, y'know?" I recounted, which brought a guffaw out of Quinn, who knocked back his glass of wine. "I didn't believe it because I know you well."

"I'm glad you didn't!" he laughed now.

"But is it true about the wild parties?" I ventured.

Quinn gave me a sideways glance and shook his head. "Where did you hear that? More newspaper crap?"

"Actually, I heard those stories from some of your high school orchestra and jazz bandmates."

"First, whoever they are, they're not my friends. Second, I went to a party in London, and The Who showed up for all of five minutes. They weren't there long enough to break up a toothpick, let alone a Stratocaster."

"So you weren't caught making out with The Princess Royal in a bathtub at the Savoy, and you didn't try to flush a photographer's head down the toilet?"

"Uh, no."

"But you did mess with that photographer?"

"He insulted my mother."

"And you didn't trash a hotel room coming down off of LSD."

"Again, no."

"And there weren't orgies of any kind."

"I wasn't going to mention the orgies. Classical musicians are always trying to be bad boys." We started laughing, and Quinn leaned in, feeding me chow mein. "I'm amazed at all the reasons people come up with to explain to themselves why I left the orchestra and disappointed them," he sighed. "Why it concerns them, I don't know."

"You'd tell me, right?"

He set down the carton and chopsticks and glanced at the poster of Florence hanging on the wall. "Such a beautiful city. I wish I could have been there with you," Quinn murmured and sighed again. "Rumors started. Ugly stuff and business—I don't want to go into right now, but it didn't help when my father showed up in London."

"Oh, geez, Quinn! I thought he promised to stay away!" I moaned.

"He always managed to find an excuse. Mostly on the

pretext of publicity for the university and the opera company. He followed us to several venues, started coming backstage, making demands, and arguing with the wrong people. He said he was there to do damage control, for what I sure as hell didn't know. Wasn't long after that the director asked me to leave. I guess they made up things and fed it to the press to make it look like it was my behavior that got me fired when in reality, I hadn't done anything at all except behave and be professional, show up for rehearsals, performances, always on time, and extra practice."

"I shouldn't have asked."

He waved it off and poured more wine into our glasses. "I'm glad someone knows the truth."

Silence replaced nervous banter and discussions about family life, catching each other up. Our conversation wandered from the mundane to questions unasked and unanswered, yet the only question not broached where it concerned us was *"Why?"*

When there was nothing left to say, we looked at one another for the longest time, noticing similarities and differences between the boy and the girl we were drawn to seven years earlier, to the man and woman we were now.

I wanted him to take me in his arms, kiss me, seduce me, and suggest we move to the bedroom.

He read my mind.

Quinn drew me into his arms and held me close. I felt that same sweet excitement and anticipation as before when we first kissed. The spark was still there three years after the painful farewell.

Dennis had always said it was meant to be…

Still warm and soft, still gentle.

I melted with every kiss and touch, and when he pulled me off the sofa and led me towards the bedroom, I was glad that there would be no parents coming upstairs or telephone ringing, no family crisis.

There was no fear.
There was only complete love.

CHAPTER 6

I WAS DELICIOUSLY DROWSY and warm, tucked under the blankets and quilts and wrapped entirely in Quinn's arms. How good it was to inhale his familiar scent—one I had not forgotten—and to listen to the steady rise and fall of his breathing, his heartbeat. An occasional gust of snoring. Sleep was beginning to overwhelm me when Quinn slid out of bed. At first, I supposed that he would dress rapidly and leave, make an excuse that it was a work night, and slip away, but moments later, I heard the toilet flush and then the scuff of footsteps and a light going on in the living room. The strains of the *Fantasia on a Theme by Thomas Tallis* drifted into the bedroom, and I smiled. Moments later, Quinn was beside me again.

"This is how it's supposed to be, Faery Princess," he whispered as he took me in his arms.

How disappointed I was to find things differently when I woke in The Curiosity Shop.

Lifting my head from the pillow I'd made of a sweater, I looked around, frowning. But once again, I felt rested, and a heaviness lifted.

The Proprietress stood over me, arms folded across her breasts, staring over her glasses. She thrust a handkerchief at me.

"Who would have thought that you drool?" she sighed. "Come on, then. I don't need to tell you."

I was at the counter, and the lapis book was brought from the display case and set before me, the key offered. I unlocked the book, and The Proprietress placed another gold star, then another, and yet another, on separate pages.

Each star was consecutively larger than the first until the very last filled the handmade paper page to which it had been affixed.

"You've made some progress, Alice," she said with a rare smile. "Go along."

I spun the rack and chose a timetable. I didn't like what I saw there, but even so, I nodded, took my things, and set off for the train station. I was again on the train for Berkeley—the same compartment and the same conductor who looked like Jack Lemmon—he whistled *Since I Fell for You* as he entered the compartment.

Surrendering my ticket book and hoping for at least a 'D' ride, I asked how he was getting on. He stopped whistling and held the ticket to the light for closer inspection.

"What's the matter?" I wanted to know and reached for the ticket. He held it away from me, clucking his tongue.

"Dear, oh dear!" he sighed. "This is regrettable. Something isn't right here."

The Conductor twisted about and punched a button on the wall so that an alarm wailed—an irritating buzz that wasn't shut off until I whacked the radio clock alarm on my nightstand. I would have pulled the covers over my head but for Quinn, who had turned over in bed and threw an arm over me.

"Hi," he greeted sleepily and with a kiss.

"Hi. Did you sleep well?"

"The best in years, truth be told."

Quinn pushed the pillows up against the headboard and brought me with him when he sat up. We nestled as the sun rose.

"Do you want to stay for breakfast?"

"I wish I could," he said, kissing my brow. "I have a nine-thirty audition in the city. The Symphony. Wish me luck?"

"Here's something for luck," I whispered. The kiss led to lovemaking that was unrestrained, gentle, yet passionate. He lay in my arms after, and soon I could hear snoring. He'd fallen back to sleep. I was ready to join him when Quinn groaned as the alarm went off again and, laughing, said, "*No!* It's not fair!"

I would have asked him what he meant when he slid out of bed and shuffled to the bathroom. "Can I use your shower?" he called over his shoulder.

"Of course!"

I had started a pot of coffee and breakfast when he came into the kitchen and nuzzled my bare neck with his five o'clock shadow, which prompted giggles. I turned around and held that exquisitely handsome face in my hands.

"Are we going to make this a habit?" I asked.

Why play games, I thought?

He didn't hesitate to respond, and I didn't notice a change in expression or his eyes.

"Let's get together and talk about that, Alice. There are some things I need you to know about. My life is one pile of shit right now, and we need an understanding. I don't want to hurt you again."

"Okay," I said nervously. "Let's talk tomorrow, okay?"

"It's a date."

He was gone a few minutes later, singing *Stairway to Heaven*, something I'd never heard him sing, and after a dozen kisses that might have led to other things if we'd both had the time. Still, something in his voice and manner wasn't right, and it was while I showered and remembered our lovemaking that I knew he would never hurt me again. The anxiety left as I drank my cup of coffee and prepared for a Friday at work, glad that it was Friday and there were only twenty-four hours or a bit more until we saw each other again.

Combing out my hair in front of the bathroom mirror,

I kept squeezing my eyes shut, hoping I'd be propelled to The Shop so I could share my good fortune with Dennis, Joan of Arc, or Richard the Third, to tell them it was the strangest and most wonderful thing to know how one word could change a course of events . . .

The doorbell rang again, and I skidded across the floor to answer it, my heart pounding.

"One last kiss, Mister Radcliffe!"

I suddenly felt ill, fear and terror rising in the pit of my stomach, my entire being. Adam, a tenor in the college choir and the briefest and most frightening of my sexual encounters, was on the doorstep.

"Hello, Alice."

His stance was angry: feet far apart, arms crossed against himself defensively. Without another word, he shoved his way into the apartment and started looking around.

"I saw him leave!" Adam growled.

"It's none of your business. We're not together anymore," I said quietly, closing the robe around me and pushing the collar up so he wouldn't see the love bites on my throat and chest.

"Who is he?"

"I said, it's none of your business. We're not together anymore."

"Who is he!"

Adam had taken me by the shoulders and gripped me so tightly I knew there'd be bruises by midday.

"What did you do? Stake out the apartment all night? Let go, Adam!"

"I think I have the right!"

"No, you don't. Let go of me, now!"

"You're a slut! He stayed here all night, didn't he?"

"Let go, I said!"

Then he struck me, and I reeled back into the coffee table, into the cartons of Chinese takeaway, nearly falling but breaking that fall by grabbing the record player. The needle skidded across the Vaughan Williams album.

"See what you've done!" I screamed at him.

"So what? You can buy another one. It's probably that boring, dull song, anyway. Don't know why you won't listen to my music. Why don't you listen to my music instead of that classical shit, that upper-class shit?"

"Learn something other than fifties pop and lounge music, and maybe I would, but that won't happen in a month of Sundays."

"It's not good enough? I'm not good enough?"

"Get out!"

"Who is he, Alice?"

"Leave, or I'm calling the police!"

"Fine. But I don't believe for one moment that you want this."

"I do—I want it bad. But not with you!"

I was shoved away, and I blocked my fall with the coat rack and clung to it, a weapon to be used.

"Let me give you something to remember me by."

Adam looked around and picked up the snow globe Quinn had given me from the bookshelf. He hefted it as if to throw, and I caught his arm and wrestled the globe out of his hand. In doing so, the globe's base struck me in the face. I felt a trickle of blood on my cheek and, without another word, ran to the bedroom and locked the door.

It seemed like an eternity in that short interval when I stood in the room and didn't move, ignoring the throbbing pain, the blood trickling down my cheek, and Adam's pounding at the door. I stared at the bed, rumpled and still warm, the impression of Quinn's head on one of the pillows.

The telephone rang. I grabbed it, waited a moment, and then, "Hello!"

"Alice? Are you alright?" The apartment house superintendent was on the phone, his voice sleepy and concerned. "What's going on down there?"

"I'm not okay," I sobbed. "Would you call the police? Please? Now?"

I unlocked the bedroom door and entered The Curiosity Shop a moment later.

The Proprietress was placing a gold star in the book. For the first time, I received a sympathetic glance from her, and that look followed me to the corner. As if nothing had happened, I began what would become my usual routine: I took notebooks and sketchbooks out of the messenger bag, set them on the table according to subject, opened up and switched on the laptop, and took a sip from the coffee mug. At the same time, I waited for the boot-up and stared at the home screen. Then I read my work from the time before and eventually started typing. Today, however, I caught my reflection in the window. I placed a finger on my left cheek and was surprised not to see or feel a scar.

Customers now came and went, and they acknowledged me, nodding deferentially, or smiling, asking how it was going and if I was settling in.

I was surprised when Joan of Arc handed me a bouquet of freesias and white lilies and said, "Well done!"

She extended a hand covered by a gauntlet and held the silver rose I still wore around my neck. "The white rose. A symbol of pure love. I wonder if he knew that?" she mused and, winking added, "He certainly felt that!"

"Alice was fortunate."

The goddess Athena had entered The Shop and handed me the snowy owl to take my face in her hands and study it. I trembled under her scrutiny but unwavering held her gray-eyed gaze. The goddess nodded with approval. "Well done, indeed!"

"We'll see," sniffed The Proprietress as she tucked the book back into the display case. She opened up a ledger— the first I'd seen her do this—and made an entry with a gold pen with a tiny, revolving cylinder on the end of it in place of an eraser. She wrote quickly and then, clucking her tongue, erased the entry. Bright streams of light shot out in all directions as the entry was wiped away cleanly.

One pale blue spark reached my corner. I watched it bob and sway, dance with every movement until my bracelet caught the sunlight as I took the kaleidoscope Quinn was handed me as we sat outside Peet's Coffees and Teas on Walnut Square.

"I found this yesterday—thought you might want it," Quinn said.

"So that's where it went to!" I laughed. "What else of mine have you got?"

Quinn kissed me and gently caressed my face. "Your heart, I hope!" Now he frowned, touching the scratch on my face where the globe struck it the morning before, the tiny welt, and the bruise. "What's all this?" he asked.

"Tripped in the bathroom, that's all."

"Poor you!" he whispered and kissed the wounds. The warmth of his lips was a salve.

He sat down and stirred what looked like a snowfall of sugar in his coffee, turning the bowl of the cup as he always did before drinking, waiting for it to cool, and in this instance, perhaps, wanting to gather his thoughts.

"How'd the audition go?" I opened.

"Waiting for a callback. I'm not holding out much hope, not with the program they've got planned for the fall. A lot of modern pieces, and my strength is with the classics."

"It's one orchestra. I've always considered you a concert cellist, a solo act."

"Those gigs are hard to come by. But thanks," he replied.

Now he drank his coffee as if it were poison, and lines appeared on his brow.

"Something the matter, Quinn?" I asked.

"What?"

"Tell me," I said, taking his hand. "Whatever it is."

"I didn't think you'd return my call," he finally said. "I wanted to call as soon as I got home yesterday, but I thought it would make me seem too desperate. I didn't think you would still care after all this time. It felt right, being with you. But,"

I forced a smile.

"There are things you need to know and understand, Alice. When you hear what I have to say, it might change how you see me, or worse, how you feel, and if you want to be with me—"

"Hey there, Alice!"

Adam's voice jarred me out of the safe cocoon I occupied when with Quinn. The old fear began to replace it. Quinn and I looked up at him; he blocked the midday sun and looked ready for a fight.

"The police officer told you to stay away," I stated.

"Alice, is this the guy…?" Quinn asked, moving closer.

"Yep. I'm the one," Adam stated. "Or I thought I was. Funny thing about Alice. She's into you for only as long as you keep it interesting in bed."

"Hey!" Quinn snapped. "There's a lady present. Show some respect!"

"I don't want to get into this, Adam," I snapped. "Just go!"

"Nope, I might have a cup of coffee, read the paper, maybe eavesdrop on a conversation. I'd love to hear if you still use the same lies you used on me."

"Why don't you leave now?" Quinn said, standing up.

"It's a free country, rich boy," Adam sneered. "I go where I want."

"Leave her alone."

"You gonna make me?"

"I just might, asshole!"

Adam threw the first punch. Despite my pleas, Quinn was equal to the challenge and attacked. They wrestled over tables and almost went through a window but avoided the street while customers and pedestrians steered clear, and I stood on the sidewalk screaming for peace. Fortunately, the cafe owner and his assistant ran out of the store and broke up the fight. Twenty-five minutes after it began, it was over, with Adam being taken away by the police.

"I can't believe you fell for a bastard like him," Quinn growled.

"Don't you start!" I fired back. "You didn't have to provoke him!"

"Provoke him? He interrupted us, and he started insulting you, Alice!"

"He's getting help. Sometimes it's best just to ignore Adam."

"Christ! Don't tell me you still have feelings for him!"

"What makes you think that?"

"I saw how you looked at him!"

"How did I look at him?" I demanded, ignoring the people that were staring and whispering.

"Isn't that Professor Radcliffe's son?" one woman said none-too-quietly to her friend as they stood on the sidewalk enjoying the show.

"That's all I need," Quinn muttered. "Are we done here?" he demanded of the police officer writing out his report. Angrily scrawling his name on the bottom of the form, Quinn glanced at me. "Well? I'm waiting."

"I don't need to justify my actions for the past two, almost three years," I began.

"Excuses aren't the best defense."

I looked away, trying to gather my thoughts and some calm.

"Well?" Quinn demanded.

What I wanted to say wouldn't leave my lips. I stood

mute, frantic, searching for an explanation for my silence.

"Silence isn't the best defense, either, but an indication of truth."

"We had broken up! Okay? What was I supposed to do? Pine over you?" I defended myself, though I didn't understand why. The words just came to mind. "You went to England and left me here!"

"I never stopped loving you! I was waiting!"

"For what? Still waiting for your father's permission?"

"Why is this happening?" he asked and walked away. I would have run after him, but the emergency medical technician shook his head. He held me back as the swirling light of the ambulance unraveled and became a pale ribbon of light that I watched mesmerized until I was looking at a heart monitor in a hospital room.

Dennis was on the bed, pierced by tubes that seemed to run to every corner of his body, his once muscular frame now skeletal. Harry was sitting in the only chair in the room and holding his hand. I was on the opposite side of the bed with Donovan beside me. We had been here for an hour, watching the monitor. A doctor and nurse stood to one side, trying to be inconspicuous.

The blue ribbon pulsed, bobbed, pulsed, and bobbed, continued for what I thought was a reassuring, long moment, and then went flat.

The tone filled up the silence.

No one moved, and no one said a word. I stared at my shoes for the longest time, hoping that if I looked up, Dennis would open his eyes and smile at me, throw a barb at me for my appearance, or criticize my choice of men with sarcasm so that I would be able to match word for word. In contrast, Harry would be looking on and pretending to be annoyed. When I finally looked at Dennis, I was amazed by how peaceful he looked and how the color had returned to his cheeks after weeks of sudden disease and pain.

Moving away from Donovan, I leaned over the bed, kissed Dennis' lips, smoothed back the hair falling on his brow, and was frightened because I could feel every bone in his skull and face.

"Harry, are you okay?" I whispered, looking over at him.

"Don't worry about me, Sweetheart," he said, though his voice cracked, and he squeezed Dennis's hand and leaned forward to kiss him.

I motioned to Donovan, suggesting we leave Harry alone to say goodbye. The doctor called the time of death, and it was then I knew I would need to call upon the strength and steel-edged determination that sustained me in times past to get through this.

Wrenching, guttural sobs came from Harry as he waved off the doctor and nurse, throwing his body over Dennis as if to protect him.

"Shouldn't we do something?" Donovan sighed, clearly put off by the show of pain and emotion. I was immobile, frozen with grief. I wanted to shout, to scream, to kick and thrash, but I couldn't move.

"Missus Trist, are you okay?" a nurse asked, a gentle hand on my shoulder. "Missus Trist?"

"What? I'm Alice Martin," I said.

"Are you okay? Do you need anything?"

I looked at her and frowned. Why did people ask if you were all right when it was apparent you weren't, and the situation was devastating?

Donovan made me sit in one of those horrible plastic bucket chairs outside the unit while he went to find a pay phone to call our friends and his family. I sat in silence and wondered if this was how it had been for my mother or father—wherever he was or wherever he had gone—and wondered how I would go.

As we left the hospital, I glanced over at Donovan and saw that his jaw was set, his driving glasses sitting perfectly on the bridge of his nose, and not a hair was out of place. His dead eyes stared straight ahead while he maneuvered the spirals and corners of the multi-level garage.

"He was just with us last year," I murmured, staring out the window and wondering why it wasn't raining. Didn't it always rain when people you loved died?

"Pardon?"

"At our wedding. He was with us. He danced with me, and laughed, caught the bouquet…"

We drove in silence for a time. Then, "Will you cry for me, Alice?" Donovan was asking now.

"What?" I couldn't believe what I'd just heard.

"Will you cry for me? When I die?"

"What kind of thing is that to say right now?" I gasped.

"I don't know. I get a feeling that all the love you've ever had is for people who have died or are dying or have gone away."

"What's that supposed to mean?"

"Just what I said."

I frowned and stared at him, then at the traffic lights at Cedar and Rose. The red lights were blinking.

Stop…stop…stop…

"Of course I'll cry!" I finally sighed. "You're my husband."

"But not someone you love. If you gave me a tenth of the love you give others—"

"—What are you talking about? I married you! I left my life, my home, my friends! I would think that's a damn good indication of love. Why are we talking about this now, anyway?"

"This is a milestone. I just want to see where it leads, Alice."

"My brother is dead, my only family, and you turn it around to yourself!"

We drove in silence for a while. I'd glance at Donovan

occasionally and wasn't surprised that the expression on his face hadn't changed or that he didn't reach out to take my hand as I thought aloud.

"I didn't say goodbye to my brother. I should have told him I loved him yesterday. Why didn't I?"

"That's not your brother anymore. It's just a pile of atoms, molecules, and tissues. Dennis is now a thought, a memory."

"Stop the car!" I ordered.

"Alice, you're grieving."

"STOP THE CAR!"

He pulled over, and I jumped out, running across the street and back toward the university. Donovan didn't follow.

I ran for what seemed forever until night turned to day and the sun rose on a winter's morning, and I was running and laughing in Quinn's forest of a backyard, trying to get to the house before Quinn. His parents' house was more of a museum than a dwelling, a miniature castle complete with a courtyard, a cloister, and a round tower. Indeed, the place was called "The Cloisters" and sat upon an eight-hundred-foot bluff overlooking Berkeley and San Francisco Bay.

I wasn't fast enough, and Quinn tackled me gently, knocking me onto the lawn and holding me down, both of us laughing hysterically.

"Say it!" Quinn commanded. "Say it, or I'll tickle you!"

"No, not again!" I screamed with laughter.

"Say it, c'mon!"

His hands under my pea coat and sweater were icy as he started to tickle. As cold as it was, I loved the feel of his hands on my skin; it was exciting, and I could tell he was getting excited too.

"Okay, okay! You are the supreme ruler and emperor of the twenty realms—and you win. Stop!!" I laughed. "You win!"

We sat up and caught our breaths. Quinn got to his feet effortlessly and then offered a hand. I lit easily into his arms, and we stood locked in an embrace under an ancient fir tree.

"I guess that'll teach you to play Risk with me, Faery Princess!" he whispered after a passionate kiss that made us both want more. The slam of a door precluded any lovemaking. Quinn moved away, pulling down my sweater and wrapping his coat around him when we heard the crunch of leaves and bracken underfoot, a pause, and then continue, fading, another slam of the door.

"Rematch! I demand a rematch!" I shouted and nodded towards the shadowy figure behind curtains at a first-floor window. After a moment, Quinn mouthed, 'Let's go,' and we did.

"Save it for tomorrow night, Loser!" he teased and then more gently, "Come on, I want to show you something."

We chased each other through the house, mindless of the medieval pillars and decoration, and scrambled upstairs to his study. I threw myself on the sofa and leaned over to switch on the television set when Quinn crooked a finger toward me from the bedroom door. I followed, and he slammed the door shut. Behind the door was an electric guitar. He gestured towards it. "Fender Stratocaster—I bought it from a Cal student. What do you think? The same guitar Jimi Hendrix plays!"

"Wow!" I touched the smooth surface and ran a finger up the strings to the fret. "Play something!"

"Thought you'd never ask," Quinn said, plugging the guitar into an amplifier dragged out of his closet and placed next to the cello. He assumed a stance I'd seen Eric Clapton take in performances and then started playing *Purple Haze*, the volume up to ear-splitting.

We bellowed the lyrics at the top of our lungs, and Quinn launched into a perfect rendition of Hendrix's riff.

He had all the notes and the style down, and I improvised a go-go dance around him.

"WHAT THE HELL ARE YOU DOING?"

The bedroom door almost exploded off its hinges when Professor Radcliffe threw it open and strode across the room, unplugging the amplifier. He looked like a raging bull with his red face and breath coming in quick, angry spurts, his chest heaving. I wondered if he wasn't going to have a heart attack. When he turned on Quinn, I saw Quinn flinch and almost drop his precious guitar.

"What did I tell you?" the Professor hissed at his son. "What... did...I...tell you!"

Quinn just glared back. He didn't make eye contact with me, for I was across the room, cowering on the window seat. He looked down at his father and glared.

"You said I could do what I wanted with my Christmas money," Quinn finally spoke calmly. He was trembling, however, and put the guitar on the bed. His clenched fists were shoved into his jeans pockets.

"I don't want that vile noise in my house. Do you understand me?"

"Yes, but I call it music. Bach, Mozart, and Verdi aren't the only musicians in the world," Quinn defended himself.

The Professor turned to me and jerked his head towards the door. "Get out!"

I glanced at Quinn, who barely nodded, and I fled, not even grabbing my book bag and purse.

Again, I ran, and again the time of day changed, as did the seasons. Suddenly a year passed, and it was late January 1973. I was on my old street in Berkeley and in front of our house. I leaned against the garage door and was grateful to hear the purring of the sewing machine, the sound of Harry in the kitchen, and Dennis' conversation with him. What I'd just experienced were nightmares. Yes! That's what they had been: bad dreams or memories that made no sense.

I knew they were neither.

This was affirmed when I saw Quinn approaching from Oxford Street.

"Hey!" he greeted after a brief kiss. "I was just coming to see you."

"You're back! When did you get back?" I demanded.

"Last week."

"And you didn't—?" I sat on the porch steps, waiting, knowing what would come next.

"We have to talk."

I gestured with my eyes and hands. He didn't sit beside me.

"Look. Alice, I know we made promises, but I've changed. I mean, my life has changed."

I didn't bother looking at him, but I knew the face was paler than usual, the eyes dark, especially when troubled, as he was now.

"I guessed as much when you didn't show up at the library. I guessed then you would break up with me, that I wouldn't see you again."

"Alice! It's not what you're thinking. I love you!"

"Don't suppose you know what I'm thinking. Remember? But you do know what's in my heart."

He stared at the sidewalk, unable to look me in the eyes. I was glad, for I knew his reasons—I wasn't ready to tell him that I knew and why, or how, I knew.

"You have to understand! I was given a provisional chair with the Royal Philharmonic. The letter arrived before I got home, and there was an impossible deadline."

"And that's why you didn't show up despite the promise."

"I didn't sleep that night—I knew what it meant. It's like an internship, and there's a lot of traveling. Alice, I'm twenty, and they've never had a cellist as young as me. If I give this up…"

"I guess we both know what this means," I murmured and looked down at a trail of ants, finding interest in them: diligent, steadfast, determined. Nothing would stand in their way.

"Alice? Alice, say something."

"When?" I asked. "When do you leave?"

"Tonight."

I slumped down and stared at nothing, felt nothing, and then I felt like I would be sick. I saw the hem of his coat, the perfect crease in his pants, and then his perfect, long hands, musician's hands, reaching for me.

"Good luck, Quinn. I wish you well," I said, keeping my voice as even as I could. I scrambled to my feet and turned to go, but he pulled me back. I was close to tears but wouldn't cry; I refused to show weakness. Quinn wanted to hold me despite my struggle to be free. I would wound him another way. I removed the white rose pendant from around my neck and was ready to give it to him when he shook his head and replaced it.

"No. Keep it. It was a gift, and I hope you'll look at it and think of me from time to time. You'll always be in my thoughts," Quinn said huskily, his voice constricted by tears and emotion. "I'll come back for you."

"Sure."

"Kiss me goodbye?"

I tasted his tears as our lips met, and I broke away first, running into the house.

"I'll come back for you!" he shouted as the screen door slammed behind me.

I didn't know then how long it would be, if at all.

Dennis barely looked up from his work as I almost knocked over the sewing machine cabinet on the way to my bedroom. He lifted the foot and studied the seams of his tie. "It's not supposed to be this way—it doesn't end this way."

"No one asked for your opinion!" I growled and ran

upstairs to The Curiosity Shop, slamming the door behind me so that a pane of glass fell out of one of the mullioned frames.

"No indeed!" said The Proprietress as she brought me a broom and dustpan. "Temper, temper, Miss Alice!"

The glass shards sparkled in the sunlight and were spattered by my tears that now flowed easily. Yes, I did cry, especially when my heart was broken. The falling drops looked like silver roses that dissolved as quickly as they appeared. Once the floor was clean, I shoved myself up from my knees and accepted the new bottle of Diet Pepsi The Proprietress handed off as I walked past her to my corner and thumped it down on the table.

"I suppose no gold star?" I murmured, daring to look at her.

"On the contrary—this is one star you've earned. Now, get your things."

"Where now?"

"As if I have to tell you! The rack, Alice!"

A brochure was removed from the rack, and I winced and nodded.

Of course.

"See you," I muttered, going out the door. Joan of Arc smiled at me as we passed, and she whispered, "It wasn't supposed to happen like that at all, Alice!"

"And be quick about it! The week is almost up!" Stomping her well-shod foot and roundly pointing out the door with the snap of a finger, The Proprietress sent me on my way.

CHAPTER 7

THE STREET LOOKED the same: the same flower boxes dangling out of windows set in buildings so close neighbors could kiss if they leaned out a bit, the same ochre walls, the same smell of diesel and garlic, the Vespas and Alfa Romeos crammed on narrow streets that twisted and stretched until they reached the Piazza Bra. The cobblestones were shiny with rain, and people walked arm and arm *in passaggio* as the sun fell below the hills, and evening came to Verona in late September.

As I walked by a shop window, Romeo and Juliet dolls displayed against a backdrop of medieval Verona caught my attention, and I shook my head.

"At least we didn't die!" I sighed.

I knew the path from the Vicolo Tre Marchetti to the Via dal Cappello as if it were a path I'd walked all my life, even though the time spent in this, the city of my dreams, had been a year, no more.

The house was exactly as I remembered it: the gatehouse with its passageway off the street opening into a courtyard of ivy-covered ancient brick and stone fragrant with roses. The bench was still there, facing the house and the balcony. The gauche souvenir shops hadn't existed when I first visited Verona in 1973, but here they were four years later, a magnet for tourists.

The museum guard pacing the courtyard looked up and smiled when I entered and sat on the bench, nodding as I sat down and took out a notebook.

"Every night, Signorina," he greeted in English.

"I brought supper—enough for two. Are you

allowed…?" I took a sack lunch out of my bag and offered a sandwich. The guard looked about and accepted it, murmuring, "*Grazie, Signorina. Molto grazie.*"

We dined silently. The guard paced back and forth and began humming a song while I sketched the courtyard between writing sentences and watched the light change as the sun dropped and glinted off the windows.

"Now is the time for lovers," the guard commented, nodding toward a couple that came through the passageway and now stood before the modern bronze statue of Juliet.

"Do it, James!" the woman giggled in an American Midwestern accent. "It's supposed to bring good luck!"

"Touch her boob? Ah hell, I'd rather grab yours!" the man teased as he reached for the woman. She jumped away and started to laugh. Finally, the man touched the statue's right breast and stepped back as if waiting for a lightning bolt or divine intervention. Rays of light sparked off the metal, highly polished by tourists' and curiosity seekers' hands over the years. The couple noticed this and embraced, enjoying a kiss in one of Italy's most romantic places. It gave me a pang of melancholia.

I glanced over and saw that the guard had shone a penlight on the statue.

"It makes people happy," he shrugged. "No harm in a bit of fun."

"What's happier than love?" I murmured, going back to my sketching.

"I think that any man with you, Signorina Alice, would be happy to death."

"I don't know what that means but thank you."

The guard nodded and sighed that it was time to go home to his wife. "Don't forget to turn out the lights and lock the door!" he teased as he entered the office. The couple retraced their steps to the narrow street. No sooner had they left than a man entered the courtyard, stopped just under the balcony, and glanced up.

"*Not* fourteenth century," he grumbled aloud. "*Not* part of the original house."

He took only a moment's reflection there, then pivoted on a foot and looked at me, surprised.

"Some say it's a horse trough," I said, pointing at the balcony with a carrot stick. "Wait, no, that's Juliet's tomb. This, they think, was added on in the nineteenth century. I've heard it said. Read it."

He stared at me for the longest time, and the serious expression on his face softened to a smile.

Now he studied the ivy-covered walls, the *pastiglia* medallions on the house's façade, the *graffiti* someone had left. After every review, he would turn slightly, look at me intensely, and smile as if waiting for a comment. It was a beautiful smile.

But it wasn't Quinn's.

He was Doctor Donovan Trist, archeologist, and Professor of Antiquities at Brown University, emphasizing *doctor*, and this was where we met.

Yes, he could have been Quinn's older brother for the similarity in hair, coloring, build, and eyes, but as I would learn, he had a cold personality, suspicious nature, and too much self-love.

The attraction was purely carnal.

I knew who and what he was.

Would I receive a gold star for what I felt in my heart and soul right then?

Donovan approached me and then stopped, spun about, and took a camera from his pocket—one of those skinny Instamatic jobs with the flash bulb larger than the camera itself—and looked around as if trying to decide.

"If you stand at the entrance of the gatehouse, that passage leading out into the street, you'll get a better shot—just over there, you see," I suggested. "The light comes down, and the mist—better in the morning, though."

He glanced over, waiting.

"Take the shot now while the light's good," I said as I gathered my things and started out. "G'night. Enjoy."

I heard his footsteps in the passage and didn't turn to respond to his calls until out in the street and halfway to the Scaligeri Tombs.

"You wouldn't happen to know any other good places to shoot?" he asked, breathless.

"A few—this one's pretty good." I gestured towards the tombs.

"Donovan Trist," he introduced himself, a hand extended.

"Alice Martin."

"You're the first person I've encountered who knows anything about Verona."

"The guidebooks don't tell you some things. You have to read histories."

"On vacation?"

No, I wasn't. Once more, I was trying to forget…again…

"Yes," I lied.

I looked at my watch and down the street as if waiting for someone. Donovan was smiling down at me, waiting.

"You?" I finally asked.

"I'm here for a conference," Donovan said. "The International Congress of Antiquities is meeting. You wouldn't happen to know anything about the excavations at the Castelvecchio? I could use some more material for my lecture tomorrow."

His attempt at a jest failed to amuse or impress me. "Sorry, I haven't been to the castle. That's on my schedule tomorrow."

"Would you like to attend the lecture?" he blurted out.

"Can't. I'm working on a paper."

Well, it wasn't truly a lie now; I was working on the Ph.D. thesis in my head.

"I'm also doing research on the della Scala—that one. It's Cangrande della Scala."

I pointed to the tomb over the door of Santa Maria dell'Antica, the chapel outside the ornate, gothic funerary monuments of the family that ruled Verona in the Middle Ages.

"Ah!" That answer won me a few points. "Historian?"

"Graduate student—medieval studies."

"Harvard, Yale?"

"Berkeley."

"I spent a summer in Berkeley. It was for a seminar with Doctor Charles Gordston and his dig in Sepphoris."

"Yeah, the town near Nazareth, the one destroyed by the Romans in the first century. We've got some of the artifacts."

His face brightened. "You're an archeologist!"

"Sorry, no. Are you?"

"Yes, I'm in the History Department at Brown. Professor of Antiquities."

Yes, Brown—the chair he fought and clawed his way to when his father's power and position in Rhode Island couldn't or wouldn't help him; the excavations in the Middle East: these were his great passions and mistresses. Remembering how the conversation continued, I wanted to turn and walk the other way, but out of the corner of my eye, I saw Dennis, The Proprietress, Richard the Third, and Joan of Arc standing across the street, watching. They shook their heads 'no' one at a time.

I forced a smile and extended a hand. "It was nice to meet you, Mr. Trist."

"Doctor Trist." There was a bit too much emphasis on 'doctor' for my liking.

My hand was still extended. "Well then, Doctor Trist. Enjoy your stay in Verona."

I was at the corner of the Via dal Cappello and heading toward the Piazza dell'Erbe when I heard the footsteps again. This time, my name was shouted, and an elderly gentleman passing by chuckled, "*Amore, amore!*" to himself.

"Alice!" Donovan was panting for breath. "Alice, if you're not in town with anyone, or seeing anyone, have dinner with me tomorrow night," he suggested. His face was earnest, boyish, and sweet. "That is if you can spare time from your paper. I'm staying at the Albergo Dante. We could have dinner there. So…?"

Again, I looked up and down the street, looking for an Amtrak train or The Curiosity Shop. He was waiting; his expression hadn't changed. I was ready to turn him down, to avoid regret and unhappiness, and hopefully return to a happier life, when Dennis appeared and held up a sign that read, "Changing history entirely is NEVER a good idea!"

"What time?" I asked brightly.

Donovan wore a look of shock on his face.

"What-time-should-I-meet-you?" I said slowly, making sure he understood me.

"Five o'clock?"

Dennis, Richard, Joan, and The Proprietress now held up a billboard-sized poster that read, "Well done, YOU!" Ignoring them, I nodded goodbye to Donovan and found myself looking back.

He waved and turned to go and did a "look back" of his own.

My heart felt lighter, and my step quicker. A smile came easily to my lips, yet in the deepest recesses of my heart, I ached and was full of uncertainty, feeling as if I were going to commit the worst kind of betrayal.

Why did I care?

I thought and rationalized that Quinn was undoubtedly making up for lost time. I was under no obligation to him.

He never came back for me!

He made assumptions on that disastrous Saturday

coffee date, never returned for an explanation, and didn't ask for one. Instead, he disappeared to England.

While showering, I washed away the hurt, not the memory. As I selected an outfit, I replaced the silver rose around my neck with a strand of iridescent crystal beads.

"It takes one love to appreciate and mend another," Joan of Arc whispered as I closed the door to my hotel room. "Two wrongs make a right!"

"Whatever does she mean?" I asked myself in the elevator.

The Albergo Dante was not far from where we stood the evening before, off the Piazza dell'Erbe as it happened, a fourteenth-century townhouse converted into a lovely first-class hotel. My arrival was met with smiles from the desk clerks and a large bouquet of white roses. One of the clerks almost tripped over himself to escort me to the dining room, where I was told Donovan waited. He leaped to his feet and stared when I entered. *Gaped* was a better word, for I'd decided against my usual co-ed look of sweater, jeans, and clogs and wore a shirtwaist dress of plum silk, with pumps, a light woolen lace shawl, and carried a simple evening bag. The dress was unbuttoned just enough to reveal a silk camisole underneath and a bit of cleavage. My hair was swept up in a chignon. I had decided to make this sacrifice worth my while and his.

"Alice!" he exclaimed. "Wow! You look, well, wow!"

"Thank you. And thank you for the flowers. I'm partial to white and yellow bouquets."

"I saw the silver rose you wore, and I thought, white roses—oh! You're not wearing it," he said, seating me and then sitting at the opposite end of the table. A waiter brought two menus and discreetly stepped away. "Shall I order for us?" Donovan asked, winking.

I glanced at the menu and shook my head, motioned with a hand to the waiter who was immediately at my side. *"Per il primo corso, vorrei che gli gnocchi, poi, lesso con la peará—fa che vengono con la polenta? Fragole e crema per il dessert.*" I said in Italian, adding, "*e un bottiglia de Valpolicella, per favore?*"

"*Subito, Signorina!*" the waiter answered, smiling, and looked to Donovan, whose face had gone dark.

"*Si, io sono lo stesso,*" he responded quietly.

Once the waiter disappeared into the kitchen, I helped myself to the bread and dish of olive oil and looked at Donovan questioningly.

"Oh dear, I've already got black marks against me!" I quipped.

"No black marks at all," said Donovan as he leaned closer in his chair. "I was expecting someone different."

"I don't need someone to order my food, though I enjoy the door being opened for me or a chair pulled out. I can stand compliments and hold my own in a fight."

"A liberated woman!" Donovan cried with sarcasm coloring the words.

"No, just Alice."

I glanced around the dining room, pleased that the proprietor hadn't ruined the simple Italian gothic interior with baroque, rococo, or Victorian décor, and nodded, smiling to myself.

"Interesting room, isn't it? I wasn't expecting something so austere," Donovan commented.

"I'm pleased the owner hasn't turned this hotel into a baroque wedding cake. I love the simplicity of Gothic arches and Romanesque architecture. I'm guessing this townhouse is a little of both," I said.

"It reminds me of The Cloisters in New York."

"You've been there?"

"It was like a playground for me, growing up."

"How lucky for you! I've wanted to visit since I discovered it existed," I said. "We have nothing like it in Berkeley. Well, there's the Hume Castle up in the hills, also called The Cloisters, built in the twenties. Sorry! Tell me if I'm boring you."

Why don't you tell him who lived there, Alice?

"You're not boring. You're refreshing. I don't meet many women interested in medieval architecture or history, at least, none as beautiful as you."

"You're making points here, Mr. Trist."

"*Doctor* Trist."

Dinner and a fine bottle of Valpolicella—a local red wine I cherished—were brought. From the look on Donovan's face, he was pleasantly surprised at the local dishes placed before him: first gnocchi and later boiled meats in a peppery bread sauce. He was even more delighted with the wine, which he poured into two glasses. We dined quietly, and then Donovan put down his knife and fork.

"Something wrong?" I wanted to know.

"What if I told you I know a few people at The Cloisters and could introduce you to the curator? They've got fellowships for doctoral students."

"I couldn't impose. I want my work to recommend me. I'm sorry, that was rude."

Donovan sat back in his chair and regarded me with his dark eyes and enigmatic smile. After that night, I always wondered what he was smiling about.

But there was no hidden agenda or secret in how he looked at me.

"No, I don't blame you. You don't know me from Adam, and here I am, offering to help. Though, if we were in an interview at Brown, I would make the same offer."

"But then you wouldn't get dinner," I teased now.

"I'd find a way to invite you to a working dinner, a dinner meeting,"

"And I'd probably have to think about it, at least until I knew if your intentions were academic and honorable."

"The words most men don't want to hear!" he laughed, charging our glasses again. "We don't like being just friends or honorable."

"He says as he fills her glass up with yet more wine,"

Donovan guffawed and playfully put the bottle on the empty table beside us. I grabbed it, and he laughed even harder.

"You are so different from the girls I grew up with."

"Where was that?"

"Originally New York. My parents moved to Rhode Island when I was thirteen. You?"

"California. Born and raised in Berkeley, but my dad's job had us living in England for a while."

"Diplomatic corps, I guess?"

"Architect. He went over to help rebuild London. And your dad?"

He waited a moment, and I thought at the time he was savoring a bite of the gnocchi, but I knew he was debating whether to tell me about his family—some of the scariest, wealthiest people on earth. "Senator from Rhode Island," Donovan sighed, and the look on his face told me he regretted that revelation.

"Wow," was all I could say at first, and then after a moment of thought, "Wait a minute! Is he the guy that stood up on the Senate floor and called Johnson all those names and demanded an end to the war?"

"It made him a hero in the anti-war movement."

"And what were your feelings about that?"

"I had better things to do than worry about getting drafted."

This was the first revelation of his conservative leanings, which I thought strange for someone who listened to Dylan and the Grateful Dead, Country Joe and the Fish and spent hours stoned. I learned later that it was a clever smokescreen. It didn't matter then, for I remembered how different my parents were politically and idealistically, and theirs had been a match made in heaven.

"Until something went wrong," The Proprietress commented from her table opposite ours.

I glanced to see if Donovan was aware of her presence, and he was gone, as was the Albergo Dante dining room, when The Curiosity Shop materialized around me.

"I'm surprised you're so naïve at twenty-three," Richard the Third commented in passing.

"Says the monarch who couldn't trust his friends!" I sniped.

"Unkind, Alice Rose!"

"I have to agree," Marie Antoinette said from her card game with Sigmund Freud. "You've had your heart broken, what, once? Twice? I'm surprised you're seeing him so favorably, Alice—Doctor Freud! Where did that ace come from?"

"My God and Saints! Enough of that, if you please!" Joan of Arc interrupted. "Remember, Alice doesn't have a choice here."

"She'll figure it out. Eventually," Tyrone Power joined in.

"I don't know," sighed Athena, "look how long it's taken her to get over Quinn."

"Is she over Quinn?" Richard asked.

"She thinks she is," sniffed The Proprietress.

"It ain't over 'til the fat lady sings!"

Everyone in The Shop turned at the sound of Yogi Berra's voice, stared rudely, and then ignored him. He skulked out.

"Well, if you want my opinion," Sigmund Freud started.

"No!" a dozen voices cried in unison, including mine.

"Stop talking about me as if I'm not in the room," I demanded.

"You're not," The Proprietress sighed.

"What?"

"You're not in the room."

With a snap of her fingers, I was back in the dining

room.

"…so after Harvard, I spent some time in Petra with the British dig and then applied to Brown, and there it is."

Donovan poured the remaining wine into his glass and considered me over the crystal rim.

"I know I've done something to offend you, so why don't you tell me?" I asked nervously.

"You've done nothing at all—just wondering how boring I am to someone as charming and attractive as you."

"I do feel a bit like Eliza Doolittle right now."

"You're not at all like Eliza, and I bet I could learn a thing or two from Alice Martin," he said in a silky, husky voice. "Let's go for a walk. I want to hear all about lovely Alice."

Verona was a city made for romantic walks. It had neither the crowds nor the attractions of its larger, more popular sisters, Florence and Rome, the sophistication of Milan or Venice. It had, like them, small, narrow streets down which to walk on warm summer nights, magnificent buildings to pause and marvel at, and a lovely river to stroll across. We chose the Ponte Scaligeri, the bridge to the "old castle," Il Castelvecchio.

Something happened that evening. Whether hindsight or the maturity of thought and character, I could claim that when this strange journey into my soul began, Donovan seemed gentle and caring now, less of a pompous ass and snob, less self-absorbed and arrogant than I remembered. He listened to what I had to say; he seemed genuinely interested in the life of a young woman in her twenties who still looked at the world for its endless possibilities rather than all of the fathomless disappointments lurking in the shadows. Donovan was charming and offered genuine flattery and was very attentive. By the end of the evening, we were holding hands when his arm didn't slip around my waist or when he wasn't offering a lingering whisper in my ear or touch

I hadn't felt this happy in months...

I didn't care that it would all burst like a balloon over time. I only cared about that moment, that night, right then.

We stood in the hotel lobby waiting for my elevator when Donovan took my hand and kissed it.

"Good night, Alice," he whispered.

"Good night. Thank you."

"Did you have a lovely time?"

It was a prompt, and for a moment put me off. Donovan was like a parent instructing a child on manners.

"I did."

"And would you like to see me again?"

Then he drew me close and we kissed, first hesitantly and then with a frightening passion.

I wanted to swoon from the heat of the kiss, his sensual, innocent touch, and his words. But I knew better.

Or did I?

"As much as I want to, I'm leaving tomorrow night. I've got lots to do."

"Is this the brush off? Anything I can do to make you change your mind? Shit, I'm coming on too fast, aren't I?"

"No. Look, I'm sorry. Maybe you were expecting me to be something or someone else."

The elevator bell rang, and I slipped into the car. When the doors opened again, I was in The Shop.

The Proprietress looked up when the doorbell jangled, and she greeted me with a scowl, returning to a quarrel she was having with Sigmund Freud over a saffron velvet book. I had all but forgotten them when I started typing on the laptop.

And then Freud approached, smiling at me over his spectacles. I glanced up, brows raised in the universal and timeless sign for *"What??"*

The smile annoyed. "So. Would you like to talk about

it, Alice?" Freud queried.

"No. Go away."

Conversations ended, and the room fell silent. Freud had a look of astonishment on his face. Athena put down the copy of Burkhardt's *The Civilization of the Renaissance in Italy* she was reading; Richard the Third was pouring coffee for himself and had managed to drip the piping hot liquid on Tyrone Power's hand when he turned to stare. The sleeping great snowy owl woke and hooted.

Joan of Arc looked at me sympathetically and scowled at everyone else.

"What—did—you—just—say?" The Proprietress came from around the counter and stood over me.

"I said no." I shrugged. "Maybe I should have left things the way they were," I said quietly. "I know what's going to happen. I know what will happen, and leaving well enough alone is better. No one will get hurt!"

The Proprietress drew an amber bottle from a pocket, a glass prescription bottle like those from my childhood. The label looked official, but the word MISERY covered every inch of it in large black letters.

"These are hard pills to swallow!"

The bottle was slammed down on the table, and I ignored it until I noticed my brother out of the corner of my eye, and then I ignored him. He came over, pulled out the chair at the table beside me, and sat down, offering the slice of cheesecake he held.

"Made it just this morning 'specially for you. How are you, my faery princess?" he greeted.

"I have no idea what's going on," I admitted. "I want to go home. But I don't know, at this point, where home is!"

It was difficult not to look at him, though I tried my best to avoid eye contact and continue typing.

He pushed the bottle towards me, just a tiny nudge, and his large blue eyes twinkled, like when we were children on Christmas morning, fighting our way downstairs to look under the tree. Or when he saw me in my senior prom dress, the one he designed, what we called his Renaissance masterpiece, the dress Quinn said he never forgot…

Unfortunately, I was not propelled into my prom night. I was still at The Shop. Dennis Martin, my lovely, wonderful Dennis, looking just as he did when he was twenty-five, with his curling black hair so much like Mom's and his Scandinavian-English features of wide-set eyes, straight nose, and thin mouth with dimples, was sitting at my left.

My typing increased in speed to mask the trembling in my hands.

No, I thought. No more!

"You fight the battles you can win and choose the ditch you die in," Dennis said. "Remember Dad saying that?"

"What good does that do me? Where's Dad? Why haven't I run into him?"

"He ran away. I'm pretty sure of it. That disappearing act he did, the stories that went around—being blown up in an IRA bomb attack, going underground, locked up in a gulag, all of it, was, forgive me, a smokescreen. He had a chance to set things right, just as you do, Alice, but he decided we weren't worth the effort. I took my turn—now it's yours."

"I've already changed things. I'm sure of it."

"Two wrongs will make a right, in this case."

"What?"

I looked up, and he was gone.

The Proprietress was glaring at me.

"Oh, eat your cake!" Marie Antoinette sighed en route to the coffee machine.

"Back to Verona, I suppose?" I asked The Proprietress when I finished licking the cake crumbs off the fork.

She pointed to the door through which was now the elevator car at my hotel in Verona. As I turned to press the button for my floor, Donovan took my hand and gently pulled me into an alcove, away from the sight of hotel guests and staff and into his arms for another smoldering kiss. "Maybe you can give me something to remember you by?" he whispered, leaning in again.

I placed my hands against his sports coat and smiled up at him. "I'm going to Florence and will be there for a few months. Any chance you might be going soon?"

I knew him, knew what drove him, and knew to fear him. But I didn't care, for I suddenly couldn't wait to have another date, talk about mutual yet separate interests, receive the attention a woman always receives in the first weeks of courtship, and know that his eyes would follow me out of the room. You see, what he did next began the thaw, and I thought I now understood what Dennis meant.

Donovan was looking at me tenderly and making eye contact, but it was what he said and did.

And I didn't remember that.

"I'll change my plans."

"You'd do that?" I sounded incredulous because I was.

"I want to. I have to see you again. I want to. I have some business to finish up here, and then I'll join you in Florence. It's a date?"

"Sure," I said, allowing a petal-soft kiss on my mouth. "As long as it's friendly and honorable."

"Can't wait!" he laughed, but not unkindly.

"I'll be at the Albergo dell'Fiore in the Via Ricasoli."

We kissed a long, lingering, parting kiss. Finally, I broke away and waved goodbye as I stepped back into the elevator car and rode up to the third floor, returning again to The Shop.

As I entered, everyone sighed with relief, as if the room had expanded and contracted. When they started to applaud, I glared. "Stuff it!" I growled and sat down, looking out the window at The Village high street.

It was midday—when the sun warmed the stones and shone through the impossibly beautiful *flora* in gardens and on fences, making everything look like it was stained glass, similar to the windows in the church at the end of the high street. I was mesmerized by their glowing colors, so I slammed the laptop closed, picked up my sweater, and headed toward the door.

"Going for a stroll?" Dennis asked, joining me.

"Alone, Denny."

I saw The Proprietress smile as I left The Shop.

Once out in the high street, I waited as if expecting the railway station to roll up, The Village transform into my high school, or family members long passed come out of the little shops with their purchases in wicker market baskets. The same people that came in and out of my dreams came and went out of The Shops and smiled in greeting as they passed. No one had unwanted advice to impart; no one spewed criticism. Instead, there were smiles and compliments.

"That's a pretty color on you, Alice," said Thomas Hardy as he left the bookshop carrying one of my titles.

"Yes, love certainly suits her," added George Eliot in passing.

"But who is that she loves?" Athena wanted to know. "And what would she think if she knew how many men held torches for her over the years?"

"Ah, but the candle she holds, well, that one is burning bright!" Thomas Cranmer commented.

"She's an intelligent girl—beautiful, accomplished, good sense of style and humor," remarked President Woodrow Wilson pausing beside me as I waited for the streetlight. "She'll figure it out. Oh, and there's a concert at the church this afternoon. You wouldn't want to miss that."

I walked to the church.

Like everything else in The Village, it was an architectural jumble of medieval, Tudor, and Victorian architecture, leaning more towards Romanesque. As I passed through the lichgate and walked up the path to the covered porch, I heard the strains of *Tallis' Third Tune* being played on an organ. The church door was open, and I stepped into the nave, one that looked like Saint Bartholomew the Great in London: a semi-circle nave with three tiers of columns in the sanctuary behind the great altar and arched windows soaring into a vaulted ceiling.

A man dressed in cassock and surplice was at the organ, lost in the exquisite music he was playing. I slid into a pew and sat in rapt attention, recognizing each note, phrase, and chord. I did not initially see the woman at the altar, assuming she was one of the altar guild ladies.

"What do you think of these flowers? Too much? I mean, it's not Easter yet, is it?"

The Proprietress was arranging lilies and white roses with yellow freesias in tall vases that resembled angels kneeling, the flowers spilling out of the bowls on their Purbeck marble shoulders. She looked around the vase she was working on and smiled, then crooked her head toward the organist.

"It's polite to give him something for his trouble, Alice," she hinted. "Go on. It'll be a treat for both of you."

I slid out of the pew and remembered I hadn't brought my purse. Patting the pockets of my cardigan, I felt and heard the jingle of coins. They were British pounds. I hefted one and closed my fingers around it as I approached the quire where the organ stood.

The organist finished with a simple chord, and I stepped up to the bench, saying, "That was lovely—my favorite hymn. Thank you," and held out the coin.

"I know. That's why I played it."

Quinn spun around the bench to face me and winked.

"Oh my God, you're…"

"Glad to see you? What do you think? How are you, Faery Princess?" Now he eased off the bench, and I saw he looked about fifty years old in a better light. He was still handsome, though lines were starting on his face, and his hair was salt-and-pepper, leaning heavily on the salt, and he wore a pair of reading glasses that he removed and put in his cassock pocket.

"You waited," he said while sorting through sheet music and putting it in a cupboard by the sacristy door.

"Well, it's rude to interrupt someone while they're playing," I began.

"My father never paid attention to that rule, did he?"

"*Purple Haze*…" I murmured.

"No, what I'm saying is, you waited."

I laughed nervously. "No, I didn't. You know that."

Quinn paused and turned to look at me. His face was so beautiful, and the tender glance was loving. "Yes, I do, Faery Princess. I also know that despite everything, you kept something for me in that amazing heart of yours, and you didn't have to."

"You just don't—you can't throw something away," I stammered, fighting tears.

Quinn reached up, touched my cheek as he used to, brushed the hair off my face, and kissed me.

"You've got a bumpy ride ahead of you, Alice Rose. Remember: I'll ride to the lists for you," he whispered.

"Still my champion?" I teased, accepting another kiss.

"I wish! Hey, where's the silver rose? Never mind. I understand."

"Quinn, say the word…"

"I already have," he said, embracing me. "Things must be put in place, and it won't be easy." He smiled down, releasing me. "I think you'd better go. You have a dinner reservation."

"In Florence," I sighed.

He nodded and winked, and as I left the church, he called, "Alice, wait!"

I stopped on the porch and wished the pounding in my heart and head would go away, the trembling in my hands abate, made worse as Quinn approached.

"What is it?" I asked, fumbling in my pocket. My fingers clutched a pound and slid it back and forth like a worry stone.

"Don't worry about me. I'll get through this, and so will you," Quinn said. "No matter what, I understand."

I held his hand as I went down the steps, refusing to let go until I reached the last one. What surprised me was how reluctant Quinn was to release me, but he did, and I walked down to the railway station, looking back once to discover that he was still there, watching.

CHAPTER 8

I RETURNED TO Florence.

In a city as charmed and beautiful as this and where every stone breathed the history I was enamored of, I lived at home in another country. I was trying to fill a void with art and history, hoping for a moment worthy of Jane Austen—one where Elizabeth Bennet arrives at Pemberley and runs into Mr. Darcy—but nothing of the sort happened.

Quinn Radcliffe would not be coming around corners or standing before the old masters in museum galleries.

Everyone told me to get on with my life, so once more, I got on a plane and then a train to escape what I would soon learn that I could not—and would not. And I managed to live all the same.

La Buca Niccolini, a restaurant in the Via Ricasoli, became my haunt. Dinner was always a simple dish of roasted chicken, risotto, and vegetables. The proprietor and waiter soon recognized me after a week of nightly visits, and when I walked into the dining room, there was no reason to request a menu. I always ordered the same dish. After dinner, I walked back to the hotel. My route was the longest and most challenging possible because I wanted to tire myself out in order to fall asleep immediately and hopefully not dream or wake in the middle of the night with that sinking feeling of knowing I was alone.

My research helped me focus on achieving a primary goal of a doctorate in History and a publishing contract or teaching with a university. While I perused libraries and archives armed with my notebooks, sketchbooks, and the all-important and necessary letters of introduction from the university, I received invitations to dinner and other less polite offers, all of which were ignored.

A month had passed since my arrival, and Donovan left no telephone call or message at the front desk. Why didn't that surprise me? In five years, I'd gone out on many first dates, always looking for someone special or something wonderful and coming up with nothing.

Had I changed my life's course of events in Verona? Not exactly.

Things started to happen.

On my *passaggio* one evening, I paused before an advertisement displayed in a Via Tornabuoni boutique window. The illustration was a detail from Ghirlandaio's Santa Maria Novella frescoes: a portrait of Ludovica Tornabuoni in *The Birth of the Virgin*. I smiled, for the dress Ludovica wore had been the inspiration for my prom gown.

"You were beautiful and enchanting."

Turning, I smiled at Joan of Arc, standing to my right and studying the poster with me.

"Her life wasn't unlike yours, I think," Joan continued.

"That is a certainty!"

Joan and I glanced to the left and saw the pretty blonde girl in the portrait, dressed in her mauve-colored gown, standing with us on the street.

"Ludovica!" I exclaimed.

"Cecilia," the pretty girl corrected. "Everyone *thinks* that's Ludovica, but it's me. No one knows about me other than I wear a pretty dress in one of Maestro Ghirlandaio's frescoes at Santa Maria Novella," she said. Then, looking up at the poster, "And what is this? What is an exhibition?"

"Experts on the subject of Florentine painting during the Renaissance and Domenico Ghirlandaio will speak to an interested audience, and they, the audience, will review the frescoes," I explained.

"I already know the story of the painting and Messer Ghirlandaio. I'd much rather go to the Mercato San Lorenzo. Or here," Cecilia waved a hand at one of the shops. Prada! How could I not? We slipped in with no one on the street noticing us and went through to The Curiosity Shop.

"Ah! *Signorina, buon giorno! Come stai?*" The Proprietress greeted us as we entered, removing her glasses and primping her hair. "Would you like a cup of coffee or tea? We have biscuits—the shortbread you like."

Cecilia waved her off and made straight for my table, where she sat down with Joan, reached for my sketchbook, and started flipping through it.

"You'll want to know everything," Cecilia sighed. "Everyone does."

"Well, not particularly…."

Glaring at me for the impertinent comment, Cecilia found a drawing and tapped it. "This is lovely, and this, well, I like your brother's rendition. It's something I would have worn to meet my lover."

"Get on with it!" Joan sniped.

"I am the youngest of the Tornabuoni daughters. You know my sisters-in-law Giovanna degli Albizzi and Ludovica. Maestro Ghirlandaio favored them for his work. I was disgraced, but my mother insisted that I be portrayed somehow, so he put me in that fresco with my aunt Lucrezia, and they made me wear what would have been my wedding clothes."

My brows were raised, and I was about to speak when Joan held up her hand for silence.

"I was contracted to marry one of the Albizzi sons, but I refused. I had taken a lover, you see, the son of a painter. My parents forbade me to see him, but we ran away together and were caught. They discovered I was with child, and my lover was executed in the courtyard of the Palazzo Vecchio. Rather than take up the veil and go to a convent or suffer the flames of the stake, I took poison. The portrait was done after my death. In retrospect, I handled it quite badly, don't you think, Joan?"

Joan shook her head and got up from the table. "That wasn't what I hoped you would share, Cecilia," she sighed. "Always the same story... she thinks she's the inspiration for Romeo and Juliet."

"I think you understand, Alice," Cecilia said, taking my hands. "One must always be ready to salvage love from a pyre of unhappiness!"

"Oh, please!" Richard the Third moaned and snapped his copy of the *New York Times*. "Bless the angels and saints Master Shakespeare isn't around to borrow that line."

"Cecilia!" The Proprietress hissed. "What did I tell you?"

Cecilia Tornabuoni glanced at me and tapped the sketchbook drawing before she hurried out of The Shop. I looked down at the drawing and smiled, for it became an advertisement for Zeffirelli's *Romeo and Juliet* in a Vogue magazine circa 1970, sitting on the top of a pile of magazines cluttering my bed.

"There's an idea," Dennis said, taking the magazine and studying the photographs carefully. "We could do something like this!"

"Oh please, Dennis, no!" I moaned.

"Why not? Not this little red number Olivia wore?" He tapped the iconic photograph of Romeo and Juliet meeting at the ball. "That's your color. Not everyone can wear that shade of red."

"Everyone will know where I got the idea, and second-period English will be a living hell," I groaned, rolling over the bed and retrieving another magazine from the floor. "Claudia and Janine will tease me unmercifully:

'Oh, you look like Juliet, Alice! What are you writing, Alice? Are you writing a play, Alice? Does 'Q' stand for Quinn and queer, Alice?' Too bad murder is illegal—what about this?" I asked, pointing.

"Barbarella it isn't, sweetie! However much it would rev up the already hyperactive hormones in your drop-dead gorgeous boyfriend. You'd be expelled if you showed up at the Claremont in that dress!"

Dennis flipped a page to a layout of Twiggy in the latest mod couture. "You've got legs and an outtasight body—what could be better than a mini? A cloud of chiffon and a hint of the thinnest, lightest silk, a bit of sparkle in pale peach, baby blue, or lilac? Even better, Faery Princess: a burgundy. Who wears burgundy at a spring prom?"

"No one. And not me. Everyone will be wearing a tent dress or mini, and I don't want to be everyone."

"Hold the phone, Mary!" Dennis said, grabbing a book from the shelf, flipping through pages, and then holding up a plate: Cecilia Tornabuoni in her pale pink and silver gown. He then took my sketchbook and colored pencils and went to work. Moments later, he had a modern version of the dress. It was a high-waisted, sashed gown, more circa 1914 than mid-fifteenth century; an a-line float in what looked like layers of sheer fabric, like a ballerina's costume, coming a few inches above the ankles, a bit higher in front than the back for the illusion of a train.

"Rather than heavy brocade or velvet, I'm thinking a silk chiffon or charmeuse overdress in pale apricot with a silver crepe chemise as an underdress so that it flows. It may be a-line and like a tent, but with the sash a few inches below your bust and with your figure, it will drape nicely and skim your curves—or something with a bit of silver thread woven in so it catches the light. You can wear a sheer peasant-style shirt under it, in silver, low cut if you want, but not so low that Quinn is staring at your girls all night," Dennis explained. "The overdress will be slashed bodice to knee on the side seams so the silver can come through, the front will have a V-shaped neckline, the underdress will have a square *décolleté*, and if we can do it, some beading with crystals and pearls. Silver slippers or silver Mary Janes. No, for this, I think silver slippers, Cinderella."

"Perfect!"

That's what Quinn said when he arrived several weeks later to escort me to the prom. His cummerbund and bow tie was made of the same silver as the underdress, and he proudly wore them with his tuxedo.

"He *owns* that?" Dennis hissed in a delighted tone as he followed me downstairs. "You said his parents were well off, but you didn't say they were rich! That must be Bill Blass or Jermyn's, or that new designer from Italy, Giorgio Armani!"

"They've got some money," I answered. "They live in the old Hume house on Buena Vista."

"The castle? My God, Faery Princess, it's no wonder you fell in love with him!"

"His house has nothing to do with why I love him or his tuxedo."

"Nobody owns a tux—they rent them!"

"He has to attend opera functions with his family, and there are the concerts and auditions his father drags him to every week."

Dennis was going to make another comment when we reached the landing, and I playfully kicked him before we went down silently, arm in arm. We were almost to the bottom of the stairs when Dennis cleared his throat. Harry and Quinn turned, and our collaboration and hard work were successful from the looks on their faces.

"Sweetheart! You look amazing!" Harry exclaimed softly.

Quinn's smile said it all. "Perfect!" he murmured as he

stepped forward. In a theatrical moment, he kissed my hand, whispering, "My lady and my love!"

"You're making me blush," I admitted, forgetting that embarrassment when Quinn handed me a bouquet of white and pale apricot-hued calla lilies.

"I wanted real flowers, not one of those half-dead carnations that stink like a freezer," he explained as we posed for photographs.

He couldn't take his eyes off of me as we walked down the steps to his mother's Volkswagen Beetle, and then we drove up to the Claremont Hotel where Quinn's Senior Prom was being held that year.

We were among the last to arrive. The music was up loud, and students were out in front with china plates filled with food and glasses of something bubbly, so we knew the buffet table was already picked over. The tables closest to the stage would be taken. A few of Quinn's orchestra mates were standing at the entrance to the ballroom and sharing a contraband cigarette when Quinn escorted me upstairs.

"Holy shit, Radcliffe!" one of the boys exclaimed as we passed by. "How did you score that?"

"Fox-*eey*!" another said. "Tasty little morsel…"

Quinn suddenly wheeled, and I stumbled, still attached to his arm. "Hey! Show a little respect for the lady!" he growled at them.

"Ladies now, is it? Thought it used to be gentlemen," said a blonde guy who came out of the shadows. He was wearing a Carnaby Street suit—a 'mod' style of several years past—and was smoking a joint. Anthony Smollers, the guy from the school corridor. "Change teams, Radcliffe?"

"Don't know what you're talking about," Quinn grumbled as we turned to go in.

"You did back in July!"

We ignored the snickering and comments and went

inside, taking a table as far away as possible from the popular kids up by the stage, which meant we sat alone in a corner. Quinn seated me and then went to the buffet, bringing back an assortment of vegetables, chicken wings, other finger food, and two glasses of sparkling apple cider.

"Is there something I should know?" I dared to ask.

"No. You know all there is to know." He growled, throwing himself into a chair.

"Don't let it get to you," I murmured as we ate and watched other couples dancing.

"I don't like it when guys comment like that about you," he said a little too forcefully.

"I can take care of myself."

"Yeah, well, I know what they're thinking—and I've heard the locker room talk. I didn't know my girlfriend was so popular!"

"Neither did I—and I don't want to spoil the evening talking about idiots and trolls like those guys outside. They're just jealous, don't you see? Do you want to dance?"

"Let's go."

We danced to *Nights in White Satin* and then *Yesterday*. These melancholy favorites of mine were perfect for the evening that was made memorable when Quinn kept whispering, "I love you!" as we swayed back and forth, locked in an embrace. The chaperones interrupted other couples dancing so close you couldn't see the light between them, but Quinn and I were ignored. As we returned to our table, the Senior Class President caught my hand, winked, and said, "You're so beautiful, Alice." Quinn immediately went on the defensive but looked as surprised as I did when he put out his hand to Quinn. "You're a lucky guy, Quinn."

"Don't I know it?" Quinn said, smiling.

We sat at the table for most of the evening, and Quinn kept whispering how beautiful I was. "I am so very lucky," he murmured in my ear, taking my hands and kissing them.

When he brought me home, Quinn walked me to the door and gave me one of the most passionate kisses I would ever receive. I would remember the look of passion mingled with sweetness, and it haunted me as I went inside from the front porch to The Curiosity Shop. Hildegard von Bingen was watering the flower boxes full of calla lilies, white and yellow roses, and white and yellow freesias.

"You forgot this," she said as she paused mid-stream, holding my tour guide. I accepted the book and returned to Florence before the art exhibition poster. Glancing at the advertisement, I smiled, knowing Cecilia's secret and the reason for the bemused expression on her pretty face.

Enzo, the night clerk, was at the desk reading a paper when I arrived hours later. He smiled and handed me that day's mail.

"*Grazie*, Enzo," I said absently, sorting through letters from Dennis, Harry, and colleagues from graduate school.

"Oh! I almost forgot. A gentleman called for you," he said and, in doing so, picked up the paper and glanced at the desktop, started shuffling through a wire basket of forms. "A nice-looking young man, maybe about your age and with such a smile! I thought he was a Florentine, but no, American. Well-educated and nice manners. Not your typical boy from the States. I knew he was looking for you when he came in. You're a perfect pair and so beautiful— where is that letter?"

I smiled nervously and watched as Enzo continued to look, mumbling and muttering about the young man surely being from California because he seemed so outgoing and casual but friendly, like the Californians who visited Florence.

"Always the comparison with San Francisco," Enzo went on.

"Do you remember his name?" I asked, starting to feel anxious.

"Quick, I think? Is that a surname in English?"
No! Impossible!
"Here you are."

A folded square of paper came out of Enzo's suit pocket with keys, a wallet, and a handkerchief. He waited expectantly and sighed when I put the note in my pocket and waved goodbye.

Once past the lobby, I sprinted upstairs, slamming the door shut as soon as I was in my room. I didn't know if my heart was pounding from the unexpected exercise or the anticipation. Closing my eyes, I unfolded the note, whispered a prayer, and then looked down.

> *I know it's been a while. Forgive me? Donovan*
> *Trist, Hotel Cavour, +39 055 266271.*

That shock of adrenaline one gets when excited or frightened coursed through me. Our date in Verona, our plans to meet in Florence—what woman wouldn't remember a romantic evening like that?

And what woman wouldn't feel betrayed when a promise was broken?

The slip of paper quivered as I held it over the toilet bowl.

"He's making it easy for you."

Joan of Arc reached out and snatched the paper from my hand. She entered the main room and tucked the phone number in my purse.

"I don't have to call him. I don't want to," I stated flatly.

"But Alice, that would drastically change his life and yours."

"For the better, I hope!" I said, following her into the bedroom.

"Don't you see? He's letting you make a decision."

"For the first time!"

I grabbed for my purse, but Joan was quicker and held it a distance from me, saying, "You cannot change all of his life. You are a part of that history. Certain moments that make changes for the better, yes, but not all of it. If you don't call him, you might as well not exist."

"And I have to relive the bad?"

Joan sat on the loveseat, resting her chin on the hilt of her sword and watching me pace yet another circle. "How do you know it will be bad if you say and do things just a bit differently?"

"I know what he's really like," I said tersely. "And so you do!"

"There's an attraction. Admit it!"

"It's obvious why! He looks like—*him!*"

"Well, why do you think you were drawn to him? Is that a bad thing?"

"Well, yes! To be reminded of him every day. Were you ever in love, Joan? Except with God and Jesus and the saints?"

"There was a boy," Joan purred. "It was in Domremy before I heard the saints' voices," Joan purred. "I melted every time he came by our house to the fields. His hand touched my sleeve accidentally one day, and I felt like it was fire—a good fire. I could only think of him until Saint Catherine and Saint Michael put an end to all that. Fighting a man with a sword is easier than loving him."

"So you know how I'm feeling. That sense of confusion, of anticipation, of fear. You want to act on your instincts and heart, but afraid because you don't know, yet you do."

"Yes." Joan leaned forward, adding, "There's something else, perhaps?"

I looked down at my hands twisted together because I was anxious.

"Quinn said he would come back," I finally admitted.

"But he didn't. He didn't say when. What do you do in the meantime? There are forces at work here that you must address. Putting yourself in a cupboard won't give you the answers—or Quinn."

"I don't want to live through that again!"

Joan got up, sheathed the sword, and started inspecting my vanity toiletries. She kissed my cheek before she left, saying, "You know what you must do. Some sacrifices are well worth it. Trust me, I know."

I went to bed that night and didn't sleep. I could only think of Verona, Donovan, and the frightening attraction he held. I was worried now that perhaps if I blinked, I would be back in The Shop or dropped into another part of my life. I feared that Quinn would be erased from my memory, that his page would be torn from the lapis book. But no, the church bells ringing outside reminded me it was Sunday morning, and I was in Florence in July of 1977 with a battle looming before me.

"Two wrongs make a right!" I heard Dennis's voice in my ear, and when I stepped before the highly polished doors of the elevator, I saw his face. "Two wrongs, sweetie!"

"What does that mean? Why does everyone keep saying that?" I hissed at my reflection.

I pressed the button and began my descent—literally and figuratively.

"*Buon giorno, signorina*," the day clerk greeted when I entered the lobby. "*Il Professore e qui. Egli e in attesa nella sala da pranzo.*"

"*Grazie*, Tommaso. In the dining room?"

"*Si*, Signorina."

Donovan was at a corner table with coffee, breakfast pastries, and a copy of *Corriere della Sera*, the Italian national newspaper. A copy of *La Nazione* was folded beside his plate. He stood and smiled when I approached and extended my hand, which he took. And there we were, standing at arm's length, studying each other for the longest time. I searched for honesty in that handsome yet cold face; I could tell he was undressing me with his eyes, the way they kept moving from my eyes to my breasts.

"Good morning," he murmured huskily. "You look wonderful."

"Thank you, and a good morning to you."

"Did you get some sleep?"

"Not much," I admitted.

"How long was our phone call? I hope I didn't keep you up too long."

"It was good to hear from you."

He took the initiative and bussed my cheek lightly. It pleased Donovan when I returned favor for favor. "It's been too long," he murmured.

"I was beginning to think you didn't remember. Or care."

"One day I'll tell you about all the sleep I lost thinking of you."

"First tell me how you found me," I said. "I know we spoke about meeting here,"

"We did. And my life intervened."

"But," I sighed. "How did you find me?"

"I have people."

The look on my face must have been priceless, for he said then, "No, really! I, or rather, my father, has people with connections."

"Oh my God," I started to move away, but he pulled me close and kissed my brow, his scent intoxicating.

"We'll laugh about this one day. Please, join me for breakfast."

"I wouldn't call that breakfast."

"I could ask for an American breakfast or English if you prefer?"

"If it's not too much trouble. Please."

I sat and Donovan caught the attention of the waiter. "*Signor, potremmo abbiamo due colazioni Americani, per favore?*" he asked quietly in flawless Italian. "*Uova, pane tostato, salsiccia e pancetta? E rendere tale appassita.*"

"Omelets, sausage, bacon, and toast," I said happily. "The breakfast of champions. I've been dying for something like it."

"Well, don't expire yet! I need someone to show me around Florence."

Yes, Donovan had a way with people, an uncanny, almost frightening way of winning you over, of manipulating you so that you were always in complete agreement. I would learn after our whirlwind courtship that he would become unyielding and inflexible about life, such as we were to share it and become as rigid as titanium steel. And yet, it made no difference.

Then.

We said nothing while we waited for breakfast. Donovan smoked a cigarette and read the paper, and I glanced at the other patrons. He studied me from behind the financial pages, and I grew uncomfortable under his scrutiny. I was beginning to think we had no chemistry in Verona.

"Ah, here's breakfast."

The paper disappeared, and Donovan put out the cigarette, pushing his chair closer to the table but still opposite me.

A feast was set before us. Donovan watched me spread toast with marmalade and scrape the green onions off my omelet.

"Have you been here long? In Florence, I mean," I started the conversation.

"A week. My first thought was to find you. Do you want coffee or tea? They seem to have given us both."

"Coffee, please. You said you would change your plans," I commented, hinting. "I suppose that took longer than you expected?"

"Yes," he expelled the word with a belabored sigh. "I had to move some meetings around and convince some people the delays weren't crucial to our work. And I wanted to take in a few sights along the way."

"So you're in town for business and pleasure."

"Now that we're together again, yes. Yesterday I met with the team doing the excavations under the Duomo, and I told them they could do without me today as I had to see a breathtaking Madonna."

I ignored the compliment and said airily, "Oh, the Santa Reparata excavation? I've been going to the cathedral every morning before the stores, museums, and my favorite coffee bar open, and I've tried to get down the stairs to see what's going on, but I get chased away as if I was a five-year-old."

"Let me see what I can do about that."

"You don't have to go to any trouble, Donovan, really."

"Anyone who is that interested in medieval antiquities and calls me by my name is worth the trouble."

"Tell you what, I'm meeting with a colleague at the archives to discuss my thesis defense this morning, but perhaps we can meet up this afternoon about the excavation and maybe go for a walk?"

"Looking forward to it. Mind if I ask what the topic of your thesis is?"

"The Guelph and Ghibelline conflict origins and its effect on Florence."

"Obscure."

"I like a challenge."

"So do I," Donovan murmured, "like discovering the secrets of lovely Alice."

"Perhaps," I said, looking at him with my head tilted seductively yet demurely, "you can find some answers on a walk this afternoon?"

I put a slice of toast to my lips, and no sooner had I taken a bite than I was in The Curiosity Shop. Dennis was sitting at the table, his chin propped up on his hand, smiling like the Cheshire Cat, as was The Proprietress.

I raised my brows in question.

"Well done, *you!*" they exclaimed together.

"Maybe if I'd done something," I grumbled.

Expecting a summons to the travel brochure rack, or another ride on the Amtrak, I closed the laptop carefully and started putting away my things. Dennis shook his head and looked sad.

"It's not fair, is it?" he said.

"I was actually having fun and enjoying his company. There was something about him," I admitted.

"Well…you know what he's like, how he is with everyone, and yet, you want to be with him, so, well, I don't know."

"She thinks she can change him," The Proprietress sniffed.

"Why not?" I demanded. "You see how he is! He needs a makeover of the soul and mind. And if there's a possibility, even the most remote, that I can help that along, why not?"

"Why didn't you want to change Mister Radcliffe?" asked The Proprietress. "Why didn't you stop him from going to England?"

"Because I wanted him to be happy, and I wanted him to succeed despite his overbearing and bullying father and complaisant mother." Here I lowered my voice, "And because I love him."

"What? Sorry, didn't hear you, Alice,"

"Because I love him!"

Dennis and The Proprietress leaned back in their chairs. "Present tense, not past?" The Proprietress queried.

"Play it through, Alice girl," Dennis said. "Play it through. You really haven't got a choice. You have to do this. Two wrongs will make a right! Trust me, darling!"

"Can't I just alter the next few weeks…?"

"Oh, I don't think so," The Proprietress sighed. "Not this time."

I knew what was to come, and I swallowed hard. The Proprietress let her eyes slide toward the door and then, in an unexpected move, patted my hand gently as I got up to leave. When she let go, I was standing on the Ponte Vecchio near the entrance to the Vasari Corridor, waiting. A young Italian about my age sauntered up in that cocky, self-assured manner of men in discotheques and clubs who knew or assumed they knew they were going to get lucky.

"*Signorina*," he greeted, leaning over the bridge as if looking into the muddy water of the Arno. He rocked back and forth, sighing, and then looked at me. "So. You are an American?" he asked in English.

"*Cosi vuoi?*" I answered, looking about my person to ensure I wasn't carrying a tour guide or map, something that would give me away.

"You want a drink of something? Maybe come with me?"

"No."

"You're beautiful. Not many girls are pretty like you. You look like our beautiful Florentine women."

"*Grazie no, signor.*"

He leaned in and ran his fingers up my bare arm. "You say that, but don't mean it. You look like a girl who would know how to give it. So…what do you say? You let me show you how Florentine men make love."

I let him move even closer, and then I moved purposefully so that my knee connected with his groin. He staggered back, clutching himself. "*Figlia de un'cane!*" he swore.

"*Lasce me no fare, no me molesta!*" I hissed.

"*Figlia de un'cane!*" he continued to gasp, hopping about in pain. "*Lasciami in pace, è inutile cazzo!*"

"*Signorina!*"

I turned at the voice since I was the only woman on the bridge. Two *carabinieri*, police officers, had seen the exchange and now waved me over. I dropped my head in shame, ready to plead out my crime, when I noticed both were smiling.

"*Signori? Dov'e la problema?*" I inquired sweetly.

"Sometimes the bridge isn't the safest place for a pretty young woman, *Signorina,*" one of them said sympathetically.

"I was waiting for my date," I began and was relieved when Donovan showed up, joining us. He looked at me questioningly when I kissed his cheek.

"Should I ask?" he murmured.

"No," I replied, slipping my arm through his as we began our *passaggio* through Florence.

We crossed the bridge into the Oltrarno, had a coffee in a nearby café, then traveled to the Piazzale Michelangelo with its iconic view of Florence and shared a picnic lunch on the parapet.

"Yesterday, it was the march through the Uffizi and Pitti. The day before, it was a cloister walk and pub crawl, or, given our location, café crawl," I said, building a sandwich of salami, cheese, and a sourdough roll. "What's today?"

"Let's just wander."

"Hmmm, done that. Got lost in this neighborhood, only it was raining then."

"You didn't tell me you've been to Florence before."

"Once."

"For your research or writing?"

I took a bite of the sandwich and carefully thought out my response. "To forget. Strange that the most romantic city in the world would be a place to forget."

"And did you?"

"Yes, I think I did. Now I think I did."

I could tell that answer pleased Donovan, for he nodded and paid particular attention to his sandwich and can of soda. I'd learned already that when he was pleased, he said nothing. And so we ate our lunch in silence and studied the landscape.

"Do you ever wonder what it would have been like to be a part of the construction of that?" Donovan asked between bites, pointing with his sourdough roll towards the *cupola* of Santa Maria dell'Fiore, the magnificent dome of the cathedral that dominated the skyline.

"It would make an interesting read, maybe even a novel," I commented.

"Do you have one in mind?"

"Oh, I have several…"

"Your area of concentration is the eleventh through fourteenth centuries, correct?"

"Yes, and your memory is good."

"The History Department at Brown has an opening. You could apply for the position now if you're close to defending your dissertation. I can make an inquiry."

I started to laugh, remembering our conversation at dinner in Verona. "And what do you want in return? And will this be academic and honorable?" I asked.

"Honestly, it is a bona fide offer with no strings attached."

"No strings."

"Well, a small down payment. One kiss."

He received from me a kiss that had all the promise of our night in Verona. Holding hands, we strolled back down to Florence and found ourselves in a narrow street with vaulting and arches. The skyline of Florence, with its compass of the *Duomo,* had all but disappeared.

"Do you know where we are?" Donovan asked, spinning around to get his bearings.

"We're lost, and I've been lost here a couple of times. There's a shop—here it is!"

An antiquarian bookshop and printing press were at the end of the dark, vaulted street, a nineteenth-century style sign hanging beside the door proclaiming the proprietors, M. Cavalli e Fratelli.

"*Buon giorno,*" the elderly gentleman behind the desk greeted us. "Ah! Signorina Martin!"

"Signor Cavalli," I greeted, shaking his hand. "You remember me."

"It's hard to forget a little girl from California who appreciates Angelo Poliziano! You bought something else last week. Was it the Alberti?"

"I'm almost done with it," I said, turning to Donovan. "I purchased a first edition of theirs—*La Rime* by Poliziano and Alberti's treatise on painting. Do you know them?"

"I imagine Signorina Martin knows more about them than I do," Donovan said, reaching around me to shake Signor Cavalli's hand.

"And so you are lost again," Signor Cavalli said, winking at us.

"I know this may sound silly, but do you have an edition of Shakespeare?" I asked, offering my most beguiling smile.

"The sonnets," Donovan chimed in.

"Shakespeare! Everyone thinks he invented Italy, especially Giulietta and Romeo."

"He did a pretty good job plagiarizing bits and pieces from Bandello, dal Porto, and Brooke," I added. We then shared a pretty good laugh at Will Shakespeare's expense.

Signor Cavalli, a spry gentleman in his eighties who looked like a barn owl with his large eyes and bushy eyebrows, scratched his nose and then studied the shelves. He muttered something in Italian under his breath and then reached for a book on one of the corner shelves, blowing the dust off the little leather-bound volume. My heart started to pound when I saw the book, for it was the color of lapis lazuli and had silver engraving on the cover.

The Proprietress did not materialize, however.

"Signorina Alicia, if you want an English poet who writes lovely sonnets, why not Thomas Wyatt?" Signor

Cavalli asked. "It was found in a fourteenth-century townhouse in the Via Bentaccordia about eighty years ago. It comes from the nineteenth century."

I stared reverently at the little volume and fingered the engraving.

"How much?" Donovan asked, taking out his wallet.

"No, you shouldn't! I can pay for this," I protested.

Signor Cavalli picked up the book, flipped to a back page, and eyed Donovan carefully. "Sixty-five hundred lire, signor."

"How much?" I gasped. "That's a hundred dollars in American currency!"

"This is the very first book made in a limited run," he explained and, winking at Donovan, added, "But she's worth the price, I guess?"

The transaction was made, and when we left the bookstore, Donovan chuckled, "Was he talking about the book or you?" Then he added, "By the look on your face, I take it you know Wyatt intimately?"

"Not as well as I'd like to," I replied. "He wrote some pretty romantic poetry."

"Maybe you'll read some to me later. After dinner?"

"I could do that."

"In Fiesole. C'mon."

We spent the rest of the day above Florence in Fiesole, wandering the ancient Roman ruins, touring the Medici villas, and finally having supper on the terrace of the Café San Francesco with the spectacular view of Florence in the distance. While I enjoyed *ravioli* made with butternut squash, and Donovan attacked *bistecca alla Fiorentina*, a steak grilled with mustard and peppercorns, with great relish, I thumbed through the book.

"Have you found anything you like?" he asked, charging our wine glasses with vintage Chianti.

"Plenty," I said, looking up and meeting his smile with one of my own.

The light was fading, and the waiter brought over candles set in Chianti bottles wrapped in straw, placing them before me. Cheese and fruit were brought, and Donovan pulled his chair around to sit closer.

"Ah, here's something," I murmured and then began:

And wilt thou leave me thus? That hath lov'd thee so long? In wealth and woe among:

And is thy heart so strong as for to leave me thus? Say nay! Say nay!

And wilt thou leave me thus? That hath given thee my heart, Never for to depart;

Neither for pain nor smart: And wilt thou leave me thus? Say nay! Say nay! And wilt thou leave me thus?

I silently read the words to Wyatt's love song again. Then aloud, "Wow…"

"They say Wyatt was in love with Anne Boleyn when he wrote that, and they were lovers—he lost his head over her."

"No, Anne lost *hers*," I quipped. Turning the page, I said, "I recognize this one!" I began to read with Donovan now looking over my shoulder:

In thin array, after a pleasant guise,

When her loose gown did from her shoulders fall, And she me caught in her arms long and small, And therewithal sweetly did me kiss,

And softly said, 'Dear heart, how like you this?'

I put the book down and pushed away from the table. Donovan poured another glass of wine and studied me carefully as if making a note of every curve and line of my body and consigning them to memory.

"I wonder if he would have been happy with Anne if he'd been given a chance, and she with him." I pondered aloud. "Though what good does it do them now? Wondering doesn't make it happen. Actions do."

"Dear heart, how like you this?" Donovan murmured and leaned in for a kiss that made my heart pound. He drew his hand up my arm to my neck, where it rested while he kissed me again, and then slid down to rest lightly on my breast while he kissed my neck.

"And wilt thou leave me thus? Say nay, say nay!" he whispered.

We both wanted what was obvious by glance and touch, so we sped back to Florence. Neither of us had to speak; neither had to ask.

A full moon shone through an open window in his hotel room, allowing in what little air there was to inhale on that stifling summer's night. I was leaning on the sill, watching the skyline, and waiting. However much I had wanted to throw myself in his arms when we arrived, I thought better of those actions. Fortunately, Donovan had gone downstairs for a bottle of wine—as if we needed any more—and I was instructed not to go anywhere...

"... *Don't go anywhere.*"

I was in Quinn's bed on that afternoon so long ago. The romantic, universe-stopping moment, *the* moment, the moment every girl fantasizes about, dreams about, was anything but.

Too bad all the songs and poetry didn't tell a girl about the fumbling, the awkwardness, and for me, the blood.

Quinn returned with a damp, warm washcloth and towel from the bathroom. I tried not to stare—he was so beautiful, and with the tousled, mussed-up hair, the towel wrapped around his hips and midsection, and the muscular physique, it was hard to think of him as a shy, sensitive musician. He wasn't one of the popular boys who lettered in sports and spent all summer as lifeguards at the Strawberry Creek Pool, worshipped by girls like me but always going for the most beautiful and popular girls that were nothing like me.

Quinn tried not to stare at my naked body—I was nothing to look at, trust me—and kept his eyes locked on mine as I accepted the washcloth and towel; then he turned away and put on a bathrobe while I washed up, giving me privacy.

"What do I do about the sheets and blanket?" I asked, trying to put on a brave, sophisticated face yet wincing from the touch of the washcloth on the sore places between my legs. "I'm sorry, Quinn. It must have been awful for you and with me being nothing like what you imagined. Or hoped."

He turned and pounced on the bed, gathering me in his arms. "No, no! You're fine—you didn't do anything wrong. If anything, I was just too excited and too much in a hurry. Don't worry about the bed linens—I can wash them before my parents get home. I can say I spilled a can of soda or a cup of coffee on them."

Then I started to cry earnestly, snuffling and wiping my nose on the towel as if I were six years old.

"Oh geez, no! Oh, my Faery Princess, there's nothing wrong, I promise! Please don't cry, Alice! You were wonderful and loving. I can't wait for next time."

"There'll be a next time?" I asked, looking at him as I wiped my eyes.

"What do you think? I love you. We can only get better together."

Despite his reassurance, I turned away and buried my face in the pillows to weep even harder. Then I heard him plucking a few notes on his guitar and singing *Here Comes the Sun*.

I sat up and smiled, looking across the bedroom to where Quinn was sitting on the window seat.

"And I say it's alright!" I sang with him.

He nodded and smiled back, continuing to sing. Wrapping myself up in a sheet, I went to him and sang, "Sun, sun, sun, here we come!" Quinn joined in on the harmony as I skipped lightly to the bathroom. While he continued to sing in his silky, smooth bari-tenor voice, I washed up properly. I felt better now and looked in the mirror, expecting to see someone new and different, someone sophisticated, because I was truly a woman now—a woman who was loved despite everything.

I didn't see the fresh-faced seventeen-year-old; I saw myself at twenty-four, staring at my reflection in a window in the Hotel Cavour in Florence.

"And I say it's alright," I whispered.

A pitcher and bowl were on a table by the window. I undressed, gently patting my face and naked torso with a rosemary-scented washcloth to remove the grime and sweat of the day's sticky heat, and then slid the silk print dress back over my head and shoulders. I was shaking out my hair when the door behind me opened. Donovan had quietly entered and placed a tray on a table.

I turned, and it was quite apparent by the look on Donovan's face and the inward draw of his breath that the translucent, thin fabric of the dress was all that lay against my skin, thanks to the moonlight streaming down into the room.

A trembling hand now brushed my cheek and neck while the other drew me close for a kiss full of heat and longing. I wanted him to slide the dress off my shoulders and let it slip to the floor in a cloud. I could tell from the growing intensity of our kisses and embraces that he found the gossamer silk as exciting as the touch of my skin, the anticipation of what we would share as powerful as an aphrodisiac.

It soon became too much for both of us, and we tumbled onto the bed. Donovan all but tore off his clothes and my dress. The breeze that had come up was tantalizing on my skin but not as electric as Donovan's lips and hands as they sought to learn every curve, every sinew. We went after one another so hungrily, so forcefully, that our climax was an explosion.

"And will you leave me thus? Say nay, nay!" Donovan gasped, and we both laughed.

I was exhausted and content to stay curled up in his arms and was glad when he pulled up the sheet and blanket when the breeze made us shiver from our cooling sweat. He ran a languorous hand up and down my back, from the small of it to the nape of my neck.

"I couldn't tell but am I your first?" he asked after a while, just as I was going to sleep.

The question put me off, and I'm sure he felt me go rigid in his arms and surely must have guessed when I moved away.

"Does it matter?" I wanted to know.

"I'm old-fashioned about some things."

"All your conquests must be virgins?" I laughed.

"A time-honored tradition with the Trist family—taking the maidenheads of the commons and nobility."

"Let me guess, *primo noctus?*"

"I'm almost positive that was the case in the twelfth century. Lots of Trists in Suffolk!"

"Well, could your virgin lover do this?"

My delicate placement of hand and lips made him gasp and pull me down on top of him, and soon we were at it again.

It was that way all night and into the next dawn. In the coming weeks, we'd meet for dinner and continue the sexual exploration we both sought and demanded from one another. Conversations about our lives and dreams punctuated our couplings; we never ventured into the past, spoke of the people in them, especially those we loved or left, or tore our hearts in pieces.

Those erotic nights would haunt me on the plane back to California, as did his smile as we parted, and later still when he didn't answer the letters or phone calls.

When I discovered that I had fallen in love and was betrayed. Again.

CHAPTER 9

"WELL, WHAT DID you expect?"

The Proprietress placed another gold star in my book and locked it up. She smirked and raised a brow, wondering why I was still at the counter.

"I get a star for being a whore?" I asked.

"Listen to you! It was the '70s—free love, love freely, love the one you're with? Remember?"

I waited, hoping she would say something else, offer encouragement or remind me the past was all about the future or something like it. Instead, she pulled out the ledger and her disco ball pen and made entries. The light of the ball flickered and glowed until it was a Christmas ornament that I had just placed near the top of the tree in Dennis' living room.

"A little more to the left," Harry said. "Like your politics."

"Funny," I responded but did what he asked and moved like a robot to the crate of decorations on the floor, taking my time in selecting the next one.

"Are you coming down with something?" Harry asked. "Decorating the tree used to be a favorite indoor sport."

"I'm okay."

"I guess home is a bit colorless once you've lived in Florence."

"Just strange."

"You had fun, though?" Harry teased. "I mean, look at you! It's like Sabrina's transformation when she returns from Paris!"

I might have been a historian with a doctorate weeks away, but I was also an *artiste* and a willing slave to fashion. He was referring to the more sophisticated style I'd picked up in Florence: a Chanel suit jacket with a pair of skinny jeans and white silk peasant blouse, a pair of Ferragamo wedges. No proper, preppy tweed skirts and Shetland cardigans with sensible shoes for this independent, heartbroken woman.

"Harry, leave the poor girl alone," Dennis sighed with mock annoyance as he entered the room with a tray of snacks and drinks. He winked, passing me a glass of wine, and gestured with his free hand. "The chunky, bohemian necklaces work with that. You are definitely my sister, Sister!"

"Thanks," I said, kissing Dennis as he scooted past me. I noticed, however, that the usual robust color was gone from his face, and he looked tired. "Look at you," I quipped. "If I didn't know you were faithful to this loser here, I'd swear you were spending way too many late nights at Henry Africa's."

"Please, if I want to go to a meat market, I'll go to Louie's for prime rib," Dennis answered, starting to re-decorate the tree, moving the ornaments and tinsel I'd just placed. "It's the job, that's all."

"Business must be good."

"Got a contract with two exclusive men's shops on Union Street—it will be a merry Christmas, that's for sure."

"I met some people at Chanel and Ferragamo if it would help sales," I began, but the doorbell ringing stopped further interrogation. The postman had arrived with Christmas packages and mail. Once the parcels had been placed under the tree, I sorted the Christmas cards and letters for each of us and was surprised to see the familiar penmanship on one large Christmas card, and gasped when I came to an envelope addressed to me. It was from Donovan.

"Must be from Quinn. I heard he was back in town," Harry said as I ran upstairs to my old room with my mail.

I unfolded the letter tucked inside the generic, tasteless corporate Christmas card, written in a childish scrawl— eight pages back and front—and couldn't believe what I read. "Slimy bastard!" I growled and tossed the letter into the wastepaper basket.

"Not so fast!"

Richard the Third was sitting on the edge of my bed, playing with the kaleidoscope.

"*What?*" I whined.

"If anyone knows anything about being screwed over, it would be me," the maligned monarch said. "When your brother said two wrongs make a right, that's what he meant."

"I don't remember asking your opinion, Your Grace!" I sniffed as I started to open the large Christmas card.

"Call me Dickon. All my friends do."

"I don't remember asking your opinion, Your Grace."

"No need to be rude, Alice," Richard sighed in a sing-song voice. "The week is almost up, and it's almost closing time."

Closing time?

"Let me give you a hint." Joan of Arc entered my room with a plate of food and drinks from Dennis' party spread. She offered some to Richard and savored one of Harry's famous miniature mushroom quiches before continuing. "Some things you have to follow through to the very end before you can tamper with, how do you say it, the settings."

"Oh no, look what she's doing!" Richard said, pointing with a *biscotti*. "Take it from her! Take it!"

"You need to go away," I said, protecting the Christmas card from their grasping hands.

"Alice, don't!" Joan wailed, but it was too late. I had

admired the Fra Filippo Lippi *Madonna and Child with Angels* on the front, read the holiday greeting text—and the personal letter from Jane Radcliffe.

"Now it will only take longer, you silly little girl!" Richard grumbled and took Joan's hand on the way out—but not before taking the food with him.

"Pity! There was just a little bit of time to go," I heard Joan say.

I took Donovan's letter and tore it into confetti, watching it sail down into the wastepaper basket.

"Where are you off to?" Harry asked when I returned downstairs.

"Going to see a friend," I said, grabbing my coat and purse.

"Didn't know Quinn was in town," Dennis said under his breath but loud enough to hear. He was still re-decorating the tree and struggling with strands of tinsel.

"Didn't say it was Quinn. I'll be back for the party. And for God's sake, would you leave that tree alone?"

I'd walked the path more than a hundred times, climbing through the Berkeley Hills to the narrow, winding street upon which the castle sat. Yet, my stomach was in knots when I rounded the corner and saw the round tower, the overgrown backyard, and the west-facing windows of Quinn's study and bedroom. My palms were sweating and trembling when I rang the doorbell and when Jane Radcliffe opened the door. She quickly removed the reading glasses on the end of her nose and held out her arms for an embrace.

"Here's the faery princess!" she greeted. "You got the card! Wonderful!"

"How are you?" I asked.

"Never mind about me—how are you? It's been ages!" she cried happily and turned, saying, "Andrew! Andrew, come and see who's here!"

I was brought into the spacious yet intimate and warm

living room where a perfectly decorated Christmas tree stood beside a hearth equally beautiful in holiday wreaths and ornaments. I felt no pain or remorse when I glanced at the portrait of Quinn that hung in a place of honor with other family photographs. That rush of adrenalin came, however, when I saw our high school prom and senior portraits and the snaps of family events to which I'd been invited and wondered why, so many years later, they were still on the walls and over to the mantle.

Professor Radcliffe came from the kitchen with a bowl and wire whisk dripping with icing—the Christmas cookies, of course. Making them was always a grand production and was followed by an equally splendid supper. Noticeably absent were the Christmas carols playing on the stereo; in their place was Bach's *Sleepers Awake*. I thought it a bit strange, for the piece had connotations of Easter and not Christmas.

The Professor's eyes lit, and he grinned as Mrs. Radcliffe gave me a gentle shove forward to accept his bear hug.

"Well, this is the loveliest Christmas package ever, isn't it, Janie?" the Professor Laughed. "Alice Martin, where did you go? We've missed you terribly."

"Italy," I said sheepishly. "And grad school—almost have the Ph.D. in my grasp. I defend my dissertation in January."

"Wonderful!" the Professor crowed.

"She's been quite the busy girl!" Mrs. Radcliffe said, her voice full of pride as if I was her daughter. I wondered if there would ever be a time when I could tell her how much I wished it could be so.

"Too busy to see friends?" he asked. "Well, I hope you don't make a habit of it. Sit down! Have a cup of tea with us or a drink. And don't say no!"

How strange and wonderful it was to be in that house; little had changed in almost a decade. Even the delicious aromas from the kitchen were the same. While the Professor went back into the kitchen to put the kettle on and make up a tray for high tea, I glanced around for other traces of the one person absent or signs that he had a different life, different pursuits, or someone else.

"He's in England, back with the Philharmonic," Mrs. Radcliffe said as if reading my thoughts.

"But I thought…."

"When the Conductor retired, and Sir Ralph Evers was brought in, he invited Quinn back. The stories of his bad boy nights were all lies. And he's already done well for himself. There's talk of his becoming the Conductor one day." Mrs. Radcliffe now explained. She went to the stereo and turned up the volume a bit. "Now, who do you suppose that is, playing?"

I frowned, listening for clues. Then I felt a pang of memory, and tears started welling in my eyes.

"He didn't break up his cello in a hotel room after a drunken orgy with half of the brass section," the Professor said as he returned with our tea. "The former Conductor wanted everyone to believe that to hide his own misconduct. It kept the London tabloids running for weeks at my boy's expense!" The Professor patted my shoulder when he read the look of horror and disbelief on my face.

"Quinn said something like that when I saw him last. Before I left for Italy." I glanced at the Professor and then Jane. "He won't be home for Christmas?"

"We don't know," Mrs. Radcliffe sighed. "He's made a habit of showing up at the oddest times. The orchestra is touring again, so we never know for certain. But you! Andrew's right—you are a wonderful Christmas gift. Graduate school and the dissertation, and Italy! I'm sure there are more surprises from Alice Martin."

"Believe me," I murmured.

"What will you do when you have the doctorate?"

"I was given an offer, Brown University, but I haven't acted on it."

"What happened to the writing? And the designing? You have such talent, Dear!" Mrs. Radcliffe asked. She clucked her tongue at the Professor now. "Darling, you know Alice doesn't drink her tea like that!" Then to me, "Lemon and sugar, am I right?"

"Yes, thank you. Excellent memory."

She took away the cup that had been offered and now poured another, putting in equal amounts of lemon and sugar and placing several cookies on my plate: angels and snowmen, which had been Quinn's favorites and mine. Then she glanced up quizzically, waiting.

"I'm writing still. Not published, except a few papers on obscure medieval personalities no one knows or cares about, and there's my dissertation, which is the Guelph-Ghibelline conflict," I continued.

"Romeo and Juliet…" the Professor chuckled.

I shot him an evil look and said, "Politics and governments today were shaped by it. If it hadn't been for that conflict, would Dante have written some of his finest work? Or Florence and the Italian city-states rise as key players in European politics?"

"Ouch, I sit corrected!" the Professor said, chuckling again. "Dinners were always interesting when the Faery Princess graced us. Do you remember that game of Risk?"

"Yes, and what happened after," I quipped. "I remember you didn't appreciate Jimi Hendrix."

The Professor's face drained of color, and he started to absently stir his tea so that it made an annoying ring. Mrs. Radcliffe leaned over to stop him.

"Is that why you went to Italy?" she asked. "The interest in medieval history, your dissertation?"

I took a sip of the *Constant Comment* and avoided their expectant faces. It didn't surprise me that Richard and Joan were staring at me from the bottom of the teacup and shaking their heads in warning, which I ignored.

"No, I went to heal a broken heart and had it broken again."

"Oh, dear! And I thought you two parted as friends?" Mrs. Radcliffe moaned sympathetically.

"Yes…we heard about the incident outside Peet's," the Professor said into his cup.

Again, I shot the Professor a look, a bit more poisonous than the first.

"Do you suppose I'm talking about Quinn?" I lied. "Truth be told, I met someone. An archeologist from Brown University. He's the director of a new department opening in the new year. The Center for Old World Archaeology and Art."

"Ah, that's how you got the invitation."

"Yes, ProfeOr Radcliffe, it is. But my work will stand on its own merits. I wouldn't need him to put in a good word. He made an offer, and I thanked him for it, but I didn't accept it."

"A whirlwind romance, I take it?" Mrs. Radcliffe asked gently.

"That's all it was. And that's that."

When I set the Wedgewood teacup into its saucer, I looked up and saw that the Professor was studying me, though I was surprised the look didn't come from his wife. It was a careful assessment, born of pity and concern in equal parts.

"Poor you!" he said, leaning in to kiss my cheek. "Life hasn't given you many breaks, has it?"

"When all's said and done, I think it's more about what I did with the ones given me, don't you think?" I replied.

Mrs. Radcliffe smiled and nodded. The Professor was ready to add his thoughts when the telephone rang, and he heaved himself off the sofa to answer it.

"May I ask something?" I said low to Mrs. Radcliffe

when he was out of the room.

"Of course."

"The pictures of Quinn and me. It was almost ten years ago. I would think, after all this time, you'd put them away. Or something."

"I was going to take them down and store them, but Quinn objected and asked to have them left where they are."

"But his other girlfriends. Surely they'd object?"

"No," she said, offering a smile that was so much like Quinn's it was painful to see. "Oh, there's been a girl or two, very briefly, mind. He never brought them home. I really don't think he has the time or interest, or there's been anyone he'd make time for. If I dare to bring it up, his words on the subject are 'if only.' I didn't want to speculate on what it meant, but now that you're here, I can guess."

I knew what it meant, and I felt like the wind had been punched out of me or someone had placed me in a vice and turned the lever.

"Gosh! Look at the time!" I chirped. "I've got to run. Dennis and Harry are expecting me back for their annual Christmas bash — of all my sins tardiness is the worst in their eyes."

"How is your brother?" Mrs. Radcliffe wanted to know. "I saw him at the market just yesterday, and he looked so pale, and he's lost so much weight."

"It's the business, I suppose," I shrugged as we walked to the door. "He's got two new Union Street clients. Haberdashers with exclusive clientele. From what Harry says, he barely has time to sleep, but he's doing very well, and there's talk of expanding, and now that he's got the Macy's account, Magnin's won't be far behind. He's got a studio on Walnut Square now."

She looked as if she didn't believe me. I hardly believed it myself.

"Well," I said breezily, "Merry Christmas! It was nice to see you after all this time."

"Alice, it has been too long. Maybe we can get together in the new year?" Mrs. Radcliffe suggested.

"Now that's a wonderful idea!" The Professor had returned with a slip of paper in his hand, which he gave to Mrs. Radcliffe when he thought I wasn't looking. She flushed and tucked it into a pocket. He turned his attention to me now, saying, "Why not come to the gala at the Opera House on New Year's Eve, and we can ring in 1978 together! I can get box seats!"

I was tying the belt to my heavy winter coat when I took a breath and said, "No, I don't think that would be good for any of us."

Most definitely and assuredly NOT what I'd said that Christmas of 1977…

"Going back to Italy, then?" the Professor asked.

"No."

I craned my neck to look him in the face. He was wearing a dopey smile and ready to attempt cajoling when I said, "I heard what you said to Quinn. I was in the next room. I know what you've done, Professor."

"What I've done?" he laughed, looking at Mrs. Radcliffe first and then me.

"If anyone should take the blame for what happened, well…."

"That was ages ago, and he's forgiven his father," Mrs. Radcliffe spoke up.

"I'm sorry, this might sound harsh, but has he forgiven you?" I asked her.

"What are you talking about?" the Professor demanded.

"Christmas Eve of 1972. Quinn proposed marriage, and I accepted. We were going to wait until we finished school. You didn't think much of our plans."

"Alice, that was, what, five, six years ago? Have you

been holding a grudge—no, wait! A torch! Have you been carrying a torch all this time? I'm surprised the house hasn't burned down!" the Professor chuckled, though Mrs. Radcliffe and I failed to understand his humor.

"I want to know whose ego you're trying to build up. How many people, besides your son, have you hurt trying to out-do us all?"

He came at me then, and before Mrs. Radcliffe could prevent it, I was shoved against the china cabinet. The Professor was too close, and I was scared, especially when Mrs. Radcliffe gasped, "Andrew, not her!"

"It was you, wasn't it?" I whispered after catching my breath. "You gave him the black eye!"

"Andrew, let her go! I think you've had too much to drink!"

I continued to look up at him and waited to see who would blink first. My breathing was shallow and ragged, and the sweat on my face mingled with tears.

The Professor released me, but I would never forget the darkness in those eyes.

"See you around, Alice," he said quietly, leaving the room.

I chalked up my unkindness to payback of sorts. It certainly took them by surprise. I was at the door and ready to leave when Mrs. Radcliffe embraced me tightly. She wasn't one for demonstrations of affection and surprised me by saying, "I should have done something, Sweetheart! Forgive me!"

I was still pondering her words when I walked down the street and the hill, keeping my eyes on the dirt path and sidewalk, controlling the urge to cry. I didn't notice the taxi climbing up the hill or its passenger craning to get a better look until the cab sped by. The further I walked from the castle, the worse I felt, and I was miserable by the time I was in my neighborhood and arrived at my house.

CHAPTER 10

BRENDA LEE'S *ROCKIN'* '*Round the Christmas Tree* was already cranked up to blasting on the stereo, and from the laughter, it was safe to guess that the party had started without me. I could see Dennis and Harry's friends and Harry's parents gathered in the living room and the frenzied blinking of the Christmas lights. All that happiness and goodwill towards all put me in a foul mood unsuitable for the holiday. However, rather than go in through the front door, I opened the garden gate and entered The Curiosity Shop.

"That's *that?*" The Proprietress demanded as she pounded a very large star into my book, made an entry in her ledger, and handed off a Diet Pepsi. "The truth will set you free, Alice!"

"I wasn't about to tell Quinn's parents it was two months of non-stop sex and groping, of trying to screw Quinn out of my head!" I argued. "I'm a bit more discreet than that!"

"And do you think they would care—when most likely he was doing the same?" The Proprietress said and waved me away.

I fought to keep the image out of my head: Quinn working the crowd in a Paris or London discotheque or wherever he was living for most of the year, charming every woman in the house and working his way up to the tallest, leggiest, and blondest eighteen-year-old. It was his life, and he could live it as he wished. And I had mine…

"It never works, does it?" Marie Antoinette mournfully asked as she joined me. "But the sex was fantastic, yes?"

"If you don't mind?" I demanded, flicking my hand toward her as if she was an insect to be shooed away.

"Tell her!" Marie Antoinette insisted, directing The Proprietress with a glittering, bejeweled hand.

"She'll find out soon enough," sniffed The Proprietress.

"Find out what?"

"Your train leaves in fifteen minutes, my dear," Hildegard von Bingen said as she placed a bouquet on my table and offered one perfect, white lily.

I didn't have to pack up the laptop or my belongings. Richard the Third was handing me the messenger bag and my purse as I crossed to the door and took a whack at the brochure carousel as I went out again, not bothering to take any publication that whizzed by me. I trudged down the street to the station and met up with Dennis on the way. He hailed me over, and I grimaced as we passed one another. I didn't feel right and wished the train I boarded would take me back to wherever I was supposed to be.

"It's been an adventure, hasn't it?" Jack Lemmon commented as he punched a ticket that materialized out of my pocket. "Ah! A 'C' ride! Well, this will be interesting, isn't it, Miss?"

"If I asked a question, you'd answer truthfully, wouldn't you?" I queried, taking his sleeve to prevent him from leaving.

"It would depend on what you want to know, Miss."

"Why am I being put through this? What did I do wrong? What is all this about?"

"I was going to ask you the same thing," he said, winking. And off he went again, humming *A Time for Us*.

The delicious smells from the dining car refused to lure me away. I slumped down on the seat and stared out the window, watching my life—or vignettes from it—glide by as the train started up and left the station.

There was my fourth birthday when I cried and ran upstairs to hide from the people singing *Happy Birthday*. I wore a pink organza dress with petticoats and black patent leather shoes and sobbed while I clutched a little red toy piano. How long did I stay upstairs banging on those poor little keys, waiting for everyone to go home?

There was the house in Westminster in London where we lived while my father worked with an architectural firm helping to rebuild London—I was sitting on the stoop with knees drawn up, watching the high street, and waiting for my father to come home. I was never told why he didn't. I remember my mother stopped crying after that. There we were, landing at the Oakland Airport to start yet another new chapter in life several months later...

The scenes were blurring now, and soon they were like Jackson Pollack's paint splatters on a canvas and then gobs of creamy watercolor squeezed out of tubes until they became bright, hot wildflowers in a field somewhere on the English coast, the roofs and spires of a village nearby. My heart began to pound in anticipation. I felt the train slow and started gathering up my things.

"What are you doing?" the Conductor demanded as I exited the compartment.

"I want to get off here—I know this place."

"This is not your stop today," he stated.

"Please!"

"Miss Martin, your ticket says—"

"I want to get off here! Now!"

"But not today, Alice. Two wrongs will make a right."

"Not today!" I shouted. "Not ever!"

"What?"

"Stop saying that!"

"What?"

I was facing Donovan now. He was standing on the doorstep, a large bouquet of white flowers in his arms. Behind me, Dennis and Harry's Christmas party was in high gear. Donovan repeated his question with a tone of disbelief as if my invitation to go straight to Hell or back to wherever he came from was a joke. He repeated himself a little louder for all the noise.

"What? I didn't hear you, sorry!" he shouted.

"I said, you've got your nerve!"

"It sounded like 'Go to Hell, you slimy bastard.'"

"Then you heard me right!"

"I know I should have replied to your letters," Donovan was saying now, following me through the living room to the kitchen, where I searched for something to put the flowers in, as much as I wanted to dump them into the trash or shove them down the garbage disposal—along with Donovan's head.

"Doesn't look like you broke your hand," I said, pulling out one of my mother's Waterford crystal vases from a cupboard and barely missing his head with it as I jumped down from the kitchen stool. "What are you doing here, anyway? Haven't you got a tomb to dig up somewhere?"

"I wanted to see you, of course, and I'm giving a lecture series at the university for the winter session. I'm here to review the syllabus, meet the staff, and sign the paperwork."

"So stopping by Berkeley was an afterthought."

"I was in town—wait, no! Alice!"

"Is that…?" Dennis queried as we passed by.

"No, it isn't!" I snapped on my way to the living room.

"For a moment, I thought he was Quinn," Harry murmured. "That torch burns brightly, doesn't it?"

"Shut up, Harry!" I said.

Donovan and I negotiated the crowd in the living room to place the flowers on the mantle in a spot not taken by empties and half-full tumblers and highballs, shot glasses and paper cups, and plates of food.

"Nice job," Donovan complimented my arranging

skills.

"The door's that way—nice seeing you again."

He didn't take the hint. Donovan followed me upstairs, and once we were behind the bedroom door and could hear one another, I had nothing to say. Donovan approached tentatively, his arms outstretched, but the look I threw made him stop. He stood on the little rag carpet in the middle of the room, hands in pockets, looking about as if being in a feminine bedroom was something new to him.

"I owe you an explanation, at least," he sighed when the silence was unbearable and only brought more tension.

"You've come a long way to offer it, or did it just come to mind since you were going to be in San Francisco anyway?"

"Look, a lot is going on. I've been out of the country. There were no phones."

"Let me guess—back at Petra."

"Yes, but there was more I had to deal with."

"Go on."

I knew what it was; the first of many sins committed, and the confession was just as surprising now as it had been then. I watched Donovan pace and then sit on the bed, gingerly shoving one of my stuffed animals aside as if it would bite.

"I had to break it off with another woman," he said. "I knew I had to break it off when you left Florence. I went home in love with you, Alice. I couldn't sleep, I barely ate, and all I could think about was you."

"I *knew* it!" I squealed. "Well, thank you very much for turning me into a whore!"

"Did you hear what I just said? I couldn't sleep! I barely ate! All I thought about was you! Alice, don't belittle yourself."

"Please!" I sighed, throwing myself on the window seat.

"As soon as I returned to Providence, I told her. I told

her the engagement was off."

"*You cheated on your fiancée with me?!*" I shrieked. "Get out!"

"You have to understand!" Donovan cried, kneeling beside me now. "We'd been together for years, and it was just assumed—Alice, listen to me!"

I'd strode to the door and wrenched it open. "Let me guess, the senator and your mother weren't too keen on your being with a poor little nobody like me?"

"Well, yes."

"Save it. I've already lived through that nightmare. Now just go. Please. Don't make me ask a third time."

"I told them it didn't matter what they thought. I even told them to withhold the money for the digs, the research, put the brakes on the new library at Brown."

"Christ in heaven! You're getting a building named after you?"

"It doesn't matter! I want you."

"And will you tell this sad little story to the next girl that comes along?"

"Alice!"

He slammed the door shut and grabbed me by the shoulders. I was suddenly afraid, yet I didn't try to escape. I was sure he wouldn't strike me as Adam might have. And he didn't. He just studied my face, his own screwed up in pain, in uncertainty—as if he was trying to find the right words to say, and in doing so, his features became soft and genuinely became the mirror image of Quinn, the reason I was first attracted to him.

"Maybe this isn't a good idea after all," Donovan whispered. "I can't pretend to know what's in your mind."

"What?"

"I thought I knew what was in your heart. At least, I thought I did."

He gave me a chaste little kiss on the brow and slipped out of the bedroom as if we'd done something clandestine, something shameful.

The sensation of lightness came over me again, and I wanted to spin happily like Maria in *The Sound of Music* or Mary in the opening titles of *The Mary Tyler Moore Show*, but I didn't. I went to my bag and dug around in the depths of it, retrieving a little leather-bound volume—a notebook he'd bought in the Mercato San Lorenzo, and tossed it into the wastepaper basket along with the photographs of us on the Ponte Vecchio at sunset.

"Not a good idea!" Joan of Arc had materialized and was looking at the contents of the wastepaper basket.

"Too bad," I said, turning to the mirror, unpinning my hair from its chignon, and brushing it out until it crackled from the dry winter air. "Maybe I've decided that this is as far as I want to go with patching up holes."

"Is it?"

"Don't say next that two wrongs will make a right! I'm sick of hearing it!"

"I don't have to—you already did," Joan sighed as she prepared to leave. "And you know we're right."

Joan disappeared as quickly as she materialized, and after she left, I slowed the frantic pace of my grooming, staring at myself in the mirror. I stopped and put the brush down, staring at the reflection of the unhappy young woman facing me.

"This is ridiculous!" I hissed at her. "What's done is done!"

"Not exactly," I heard The Proprietress whisper in my ear. "Play it through, Alice! There's not much more you have to do!"

Sighing, I curled up on the bed and went through old photo albums, knowing it was a bad idea, and soon cried myself to sleep, waking around midnight. I was miserable and hungry and went downstairs to see if anything was left over from the party.

"There you are! I thought you went off with your

friend—are you okay?" Dennis said, meeting me on the first-floor landing.

"Peachy. Anything left to eat? I'm starving."

"Your friend and I were never properly introduced."

"I didn't think there'd be a reason to," I said, trying to get past.

"At least a name and a reason why not."

"He was my last tango in Florence."

"How are you, Sweetheart?"

"I don't know."

"Maybe it would help a bit if you weren't attracted to or didn't bring home guys that look like or are Quinn's evil twin—geez, oh no! Oh God, and here I was trying to compliment your taste in men."

I had slumped down on the stairs and put my head on my knees, desperately trying to keep from crying.

"I hate it when you're right!" I sobbed, trying to keep from laughing. "You're always right!"

"And I'll have to hear about it for weeks," Harry sighed as he joined us. "You think I'm kidding, don't you? Well, come on, we've got an early Christmas present for you. Then you can tell Dennis he's right. Again."

Harry held out a hand and lifted me off the stairs. That hand now went up around my face and covered my eyes. They escorted me one stair at a time down to the living room and through the house that was now quiet. We kicked aside paper cups and cans on our way into the kitchen and almost knocked over the laundry basket on the back porch.

"What are you up to?" I giggled.

"Just one more step, annnd...open your eyes!"

"Merry Christmas!"

Quinn's voice startled me, and I opened my eyes, looking at our reflections in his bedroom mirror. It was several years earlier, the winter of 1972, and we were both home from college for Christmas, Quinn from Oxford, I from Cornell. Quinn stood behind me, holding an exquisite silver cross studded with garnets to my neck and fastening the clasp of the heavy filigree chain from which it was suspended.

My hand touched the stones that caught fire in the light.

I'd never owned anything as beautiful as this.

"I saw this, and I thought of you. It was in an antique jewelry shop in Oxford near my apartment. Couldn't pass it up!"

"It's gorgeous! Quinn, thank you! I've never owned real gemstones. And this is so beautiful, so perfect…"

"That look says it all," he murmured in my ear.

"I'm sorry I don't have anything as nice for you."

I slipped away and reached for my school bag, retrieving a clumsily wrapped package. "I made these. Sorry about the packaging. I can choose the paper and ribbon, the colors, but putting it all together and making it look like something from The Emporium or Capwell's, that I can't do," I confessed and handed over the Christmas gift.

It didn't matter to Quinn. He laughed happily and hurled himself on the bed to attack the package greedily, gasping in delight when he discovered a small teddy bear of silky white fur and a sweater I'd spent all summer knitting. The wine-colored wool was a perfect choice, given his dark good looks.

"You said you'd never had a teddy bear or a pet, so I had Dennis help me make one. But I knitted the sweater myself."

"I have a pet! What do we call him?" Quinn said delightedly.

"I kept thinking of Frodo from *Lord of the Rings* when I made it. Guess it's the hairy feet."

"Frodo it is. Is that bow tie he's wearing some of the fabric from our prom?"

"The same. Dennis's idea—make the magic last forever, he said, or something like it. I told him not to, but he said to go along with it. You know Dennis."

"Let's see this sweater!"

He pulled off the expensive sweater he'd had on and replaced it with my poor offering. Though a bit long and wide in the shoulders, it fit, but he did look handsome wearing my gift.

"Wow, so soft. And you made both of these," Quinn said as he studied the bear first and then ran a hand lovingly up the left arm of the sweater. "I'll sleep with both tonight," he whispered between kisses. "It'll be like you're with me."

After a long, lingering kiss and an embrace, he said, "C'mon, I have another surprise," and took my hand.

We went into the backyard, where a little fir tree planted in a ceramic pot was dwarfed by pine and eucalyptus trees. It was sweet for all that it looked like something Charlie Brown would have decorated. The ornaments were photos of us and pictures from Zeffirelli's *Romeo & Juliet* glued to wooden disks with decoupage. Some were embellished with gold leaf and pasted-on colored glass beads. Velvet ribbons from the notions counter at the local fabric stores were tied on the branches and draped like tinsel. Crowning the tree was a medieval lady with a harp and a knight with a sword and shield.

"Quinn!" I exclaimed in delight. "How long did it take you—and how did you?"

"Well, Dennis was Santa Claus for both of us this year. I told him what I wanted and picked the photos and the colors. You like it, then?"

"Love it!"

"Maybe you'll put it in your dorm room when you return to Cornell?"

"I hope there'll be room for it. I hope I don't kill it!"

Quinn leaned in and whispered, "Thought of that. It's

not a real tree, but every thought that went into it is very real."

I cooed and giggled at every ornament and decoration, especially the lady and knight.

Quinn wrapped me in his arms while we kissed. There was something different in that kiss, and I looked at him questioningly. He touched my face and said softly, "I've been thinking, Alice, let's get married after school. I love you and hope you feel the same way about me. It's two years away for you, but it's possible. People get married in college all the time. I want it to be. I know it can be! After college, I could get work in New York, maybe teach at the School for the Performing Arts or audition for the New York Philharmonic. That way, we'd be together while you finish up your degree. I've always wanted to live in New York," he rambled. "I think we can do this."

"So do I."

"That's a yes?"

"Pretty much."

"I guess that wasn't a traditional proposal, either."

"Well, feel free to get down in the mud if you want to," I quipped.

Quinn took the bait, and when I tried to stop him from kneeling on the rain-soaked ground, we both lost our footing and skidded to our knees. We hugged and laughed, the laughter that came from anxiety being dispelled, from joy realized. Our laughter now haunted me as I sat in my corner of The Curiosity Shop, tears spilling from their ducts.

I reached into my purse and took out a cosmetic bag holding a lipstick tube and the cross. So many years later, the garnets had not lost their beauty; the silver findings and chain were still brilliant. I slipped it around my neck and studied it, watching rays of sunlight spark off the stones. Joan of Arc slid into the chair next to me and touched the cross with a delicate finger as if the stones were too sharp or they might scorch.

"So very beautiful. Aren't you glad you kept it?"

I nodded and tried a smile. I took a notebook out of my messenger bag and flipped through sketches of clothing and costumes, drawings of medieval villages, and tomb sculptures, turning to the page where I'd drawn my idea for a wedding dress.

"I had a dress like this once."

The woman's voice was unfamiliar: soft and low, almost like my mother's. I glanced up and was taken aback by the extraordinary patrician beauty of this medieval lady smiling at me. She tapped the drawing with a bejeweled finger, her hands equally beautiful. Joan deferred to her as she sat down, pulling her *New York Times Book Review* closer and trying hard to ignore the stunning woman, calling her "*La Reine Alieanor.*"

"What would you use to make this dress? A silk brocade or velvet? Perhaps velvet bands on the sleeves and the dress sewn of a rich fabric in red?"

"It was my wedding dress. I thought silk and lace, shades of ivory and iridescent pearl gray, the underdress in silk with heavy French lace over it. Pearl buttons on the sleeves, a small train," I said, feeling quite comfortable explaining my design to her.

"And did you wear it?" she asked kindly.

From behind her counter, The Proprietress guffawed and then excused herself. As customers approached, she took out little volumes from the display cases, the sheets of gold stars coming out of a drawer and disappearing out of sight just as quickly. The lapis-colored book stayed on its shelf.

"Nothing to say?" I spoke up now, glaring at her.

"I beg your pardon?" Joan asked, looking up from her reading.

"I wasn't speaking to you," I hissed. "You all know it was my wedding dress!"

"But it was the wrong groom!" sighed Marie Antoinette as she joined us.

"This is what happens when you give yourself completely to a man," the lady said. "Let me tell you, Alice, had I known what Henry Plantagenet was going to put me through, I would have stayed with King Louis, but then, history would have been written differently, and you would know about that, wouldn't you? I'm Eleanor, a queen of England."

Eleanor of Aquitaine glanced over at the *Review* and tapped an advertisement for one of her many biographies. "Didn't you write this book, Alice?"

"In one of her better years," Joan offered and shrank back when I pointed my index finger at her, warning.

"Thank you, by the way, for portraying me in such a favorable light," Eleanor continued and winked as if we had a secret. "I'm not the fast and loose harlot some historians make me out to be."

Again The Proprietress guffawed. She composed herself and now took to making entries in her ledger.

"One of the problems of writing about the past and living in it," The Proprietress spoke up, "is not seeing how important today and the future are. Sometimes, we are so afraid of making changes for the better the opportunity slips away."

"I think what she's trying to say, Alice, is that you need to get back on that train before it's too late," Joan offered.

"Don't forget your map!" Eleanor of Aquitaine said as she followed me and took a map from the brochure rack.

I ignored it and her, all of them, as I went out the door and crossed the street to Post Street in San Francisco and walked up to Dearmont's, the antiquarian bookseller off Union Square where I'd worked during holidays and summers since college. The store owner, Percy Dearmont, glanced up from his reading when I entered and slid behind my desk in our shared office.

"Late…"

"And in five weeks, you'll be dead, and I'll be out of a job," I muttered, slamming the desk drawer on my purse.

"Sorry, didn't hear you."

"Nothing," I sighed and untangled the purse strap from the drawer edge.

I didn't particularly appreciate knowing the future; I wouldn't say I liked knowing I could change my share of it if I desired, and the opportunity lent itself.

The vase of flowers on the coffee table caught my attention. You could tell the time of year by whatever Percy plucked from his Marin County garden and put in that vase. Camellias were stuffed among holly and ivy, some greens. It was winter still, and I knew the date and the hour. I knew what would happen that day.

The morning passed uneventfully. Two customers, no more. I often wondered how Percy managed to keep the doors open and pay the generous salaries he offered. After his sudden death in a cable car accident, I learned he was obscenely wealthy; the bookstore was something that amused himself and his clientele, who were friends of the family or acquaintances from one of the high-end restaurants or bars in the city. Every day was the same: Percy would read *The New Yorker,* and I would unpack books delivered from all over the world and appraise and catalog them, longing for my lunch hour when I could read some of them while seated on a bench at Union Square.

That day had a twist.

The doorbell rang, and neither of us looked up to see if it was the morning delivery or a customer. Percy was still engrossed in *The New Yorker*, and I was cataloging the week's latest acquisitions: late nineteenth-century folios of Audubon illustrations. The receptionist was too cheery in her greeting, and I supposed the bottled water guy had arrived and was flirting with her. Then I heard her say, "She's right there—where the door is open. Just knock."

"Hello, Alice."

I looked up sharply from the typewriter and saw Donovan standing in the doorway. Percy had come to attention, assessing this tall, dark, handsome stranger. He glanced at me and, from behind the magazine, made the 'okay' sign with his fingers.

A bouquet of white flowers was offered sheepishly, and I handed it off to one of the assistants passing through with a stack of books. "Put them in water, would you?" I asked sweetly.

"It isn't hard to imagine you in a place like this," Donovan said. "It fits you perfectly."

"Then you can guess where I imagine you," I muttered, returning to my work.

Donovan stood there for the longest time watching me type, and Percy kept giving me looks that said, 'Be nice to the gorgeous man.'

"I tried to stay away. Okay, yes, I know you made it clear," Donovan started, but I gave him 'The Look.' I threw one at Percy, who was watching as if it was a soap opera (which it was).

Percy coughed and made an excuse to check inventory.

"You went by my brother's, I guess?"

"Well, yeah, it was my only address for you,"

"That's the only way you could have known where to find me."

"Alice, I know—"

"You're wasting your time."

"I don't think I am, but would you at least look at me, talk to me?" he asked. "Just tell me—something."

I took off my reading glasses and looked up. I remembered the expression on his face from our first night together in Florence. A pang of longing and remembrance shot through me, and I began to feel pity for Donovan.

"Not here. Not now," I said quietly and with control.

"Meet me for dinner. I'm at the hotel across the street, The Saint Francis."

"No."

"I don't give up easily," Donovan whispered as he retreated. I was glad he didn't see how it affected me, how I blushed and felt like I did in Verona on our first date.

He was back the next day.

And the next.

Finally, I gave in, more out of curiosity than a genuine desire to hear what he had to say, what excuse he could conjure up for the weeks of silence after the breathless, romantic promises whispered in bed in Florence when I was almost ready to believe again, hope that love was possible, and my broken heart had mended at last.

Donovan was waiting on the doorstep when I arrived at the bookshop that morning.

"All right!" I sighed, not letting him speak. "I'll see you at seven."

"Thanks. See you then," Donovan said quietly, a bit surprised. "Uh, do you have time for coffee? Now?"

"What do you think?"

"Sorry. See you tonight."

"Donovan!"

He turned, his face shining with expectation.

"No promises."

Unlike our first date, I didn't take care with my appearance. That morning I'd met with a client in a toney neighborhood of San Francisco, St. Francis Wood, so I kept the day's corporate look: my safe navy blue 'dress for success' business suit and prim ivory blouse with sensible pumps, hair pulled back in a low ponytail. It was a clear message that I meant to be as severe and cold as my appearance.

I passed like a nun or a corporate attorney under the Christmas lights and decorations, the ebullient shoppers pushing their way and being carried from one department store to the next. The doorman at The Saint Francis tipped his hat and opened the door for me as I approached. A wave of nostalgia washed over me as I inhaled the spice-scented air of the lobby and took in the warmth from the fireplace. As a child, my mother took me here to admire the lobby decorations and have a cup of hot chocolate in the lounge after seeing Santa Claus at Macy's. She used to say it was our one extravagance.

But Donovan was nowhere to be seen.

"Are there any messages for Alice Martin?" I asked the desk clerk after fifteen minutes had passed.

"No, Miss." The clerk thoroughly searched the counter and boxes behind him and shook his head. Nodding, I paced another circle. I kept glancing at my watch and pacing the carpet until the concierge invited me to the lounge, where I took a table near the door to watch, nursing a gin and tonic. An hour passed before I decided I'd made a fool of myself. As I was leaving, Donovan entered the lobby, strolling towards the elevators.

"Hello," I greeted. "Did you forget?"

He looked up when he heard my voice and frowned, reaching for the elevator buttons.

"Donovan?"

Now his face drained of color, and he forced a smile. "Alice!"

Pivoting on my heels, I left the hotel. Outside on Powell Street, I hailed a taxi and was taken directly to The Curiosity Shop.

"Well done, you!"

I glanced up wearily and saw Richard the Third sitting at my table and pouring himself a glass of champagne.

"Something's changed," I muttered, looking around.

"Indeed. That would be you, Alice Rose. I wish I

could choose my friends and lovers wisely when it mattered," Richard said.

"But you know what happens!"

"Yes, some things can't be prevented—but you can make some events work to your advantage. Of course, had I known then what I know now about my circumstance, well...."

"You had your chance," The Proprietress sniffed, violently stamping a page in a book. "It isn't about you, Your Grace. This week is for Alice."

"The week is almost up!" Richard protested.

"What happens at the end of the week?" I wanted to know, looking around. From Tyrone Power with his volume of Shelley to Joan of Arc still poring over The *New York Times Book Review*, everyone became very interested in what they were reading or doing and ignored me.

The Proprietress snapped her fingers and pointed out the door where a taxi waited on Powell Street in San Francisco. I was taking the door handle when I heard Donovan's shout.

"Alice, please wait!" he shouted, almost knocking an elderly couple down the entrance steps as he vaulted from the hotel lobby.

"Drive on," I said to the cabbie. I watched my ride home disappear into the traffic on Powell Street and then turned questioningly on Donovan.

"People make mistakes," he said and took from his coat pocket an envelope upon which my name was written in his hand. He gave it to me, adding: "It would have helped and done me a world of good if I'd remembered to give it to the desk clerk!"

It was a moment before I took the envelope and removed the note from it.

Please don't think I'm a jerk or asshole — I had a last-minute meeting.

Wait for me in the lobby, and I'll make it up to you. D.

After a long moment during which I stared at my shoes, and my cheeks burned, I muttered, "I was in the lounge."

"And I was looking for you in the lobby."

We stared at each other, hands in our pockets, until I started laughing, and Donovan joined in.

"Do you want to get something to eat?" he asked. "I can get us a table upstairs at Victor's."

"Victor's? I'm not dressed for it."

"Well, how 'bout my room? You won't need an evening gown for that—or clothes!" he murmured, leaning in for a kiss.

"Remember, I'm still mad at you," I jibed. "You'll have to earn that privilege."

"And it will be," he said, wrapping his arm around my waist. "Have you lost weight?" He glanced up and down Powell Street. "You know the neighborhood? Any ideas?"

"Are you in the mood for French cuisine? There's a *bistro* in the Financial District not far from here. *Le Central.*"

"Lead the way."

Our walk took us from Union Square east and down into the glass and granite canyon that was San Francisco's Financial District and over to Bush Street, where we managed to secure a table at the most popular restaurant in the city. We were tucked into a corner lit by candles and flickering holiday lights scattered on potted plants.

"Do you live here?" Donovan queried an hour later as we waited for the check and lingered over sweet wine.

"Berkeley."

"Why not here? This is my first time visiting San Francisco, and it's an amazing place."

"I lived here briefly with my grandmother when I was little. She lived in an apartment house on California Street near Grace Cathedral. That was after we got back," I explained.

"From where?"

"England. After my dad disappeared, we lived here until we found a house in Berkeley. I used to spend weekends with Gran—probably just to keep me out of my mother's hair while she tried to find Dad."

"You haven't heard from him or know what happened?"

"There are stories . . . most aren't true, I suppose, and no one will corroborate anything said. I have my own theory."

"Which is…?"

"I think he just left." I turned to look at Donovan, who looked back tenderly. "My parents were having a hard time. My mother wanted to come back to the States. My father wanted to open an architectural firm in London. He loved restoring old houses and buildings that were damaged in the war and liked the government contracts that kept falling into his lap. My brother and I were caught in the crossfire of their arguments. One afternoon he didn't show up. We waited for a week. The British authorities and the American embassy had no explanation. I used to sit on the stoop of our townhouse and think that if I sat there, his taxi would roll up and out he'd bound. Didn't happen. I was relieved when my mother finally stopped crying and brought us back to California."

"Maybe that's why there's a wall up around lovely Alice," Donovan murmured, leaning in for a kiss, but I dodged it.

"No, it's being mistreated by men."

"What if," Donovan whispered, sliding closer in the booth, "I helped you get over that?"

"It's not a virus, Donovan!" I laughed sadly. "If you can change the genetic predisposition of men to not look past oneself and one's needs, I'd be impressed."

"What if it was the gene pool of just one man?"

Moments ticked on before I said, "I'd be impressed."

The wine may have softened my disposition towards Donovan, but my guard was still up. We took a cab to the Montgomery Street BART Station, where he spent money for a ticket just to wait on the platform with me until my train arrived, a kind gesture, if not romantic, in my eyes.

"I wish you'd reconsider my offer," he asked, taking my hand as I glanced down the tunnel at the lights in the next station, a sign of the train's imminent arrival.

"Donovan, I enjoyed being with you tonight, but I have to sort things out. You can't just appear out of the ether and expect everything to be like it was in Florence."

"I think it can be like it was. Give me a chance? I'm trying to reconstruct genetic makeup here."

The train flew into the station, horn blaring. Donovan pulled me close for a brief kiss and stood on the platform, waving goodbye as I left on the train. I saw that image in my mind and dreamt of Florence—hot, disturbing dreams—after falling asleep on the sofa when I returned home. It made for a night of troubled sleep, which put me in a foul mood when I woke.

Someone punching the doorbell had me alert, and I yanked the door open to find Dennis and Harry on the threshold with a pink bakery box and a trio of coffees in a paper tray.

"Oh, dear!" Harry greeted. "Just getting home?"

"Not what you think or want to think," I grumbled, stepping aside to let them in.

"Oh, dear!" they sighed in unison.

"Just once, I'd like to meet on a Saturday morning and learn that you'd done something wicked and scandalous, and preferably not in a foreign country," Dennis said, kissing my cheek.

"Oh, I don't know," Harry chimed in. "It looks better on a resume if you've caused a sensation on the Continent than in Kansas because nothing would shock most Europeans these days."

"Harry!" I groaned.

"Office Christmas party last night?" Dennis hinted, handing Harry everything and gently nudging him into the kitchen.

"A date with Doctor Trist," I muttered and glared at both of them, waiting for a barb or something smartass.

"The guy who keeps showing up at the house?" Harry called over his shoulder on the way into the kitchen. "And? *And?*"

"I appreciate your concern, but let's have breakfast and save rescuing me from a rabbit hole for another day," I said and threw myself back on the sofa, clutching one of the throw pillows.

Dennis stared at me for the longest time—an uncomfortably long time. "What are you doing?" he finally asked in the sonorous whine of a parent.

"Oh God, here it comes…"

"Alice, you're miserable. You went to Italy, again, miserable, and you came back, again, miserable."

"Do you want me to return and stay there so it doesn't bother you?"

"No, but I need to know what's going on. I don't want a repeat of Dad or Mom. I can't live through that again."

"I don't drown my sorrow in booze. The only pills I take are birth control or an occasional aspirin."

"Maybe it's time to let go."

"I have."

My statement was defensive, and I could tell Dennis was ready for another lob. He threw a grenade.

"You haven't. No, don't argue! You haven't. This Doctor Trist looks and sounds like Quinn's evil twin. And Adam, the Boyfriend from Hell? Same thing. I won't bring up Jeremy, Patrick, or any of the one-week wonders you brought around. Date a blond with blue eyes—a surfer or a car mechanic. Walk away from these intellectual basket cases, Alice! Do something different and unpredictable for a change. You're miserable, and you know it."

"Get used to the 1977 model Quinn, Denny. I've pretty much decided on it. Already went for a test drive," I quipped, jumping off the sofa to change my clothes. Dennis caught my hand and pulled me onto his lap like in the old days.

"You don't sound convinced to me."

"Still working out the bugs, if you must know."

"Such as?"

I drew a long and deep breath, knowing where this would lead. Despite this, I said quietly, "Ever been attracted to someone you knew was just wrong for you for every reason possible?"

"I get it. He's not so much a Mister Goodbar but a Rocky Road. Maybe a Sugar Daddy?"

"Candy metaphors? He isn't all bad. Just bits—really, really, annoying bits."

"I bet he needed to do some serious begging or groveling to earn your forgiveness."

"Life's all about second chances—shit, you've got that face. What?"

"I don't like him. He's not the guy who should get a second chance in my book."

I bristled. "*That* guy isn't here, and Donovan is. I'm tired of being alone, and Donovan wants me."

"Not the best reasons," Dennis said as he dumped me off his lap. "Speaking of which, do you have any?"

"What?"

"Reasons."

"He's an interesting guy, Denny. He's an archeologist, intelligent, and we have interesting conversations that take interesting twists and turns and make me want to read more and be more than I am. I feel grown up around Donovan. I feel sophisticated."

"That's it? You want to be Galatea to his Pygmalion?" Dennis asked, pushing himself off the sofa to help Harry bring in our traditional Saturday morning brunch, a tray laden with pastries, scrambled eggs, sausages, bacon, fruit, and our coffee.

"C'mon, Alice!" Harry called after me as I finally went into the bedroom to change.

"I'm changing! I'll be there in a sec," I shouted back.

"I'm not talking about clothes. I'm talking about this guy!" Harry said.

"Why do you insist on calling him 'this guy'? He has a name."

"Beelzebub comes to mind," Dennis muttered. He smiled innocently at me when I returned in jeans and a tee-shirt.

"Hands off the bacon. It's mine," I said, sitting on the floor in front of the coffee table to take my fair share of the food.

"We want to know what you see in this Doctor Trist," Harry commented, adding low, "Sounds like a comic book character!" Dennis nudged him playfully.

"I told you," I said, mouth full of bacon. "He's intelligent, interesting, not bad looking you have to admit."

"You'd say that about a teaching assistant or Professor. I've heard you," Dennis said.

"Okay—the sex is incredible! He's a fantastic lover. Mind-blowing orgasms and speaking of blowing, what he does would make you melt. I swear, he knows exactly—"

"*Alice!!*" they both cried at once.

"I'll need eye drops for days to get that image out of my head. Not my little girl, not my little girl!" Harry moaned.

"That'll teach you to meddle," I answered, winking. "I know you're looking for black marks against him. So what's bugging me is this." I paused. "He's condescending, so much so that I feel like Eliza Doolittle a bit more than I should."

"That's it?" Dennis queried, baiting me.

"He doesn't pay attention sometimes. It's as if he's waiting for me to finish what I'm saying so he can top it with something or prove me wrong—instruct me as if I was intellectually his inferior."

"Which you are not," Harry interjected, patting my hand.

Again I hesitated. "I always feel I have to keep my guard up with Donovan. He's not telling me the whole story. He's deadly charming like a character out of Jane Austen."

"Well, you'll have to make up your mind about this Doctor Donovan Trist, who sounds like he stepped out of a Dickens novel," Dennis said. "Maybe he's Uriah Heep's great-great-grandson. And is that a real name, anyway, Donovan Trist?"

"He's going to break my heart twice more...."

The light changed in the room as if a cloud had passed over the morning sun, and Dennis suddenly looked different and older, and I was afraid.

"Sometimes, two wrongs make a right, Faery Princess. Let's eat."

"*What?!*" I squeaked. "What did you say?"

Dennis got up and headed towards the kitchen. I followed him straight into The Curiosity Shop.

"Alice!" The Proprietress snapped, grabbing my arm as I passed by the counter. "One never divulges what one knows! That changes everything. Not everything should change. Remember that, will you, child?" She took my book from its shelf and placed a minuscule gold star on a page, carefully and deliberately, as if wanting me to pay close attention to her actions. "Time is short. Time is running out. There's only so much people can do, Alice."

"I'll go back," I offered.

"You're agreeing with me?" The Proprietress asked, feigning shock.

Dennis was at my side then. "She'll let you think that,"

he said, winking at me. And then, taking my hand, said, "We haven't gone for a walk together in a while."

Out in the high street, I marveled at the brilliance of the sun, the deep blue sky, and the songbirds perched on every branch. On a day like this, The Village looked every inch like Castle Combe in Wiltshire, with cottages and shops made of thick stone with split stone shingled roofs. Charming front yard gardens were teeming with hollyhocks and roses, Canterbury bells, daffodils, and lilies, a village from my dreams, someplace I'd always wanted to live. The dreamlike quality continued, too, for as soon as I thought of someone, they would appear on the street: here was Jane Austen walking with Mr. Darcy, Joan of Arc was window shopping with Marie Antoinette, and there was Quinn Radcliffe at the corner by the little church.

CHAPTER 11

DENNIS TIGHTENED HIS grip on my hand as we walked towards the church, ignoring the whispers and stares of such luminaries as Marilyn Monroe and Queen Elizabeth the First, the composer of the Tallis *Fantasia*, Ralph Vaughan Williams, and Otis Redding, who was singing *Here Comes the Sun*.

"You have to do this," Dennis whispered as we moved closer. Then he was gone, and I was left to face Donovan, not Quinn, alone.

Once again, the scenery changed, but rather than the creamy, rich strands of watercolor and oil paints, shards of brightly colored glass fell around me like snowflakes, and I was moving at a fast clip through Union Square.

It was Friday night that week before Christmas in 1977, and it was another disappointment.

I could hear Donovan's feet on the pavement, his calls for me to stop. Under the Christmas tree, a Salvation Army band played *Good King Wenceslas*, and carolers in Dickensian costumes warbled *Silent Night* while strolling among hedges and weary shoppers.

"Alice, please!"

"All you do is plead!" I shouted. "Why don't you think before you act or think of a more convincing lie?"

"Let me explain!" he begged, catching me up halfway through the square.

We stared at each other for the longest, most uncomfortable time. I grew tired of waiting and snapped, "I'm here. Say what you have to say."

"She's a grad student in my lecture series. The class

wanted to go for drinks."

"It looked like you were celebrating pretty hard!"

"Look, I'm pretty drunk right now, not in my right mind."

"Finally, the truth! Bye, Donovan."

I started down Stockton Street towards the BART Station.

"But I'm sober enough to know I've hurt you, Alice!" he called. "Please! Stay and listen!"

Spinning about, I stood upstream of pedestrians shoving their way past me to get to the nearest sale and waited.

"Why? It'll be more of the same excuses."

"Please, sit down. Hear what I have to say," Donovan said, gesturing towards a bench facing the square's southern end and fronting Macy's. "I'm making a promise to you, Alice, here and now. I'm baring my soul to you. I can be a sonofabitch. I'm careless about others' feelings."

"Clearly! There really is truth in wine."

"But I want to change. I do. All I can see is your loveliness, and know that is what I want — your loveliness of person and soul. I love you. If you could see your way to forgive me, of loving me,"

"Could you say that while sober, Donovan? You see, it dawned on me last night at my brother's that you need an awful lot of wine to say what you think and mean. I noticed that in Florence, too. I came from that—both parents. I don't want that in my life anymore."

"I'll get help."

"Would you?"

"For you, yes."

"For yourself, Donovan. Would you?"

"Yes!"

I watched a couple cross the square hand in hand, laughing, their heads close. The man was hanging on to his sweetheart's every word.

"Could you be like that?" I queried, nodding toward the couple.

"Him?" Donovan was pointing at the man and looking at me.

"Could you give me that kind of attention?"

"I did!"

"Could you do it without expecting something in return? Do it just because you want to? Because you know it would make me happy, make me smile? Listen to me? You see, all a woman ever wants is to be appreciated, to have someone's attention and sympathy when she's troubled. And once in a while, to have her own way. And could you do it sober?"

Donovan reached for my hand, drew me to the bench, and sat close.

"For you, yes," he said at last.

"And time," I added as he leaned in to kiss me. "Time to decide if it's right."

"We have our whole lives…now kiss me, Alice!"

"You hurt me. Some wounds take longer to heal."

"Never again, I promise!"

I let him kiss me then and moved away. We sat silently and detached as if we were two strangers waiting for a Muni bus, watching people come and go, hearing snatches of conversation, pretending the other wasn't there.

Did Donovan want to be one of those couples walking arm in arm across the square, whispering to one another and planting kisses on foreheads and cheeks, laughing about little secrets, private little jokes?

I wondered.

"It's early still—we could catch a movie or a late dinner," he offered. "I could use some food in me right about now."

"Or we could take a cab to the opera house to see this new production of Balanchine's *Jewels* you said you were dying to see," I hinted, my voice as soft as my expression.

"Oh geez, I didn't think you'd get the tickets!" he sighed and then caught himself, looking away quickly.

"I didn't get dressed up for a movie. We had tickets for the ballet. You should have said something if you didn't want to go to the ballet."

"If I had, we would have had this argument yesterday."

"This isn't the best of ideas. I can see it now," I sighed and slid off the bench. Without a goodbye, I hailed a taxi and got in. When I arrived home forty-five minutes later, the phone was ringing. In one movement, I disconnected the phone from the jack and threw it on the floor.

Imagine my surprise when the phone kept ringing.

I stared at it, hoping it wouldn't grow fangs or chase me around the living room. It wouldn't stop ringing until I picked up the receiver.

"Alice! Come into the kitchen!"

I obeyed The Proprietress and sheepishly pushed open the kitchen door to find myself at The Shop.

"What are you doing?" Sigmund Freud demanded.

"I was going to ask the same thing!" Marie Antoinette added.

"What do you expect when you don't tell her the rules?" Joan of Arc defended.

"That's what she'd you'd like to think—that she doesn't know what she's doing," Richard the Third chimed in.

"Where's my stuff?" I went to the corner table and found it empty. "That's it! I've had enough. I want to go home. Now!"

"Silly child!" The Proprietress snapped. "Whether you like it or not, you are home. For now."

"No!" I shouted, approaching the counter. Everyone turned and gaped. "I make an end of it here and now! Dennis said I could have 'do-overs,' to change little things so that eventually they change the whole because people change. But not Donovan! He wouldn't change then. Why would you think he'd change now?"

"But you did," The Proprietress answered not unkindly. "It's like watching a butterfly come out of its chrysalis."

"Alice," Joan softly said as she came to my side, "you're changing history. You aren't allowed to do that. Not all of it. Moments and seconds, yes, but not all of it. If you leave now, all that comes after won't happen!"

"I said no!"

I went to my table and waited for my laptop and bag to appear; for Dennis to come in and explain matters. All I received were inquisitive glances, if that at all. Everyone seemed to avoid me, everyone but Joan. "Surely you have some sort of power," I pleaded with her, and then, gesturing toward The Proprietress, "What about her? Doesn't she have any pull? Can't you just let me go home and leave things exactly as they are now?"

"Where would the good be in that?" Athena queried. Her snowy owl hopped from the gloved hand upon which it had been perched and lighted into my lap, where it immediately fell asleep. "He's never done that before," the goddess commented and smiled.

"I won't have to live through it again. That's the good of it!" I sniped.

"What about everyone else?" asked Joan.

"All that comes after, Alice, will not be," Athena said.

I sighed and stroked the owl's soft and silken back so that it made cooing sounds.

"And it must, I suppose. I understand," I said quietly, picking up the bird and handing it to Athena.

Joan tried to embrace me, but I shook my head and whispered "no," and went out into The Village, walking across the street to the bookshop where a bench was outside the door. I sat down and began to weep and continued until I looked up and saw Quinn.

He was where I always saw him in The Village: down the street near the church, always too far to reach. He smiled sadly and stood there for the longest time until he raised a hand in a tentative farewell before going to the church.

It was enough to send me back to The Shop. No sooner had I entered than Hildegard von Bingen offered a bouquet, and when I glanced up after inhaling the lovely fragrance and started to offer thanks, I was staring at Donovan, who was waiting on my doorstep.

"Keep this up, and I'm going to hate white flowers," I grumbled at him.

"We can't end it this way, Alice," Donovan said.

"I already did, and you'll have to live with it."

"Then shut the door."

"What?"

"I said, shut the door—if you're ready to end what could have been the best thing in our lives," Donovan said. "If you believe you did, you would have slammed the door in my face."

I slammed the door in his face.

The cacophony of the doorbell frantically ringing, the tea kettle shrieking in the kitchen, and Donovan's desperate pleading brought on a sudden headache.

I never had headaches!

Something was wrong.

With hands over my ears, I ran to the bedroom and dived under the mountain of quilts and blankets, burrowing deep into the pillows, breathing slowly and deeply as my mother had taught me when I was a little girl and frightened of thunderstorms. Soon I began to relax, and behind my eyelids, I saw bright wavering lights, soft, soothing colors in Easter Egg pastels, and paisley patterns that danced with my heartbeat.

Oh no, I thought, this is the end time for me. This is now. There would be no more visits to The Curiosity

Shop, no train journeys…

As I felt the panic rise in my chest, I also felt weary—bone-weary, to be precise. I wanted to stay awake until the last moment, but my eyelids were made of lead, and I closed them and waited…

I felt a gentle kiss and opened my eyes. I found myself in Quinn's bed on Christmas Day of 1972. Quinn was pulling on the sweater I'd given him, raking his hands through his hair.

"Oh geez, for a moment, I thought…" I caught myself and ended the sentence by asking, "What time is it?"

"Past four—and my parents are finally home. Better get dressed, Faery Princess. It's our big moment!"

"Want me to come with you when you tell them?" I asked, coming out of the bathroom dressed and brushing my hair. Quinn was making up the bed, and I smiled when I saw that Frodo was placed on what we considered my pillow.

"I'll bring you in triumphantly after I break the good news," Quinn said, taking my hand as we skipped down the stairs one floor to Professor and Mrs. Radcliffe's private rooms. "Why don't you wait in there," Quinn gestured with his chin to the little family room next to the Professor's study. He kissed my hand and, smoothing back his hair, fixing his collar as if he were going to a job interview, knocked on the study door. I waited until he was inside before throwing myself into the Barcalounger with a copy of an old *Life* magazine.

I knew what would happen next, yet I was still as unprepared as I had been all those years ago. Quinn's shout startled me first.

"Why?"

"Because I don't believe you're ready to give up a promising career as a concert cellist! She's your first girlfriend, Tarquin!" the Professor shouted back. "Are you willing to saddle yourself to a girl so young herself? What happens when the children start coming—oh, Lord, bloody hell! She's pregnant!"

"No! I respect her too much—I love her too much to let something like that happen! Don't you care that I love her? We're a perfect fit! I can't imagine my life without her."

"Infatuation does this, Quinn—we all have first loves," Mrs. Radcliffe interjected in her low, Claire Bloom-like voice. She continued: "You say this now, feel this way now, but what happens when you return to Oxford? She's going back to New York after the holidays. Do you think both of you can wait, especially when the separations get longer? If what you've told me about her plans, there's graduate school for Alice. That will be necessary if she wants a university department chair, and if you get that position with the orchestra, there's the touring. Separation is lonely, and you can't expect someone to sit at home every Saturday night, especially someone as pretty and vivacious as Alice. And does she expect you to do the same? I see how girls look at you and you at them. You should take time, consider all the possibilities, and weigh all the pluses and minuses. Maybe you need someone closer to your interests and your social status. It would help your career."

"And have a loveless marriage like you and Father?" Quinn snapped at her. "I guess going to bed with a fifth of vodka and copies of *The New Yorker* and *Psychology Today* is more pleasant than giving it up to your husband at least once a month!"

"That was unnecessary and cruel," Mrs. Radcliffe said. The voice and tone were unemotional.

"So is this reaction. I thought you'd be happy. I know you like Alice."

"Why limit yourself to one girl, Quinn?" the Professor asked. "Doctor Barton on the music department faculty has a lovely daughter near your age. She's also attending school in England and will be auditioning for the Philharmonic. I think you'd have more in common with the Bartons."

"Than with an orphan girl?"

"Oh, really, Quinn! Is that fair?" Mrs. Radcliffe was asking.

"C'mon! Don't deny you've always wanted to know what happened to her father. Was he really an architectural engineer, or did he disappear into East Germany or a gulag while working undercover for the CIA? And did her mother die of cancer, or did she drink herself to death?" Quinn snapped. "No matter which story floating around the Co-Op or the Berkeley Women's Club you want to believe, I guess either don't look good on the society page of the Times!"

There was a pause, and then I heard the words that nailed the coffin shut.

"I'm twenty now. I'm old enough to be drafted. I'm old enough to make up my mind about what I want and who I want!"

"True, but how will you live?" the Professor asked.

"I've got my savings, and there's the trust—I can get a job. Music isn't the only thing I can do."

"No savings, no trust. You don't get to touch that money until you're twenty-five."

"Wait! Grandpa Salimbieni made no condition on when I got the money! Mother, that's your money, too! You're not going to let him do this!"

"Darling, we had to secure your future," Mrs. Radcliffe purred.

"I had our lawyer make the provision. It was advised," the Professor replied.

"You bastard!"

"Watch your mouth, young man!"

"I don't need the money. I can get a job."

"How do you pay for school? You'd leave Oxford

with two years left? Not a smart move, Tarquin."

"Fuck Oxford and fuck you!"

I heard his angry footsteps and the door opening and hid behind the magazine.

"Get back here!" the Professor growled.

The door slammed shut.

"Quinn, please," Mrs. Radcliffe implored. "We know how you're feeling."

"That would be impossible. You haven't got souls!"

"I can make things more difficult by placing some calls," the Professor sniped.

"You'd do that to your own son?" Quinn shouted. "The Royal Philharmonic is one orchestra. I can audition for others."

"As I said, Tarquin, I can make a few calls. I'm telling you now to reconsider. Wait a while. This passion for the girl may be a fleeting thing."

"The *girl*? She is Alice!"

"She wouldn't mean a thing to you if she hadn't given it up!" the Professor was shouting now.

"Bastard! You think that's all I care about?" Quinn yelled at his father.

"You sound desperate, Tarquin. Has she given you an ultimatum? Told you she wouldn't put out or leave if you don't marry her?"

That was all I could stand. I ran down the stairs and was almost to the front door when I heard Quinn's shouts.

"Alice? Alice! Where'd you go? Alice!"

"Here, Quinn!"

My hand was on the doorknob when he appeared on the landing. "Hey! Where are you going?"

I wiped the tears off my face and turned, smiling. "Your father can shout, can't he?"

"Stay for a bit. We've got to talk. C'mon."

Swallowing more tears and the lump in my throat, I agreed, for why delay the inevitable, I thought? Yet we didn't utter a word once upstairs in his study. He threw himself into the overstuffed chair, not saying a word. I pretended to be interested in one of the musical compositions he'd left on the coffee table. It was a transcript of the *Fantasia* he'd written out in his precise, almost perfect hand, for I recognized the notes and willed them from memory to hear the lush, romantic music in my head when the painful, uncomfortable silence between us was too much to bear. He'd added tiny flowers and scrolls in the margins to make it look like an illuminated manuscript page. At the bottom, he'd written, *A Proposal of Marriage to my Love, Alice.*

"What's this?" I asked, trying to fight a new wave of tears.

"Oh. That. I was going to propose on New Year's Day, officially, but I decided . . . doesn't matter now, does it?" Quinn took the pages, looked at them, and tossed them back on the table.

When the silence became too much, I started up. "I should be getting home—Christmas dinner is always at seven, and it's probably waiting."

As I walked past him to get my purse and coat, Quinn pulled me onto his lap and held me tight so I could barely breathe. I let him hold me while he silently wept. His tears fell on my breast, making me hold him even tighter.

"Do you want to come to the house? Dennis and Harry would be thrilled."

"Yeah, let's go," he whispered.

We walked back to my house in silence and, holding hands, slipped in unnoticed by everyone but Dennis. Harry and his parents were in the midst of a present-opening frenzy in the living room. Dennis waved us over, but I shook my head, as did Quinn. My brother came over with two glasses of champagne, stopped short when he saw our faces and downed one flute, then the other.

"Didn't go as well as you expected, I guess," Dennis

hinted.

"Not at all," Quinn whispered.

"Jesus! I am so sorry! Maybe if I talked to them?"

"No, but thanks," Quinn said and, after patting him on the shoulder, followed me up to my room, where the bone-numbing silence took over again. We lay on the bed wrapped in misery and one of my afghans.

"You probably think I'm a sissy or something," Quinn said.

"No! Why would you even say that?"

"I could have stood up to my father, Alice!"

"I think you did, or as best you could, given the circumstance. He's a hard man, Quinn—and a bastard and a bully. Sorry, but it had to be said."

The lightness overwhelmed me, though I felt like someone was punching my chest, and I wanted to run as far away as possible from him.

Why?

Quinn was the one constant in my life! Why should I be afraid of him?

He looked at me and smiled. "No, you're right," he said, taking my hands. "Alice…"

"Yeah?"

"This may sound crazy — but what if we went away together?"

"You mean like eloped?"

"Yes. I've got enough money that you could come with me to England. There's a music school I do volunteer work at in Oxford, and maybe they would hire me as a teacher."

"Hey, lovebirds! Are you coming down for dinner?" Harry had popped his head around the door, and we bolted upright at the sound of his voice, ready to protest that we weren't doing anything.

"Sure, we'll be down in a minute," Quinn answered.

"Great! My mother wants to meet this tall, dark, and

handsome feller," Harry teased and winked before he slipped away.

Dennis had cleaned up the dining room and turned it back into the room it was meant to be. As was the Royal Doulton china and Waterford crystal, the lace tablecloth from Sweden was brought out of storage. Quinn and I raised our brows at the Norman Rockwell scene before us and sat down at the only empty spaces at the table. Dennis knew that Quinn would return with me and had broken his etiquette, allowing us to sit together. Harry's Mom watched as I sat down and glanced around at the others: Harry's Dad, Dennis, and Harry, Quinn.

"Well, Alice Rose," Harry's Mom cooed, "I always thought you were pretty, but love certainly has added to that beauty!"

"Thanks," I said, glancing nervously at Quinn, who winked.

"Yeah, we haven't had to worry about bikers and stoners since Quinn stole her heart," Dennis quipped. "Mashed potatoes, Faery Princess?"

"Pile 'em on!" I muttered. Dennis knew that mashed potatoes were my comfort food.

"Harry says you're at Cornell now?" Harry's Dad pleasantly asked, passing the green beans, olive oil, and pine nuts dish.

"Second year. Just finished the fall and winter."

"Music, like your young man here?"

"I've got some composition courses, choir, but my major right now is History with a minor in Performing Arts. Theater," I answered and smiled on cue with all the enthusiasm of a robot.

"That's right!" Harry's Mom interjected. "You did the costumes for the Live Oak Shakespeare Festival!"

"Only one of the plays. A union person supervised me. Don't have enough credits for union membership, but I'm getting there."

"And you! Andrew Radcliffe's son! Everyone who loves opera knows Radcliffe!" Harry's Mom batted her eyelashes at Quinn. "I hear you're at Oxford? And you're an intern at the Royal Philharmonic?"

"Guilty of both, Missus Davidson," Quinn answered.

"Well, Harry says you two are proof that long-distance romances work and that absence makes the heart grow fonder!"

Under the table, we held hands, fearing we might lose the other if we let go.

The party broke up around midnight, and though Quinn offered to walk home, Dennis would have none of it and offered him a lift. While keys and coats were fetched, goodbyes with the Davidsons exchanged, Quinn and I stood apart in the vestibule and kissed goodbye. "Think about what I said," Quinn whispered as he nuzzled my ear. "I go back the day after tomorrow. Come with me!"

"Just tell me where to meet you," I said breathlessly between kisses growing hot and desperate.

"C'mon, break it up, you two. Say goodnight," Dennis teased.

"Promise me, Alice!" Quinn murmured as he followed the Davidsons out.

I avoided Dennis' suspicious glance as they got into the Volkswagen bus and stood on the porch to watch as the car drove off, Quinn turning around to wave goodbye. When I woke the next day, Harry delivered a letter that had been slipped into the mailbox.

Library downtown tomorrow—newspaper room at 1:00. It's all arranged. I LOVE YOU!

It was the longest day of my life, and to make it worse, Quinn didn't come by, and I made no effort to see him, which made it all the more suspicious to Dennis and Harry, especially when they asked if we fought and I answered with a non-committal shrug and changed the conversation.

Neither Dennis nor Harry paid any attention to the school bag I took out of the house the day of my departure, as it would have been unusual if I carried around something smaller. My stomach was in knots, and I felt like crying. Of course I'd come back! I wasn't running away from my family; I was running to the man I loved beyond all else, and I was helping him.

I was his knight in shining armor.

Taking a deep breath and wishing my heart would stop pounding so hard, I walked down to the main library downtown. The newspaper room was quiet, and I settled into one of the overstuffed chairs that stank of old men and ink, taking an old edition of *The New York Times* from the stack to read.

But I couldn't read.

My heart was pounding, and every clip of a heel on the linoleum floor or a scuff across the worn carpet set my nerves on edge. I waited for the scent of Quinn's cologne and to hear his cheerful 'hello.'

I waited for two and then three hours.

Back at home, no one thought anything was amiss; nothing was different. Dennis did notice how quiet I was as we made dinner, and I set the table.

"Did Quinn go back to Oxford this morning?" Dennis queried.

"Yesterday, I think. I hate it when he leaves."

"I bet he's glad to get away," Harry said, hastily adding when Dennis glared at him, "From his parents, Alice! From his parents, not you! I mean, what kind of parents leave their son alone on Christmas Day to do God knows what when he comes home all the way from England?"

"Parents like Andrew and Jane Radcliffe. He didn't mind. It was their gift to Quinn, I suppose. Besides, making love when no one's in the house is easier, isn't it? Certainly was for us," I said. "Mashed potatoes, please?"

I was surprised then and now by how calmly I had taken it. Certainly calmer than Dennis and Harry were now after that little confession.

Perhaps, too, it came from a deeply repressed understanding that it just wasn't meant to be…

CHAPTER 12

"BUT IT *WAS!*" Eleanor of Aquitaine sighed.

The women in The Shop flocked to my table and watched with sympathetic eyes as I sat down and reached for the coffee mug. Athena's snowy owl hooted and billowed, set down in my lap, and tucked itself in. Joan of Arc made her way through the little group and claimed the chair beside me, as Marie Antoinette tried but was shooed away by Queen Eleanor. Mary Magdalene, a newcomer to the group, glared at Richard the Third when he sympathetically tendered a slice of angel food cake with strawberries. She sent him sulking to another corner.

"What was it about Quinn?" Mary gently asked.

"Everything!" the women sighed in unison.

"You don't seem heartbroken."

All eyes were now on Athena, who claimed the owl and placed it on her shoulder.

"I knew it was going happen," I said, trying to ignore the icy stare she was throwing my way.

"Then. Not now, you silly milkmaid!" exclaimed Athena.

"How very rude!" sniffed Marie Antoinette.

'I was asking a question—"

"Yes, even then. And no, that wasn't a question," I replied.

"Every woman knows that," Eleanor interjected. "Things are said, and habits change."

"Every woman knows she would be a fool not to try to stop him!" Athena snapped.

"What could she have done? She had no money, no

position, no room or board!" Eleanor argued. "She was left at his mercy!"

"More like the mercy of his parents," Richard spoke up.

"Your Grace has hit upon it directly," Eleanor said, smiling at him.

"A very direct hit!" he said.

"Be that as it may," I interrupted, "you know when the cause is lost, but you never give up hope. You just move on. And you wonder…"

"Let that be the end of the discussion!" Eleanor crowed and shot a venomous look at the goddess.

"For now," Athena purred.

"You heard her," I sniped at the ladies. "End of discussion. There's nothing else to say. Go have a PopTart or something."

Left alone, I resumed the transcription of my notes from Villeharduin and de Joinville into the text of a footnote. I ignored Joan, still seated beside me, her chin propped up on her hand and staring.

"What you didn't say is much more important than what you did, and you and I, and perhaps Richard over there, know that that unspoken comment is the truth."

"I'm frightened now. I've changed so much," I confessed.

"Yes, you have, and for the benefit of all!" Joan exclaimed, patting my shoulder.

The Proprietress cleared her throat and then started organizing the display cases. "But are we speaking of Alice or history?" she interjected.

"Or both," was my reply.

"Remember what your brother said. Two wrongs, in this case, make a right."

"Why does everyone keep saying that? What?" I demanded of her. "How can it be?"

The Proprietress crooked her finger in my direction as

she took my book out of its case. "The first step is asking questions and asking why. Congratulations, you're not like some people, after all. It annoys you so much that you have to ask."

She opened the book and pointed to a page not decorated with an enormous gold star but with a neat, flowing italic script. Her finger tapped the page, and I read words in my hand: I was saving myself from Quinn's parents and saving him from more significant hurt.

I understood—only just.

"That's one wrong, I guess," I sighed. "Where's the other?"

She pointed to the door. Joan looked apprehensive, frowning, and I thought I heard her call out as I passed the threshold. Whatever it was, it was too late. The warmth I felt now was delicious. I found myself in a shower of golden light that transformed into soft peach, lavender, and palest blue, while diamonds showered down upon me, which soon became the warm water from my shower. I had returned to my apartment in Normandy Village in Berkeley during Christmas of 1977.

Donovan was sitting on the top of the stairs outside my apartment when I went out to check for mail.

"You've been here all this time?" I demanded, incredulous. How long had it been since I slammed the door on his face?

"Yes, and I passed your landlord a twenty not to call the police—only kidding! I'm kidding, Alice!" I brushed past him, and he caught my hand. "What more can I do to prove I'm sorry and that I'll never hurt you again?"

My look was made of flint, but inside I was melting. He lifted my chin to see my eyes, and I looked away at first, but the soulful glance, the softness I held in those eyes…

"Come back this evening, and we'll talk."

I was genuinely surprised when he showed up at six

o'clock that night. Thankfully there were no white flowers in his arms, only a bottle of Pellegrino.

"This is my pledge," he said, handing the bottle to me. "If you will give me the courtesy of a fair hearing, I promise more."

"Come in," I said. The tone was unemotional though my insides were quaking. I was glad to see him, but I wouldn't let it show. I would not be so easily won.

He followed me into the living room and stood at the threshold as if waiting, then took a place on the sofa. I could sense that he followed me with his eyes as I came around and sat on the loveseat across from him. Without prompting, he leaned forward a little, his forearms on knees and hands clasped together, penitential, if anything.

"I've made so many mistakes in my life. I pretended it didn't matter until I realized how badly I hurt you," he began. "I would do and say things to get what I wanted because I knew I could and could get away with it."

That made me look up and feel ethereal, a joy almost bursting through my heart. Indeed, it was pounding furiously.

"Until now," Donovan said softly.

He stared me straight in the eyes, and neither of us flinched. The eyes were soft and loving and, for once, not undressing me or taking account of my faults.

I rose, reached for two wine glasses in the hutch cabinet, and brought them back to the coffee table, opening the bottle of Pellegrino, pouring the sparkling water, and watching it fizz and grow still.

"It's not wine…" I murmured.

"My first promise."

"And the second?" I asked, smiling.

He leaned across the table so our lips almost touched and whispered, "To take our time, Alice." And then he moved away, winking.

It took me by surprise, but it was delightful. I took a

sip of the water and set my glass down. "Stay for dinner?"

"Sure."

"I'll throw something together. Everything goes with water, right?"

Donovan threw back his head and laughed for the first time since our reunion, a hearty laugh that seemed forced.

While I quickly assembled a dinner in the kitchen, Donovan explored the living room, calling out approving critiques of my decorating efforts and my choice of art and books.

"Hey!" he called. "This guy could be my twin!"

Closing the oven door with my foot, I removed the apron and went in to see what caught his attention. Donovan held a framed snapshot of Quinn and me standing in front of Holbrook Library across from the Pacific School of Religion Chapel on Holy Hill.

"That's a family friend," I said as I took the photo out of his hands and replaced it on the shelf where he found it.

"Friend? Standing pretty close to you for just a friend," Donovan teased, or so I thought. His smile chilled to brittle.

"Yes, a gay friend…"

"…Wait, wait, wait! Back up the truck, Mary!"

Dennis was waving his hands and shaking his head as I suddenly slumped into my chair in The Curiosity Shop, feeling like I had just fallen out of the sky. "Why on earth did you tell him that?" he demanded, his voice rising painfully.

"It was the first thing that popped into my head!" I pleaded, staring first at Dennis, then Joan, who had gripped the pommel of her sword a little too quickly for my liking, and then Marie Antoinette, who stopped in mid-bite, her Danish suspended by a dainty thumb and forefinger. Richard, working on his crossword, muttered, "Wrong answer!"

"Oh, for God's sake, send her back!" Dennis moaned.

"Get it right, Alice," Richard advised, erasing his latest entry on the crossword. "You only get this one chance…"

"Wait!" I cried, and when I blinked, I was staring up at Donovan, who stared back with a more familiar look: narrowed, dark eyes and a smirk on his lips.

"This is the friend you wanted to forget?" he queried.

"He went to England for college, we broke up during the winter break of his third year, my second at Cornell, and he's now a cellist with the Royal Philharmonic."

Donovan studied my face, perhaps searching for the indication of a love still burning, tears to prove that it wasn't over, at least in my heart or mind. He glanced at the photo and nodded.

"Yeah, college will do that. Let's eat," he said, smiling.

Dinner was pleasant; the conversation was mainly about Donovan's excavations at Petra and those at a castle in the Tuscan mountains, which I peppered with questions and comments. I noted he didn't ask about the dissertation I would defend in three weeks, my plans once the doctorate was conferred, or anything else that concerned my life. To his credit, Donovan helped with the washing up, and afterward, we brought our dessert into the living room.

"Let's have some music," Donovan suggested and crouched by the stereo to thumb through my collection of rock n' roll, classical, and medieval recordings. He found a record and put it on the stereo turntable, waiting until the disk started before moving away. The first in a suite of medieval *chansons* and dances by David Munrow's Early Music Consort filled the silence—a *pavane*. "A lot of Middle Eastern influence in the music, don't you think?" he queried as we sat and shared a massive slice of chocolate cake.

"The Crusaders brought the instruments and the music back from the Holy Land," I commented, feeding him the last frosting and crumbs.

He now leaned back with his head on the sofa pillows, eyes closed, listening. Suddenly he said, "I can picture you at Petra, the sun on your skin."

"Picking the sand out of my teeth and hair," I jibed, and as I had hoped, the overly serious Donovan laughed.

He turned to look at me; the dark eyes were soft and loving, sensual. "I picture you at sunset, just when it starts to cool—just a bit. The violets and oranges of the last rays, the warmth of the day making you…." Donovan didn't finish the sentence but reached out and pushed my hair back, kissing my cheek and neck, fingers gently sliding down the shoulder curve inside my blouse to the swell of my breasts.

"Incandescent?" I murmured between soft kisses.

"I can see you in the tent, the silk curtains brushing up against your body as the breeze stirs them."

"Pillows and carpets, perhaps some incense?"

"If you want!" he said huskily, adding, "Hold that thought!"

Donovan slid off the sofa, picked up his coat, and walked towards the door.

"You're going?" I asked, running to catch up.

"Disappointed?" he asked, winking. Before I could say another word, Donovan lightly bussed my forehead and said, "We take our time because we have time. Right? See you tomorrow night if there's nothing else going on."

I felt lightness and joy as I turned and took my chair at the table in The Curiosity Shop, smiling victoriously.

"What has become of our darling Alice?" Marie Antoinette teased, offering a slice of apple pie. "Before, she didn't want to change the leopard's spots, and now she can't wait to jump into bed with them! Well, Alice Rose?"

"Isn't that supposed to be cake?" I quipped.

"My, my, isn't Alice clever!" The Proprietress spoke up. "She thinks she has him wrapped around her finger! Be careful he doesn't cut off the circulation!"

I was ready to snipe at her, conjuring some fairly tart language and almost physically impossible things she could do with her stars, books, and parquetry casks, when The Shop came to a standstill. All heads turned to the door.

"Hello, I don't believe we've met," said the sloe-eyed, dark-haired woman strolling towards me. She was not exceptionally beautiful, but her low voice and how she carried herself made her attractive. I noted the French style of dress and the horseshoe coif of the early sixteenth century and could not take my eyes off the bandana she wore around her neck. Around that slender neck was the famous golden letter 'B' and three teardrop pearls suspended from a pearl choker.

Anne Boleyn extended a hand in greeting. I took it and was surprised by the strength and warmth.

"We meet at last, Alice Martin! Your brother said you'd be here by now," she said, lifting my chin with her long, bejeweled fingers to study my face. "Ah, yes! You are stunning. Beautiful, even. Dennis never lies."

"Dennis talked to you about me?"

"What a charming young man and such a talent with needle and thread! He made this dress. What do you think?"

She took a spin, and the rich fabric swirled around her, a stream of scarlet velvet and gold that flashed and burned in the sunlight streaming through the windows.

"Wait, isn't that the dress Jane Seymour wore for the Holbein portrait?" I wanted to know.

Anne stumbled to a halt. "Stupid little cow!" she hissed and started to move away, carefully smoothing the fabric of her skirts.

"I'm sorry, I didn't mean to offend . . ."

"Not you! The stupid little whey-faced whore that got me killed!" Anne grumbled.

"Please," I offered a chair.

Anne sat down and glanced over at Marie Antoinette,

who pointed at Anne's neck and said, "Nice touch that, the kerchief."

"I'm sure you have advice for me, too," I said to Anne as I opened the laptop and pressed the power button. "No sooner do I think about someone than they appear and give me advice for the lovelorn, though each of them," (here I shot looks at every man and woman, real, imaginary—damn, they were all unreal and dead), "is living in a glass house. Their experiences with love are, were, no better than mine!" I turned to Richard, who was about to speak when I added, "Present company included, Your Grace!"

"I should hope so!" He sniffed.

I smiled up at Anne Boleyn. "So tell me, Anne. What jewels of experience can you give me so I can deal with whatever is next on my itinerary?"

Anne watched the laptop boot up and nodded. "So much better than pen and ink," she said. "Just think of the sonnets Thomas might have written for me—Thomas Wyatt?"

"I know his work."

"Mistress Boleyn," The Proprietress hinted. "It's not always about you."

Anne brightened, turning to face me, her black eyes sparkling. "Ah, advice! I thought I could change Henry and make him love me. And what did I do but give him what he didn't want? A little girl!"

"That daughter was worth ten boys," I muttered.

"It truly is impossible for a leopard to change his spots. I could have given him sons, but it wouldn't have mattered. Harry was tired of me the night after our first union. I'm surprised I lasted three years—are you writing this down?"

"No, I'm writing a history of the Fourth Crusade, but I am listening."

"Horrible subject and such a scandal! What does one

do with Venetians? They saw to the destruction of Constantinople," Anne sniffed.

"Alice knows that, and I don't think she cares about your opinion on the matter," Joan said.

"If - you - *please?*" Anne snapped back, glaring, and then turned to me and smiled. "Let me be brief. Never give away your heart. They're not worth it! Not a single man."

"*Mon Dieu!* Is that all you have to say?" Joan exclaimed.

"I could have told you she was going to say that," Richard muttered.

"So could I," I echoed, smiling at the maligned English queen. "But there is hope."

"*What?!*"

The exclamation in unison by everyone in The Shop was like a Greek chorus and made me smile. I said brightly, "You see that there *is* hope, don't you?"

"Unbelievable!" Eleanor of Aquitaine cried.

"My, how you've changed your tune!" The Proprietress sighed. "Where are the fear and caution?"

"You told me I had to play it through," I said. "I'm only doing what I'm told, and hopefully—"

"Goodness! Look at the time!" The Proprietress exclaimed as she took an anniversary clock out of a display case and set it on one of the counters. "Alice, I know you'd love to stay and chat. Tell us that, on the one hand, what an evil man Donovan Trist was and how very much you wanted to erase him from your history, and on the other hand, how the physical attraction makes you willing to overlook such flaws, how you now see there is the hope of redemption and restoration,"

"Now, wait a minute! You don't know that!" I protested.

"Don't I, darling girl? Now's not the time to start a quarrel. Time is short, and you must be going," The

Proprietress said. She waved goodbye as I left The Curiosity Shop and walked down the high street to the train station. As usual, the train pulled away as I entered my solitary compartment and settled in.

"We're all hoping for the very best, Miss Martin," the Conductor said as we negotiated our usual transaction. "Ah! A 'D' ride. Things will be getting interesting—but you already know that. You know where to go for dinner."

Frowning, I opened the door and watched him work his way down the train. He left the compartment whistling Jacques Brel's *If You Go Away*. The song was in my head for the rest of the journey, and when the train whistle blew, it was the tea kettle on my kitchen stove, and I was listening to the song on the radio as I spent a rainy Saturday afternoon alone.

I was warm and contented, fresh from the luxury of a bubble bath, the apartment scented with my trademark scent of Elixir of Love Number 1. Curled up on the sofa, I had job applications and notebooks scattered around me, Sammie sleeping on my feet. The rain was a pleasant mantra, white noise to help me write essays extolling my virtues as a Doctor of Philosophy in History and why I should be hired to teach and write at various universities.

The only university I hadn't applied to was Brown in Providence, Rhode Island.

It was going on four o'clock when the doorbell rang. I grabbed my wallet and shushed Sammie as he yapped and slid on the polished wood floors as we went to get the takeaway dinner ordered from China Station.

"Hi." Donovan raised his hands in supplication and said, "I know we had a date tonight, but I wanted to see you now. Couldn't wait, really. I wanted to hear your laugh and see your lovely eyes."

That took me by surprise. I found that all I could do was smile.

He looked miserable, expelling a sigh, then shoved his

hands in his coat pockets and glanced around nervously. "I was trying to be romantic … I can go if this isn't what you want."

"Oh, sorry! Please, come out of the rain. I'm sorry. I was expecting cashew chicken, chow mein, and broccoli beef, but you'll have to do."

"Funny," Donovan quipped as he followed me into the apartment.

Moments later, Donovan was warming himself in front of the wall heater in the living room while I hung up his sodden raincoat and umbrella in the bathroom and then just as quickly switched on the coffee maker. "Who knew California could be this cold?" he jested.

"Mark Twain!" I called back.

"Ah yes, didn't he say the coldest winter he ever spent was July in San Francisco?" Donovan remarked, then suddenly shouted, "Waterhouse!"

"Pardon?"

"The paintings here. The prints on the wall. John William Waterhouse. And I see you like Edward Coley Burne-Jones, too."

He was admiring the prints of *Fair Rosamund, Juliet,* and *Love Among the Ruins*, works with medieval themes by my favorite Pre-Raphaelite painters. *Fair Rosamund* was a medieval damsel looking out a castle window at the column of knights approaching in the distance; *Juliet* was a profile portrait of a pensive-looking young girl in medieval clothing. *Love Among the Ruins* was Edward Coley Burne-Jones' masterpiece: two lovers clinging to one another in the ruins of an ancient palace or castle, the colors vibrant. These works hung over the dormant living room fireplace alongside my poor offerings in watercolor and ink.

"Gifts from a friend. I wrote a paper on the Pre-Raphaelites that year," I said when I brought him a cup of steaming hot coffee.

"The friend you tried to forget?"

"Yes, if you must know!" I chuckled.

"And this pensive young man must be the mysterious friend?" He was pointing to a portrait of Quinn grouped with other artwork.

"The same."

Donovan glanced at me and then leaned in to study my work. "This is very good. I'd forgotten how incredibly talented you are. Jesus! You drew every single hair!"

"Thanks. Look on the wall to the right of *Fair Rosamund*."

"I'm looking...hey! That's *me!*"

"I based it on the sketch I drew while we toured the Palazzo Davanzati. Remember? In Florence?"

"I remember the courtyard . . . wow! Watercolor?"

"Yes. I was going to send it to you as a gift, but then I never heard from you—okay, that's forgotten. But it's yours if you want it."

"No, no, I like that it's hanging on the wall in your apartment. Keep it here," Donovan said, stepping back to view it from a different angle. "Wow, do I really look like that?"

"You mean that good? Yes."

The answer pleased him, for Donovan's dimples increased, and his smile was genuine. It might have been Quinn standing near the coffee table admiring himself. But then, Quinn wouldn't have dwelt on how he appeared to others in his portrait. He would have shrugged and remarked on the technique of light and shadow that made the arched stairwells and galleries of the famous courtyard in the fourteenth-century Florentine townhouse look like an Escher print or teased me about wanting to rent rooms there.

The doorbell rang and saved us from what I knew would be an awkward exchange, for Donovan was now looking at the photo of Quinn and me that had caught his attention the day before.

"That'll be dinner," I said, going for my wallet again. Donovan was quicker; moments later, the bags of takeaway cartons were being unpacked on the kitchen table.

"Consider this a date," he said, winking.

"You've caught me by surprise. I hoped to have this place cleaned up before tonight."

"Sorry! My bad timing, as usual," Donovan said, a tinge of disappointment in his voice.

"No, not at all. I spent most of the morning working on a surprise. I figured I'd show it to you when we returned from the movie."

"For me?" he said skeptically, then, "Seriously, for me?"

"That's what I said."

"Oh."

I turned and frowned. "Donovan, are you okay?"

"Want the truth? I haven't had a drink in twenty-eight hours."

"Twenty-eight—?"

"I did it for you."

I kissed him on the cheek, saying, "Thank you, but I insist you do it for yourself. That will make me very happy."

While I served up equal portions, I noticed he was observing me; his expression was sad.

"Please . . . tell me."

"What?" he asked, distracted.

"Something's the matter. Where's the urbane, erudite, and cocky archeologist that swept me off my feet and into his bed in Florence?"

"Let me know if you find him. I've been looking all day. I think he's corked up in a bottle somewhere!" Donovan replied half in jest.

"I could get used to this new guy sitting at my kitchen table."

"The guy who looks like the evil twin of the guy you're trying to forget?"

"I don't know if he's evil, but I'm here with him."

Donovan scowled at the food before him and glanced at the chopsticks I handed over. "Could I get a fork? I want to keep this urbane, witty, handsome evil twin guy thing going, and I can't do it with chow mein in my lap."

A fork was traded for the chopsticks, and we dug in. Donovan inhaled the food as if he hadn't eaten for days and was reaching for the carton of cashew chicken when he paused and picked up a monograph stacked on top of a pile of books at one end of the table.

"Sorry, I wanted to straighten things up. Someday I'll have a proper office," I apologized and reached for the monograph.

Donovan shook his head and flipped through the pages. "No, no! This is good, Alice! Historical origins of the Guelph Ghibelline conflict and how it shaped the Italian city-states. You couldn't have chosen a more obscure but fascinating topic."

"And I'm defending it in three weeks."

His eyes nearly popped. "This is your doctoral thesis?"

"The basis for it, anyway. I wrote that during my first trip to Italy, and a small scholarly press published it in their quarterly. I took the introduction, discussion, and conclusion, most of the footnotes, and worked them into something more in-depth and researched. I expanded the bibliography and appendices. My dissertation is nothing like this. I'm taking a big risk if my advisor happened to see it," I rambled, happy he was listening and I could talk about my work. "I'm sure you've published papers in more recognized journals. Weren't photos of the Petra excavations published in *National Geographic* last month?"

"Yes, but they weren't my photos."

"And there was an article about Petra and the work at Santa Reparata in *Newsweek*. I immediately thought of you when I read it."

"Wasn't my work." He held up one of my costume sketches for a local theater group. "Let me guess, part of the thesis?" he teased.

"Part of my employment. When I'm not working at the bookshop, I design costumes for local groups—the best money I ever spent getting that union card. It pays for this place."

He picked up one of the spare chopsticks and started pushing cashews around on his plate as if it were a billiard game, then pushed it away, sat back in his chair, and drank the sparkling water. "I wonder if you aren't too intelligent for me," Donovan murmured.

"What do you mean?" I laughed. Inwardly, I was starting to feel ill, as if the big brush-off was coming.

It wasn't supposed to go this way!

"What did I do to attract someone as beautiful, clever, and smart—"

"You said hello to me in Verona and ran down the street to find out my name," I whispered, my face close, and then I kissed his cheek.

"I'm the kind of guy who finds courage in a bottle," Donovan said quietly. "All the girls I've ever dated were drunken pickups in bars or daughters of my parents' friends. Everything neatly arranged. I never had to do anything on my own to attract someone."

"Have you looked in a mirror lately, Doctor Trist?" I said, giggling.

"I never knew if that was the real attraction!" Donovan suddenly laughed, but the laughter was bitter. "They saw Senator Trist's son, the rich boy from Long Island and Rhode Island, the Hamptons, the guy you'd get your picture taken with at a club on Saturday night, and it would be in the tabloids that Sunday."

Donovan did something uncharacteristic then. He raised my chin with a finger and looked at me without judgment or appraisal. I felt a chill ride through me as if something had been stripped away, and I suddenly felt vulnerable and strangely sympathetic.

"I wouldn't have had the guts to say hello to you if I hadn't already drunk a few glasses of wine that afternoon," he admitted.

"But you did, and here we are."

I wanted to kiss him then, and I did. I stood, hand held out. "Let me show you something."

I had transformed my bedroom into a desert sheik's tent, with carpets, pillows, and yards of silk falling from the ceiling and walls. I'd changed the lights so that the room looked as if it was in a never-ending sunset; all that was missing was a gentle evening breeze and the perfume of incense. I took care of that by placing a cone of frankincense in a bowl and putting a match to it so that evocative and exotic smoke started to rise, then turned on a small fan to make the hangings dance.

Donovan nodded and strolled around the room as if it was a museum exhibit, running his fingers against the silk, touching the Middle Eastern trinkets and décor I'd purchased at Cost Plus just that day. "You've got the feel of it, the colors and lighting—I guess that comes from your theater work and penchant for research," he said. "The lighting is good. It does look like a spring sunset in the desert. All that's missing are the camels and sand." He stopped before me, smiling. "But I'm glad they're not here."

"Is this what you imagined?" I whispered as one of the panels skimmed my body when I slid out of the bathrobe.

The Donovan I remembered took me in his arms.

The mere physicality of his lovemaking and how I responded made me want to be with Donovan. There was no tenderness, just urgency. That was the most significant attraction to him. Dennis once said he knew couples whose relationships were purely physical and nothing else.

I supposed that would be Donovan and me. When all else in our lives fell apart or strained to the point of snapping, we still knew what kept us together.

"Have I redeemed myself?" Donovan asked hours later while we were still among the pillows and tangled in yards of silk, and dawn was breaking.

"Well," I said, turning in his arms to face him, "that's something you'll have to ask of yourself."

"Ah, my beautiful, charming, incredibly sexy Alice has turned philosophical."

"First, I belong to no one. Second, there's no philosophy in one speaking their mind. Only truth. I'm doing what I should have done in Florence. Speaking my mind."

Donovan started to laugh. "I wasn't expecting a manifesto, Alice! Did you take something that said 'drink me' and have it turn you into a raging feminist?" He noticed the steel cast to my eyes and plopped his head back on the pillows. "I'm going to pay for that, aren't I? I should not have said that. I shouldn't have said that. Sorry!"

"It's a start," I said, kissing his mouth before I grabbed my robe and slid off the pillows, adding over the shoulder, "and you gave me what every woman wants. To hear a man say he's sorry and say he was wrong. Consider that redemption. There's hope for you yet!"

Not what I had said that winter of 1977!

"I meant it!" he called after me as I disappeared into the bathroom, and when I emerged, the sun was breaking and shooting rays of bright saffron into the apartment. The light picked up the last of the incense smoke and made it dance rapidly. I knew what was about to happen.

"No!"

The voice was mine, but I didn't know from where it came. Pressure started to overwhelm me, that sensation of being in a vice grip. The light danced and weaved as if captured in a lava lamp.

I heard voices and strange electronic noises, rapid footsteps. The sensation of pressure and now lightness was replaced by fear, a panic I'd never experienced before.

I moved away from the light and was face to face with The Proprietress.

She pointed at me with a perfectly manicured nail, and I followed her to the counter. The lapis lazuli book was lying open on the velvet pillow. Everyone in The Shop was quiet, watching me. Even Richard the Third had put his crossword puzzle down and was staring.

"Go ahead," I sighed. "Say it! Say I'm a fool because it will come around badly. Tell me I can't change everything! Even Jesus forgave those who persecuted him. So why can't I forgive a jerk like Donovan?"

The Shop erupted in cheers.

Rather than speak, The Proprietress wrote in the book with a beautiful pen of sparkling diamonds. The ink that flowed from the nib was iridescent plum. She held up the book so that I could read the words:

Καλοψημένος, Alice Rose! Καλοψημένος, εσείς!

Translated, it meant: *Well done, Alice Rose! Well done, you!*

"Don't look so surprised, Alice," Cecilia Tornabuoni said as I went to my table and was joined by Anne Boleyn, Joan of Arc, and Cecilia. "We were wondering whether this kitten had claws."

"A lot of good it did me then!" I said.

"It's difficult to fight back," Anne sighed.

"Especially when you fall into bed together, he does things that make you want to forget the pain. You want to ignore the dark side of him," Joan added.

We all turned and stared at Joan. She shrugged.

"Do you speak metaphorically of the ugliness and abuse that came later?" Hildegard von Bingen asked.

"Or using sex as a means of control?" Cecilia added.

"What do you think?" I hissed.

"Has anyone noticed how petulant Alice gets when she returns?" Richard murmured.

"I was noticing that," Anne piped in. "One would think she would be happy with her conquest."

"It was hardly that!" I sniped.

"Hardly anything," Cecilia added, and she placed a slice of angel food cake with strawberries and whipped cream in front of me, pushing it forward and nodding. Rather than indulge in my favorite dessert, I put my chin in my palm and stared into the street. Dennis was with Sir Walter Raleigh. They were discussing a map unfurled before them as they walked towards The Shop. Moments later, Dennis arrived and slid onto his chair beside me.

"I know you're curious," Dennis said, attacking the cake with great abandon.

"So?"

"We were wondering what the best path to Alice's heart was," Sir Walter Raleigh said, winking.

"That would be honesty and love," Joan commented, winking as I nodded at her.

"The path to that place is pretty steep and rocky. It'll cost you," Dennis replied and pointed with his fork towards my reflection in the window, which slowly morphed into a younger Alice standing before my bathroom mirror, combing my hair. Donovan was standing beside me, smoothing lotion into his day-old beard.

"Any chance of stopping by tomorrow?" I asked, our movements and mannerisms those of a couple married decades rather than lovers rediscovered.

Donovan looked at me in the mirror, his face sad and serious. "I leave tomorrow night. I'm expected to spend Christmas with the family in New York, and then the semester starts up the week after New Year's."

He was fussing with his polo shirt, turning it wrong side out and back again before slipping it over his head.

"So…" I sighed. "Is this it?"

"That's up to you, Alice."

I turned and ran my hands up his broad, muscular back and wrapped my arms around him. "There is something good here."

"If there is, it's because of you."

"I'm glad we talked and argued. No illusions, no surprises."

Donovan looked as if he was going to speak and then held me at arm's length. "What if you came out on weekends after the holidays? You could interview for jobs, spend time with me."

Now it was my turn to be hesitant. "I don't want to land at Providence and discover that you're in Petra or somewhere in the Tuscan mountains digging out an old castle and have forgotten it's our weekend together. Or worse, in some debutante's bed."

"I just made promises to you and intend to keep them."

"Let's see that you do, Doctor Trist. Still, airfare is pretty steep, and my brother couldn't help if he wanted to."

"Let me foot the bill, and you could pay me back when you get a job at Brown or Stonybrook."

I laughed. "You're that sure I want to work on the East Coast?"

"I can get you to change your mind," Donovan started nuzzling my neck.

I pushed him off playfully, saying, "Why don't we go half and half? You come out here, then I go out there, and we'll talk about cost."

"Can't say no to that."

It was Quinn's voice, and it was Quinn beside me. We were sitting at the boarding gate at San Francisco Airport in the late summer of 1970. His parents had gone to find some coffee and yet more reading material for Quinn on his flight to London. He reached for my hand and then leaned in for a kiss, which was hesitant and brief, as strangers surrounded us in a noisy, busy place.

"Nervous?" I wanted to know.

"Hell yes, Woman!" he laughed. "I'd feel better about it if I'd chosen New York Conservatory instead."

"But Oxford! I know people who would kill for the chance…sorry, I'm not making things any better. Yeah, New York would have been good."

"New York would have been closer to you."

"Well, I've applied to Cornell, and that's closer to England than California."

"I'd like to be close now!" Quinn whispered huskily.

"This airport goes on for miles, and no decent coffee!"

Our kiss was interrupted by the Professor grousing and whining as he and Mrs. Radcliffe rejoined us. Quinn moved away when he saw his mother's sympathetic smile. He reached into his carry-on, took out a parcel, and handed it to me.

"These are for you," Quinn murmured.

"What've you got there, Alice?" the Professor asked as he looked over my shoulder while I unwrapped art prints. "Ah! Waterhouse and Burne-Jones."

Two prints were copies of *Fair Rosamund* and *Juliet* by Waterhouse, and the third was Burne-Jones' *Love Among the Ruins*. In all three, the women were pensive, waiting.

That would be me.

We had seen these works as part of an exhibit at the Legion of Honor and decided on the bus ride home that I would design an entire Shakespeare play or an opera using a Pre-Raphaelite theme inspired by these medieval ladies and Burne-Jones' melancholic lovers.

That would be us.

"You remembered," I said quietly, smiling at him.

"I never forgot the look on your face when you saw them."

Mrs. Radcliffe was bending over us now. "Sorry, darlings, it's time to go."

A stewardess had emerged from the tunnel and was at the desk. Around us, passengers were sharing goodbyes and queuing up to board the flight to Heathrow. We were no exception. I stood off to the side while Quinn said goodbye to his mother and tried not to stare when he brushed off his father's extended hand and came straight to me.

"See you at Christmas?" he whispered, leaning in for a kiss. Quinn dropped his carry-on and wrapped me tightly in his arms for a passionate farewell. "I don't want to go!" he murmured.

"I'll be here," I whispered back. "I love you!"

"I love you! God, if I could just…"

"It's for the best—at least, for right now, isn't it?" I said, my eyes sliding toward the Professor. Oxford is a long way from the Berkeley Hills!"

"You sound as unconvincing as I put on!" Quinn's laugh was forced, the words choked with tears.

Again I was held tightly and given a passionate kiss that had his parents embarrassed but left me in tears, yet elated. It was the Professor's turn not to stare, but stare he did as Quinn finally broke away after a second long kiss, and he was still looking at me as we left the terminal. It was hard to discern between jealousy and hatred.

"I think, Alice," Mrs. Radcliffe commented, linking my arm in hers, "that absence will make his heart grow fonder!"

"Looks like our faery princess has it all knit up, Jane," the Professor said, opening the door for me. As I passed through, the light changed, and the sensation of being pulled along overwhelmed me, so that I shut my eyes and wondered when this painful journey would finally end. Opening them, I was in another airport at another time, walking down the tunnel to the gate at T. L. Green Airport outside of Providence.

I emerged from the tunnel and found myself in a crowd of passengers and their friends and families exchanging the happy greetings one witnessed at airports. I got to be a part of this scene, for I saw Donovan standing off to the side.

He had a bored expression until he glanced around and saw me, and I was pleased that his face lit up. He motioned to the man standing beside him, and they started moving against the flow of foot traffic to get to me. The man held a bouquet he kept from getting crushed by holding it over their heads as they walked forward. As I approached, Donovan took them, and the man stepped back respectfully, nodding in greeting.

"I like these kinds of surprises," Donovan murmured between kisses.

"I have others, but they can wait until I get to the hotel." I winked and then batted my eyelashes seductively.

"Hotel? No, you're staying with me at the brownstone. Here, these are from Mother." Donovan handed off the bouquet and motioned to the other man. "This is Phillip, Mother's driver. He'll take us home."

"Oh."

Mother.

Home was a colonial brownstone in an upscale neighborhood of Providence. It reeked of privilege and old money, and if it looked stately and a bit foreboding from the street, inside was like a museum. I stood in the middle of the bedroom and wondered if I could sit anywhere, sure that every chair and stool, the four-poster bed, was authentic Chippendale. Phillip nodded again as he brought up my suitcase and disappeared as quickly. Donovan entered next with a vase for the flowers, which he placed on a vanity table.

"I'd have you stay in my rooms, but Mother is coming from Newport for the weekend."

"You could stop by to tuck me in, I suppose." I patted the bed, and he took the bait, tumbling me onto my back and fumbling with buttons.

"You could start wearing things with zippers!" he murmured between kisses.

I wriggled out of his arms and reached for my purse, taking two envelopes from the outside pocket. "Are you ready for the first surprise?" I asked.

"Only if we get to celebrate tonight."

"Deal. Here."

He took the envelope and chuckled when he saw the return address. "This is no surprise, but congratulations, Doctor Martin!" he exclaimed. "Look at this! Top ten in your class, too! I was never so ambitious. So? How does it feel?"

"I guess I'll get used to the title."

I gave him the second envelope, and he whooped in delight when he opened it.

"You were here last week? You didn't tell me!"

"If I had said anything, it would have ruined the surprise. That's why I've come on such short notice. I've got a final interview with the head of the History department on Monday. I made it through the preliminaries."

Donovan sat up and leaned against the bolster, bringing me with him as he read the letter. "Well, if anything, it means one thing."

"I have a shot at a chair no man or woman my age or with my level of expertise ever had in the past? That an entire curriculum will be written around my interests and knowledge?"

"No. The committee's intentions were academic and honorable."

He looked at me with the most serious face I'd ever seen, and then we both burst into laughter, remembering our date in Verona. It wasn't long before we were between the sheets and celebrating as only we knew how. We were both contented in yet another afterglow when the grandfather clock chimed six in the evening. Donovan softly swore as he dragged himself out of bed and threw on his jeans.

"Mother will be here in an hour. She's taking us to Camille's."

"Geez, I don't know if I brought anything suitable for that place," I sighed as I wrapped myself up in a sheet and went into the bathroom to start a bath—and remembered my other news.

"You're gorgeous and have a great sense of style. Anything you wear will do," Donovan answered as he headed down the hall to his rooms.

"Donovan, wait!" I called.

He turned in the hallway, smiling, glancing over the railing at the maid on the next landing with a carpet sweeper, and waved her off. She disappeared when I came out dragging the sheet. Donovan pulled me into his arms.

"You are so beautiful," he whispered, kissing the smooth bare skin of my shoulder, then my neck. "Don't tempt me, lovely Alice! It'll be difficult enough tonight with Mother here!"

"Donovan, I'm pregnant."

He released me as if I was made of kryptonite, actually recoiling, and pulled me back into my room. Once the door slammed shut, he paced the braided carpet several times, not saying a word.

I sat on the bed dejectedly, sighing, "Your reaction doesn't surprise me."

"Well, it was going to happen anyway," Donovan murmured. "I was hoping for more time, though."

"Pardon?"

Donovan looked over at me. "You're sure?" he asked quietly.

"I went to the doctor. I'm about six weeks along."

Now he looked at me differently, as if seeing something new.

"Wow," he whispered. He sat next to me and took my hand. "Are you okay?"

"The doctor says I'm fine, healthy. I'm only worried about my shot at the History Department Chair. A pregnancy might put a crimp in my plans to work at the university towards that goal."

"Do you want it?"

I paused and sighed. "Well, the chair won't be a reality for a few years, but,"

"The baby, Alice."

"Yes. It's our child. Why wouldn't I?"

"We'll just get married," he said matter-of-factly.

"Married? Now?"

"*Married!*" Mrs. Arielle Trist delightedly exclaimed when Donovan announced our news at dinner that night. I glanced sideways at him, noting the smug look on his face, and didn't hazard a guess why that was all she would hear for the time being.

Arielle was a Daughter of the American Revolution and an icon of a previous era when women swept the floors and made pies wearing perfectly pressed shirtwaist dresses, pearls, and a pair of heels or had a maid or cleaning woman do it all. Sex waited until after the marriage vows had been sworn, and conditions like mine were whispered about behind pristine lace gloves in polite society at afternoon teas. Due dates were always calculated to be near ten or eleven months after the honeymoon. Donovan told me that Arielle insisted on propriety, upholding standards and traditions, and family values. No scandal would ever taint her to the first degree, nor would she allow it to shatter the façade if something did happen to cast aspersions on the perfect, charmed life she presented to the commons. Arielle proved as much when, the year before my meeting Donovan, a news story of

Senator Trist's affair with a congressional aide broke. The young woman was pregnant, and she mysteriously disappeared. Next came photographs of the senator's visits to Bangkok whorehouses that surfaced in *People* and *The New York Daily News*. She filed for divorce and took him for every penny, ensuring her name and family were spotless. However, when Donovan's bachelor escapades made the local and national news, she turned a blind eye and always blamed the girl. It was no wonder Donovan only told her part of our truth.

Now Arielle turned her attention to me. Her porcelain features and eyes reminded me of Vivien Leigh as Scarlett O'Hara, but the resemblance ended there. She was warm, affectionate, and attentive—to her son. A thousand men could be in the room, and she would only have eyes for her only child, her "Little Man," as she called him. It was somewhat amusing, if not disturbing, that Donovan didn't seem to mind.

"We're thinking August," Donovan said, lighting a cigarette.

"We are?" I kicked him under the table. Donovan nearly gagged on the smoke.

"Wonderful!" Arielle squealed. "Oh, I've always wanted to do a wedding! Well, other than my own, of course. That's the one sad thing about having a son. No trips to the bridal salons on Fifth Avenue! May I help with the planning and arrangements, Alice? I know you don't have a family. Donovan? Are you all right?"

"Nothing to worry about. I think it was a gnat or fly. It's gone now."

"We ought to say something. That they let insects fly in . . ."

I ignored the sideways glance Donovan offered.

"Thank you, Missus Trist. I have a brother who's very good at these things," I said. "He designs menswear, and if Donovan told you anything about me besides having a history degree, I have a background in theater and make a bit of money designing theatrical costumes."

"But it would be so much fun to do it together—as I said, I never had a daughter, and well…" Arielle looked wistful now and played with her napkin, then summoned a waiter over to pour wine all around.

"I haven't given the wedding plans any thought, what with work and interviewing for positions. There's a chance I'll get the position in the History Department here at Brown, so there it is."

"When Donovan said he'd found a beautiful girl from Berkeley, I wasn't expecting such a poised and demure young woman or one so accomplished," Arielle said.

"She was expecting a hippie," Donovan quipped brightly. "You should have seen her face, Alice, when I told her how we met in Verona."

"Like Gregory Peck and Audrey Hepburn in *Roman Holiday*!" Arielle crowed.

"There's always room for disappointment," I replied, taking a drink of wine and remembering that wasn't a good idea. I did note that Donovan had refilled his glass and mine and had asked the waiter for another bottle. It was my turn to give him a look.

"This woman is amazing, Mother," Donovan said, nuzzling me affectionately. "Ph.D., author, artist, incredibly beautiful, incredibly sexy."

"Well," Arielle tittered, "Look at you! It's a good thing the wedding's set for August. Who knows what might happen?"

Indeed.

I was bemused when it did.

CHAPTER 13

When Donovan came to visit that March, I waited a day before telling him, and he looked disappointed, which I did not expect.

"Here's the doctor's report if you don't believe me."

Donovan turned from me and started making coffee, moving quietly and economically in my kitchen as if brewing something in the coffee maker was a lab experiment.

"It was a cyst. I've had them before, but this required an outpatient procedure. Some cauterizing and antibiotics. I'm going to be okay despite everything. That's if you care."

Donovan looked at the papers I held out and frowned, then turned towards me. What his expression conveyed was hard to discern. It was either shock or anger.

"Alice, what are you thinking? I didn't say—"

"That's just it. You haven't said anything one way or the other. That silence could be interpreted in many ways."

"Well, it's a shock. I wasn't expecting it…and I'm worried about you."

"You're not angry?"

Donovan put down the coffee cups and took my hands, drawing me close. "It's not something I choose to be angry about. All I can think of right now is how to please and make you happy, Alice."

I drew a breath. "What would please me most right now," I paused. "Okay, here it is. I've been thinking about it, and what would make me happy is slowing down the pace."

"Pace of what?"

"The wedding. Marriage."

"Why would you say that?"

"It's a logical choice now, isn't it? Maybe we can slow down a bit and not rush to August. I'm starting the job in Providence in September, and before that, I've got the summer seminar at the College of Ripon and York St. John. You're going back to Petra, so what's a few months more? That way, we can plan something extraordinary."

He said nothing. I went to the living room, switched on the stereo, put on an album—*Fantasia on a Theme by Thomas Tallis*—and stared out the window while listening. Donovan settled onto the sofa with his papers and notebooks.

"Are you saying you don't want to get married?" he finally asked.

"No. I just don't want to rush things. There's no reason to hurry along now, is there? And you said you wished there was more time to do things right."

"True, and I could deal with the whispering and embarrassment of calling off the wedding, but my mother? Alice, it will devastate her. It will destroy her. She's already suggested you're forcing or blackmailing me into marriage. Wait, wait! Wait a moment. Before you say anything, I've fought her every step of the way on that. I've almost convinced her that you love me. So, we might as well go through with it."

"It's not a driving test or a root canal, Donovan!" I burst out angrily. "It's our lives together! We don't just go through with it! How long before we divorced if we did this just to please someone other than ourselves?"

"That's optimistic!"

"Why can't we just live together for a while?"

"It's not something my family does. It's not something I do! That's for hippies and beatniks, people who don't care about what's important in life."

"Sounds like you're talking about me," I stated quietly.

"Shit! I didn't mean—"

"Yes, you did. Otherwise, you wouldn't have said it. Your mother thinks I'm a freak from California and all wrong for you."

"No! You misunderstand her! She's used to the girls in Newport, the Vassar, and Mount Holyoke types. You're different. You know, Alice, I don't care what others think!"

"You do."

"No, I don't!"

"Yes, I think you do. You put on this front of being free-spirited, not caring about the world and what's going on, but deep inside, you care about appearances and others' opinions. You seem conflicted and confused. Maybe that's why you drink. To pretend there's no world to tell you you're wrong."

Not what I said in 1978...

"When did you get a psychology degree, Doctor Martin?" Donovan's words were icy, if not downright sharp enough to wound.

I watched the storm raging outside, the rain and wind lashing at the window, and fought tears. "I'm asking to slow it down a bit," I said. "Let me have some time to get used to a new life in Providence."

"Just admit you don't want to marry me, damn it!" he fired back.

"That's not what I'm saying!"

When I turned to face him, I was in The Curiosity Shop, standing at the window and watching the traffic on the high street, looking over at the church, the houses, and shops, surprised that the sun was always shining here and it never seemed to rain unless my tears had something to do with it.

"That *was* what you were saying. There's no doubt of it!" Eleanor of Aquitaine said as she brought me a new bottle of Diet Pepsi.

"Why is it that men never listen?" Joan of Arc sighed.

"We do. We just never respond with what a woman wants to hear," Richard the Third spoke up, receiving murmurs of assent from Tyrone Power and Sigmund Freud.

"If we had just waited!" Tears started to well, and I turned away from everyone.

"You were trapped," Joan stated. "It became a marriage of convenience when you couldn't rekindle the love. It happens all the time."

"No, a marriage of *appearances*," Cecilia Tornabuoni chimed in. "Donovan Trist didn't want the façade taken away. He needed the support of Newport society to fund his enterprises. If it looked like he couldn't manage and hold on to an artistic, intelligent—"

"And beautiful," Richard added.

"—woman like you, Alice, how could he manage his life and career? Take control of the work at Petra or any other place?"

"Or was it lust pure and simple that you mistook for romantic love?" Athena asked. "Just as powerful and sustaining, I think. We are all born with the drive, and it needs to go somewhere. Loneliness is a cancer."

"I think she had to choose between loneliness and uncertainty and the devil she knew," Richard commented and snapped his fresh copy of *The New York Times* as if to ward off any opposition and folded the page to the crossword.

"Explain that to a family counting on the wedding of the century and one that wouldn't brook disappointment!" I groused. "Shaken or stirred, it's an impossible situation with no winners except Arielle."

"It's regrettable when people are together for a long while before they marry and the love starts to die, so they marry, hoping to relive moments and hours of passion, the laughter, and happiness," Marie Antoinette mused, bringing over a plate of pastries and setting them before me. "Sometimes it works. Many more times, it is a dismal failure."

But what if you haven't been together for more than a year?

"Or did something else make her change her mind and settle?" The Proprietress spoke up.

"Ah, but of course! And look where it led her," Marie Antoinette crowed. "Madame Alice, time for another journey!"

Marie Antoinette spun the brochure rack and pulled out two theater tickets when it stopped, and she all but shoved them in my face.

"A concert!" I exclaimed and looked up at Donovan, holding the tickets before me.

We stood in the kitchen of the three-story brownstone in Providence, a bag of groceries in my arms, Donovan home from work and burdened by books, files, and a briefcase. All these were dumped on the kitchen table, except for the tickets.

"Mother says paper is for the first wedding anniversary. These look like paper to me. Oh? Do you want these?" he said, teasing me as I tried to snatch them away. "We could make a weekend of it. Go down to New York for the concert, dinner maybe? Without my mother or Father and his new wife?"

"It sounds like a wonderful idea! Thank you!"

"You didn't have anything else planned?" he queried, brows raised anxiously.

"I was thinking of a romantic dinner at home, but this is infinitely more romantic. I haven't been to New York since our wedding."

I snatched the tickets from him and was rewarded for my persistence with a kiss.

Donovan dropped his suit jacket on one of the chairs and reached for the bottle of scotch in a cupboard over the range. A shot glass was pulled from the shelf to the left. I was ready to say something but decided against it. We would talk about breaking his promise another time. Why spoil a happy moment? I watched him pour a shot, toss it back, wash the glass, put it back on the shelf, and return the bottle of scotch to its cupboard. Donovan picked up his briefcase, books, and files and left the kitchen.

The spontaneity was fleeting.

"The last concert I attended was the Rolling Stones in 1970. Denny, Harry, some friends," I called after him while putting away groceries. "Wait! Are we going to Paul McCartney's concert?"

"Look at the tickets, Alice!" he called in a sing-song over his shoulder.

I glanced at the tickets I'd placed on the table.

The Royal Philharmonic Orchestra
With Tarquin Radcliffe Conducting
First American Appearance.

I felt like something was pushing on my chest and sat down to catch my breath, looking around to see if Donovan had returned. He was still upstairs; I heard the groan of the water heater as the shower was turned on. I stared at the tickets for the longest time, waiting for them to disappear if I touched them again.

"That was years ago," I murmured to myself. "What are the chances?"

"It may have been, but you knew nothing had changed. Well, if anything, it set the wheels in motion, didn't it?"

I frowned at Richard the Third, who stood in the doorway and held the Vaughan Williams album in his hands. I strode across the kitchen and snatched the album from him in one movement. In doing so, I was jettisoned back to The Curiosity Shop.

"That was mean and spiteful!" I growled at him.

"What? By saying what you were thinking? Or Donovan taking you to the concert?" Richard asked.

"Maybe it's time you took that side trip?" Dennis hinted, joining us.

"I only needed one more moment with him. I could have prevented—"

"—Absolutely not!" exclaimed both Richard and my brother. They jerked their heads towards the door. "Get a move on!" Richard ordered, but Dennis kissed my cheek, and Richard winked.

Out the door I went to find myself at Union Station and queued up for a train that would take me to the City of York.

CHAPTER 14

I TOOK A detour to Berkeley.

The slam of the compartment door behind me became the pop of a champagne cork; the bottle was handed to me, and I chugged a mouthful, then passed it to Harry, who poured flutes and distributed them around the dining room to our friends and neighbors. Dennis stood apart from us, drinking silently.

"Congratulations and happy birthday to Doctor Alice Martin, Doctor of Philosophy, historian, author, queen of hearts, and our faery princess!" Harry crowed as he raised his flute. His accolade was repeated, and when other praises had been sung and the topic of conversation turned to local politics and the latest movies, I went to Dennis.

"You can go back to school now and finish what you started," I said.

"Might be too late for that—the business is doing well. Besides, your success is enough for me."

"You don't sound very happy, Denny."

"That's because I know what's in the second envelope you got in the mail today."

"You went through my mail? Denny!"

"No, I took the call from the university," Dennis admitted, taking a sip and wincing. "Harry has no taste when it comes to champagnes and wines. God love him! At least he has good taste in men. Don't look at me like that! I put two and two together, okay?"

"I was waiting for the right time to tell you. I'm surprised, given that I had fierce competition from Yale, Princeton, and Stanford."

"But are they sleeping with Doctor Donovan Trist with the deep pockets?"

Dennis' voice was bitter and sarcastic.

"That was cruel but truthful," I murmured.

"This is the guy that broke your heart, Alice!"

"As did Quinn."

"Quinn wouldn't have done some of the things you said Trist has—and I don't think Quinn intentionally hurt you, either. But settling for Trist?"

"Why do you think I'm settling?"

"Because you are. You just aren't admitting it. Hope the sex is good and worth it."

"Truthful, that. Donovan isn't really a bad person, Denny. I have affection for him, enough that I want to be with him—he's asked me to marry him, and I said yes. And I thought I was pregnant, so it made sense . . ."

"Good God!" Dennis sputtered and choked on champagne while I thumped him on the back. He waved me off to wipe his face and mouth.

"But I'm not! It was a false alarm. Still, it makes sense, I think, to keep the plans."

"No, it doesn't!" Dennis muttered as he turned away and walked towards my kitchen, taking empties and plates along the way. The hallway seemed longer than it was, and I followed my brother through a tunnel that led me onto a train somewhere in the English Midlands going north. Looking around, I knew where I was headed.

The journey didn't take as long as I remembered—perhaps it was watching scenery that had, over the years, become familiar. I knew how many rocks and trees there were until the next station. The Conductor entered my compartment and waited as I took my ticket out of the book bag and handed it over for punching.

"Dinner will be served at half seven, Doctor."

"I'm not hungry. Thanks all the same."

"All the same," he responded, smiling and tipping his

cap. The Conductor moved to the next compartment as he whistled *Never Comes the Day*.

The gentle rocking of the train lulled me to sleep, which became easier as my travels or travails became more frequent. When the train lurched into a station, I sat up and glanced out the window and saw the spires and towers of York Minster.

"York, Doctor Martin!" the Conductor said after sliding open my compartment door, though he wasn't smiling. "You have five minutes."

"I'm going…"

I wandered through the station to the baggage claim and, once in possession of my suitcase, glanced around for a taxi to take me to number 50 Gillygate in Portland Street, the magnificent townhouse where I lived during the summer of 1978—a relaxing and exciting summer spent lecturing in Medieval Studies to first-year students at The College of Ripon and York St. John while undertaking research on the city's role in the rebellions against William of Normandy after the Conquest in 1066.

The townhouse was fully furnished down to food and drink. A note on the refrigerator welcomed me to the faculty and listed all the amenities provided. I puttered around, opening cupboards and closets, adding my personal touches to the two-bedroom flat that would be my home for three months before I returned to marry Donovan in August.

If I married him at all.

I was still fence-sitting on the idea, but no one knew. I gave up control of the wedding plans to Dennis and Arielle and decided to let them fight it out. I figured I had done my job if I showed up in a suitable dress.

But would I show up?

Placing a photo of Donovan near the nightstand, I picked up the telephone and was glad the phone company had already turned the service on. After dialing the number, I twisted the engagement ring cutting into my finger and removed the heavy carved band with its obscenely large emerald. The ring was tossed into the nightstand drawer, where it rolled about as I listened for the transatlantic rings.

Two, three . . . finally a pick-up.

"Hi, it's me…I arrived a while ago. You should see this place—it's straight out of Jane Austen. I love it! I'll take pictures so you can see…maybe you can help me decorate the place in Providence to duplicate the look and furnishings? Why not? The brownstone may be the family shrine, but it could stand something more than colonial drab . . . okay, okay . . . oh, a bit tired, but now that I'm here, I think I'll go out for an early dinner…What? She *what?* Well, is she okay? How many people can say they survived a fall off the stage at Lincoln Center? And at her age, too . . . hey, you brought it up! I'm not laughing. *You* are…I've got her number. I can call her—oh wait, time difference…yes, if it'll make you feel better. I'll call before I grab a bite to eat…Okay, okay! I promise . . . talk to you later. Bye."

I waited a moment, then pressed the receiver button and listened to the dial tone for the longest time. I hung up.

The Minster bells struck the hour. It was just four o'clock, and there was enough time to get in some sightseeing before dinner and spend the evening preparing for tomorrow's first day of classes.

The Lantern Tower of York Minster caught my attention when I left the flat. Like Santa Maria del Fiore, the cathedral of Florence, The Minster dominated the skyline and was a beacon. I wandered over and joined other like-minded travelers strolling through the nave, staring in awe at the windows and architecture.

I caught a flash of light glinting off a window and turned to see what it was; that three-hundred-and-sixty-degree turn placed me at The Cloisters in New York on my wedding day.

We were in one of the exhibition rooms, The Five Heroes Tapestry Room, with a Museum docent, a photographer, a wedding planner, and a seamstress. Dennis and Harry were adjusting their ties and checking the shine on their shoes. At the same time, Arielle circled me, smoothing the lace of my gown and calling attention to a loose rhinestone, Swarovski crystal, or a pearl that prompted the seamstress to swoop down and make the necessary repairs. I was standing on a bench and smiling on cue for the photographer.

"What time is it?" I asked.

"Five minutes later than the last time you asked, Faery Princess," Harry answered.

"She does look like a princess, doesn't she?" Arielle billowed. "Oh, wait until Donovan sees you!"

"If he decides to show up," I quipped. I smiled at the photographer. "Can I get down now?"

I was helped down and immediately started to pace. The heavy fabric of my gown made my progress slow, and I imagined that this was how noblewomen must have felt having to wear layers of wool, velvet, linen, and silk every day with trains longer than mine dragging in the floor rushes, the dirt and Lord knew what else. I at least had a freshly scrubbed tiled floor to walk.

To the west of where we gathered was the Chapter House, where a quartet entertained our waiting guests. We had compromised on a small guest list—one hundred and fifty altogether—most of them Donovan's guests, but they were enough to fill the chapter house. Music and conversation drifted through the medieval museum to where I waited.

"Where is he?" I snapped.

"Traffic from the city might be holding him up," Harry suggested. "It's rush hour,"

"It's Saturday!"

"Ball game at Yankee Stadium?"

Arielle was adjusting the short train for another photograph. "Darling, you know how he is, and let's be honest, everyone heard the quarrel last night."

"Thank you, Arielle. Just because you paid for most of this wedding doesn't give you the right to meddle."

The door opened, and we all turned expectantly. The priest entered and stopped short, looking at me, hands raised as if to bless. "Look at you! You are perfection!" he exclaimed.

"Thank you, Father. Any news on Donovan?"

"I've sent someone to the hotel, and we're trying to get him on the phone."

The museum director now came in with an aide. "Missus Trist, we really can't wait any longer," the director said apologetically to Arielle. "It's almost seven o'clock. It's been two hours."

"Well, something might have happened!" Arielle whined, looking around at us.

"I won't wait any longer," I said. "Sorry for your trouble and the expense, Arielle. I'll try to pay you back."

"What? Wait! Where are you going? Alice!"

I brushed by the priest and director to the door and moved as quickly as possible, making my way to the Chapter House.

"God, but you are incredible!"

I turned at the sound of his voice. Donovan was sitting on the stairs leading up to the Gothic Chapel.

My first impulse was to charge at him like a wounded animal and sink my teeth in. Instead, I approached slowly. "It's bad luck to see the bride before the wedding," I said, stopping at the stairs.

"Why is that, and where did that tradition come from?" he chuckled.

"Don't know. Maybe if the groom saw the bride

before the marriage rite and didn't like what he saw, he'd bolt."

Donovan studied my face for the longest time. "Well, that certainly isn't the case here!" He whispered. "What about the bride?"

"Given all that's been said and done this last week, you couldn't blame me. I was on my way in to tell everyone to go home. Maybe you were going to beat me to it?"

"The thought crossed my mind."

"We should have had this conversation in March," I sighed, taking the stair below his and not caring about the yards of Alençon lace flowing around us like waves.

We sat in silence. Finally, Donovan took one of my hands and said, "What are we doing? Are we so afraid of making mistakes that we're willing to make the biggest mistake of our lives and one that we'll live to regret years from now?"

"Is it getting married or walking away that would be a mistake?" I asked. "It would be a mistake if you didn't honor me after we swore our wedding vows, and I was forced to disobey."

"What do you mean?" Donovan was staring with incredulity. "I intend to honor you with my life, mind, soul, and body! I'm ready to stand up before everyone in the Chapter House who know me too well and do that. I will give you no reason whatsoever to disobey, Alice."

"Will you?" I queried with sadness in my voice and words. "You show up two hours late, and then you're here. You don't say a word."

"You gave me a lot to think about last night. Knowing how you felt several months ago, I wondered if you would be here."

"And would you have blamed me?"

"No. And I will give you no reason to doubt my sincerity. Or my love." Donovan stood and extended his hand. "Come and see."

I took his hand.

As soon as our fingers entwined and he lifted me off the stairs, I caught a flash of light—the photographer's flashbulb, I thought—until my eyes adjusted and I was back at York Minster, the light fading in the Great East Window in the Minster. A cleric in robes was standing under the lantern at the crossing. For a moment, I thought it was King Richard coming to scold or instruct, but no, it was a priest. I smiled as we passed one another, he to wherever his business should take him, I to the streets of York, to The Shambles, the oldest street in York and now a shopping district and tourist attraction.

Shops were closing up for the night, but there was a pub to the north, just as the street met King's Square, The Bitter End, to be exact, and I started for it.

No one noticed when I slipped in and took a booth near the door. The publican immediately saw that I had drink and food and introduced me to some of the locals when he learned that I was an American in York for the summer. The pub became my haunt every night after finishing lectures and grading papers. This familiar routine took an interesting turn in late July when, one Friday evening, I pulled open the door and found myself face-to-face with Quinn.

"Sorry—my God! Alice!" he exclaimed with that knee-disintegrating smile.

"Quinn! Hi! What are the odds?"

Why did I ask that? I knew what the odds were.

"Are you on vacation?"

"No, no, I'm working here through August."

"Working! What are you doing?"

"Lecturer in Medieval Studies at The College of Ripon and York St. John—just for the summer session. Then I return home and…"

"And…?"

"…and I figure out what the next chapter will be in this bad Jane Austen novel that is my life," I quipped.

Why not tell him you're going home to get married?

"So it's Doctor Martin, I guess?"

"Yes, Maestro. And you? Is the orchestra touring here?"

"No, taking some time off this week for family business. My grandmother died a few months back. I'm here to take care of the house and shop."

"Oh, Quinn! I'm so sorry. I know you and she were close."

We stepped to the pavement to allow patrons access to the door and just stared at one another for a moment. I wondered if he noticed the extra pounds I'd put on or that at the age of twenty-six, two gray hairs struggled to rise above the dirty-dishwater blonde.

He certainly improved with age. He looked thinner, but the hair was still a tousled mess. The athlete's body was still in top form from the drape of his jacket and tee shirt, and the five o'clock shadow only brought attention to the fine features of his handsome face.

"You won't believe this. I know you won't," he laughed nervously. "I was just thinking about you the other morning."

"I'm flattered," I giggled. *I was.*

"This is so great—to run into someone from home."

"I've been traveling myself."

"Italy?"

"No, with a colleague in the Middle East. And busy with school. How are your parents?"

"They're fine from what I hear," Quinn said with a dismissive shrug. We continued to smile at each other like idiots.

"I should have called you," he said suddenly. "I wanted to. Then, I thought, no, she wouldn't want to, then I got busy, and…"

"Quinn, it's forgotten. No harm, no foul."

"So, did you marry the guy?"

"Who?" I asked, wondering if he knew something. "Adam? No, I think he's doing time somewhere—most likely for assault and battery on someone else's boyfriend," I joked nervously, and Quinn laughed with the same self-consciousness.

"You're worth a good fight. Or a beating, in my case. Wow, y'know, I'm always saying the wrong things to you, Alice."

"As opposed to what you say to other girls?"

"Yeah—well, no, no—God! I did it again! What I mean to say is, what I wanted to say, is, that day wasn't what I wanted to come out of my mouth."

"Ohhh…"

We glanced about, watching the traffic in the street, staring at our shoes; finally, I looked up and saw his smile, genuine and loving. A warmth, lightness, and joy overwhelmed me.

"Yeah, I couldn't imagine you with someone like that."

"Stop while you're ahead, Quinn." I laughed.

"Listen, do you want a drink?"

Quinn pointed towards the pub, and we went inside, taking a corner booth.

"Youngest Conductor of the Royal Philharmonic," I said as we clinked glasses. "I suppose the Professor is proud."

"It's not like I care what he thinks," Quinn commented as if to himself and winked as he sipped his beer.

"If you must know—and I know you must—I told your father what I thought of him and how he ruined the best of plans."

There it was again—the sense of lightness and joy.

"My God!" Quinn whispered. "How did he take it?"

"He stared at me with those huge blue eyes and said, 'See you around, Alice,' and walked away. Haven't talked to him since, though your mother calls from time to time. She came to my birthday party this year. Denny invited her."

Quinn's glass clinked with mine again. "Well done, Alice Rose!"

"I just did it. It just came out of my mouth. Your mother was amazing. She hugged me, and well, it was amazing."

I gulped my beer and Quinn smiled. "You've got foam," he gestured with his finger to the upper lip and tentatively reached out, then wiped my lips, a delicate, sensual touch that made my heart beat faster. "You look great," he said softly.

"So do you. I like the longer hair, the five o'clock shadow."

"Do you? Thanks. It's called fatigue. We have two more performances in London, and then we close out the season, and then it's back into the studio to record. Then I'm going home for a bit," Quinn said as he split an order of fish and chips.

"Where's home these days?"

"San Anselmo, when I have the time. You? Still have that little place down on Oxford?"

"I have a bigger place in Normandy Village on Spruce."

"Normandy Village? That little place that looks like it dropped out of a fairy tale? The one you used to sketch?"

"The very same. When I turned twenty-five, I was able to take some money from the Trust, and that's what I used it for. I have the apartment facing Spruce Street, just as you enter the courtyard, with the really steep stairs. I love it. Harry and Denny want to sell the house and move to a bigger place near Walnut Square, so he doesn't have to go far to work.

"Denny's been sick—he constantly has a cold, sometimes it goes into pneumonia, and there are rashes," I explained, helping myself to the chips and offering to sprinkle some malt vinegar on the basket. "He's been to at least a dozen doctors, and nobody knows what it is, or they do, and they're not saying. He's a trooper, though, still working, still being a mother hen."

"A little more, yeah, you remember," Quinn chuckled as I sprinkled malt vinegar over the fish and chips. "I bought one of his ties. It's the knight design. Made me think of you."

"I'll let him know since he designed that one with you in mind."

"Really! I'm flattered. I really like Dennis. The next time you talk to him, tell him hello, and that I'm sorry about the illness. Y'know, I still have that cummerbund and bow tie he made to match your prom dress."

"I think I'll kill myself if you tell me you've worn them recently."

Quinn started moving the knives off the table, and we both laughed.

"It was a party for a friend's album release, okay?" he said. "And I'll never forget how beautiful you looked in that dress. You still are, you know."

"Didn't you record an album before taking over the orchestra?"

"Alice, I just told you you're beautiful!" he laughed.

"I know, I know. I'm milking it. Your parents were playing something of yours when I was at the house— *Sleepers Awake*. Funny, I knew it was you as soon as I heard it."

"That got me the conducting job. I should give you a copy of the album."

"Please, I'd love it. Have you done anything else?"

"Last year. Schubert and my first with the orchestra. Not the easiest couple of weeks. Everyone's excited about the new album since it hasn't been done in a while. I think it will be challenging. Ask me what's on the new album," Quinn said as he playfully fought for the last of the chips. Our fingers met and locked—I felt that electricity, that sweet surge of adrenaline when we touched, was glad he didn't let go. Quinn leaned forward, his face close enough for a kiss.

"*Ask* me, Alice!"

"What's on the next album, Quinn? *White Rabbit?*"

Our hands were still clasped when he leaned closer and said, "Vaughan Williams. *Lark Ascending, Greensleeves,*" he paused dramatically, "*Fantasia on a Theme by Thomas Tallis!*"

Our lips were almost touching now. "Really!" I whispered, genuinely surprised.

"No joke. I insisted."

"Really?" I was incredulous and leaned back, letting go of his hand and shaking my head in disbelief. "All these years…"

"I listen to it whenever I need inspiration, whenever I'm lonely."

"My friends say it's the most depressing music they've ever heard, and one guy—oh, it doesn't matter."

"No, it isn't. It's like a summer morning after a shower or an evening. Everything is there. The light and dark, the changes in colors. I should take you to Scarborough to show you what I mean. Most of all, it brings back good memories."

"I think of it as a friend—I know it sounds maudlin or silly, but when I need to think, while I'm writing, I like the *Fantasia.*"

"What do you think about?"

"The usual—Dennis, his health, my parents, screwing up my life in so many different configurations, do-overs."

"I wonder if you think about me."

Quinn moved in and placed his hand on mine. Again,

our faces were close.

"Yes," I whispered.

"What about when you're happy?"

"*Here Comes the Sun.*"

"*Purple Haze* when you're feeling silly?" he teased.

"That's just for go-go dancing. *White Rabbit* is for silly."

He was still leaning in, the smile softening, and I wanted him to kiss me. If I'd been more daring, I would have kissed him. I was sure Quinn expected something, the way he lingered. Finally, he tapped my nose playfully and said, "C'mon, Alice, I'll walk you home."

We strolled through the streets of York. I didn't care if it took a month and a day to reach home, for it meant Quinn would be there a bit longer. The May night was pleasant, not cold, not too warm, and the stars were scattered above us with a full moon that lit our path to Gillygate despite street lamps in The Shambles.

"I didn't ask."

"What?"

"Maybe it's just…"

"Ask!" I implored. "What?"

"I suppose you've got a couple of kids, an attorney for a husband, or an English Professor from Cal," Quinn said half in jest.

"None of the above."

"Really?" Now Quinn sounded incredulous. He glanced over and studied me carefully. "Really! Well, there's got to be someone."

"He'd like to think there was," I quipped.

"Serious, or…?"

"He'd like to think it was."

When I turned to look up, I was looking at Dennis, and we were walking down the high street in The Village past The Curiosity Shop and towards the church.

"Do you think she'll tell him the truth?" Richard the

Third asked, joining us.

"Is it your business to know?" I snapped.

"Lying to the love of her life? Never a good idea," Tyrone Power added, stepping in line behind us with Richard.

"How many of us are ready to spill our guts when we have an opportunity thrown at us as Alice had? Or, in her case, walking out of the pub?" Dennis asked, squeezing my hand as we continued to stroll. "She'll tell him and all in time. Besides, don't you remember? Things happened first."

"Can we skip this part and get to the end?" I begged.

"That would never do," Dennis said as we waited for the traffic to clear the intersection. When the last automobile and bus had gone through, I was back in The Shambles but standing at a corner with Quinn, waiting for the light to change.

"And you? Is there a lady?" I asked Quinn.

Quinn paused, and I knew what that meant. He sighed and then opened his mouth to speak and nodded. "She's a girl whose father donates a lot of money to the orchestra. We've been dating for a few months."

"Ah, sounds like an arranged marriage to keep the orchestra afloat."

"Pretty much."

"Do you sing to her, play songs to keep her smiling? Play games of Risk or read aloud from Tolkien and John Donne?"

"I follow her to social events like the Ascot and show up for photos at nightclubs. Her father is a peer. She's . . . interesting."

"Does she have a soul or a heart?"

That didn't come out how I'd wanted it, and I immediately looked up at Quinn to see if I'd inflicted any pain. He was smiling and then started laughing. "Believe me. I've been searching for them for months. If they existed, I think I would have found them by now!"

"Geez, I really stepped into it, didn't I?"

"No, no, of all the women I've been with, and there haven't been that many, so don't believe what the tabloids scream. You're the only one who really knows me. *Absolvo te*, Faery Princess."

We laughed nervously at that, and then Quinn spun around to face me, winking and walking backward as he said, "Now, your guy. What's this guy got that I haven't?"

Me, he's got me…

"A degree in archeology and a substantial stake in the dig going on at Petra, the chance to have a building named after him."

"An archeologist! Like Allan Quartermain in *King Solomon's Mines!* Remember that old movie with Stewart Granger and Deborah Kerr?"

"Sure—we saw it, what, three times? And I think Quartermain was an adventurer, not an archeologist. Handled snakes better than someone I know." I smiled at him sideways.

A sensation of lightness overwhelmed me, and I felt as if my heart had grown stronger with every breath I inhaled the longer I was with Quinn.

"Better than me? Hardly! Remember that giant garter snake we found in your sanctuary?"

"Yeah, that was pretty amazing, Quinn. I would have been more impressed if it had been real."

"How was I to know Harry put it there for an April Fool's joke?"

"I think he's finally over your ruining his best golf club on a fake reptile."

We shared the best of laughs over that, leaning into one another as we walked and laughed, remembering shrieks and giggles. As we paused for another traffic light, Quinn casually draped an arm around me and said, "I'm pretty good with plastic creepy crawlers, aren't I? I suppose your archeologist would come swinging from the rafters with a machete or something."

"Actually, I prefer the strong, silent types who quietly tell guys to back off and then walk away, the kind that defends a lady's honor above all else despite personal humiliation."

"Did that a few times and will gladly do it again if the occasion calls for it."

"Good to know."

We walked in silence for a time. His arm was still draped around my shoulders. Quinn looked down and grinned. "I guess you guys talk about Roman *sarcophagi* and *stele* at the end of the day?"

"Mostly. He works at Petra, though. Not much Roman stuff there."

"And you discuss your latest theatrical designs, or your latest book, research, how you unlock the mysteries of the Italian city-states governance, the vagrancies of the Crusades, the English backlash against the Conquest?"

"Nope. Just whatever was dug up at Petra, his latest press conference, or tour. Latest photo in *Time* or *Newsweek*. Whatever."

Quinn looked surprised. "You'd be his equal in so many things, Alice."

I stopped suddenly, and Quinn, still walking, turned and raised his brows in question.

"He isn't. He's not my equal, you see. He's not you."

"I'm flattered."

"With you, I can just be Alice. Be myself. I'm never on guard, never worrying about saying or doing the wrong things, never worried about offending extremely wealthy and class-conscious friends, colleagues, and relatives."

We were at my flat. Quinn stood on the sidewalk while I walked up the stairs to turn the key in the lock. "And yet he's got a hold on you," he said matter-of-factly.

"One that I'm trying to untie, I guess, or figure out."

The door now open, I turned and gestured with the keys. "Do you want some coffee, a nightcap?"

"I wouldn't mind some honesty."

His tone of voice and the expression on his face didn't surprise me. "C'mon," I invited.

Quinn followed while I took out cups and saucers, set up the coffee maker, and looked for a bit of courage while I was at it.

"Nice digs," he commented.

"They are, aren't they? Do you want crumpets or scones?"

"Doesn't matter. So you're here for how long again?"

"Through August. I've been here since May, and I like it. I'm hoping the university will let me return next summer."

"I'm here through the end of next week, then down to London. I told you that, didn't I?"

"To record the new album."

"The one dedicated to you."

"That's a huge honor, Quinn. You don't have to."

"It's a gift a long time coming." He studied me now, not the obdurate leer that Donovan threw at me while he undressed me in his mind and fantasized, but a critical, loving glance offered to encourage sharing secrets or a cause for unhappiness.

"I don't think he has a hold on you, Alice," Quinn said softly after a time.

I glanced up, surprised.

"I think you're being strangled. Tell me if I'm wrong—or worse, if I'm right."

The toaster oven bell went off, giving me an excuse to turn away from him and collect my thoughts. Measuring scoops of coffee, I counted them to myself and poured water into the pot, wiping my hands on the dishtowel hanging off the rack against the wall. Quinn waited. Finally, and without looking at him, I said slowly and quietly, "This isn't something I want to discuss with you right now."

"But you do want to discuss it?"

"It's been a long day, and I'm tired, and seeing you again…."

"Understood."

I was not prepared for the kiss. Quinn pulled me gently into his arms and kissed me for the longest time as if he'd saved up years of passion just for that moment.

Anticipating a confession of love, loyalty, and years of anguish, I opened my eyes and frowned at The Proprietress, wearing a pair of my mother's cat's eye eyeglasses with a beaded chain that matched her severe blue suit. She grinned like the Cheshire Cat.

"What could you have done?" The Proprietress moaned, a tinge of sarcasm in her voice.

"*Nothing!*"

It was a Greek chorus: Richard the Third, Joan of Arc, Anne Boleyn, Eleanor of Aquitaine, Marie Antoinette, Sigmund Freud, Tyrone Power, and Dennis. Having stated this, they returned to their usual business, whatever that might have been.

"So, Faery Princess, have you figured it out?" The Proprietress demanded.

"The riddle of the Sphinx? Two wrongs make a right?"

"Well, aren't you the clever girl! And?"

"…No."

The Proprietress expelled a theatrical sigh and turned her back, taking casks from the shelves and setting them carefully on the velvet square on the counter. She opened each and inspected the contents: large, shiny gems or rocks that were brilliant in color and light, solid yet fluid, as if each contained flowing water and liquid metal in different shades of whatever color the gem might be at the time. Some boxes had two, others one. The boxes that had three were opened carefully, for the light that poured from them was blinding and mesmerizing.

She took down a box carved with medieval trefoils, roses, and crosses. An ornate 'A' on the lid was entwined with an 'M.' She placed the box in the middle of the velvet square and opened it with the top facing me so I couldn't see its contents. The Proprietress sighed loudly and made an entry in the ledger before her.

"May I see what's in the box?" I asked timidly.

"No."

"I'm guessing that's my box, and whatever has been happening, all these journeys I've been taking, the changes I've been making to my life, all of it has something to do with that box and the book," I stated, my hand out.

"No."

The box went up on the shelf with the others, and The Proprietress glared at me before smiling at Sigmund Freud as he left The Shop.

"Two wrongs—not going with Quinn and settling for Donovan," I said suddenly, not backing down. "The right would be choosing one over the other. I just have to discover which is most right, but I think I already know since…."

"*No!*"

The Greek chorus had spoken.

"I'm going for a walk."

Out in the high street, I was as confused and conflicted as ever since this journey began.

The same historical persons strolled to and fro as if this was a Disneyland attraction or a Renaissance Faire somewhere in Northern California or the Midwest. As I thought of people, they appeared.

Quinn was the only person who did not.

"I'm going mad. That's what this is all about!" I muttered to myself as I walked up the street. "I'm on a Vicodin drip, and I'm hallucinating!"

"You'd like to keep believing that," said Isabella of Aragon as she walked by with Florence Nightingale.

Glaring at her over my shoulder, I went into the bookshop near the end of the street. The bell over the door tinkled thinly, and The Shopkeeper, again The Proprietress, did not turn from her book shelving. The other patrons in The Shop ignored me as well. They were browsing and thumbing through the same book: my biography.

"Read this, Albert," said suffragette leader Emma Pankhurst to Prince Albert of Saxe-Coburg and Gotha. She held the book up and tapped the page. "'She was conflicted for many years. Out of fear of loneliness and unhappiness, finally, and when all seemed to be lost, she, at last, found her bliss despite the warnings and threats he made.'"

"I believe she was in great need of emancipation, don't you, Miss Pankhurst?" the Prince commented.

"Where?" I exclaimed, grabbing the book. "Where does it say that? I have to know..."

"Silence, Miss Martin!" hissed Lewis Carroll, perched on a ladder across The Shop.

"Oh, shut up!" I snapped.

Everyone in The Shop turned and gasped. The Proprietress stared me down from above the rim of her glasses.

"Oh, please! You're all here because of me!" I proclaimed. "Each of you has something to do with my life or interests! If I wanted, I could snap my fingers, and you'd all be sent to whatever circle of Hell you came from! I think I will."

Snap!

Looking about, I smiled and nodded. Only The Proprietress was there, and Lewis Carroll perched on the ladder, who slowly, eerily, transformed into The Cheshire Cat.

"I guess I could do that if I took enough Laudanum," I muttered.

"So what will you do, Alice?" The Proprietress demanded.

"I'll have to think about that."

"Hmmm, so did Quinn."

"What?"

I went to her, unsure of what I had heard. The Proprietress was taking stacks of books out of cartons and, one by one opened covers and initialed the endpapers. She looked up, a smirk riding her lips from cheek to cheek.

"I said that Quinn Radcliffe made the very same comment—when it was his time and when he was in the same circumstance as you. He managed to figure things out quicker, though. I suppose being a musician gives one a logical edge over those who read history. And romances."

Again, the smirk.

"That's not fair! There's nothing wrong with reading history or romances!" I protested. "And are we forgetting the diva musician, the temperamental artist?"

"The heartsick and lonely young man with prodigious talent? I haven't."

"As far as I know, he wasn't conflicted about his love, not like I am—was! Will be! Oh, hell."

"You don't know that for certain."

I was about to finish a thought and decided it was better left alone. The Proprietress was waiting, however, and I said, "If all this is what I think it is, then why should I have to relive those painful moments? You said I couldn't change everything, only certain things, and I know what will happen next, and frankly, I don't want to live through that again!"

"Do you think you're the only person who's gone through this? Agonizing over what to do or say? Wanting to put things to rights?"

"I never said I was."

"I think it's time you went back and dealt with it," The Proprietress sighed. "On your way, Alice! Oh, and Alice?" she called after me. "A word of advice. Being silent and complaisant is never good in an argument and doesn't heal wounds. Remember that and what happened before. On your way."

I hurried into The Village lane and took my time getting to the railway station. The Conductor tipped his hat as I boarded the car, slammed the door shut on my compartment, and threw myself on the seat.

And then something different happened. The train went at a supersonic speed so that the scenery from my life was like the colored gels and dishes of food coloring and paint that Quinn had used for his light shows. It sped faster and faster, like an amusement park ride, so fast that I started to scream.

The scream woke me up. My heart was pounding, and I was drenched in sweat, trembling, and frightened as I lay in our bed in the brownstone in Providence. The grandfather clock in the hall struck noon.

Another day of staying in bed until noon, another day of life gone by, wasted, without purpose.

Looking over, I noticed Donovan's side hadn't been touched. He had probably slept at his office or downstairs, as had been his habit for the last week.

My entertainment during the past seven days had been staring out the window. Yesterday, the sky had been a brilliant, silvery-blue; today, the skies were leaden, and snow fell. I hated snow. I hated Christmas in Providence and longed for Berkeley's brisk, biting cold but tolerable, snowless winters.

I tried to sit up, but the pain was excruciating. I gasped and held my mid-section, grabbing a pillow to press against my abdomen as I sat up and was like this for what seemed like hours until I heard the doorbell. It took a lot of effort to scuff into my slippers and stand, and while I was trying to put on a robe, the doorbell ring became a pounding. Many painful minutes later, I opened the door to my mother-in-law.

"Sweetheart!" Arielle gasped. "What are you doing out of bed? Where's the nurse?"

"I don't know. I need to sit down—would you...?"

Arielle shooed the ever-present Phillip away and put an arm around my waist, leading me to the appropriately named fainting couch in the living room. She made sure I was comfortable, grabbed one of the afghans stacked in the corner of the sofa, and tucked it around me. I put my head back and closed my eyes, tears smarting the lids and another lump clogging my throat.

"Where is he?" she asked, sitting beside me. 'He' was spat.

"I don't know. At work, I suppose. What day is it?"

"Thursday, darling. You are so very pale—and you've lost more weight! Darling, darling, can you eat yet?"

"Don't want to, honestly."

"Honestly? Must I call Harry to come out here and look after you?" Arielle threatened but in a gentle and teasing manner.

"Please, don't! He doesn't know. I never told him, and the anniversary of Dennis' death is coming up. He doesn't need to worry about me. It's been an awful year...."

"Awful? A year in which you move to Providence, marry, land a job at a prestigious university, a husband who receives acclaim for his work and has a building named after him?"

"I suppose we won't mention my brother's death, the car accident that put me in this condition, the stories of my husband's whoring and drinking in the papers, the pending lawsuit."

"Well, aren't you one for looking at a glass half full?"

"I appreciate your coming by, but you're not helping."

"I still think you should tell Harry. He'll be furious if you don't tell him what happened."

"He'll kill Donovan, that's for sure."

"Wouldn't we all like to?" Arielle muttered under her breath.

She now fussed with the bandage on my neck, clucked her tongue at the stitches on my arm, glanced at the pillow I still held to my abdomen, then looked at me and looked away just as quickly.

"Do I look that bad? Are the black eyes gone?" I tried to jest. "I've been avoiding mirrors."

"You look remarkable, all things considered," Arielle said gently. "What did the doctors say? Yesterday was the appointment?"

"I'll mend—I can still have children."

"Well, that's some consolation, I suppose. Oh, darling Alice! I'm sorry! Don't cry, please! That was thoughtless." Arielle leaned closer to hear what I was muttering in between sobs. "New York? What did New York have to do with the accident?"

"If we hadn't gone to New York, the concert, the anniversary weekend, you know…."

"I really don't, but I suppose I can guess."

She patted my knee and smiled, offering a kiss on the cheek. "Why don't I find some soup for you? Chicken noodle soup cures almost everything, I think!"

"If it can put a car and a life back together and rewind the last eight weeks, bring it!"

I heard her gasp and the fast clip of her heels on the parquetry floor as she crossed the living room to the hallway and the kitchen. It all started going badly and yet coming together in New York, where a trip for our anniversary became a battle, and I became pregnant again…

Two weeks later, I moved with more ease, thanks to pain pills, and I was getting food to stay down. Again,

Donovan's side of the bed was untouched, and it seemed that he came and went like a ghost, for I seldom saw him now.

The nurse he employed to care for me was Gale, a gentle lady in her sixties. She was there from the moment I woke until I closed my eyes at night, the scent of her clean uniform and Chanel Number 5 as soothing as the medication given to me to help me sleep, help me heal, help me forget.

But I couldn't, and I wouldn't forget.

Somehow, I would get past it, and my life would be restored to something different but something I wanted.

How it would come about occurred to me as I walked by the room that used to be Donovan's office. At that moment, it was still a nursery. I went in and looked around. Decorating had been interrupted. The crib was left in stages of unpacking, with instruction booklet and tools lying where they were dropped; shopping bags of un-opened bumpers, quilts, blankets, and an infant's layette, were dumped on the rocking chair that still dangled a price tag. Seated on the rocking chair was an overstuffed teddy bear I'd made months earlier. Teddy Bears paraded around the walls with balloons in paws and stopped in mid-march, the wallpaper borders hanging like ribbons above the floorboards.

"I was wondering if you want to celebrate Christmas."

Donovan was standing in the doorway, a coffee mug in his hand. My expression must have been of anger and contempt, for he took a step back and hid his face as he drank.

"Why would you think that?" I wanted to know.

"Christmas was two weeks ago. Maybe get our minds off things, talk about what's next."

When I reached for the teddy bear, Donovan took it out of my hands.

"It won't do any good, Alice," he said. He still had the

bandage on his forehead, the black eye, and the stitches on his right cheek.

"Putting it all at the back of my mind won't change what happened or how I feel," I said, moving stiffly past him to the kitchen where I had started a chicken pot pie for dinner.

"We have to move on, eventually,"

He tried to take my hand, and I gently moved out of his reach, saying over my shoulder, "Did you call the support group people like you were supposed to?"

"Got caught in a meeting with the department head. He wants to know how you're doing, by the way. Sends his sympathies, love."

"Peachy, fine, and dandy," I said as I slammed the oven door. Donovan took a shot glass down from the shelf and opened a cupboard for the bottle of scotch—that wasn't there.

"You didn't have to get rid of it!" he grumbled, reaching for the bottle of tonic water.

"I had a choice. You or the scotch. I decided the scotch should go. For now."

Picking up a knife, I started chopping carrots and celery, and the movement soon became placing tarot cards on my table in The Shop. The cards were turned over and set carefully, each figure of the arcana different and seemingly real, vibrant, and alive, the colors bright as if they were painted on parchment only that morning. Anne Boleyn now rested her chin in her hands and studied the Celtic cross pattern.

"Things are looking up for you, Alice!" she declared, tapping a card—the figure of Death.

I picked up the card and looked at it, asking, "How is Death good news?"

"The cards are the opposite of what they seem. Just like your life," she sighed, ruminating over the pattern. "Aha! I thought as much. Yes, things are getting better at every moment."

Now I took a carrot stick from the plate Dennis offered and raised my brows, waiting. "I know you have something to say," I told him.

"He was lucky it wasn't his head on that butcher's block, and I wasn't around to make him answer for what he did to you and the baby!" Dennis growled and then turned to pour two cups of coffee, one for himself and one for Richard the Third. "Alice! My God, Alice! Are you alright?"

I had slumped into the chair and began to tremble violently, my throat constricting as I tried my best not to cry. Everyone in The Shop turned to stare, and no one was sympathetic except my brother.

Dennis turned to The Proprietress. "Enough is enough!" he hissed. "Can't we end this now? We should send her back."

"No. There's only a short amount of time left, and there's still much to be done, much to relive, much to change," The Proprietress responded as she took books from cases and stamped a page in each of them with a date-stamp like those used in libraries before the advent of computers and scanners. "Give her something. You know what to do."

Dennis took what looked like a medicine bottle with a dropper out of his pocket. He opened it and held it under my nose. I inhaled a lovely scent of rose and freesia, fresh air on a warm spring morning, and the sea with a tang of salt. I sat up and looked around, surprised I wasn't elsewhere.

"This has got to end sometime!" I muttered.

"Come here, Alice."

The Proprietress beckoned, and from the look in her eyes, there was no choice but to obey. She took down one of the casks and opened it to reveal three incredibly beautiful gems, large stones of unearthly quality and beauty that lay in the box. They weren't glowing or full of fluid in motion as were the others I'd seen. Their lights were faint and the colors dull. Now she looked at me squarely, saying quietly, "Do you think, Alice Martin, that you are the only person who ever suffered? Do you think you're the only woman to have her heart broken more times than ever possible and struggle to put all those pieces back together?" She picked up the gems and placed them one at a time in my hands. I shrank at their touch—cold yet burning, smooth yet rough. She took them back and put them in the cask. "Find the pieces, my girl! Two wrongs make a right."

I stopped swallowing tears and looked at her first, then my brother Dennis, and then Joan.

I understood.

I knew what they meant.

CHAPTER 15

"THAT'S NOT WHAT I meant," Dennis said as he heaved himself off my sofa as best he could, reaching for the pole lamp to support him. His color was suddenly gray, and he swayed slightly as if dizzy. I took a step, but he waved me off and walked slowly toward the kitchen.

It was April 23, 1978, and around us were the remnants of my birthday dinner and party: foil wrapping paper was scattered on the coffee table, and plates smeared with the crumbs and streaks of frosting from a three-tiered angel food cake were stacked precariously on end tables, sharing space with half-empty bottles of sparkling wine and champagne flutes. I scooped up the plates and bottles and followed Dennis.

"I'm twenty-five, Denny. If not now, when?" I responded to his comment.

"Why at all? This isn't Mom and Dad's generation," Dennis said, adding, "And they're not here to disapprove, anyway. Who says you need to get married? If you love this guy, wait a bit longer, just to see."

He bent down to open the dishwasher; even that movement was excruciating and difficult. I put an arm around him and felt his bones under the heavy sweater he wore. "It's only a matter of time," I whispered to myself, and the light in the kitchen flickered and faded. What I knew I could not share; The Proprietress warned me several times already. The pressure in my chest told me I'd taken a false step. But I knew what was to come. I knew I couldn't tell him; my life I could change. His, I could not.

"Only a matter of time before what?" Dennis groused,

pushing me off. "Hopefully when you come to your senses?"

"Something like that. Denny, I'm worried about you. You don't look well."

"I'm fine. No, I said I'm fine! Let's worry about you."

"I think you should see a doctor."

"*You* should for wanting to marry Donovan Trist. Again I ask, is that a real name?"

"Would we be having this conversation if the bridegroom in question was Tarquin Radcliffe?"

"Probably not, Faery Princess, but I would beg the question of why it took you two so long."

"A stage father and overprotective mother, priorities, Bach, Schubert, and Beethoven," I muttered as Dennis reluctantly allowed me to seat him at the kitchen table.

I started to clean up the aftermath of Harry's cooking. To placate Dennis, I put a slice of the *crostata* I'd baked before him.

"Mmmmm! Stella or Victoria Bakery?" he wanted to know.

"I beg your pardon. *I* made that!" I laughed.

"When did you learn to cook?"

"Italy."

"Ah, so it wasn't all history, archeologists, and sex marathons!"

"Funny."

"That's about all the humor in this discussion, Alice," Dennis said, digging into the pie. "Mom didn't raise you to make stupid mistakes you'll regret, and God knows how many times I've tried to keep you off that path ever since the *White Rabbit* incident. From what I know and what you've told me, this marriage you're settling for has all the earmarks of a disaster."

"I do have affection for Donovan, Dennis. I fell in love with him in Florence, and then, well, it isn't the grand passion of first love. Who knows? I think there's more than a chance that passion will be rekindled."

"And in the meantime, you grow old wondering when it will happen because men like Donovan rarely change, and suddenly you're almost sixty, and it's too late. Another slice, please?" Dennis looked all of twelve as he dug into the new slice offered; his face seemed to regain its rosy, healthy complexion.

"I think you'll love Providence," I started to chat as counters were cleared and the dishwasher unloaded of its clean dishes and loaded with the dirty. "There's a little cottage on his mother's estate in Newport. I think you'd like that, too. Now that it's ours, Donovan says I can decorate however I want, and you're the best designer I know."

"I'm the only designer you know. Harry and I can't move to the East Coast, so you can stop trying to entice me, Alice. Why can't Mister Money Bags move out here and get a job at Cal or something?"

"Because," I sighed, "I am going to accept the job at Brown University."

"What?" Harry exclaimed, coming into the kitchen at the end of that conversation.

"I knew it!" Dennis cried.

"I wasn't going to leave without telling you! I was getting around to it."

The subject of my life was ignored when Harry and I moved as one to grab Dennis as he rose from the kitchen table and suddenly collapsed. As I knelt to help him off the floor, I was bending over him at the Iceland skating rink on a Saturday afternoon in the winter of 1969. We were both laughing to the point of tears.

"Maybe we should get you a helmet," I giggled as I pushed Dennis to his feet and dragged him to the edge of the rink where he could hang on to the wall.

"Never mind the helmet," Dennis panted. "Get me something for my ass—like an ice pack!"

"Can you make it to the stands?"

"As much as my pride will allow. Stop laughing and get me something! This was the worst of ideas! Go on, Princess!"

Once I saw that Dennis could make it by himself into the stands without spilling onto the ice for the umpteenth time, I slipped off my skates and padded in socks to the lobby, walking against a new crowd of high and middle school students arriving for the Valentine's "Skate-for-Love" fundraiser. Dennis offered to be my sweetheart for the day so I could participate. Walking through the mob of chattering, happy lovebirds reminded me of the nasty breakup with Will the Pill and how horrible it was not to have anyone on Hallmark's Second Most Favorite Holiday of the Year. I averted my eyes from the bouquets and teddy bears, the balloons with "I LOVE YOU" screaming from their bloated perimeters.

Once I had the ice pack, a cup of ice cream, and a frozen Mars bar in my hands, I worked my way back to the rink and Dennis. We would soothe his sore bottom and ego and mend my broken heart with scrumptious calories.

"Hey! Alice!"

I stopped suddenly, for a boy was blocking my entrance, and when I looked up and was ready to bark orders to step out of the way, I flushed bright red. I knew it was red because my face was burning. Quinn Radcliffe was smiling down at me. I returned the favor with a weak smile.

"Hi!" I said. It came out like a squeak, and I wanted to die but mostly avoid the stares and giggling of the two nasty bitches that walked by with their latest conquests. They made my life Hell in second-period English.

"Don't mind them," Quinn said, nodding in their direction. "They only live to make people like us miserable."

"Us? Why would they do that to you?" I wanted to

know. I didn't say what I was thinking: *I mean, LOOK at you; you're gorgeous, a Greek god with those big dark eyes, knee-disintegrating smile, shoulders out to here, an athlete's body…*

"I'm a marching band and orchestra nerd."

"Nerd?"

"Somebody who's not cool—hey, are you with anyone?"

I pointed to Dennis, sitting in the bleachers. "My brother."

Quinn glanced over my shoulder and nodded. "Oh, so I guess he wouldn't want you to have company or anything."

"I don't—oh! No, please! Join us. I don't think he'll mind."

"I don't want to intrude or anything."

"You won't. C'mon."

I led the way through another mob of students to where Dennis waited. He looked as bored and detached as I'd ever seen him, and we weren't even at a Giants game, nor was he being forced to play Risk.

"Hey Denny, how are we?" I cooed, climbing up to where he was seated. Dennis had that look on his face, the one that was a portent of whining and self-pity, but it transformed into something akin to delight when he saw Quinn, who sat next to me.

"I'm going to have a bruise down to my ankle, I know it," Dennis said, taking the ice pack from me and sitting on it. He smiled at Quinn and then glanced at me, waiting.

"Hi, I'm Quinn," Quinn introduced himself.

"Where are my manners?" I apologized. "Denny, this is Quinn Radcliffe. Quinn, my brother Dennis, who's home from college. Winter break."

"Nice to meet you," Quinn greeted, leaning over me to shake Dennis' hand. They kept shaking hands, though I didn't mind, for Quinn was very close. I gently extricated Dennis' hand when Quinn started looking nervous, and

Dennis kept staring at him.

"Radcliffe? Any relation to Andrew Radcliffe of the Metropolitan Opera?" Dennis asked.

"He's my dad. He's with the San Francisco Opera now."

"That's why you look so familiar! I saw your father in *La Boehme!* The best portrayal of Rodolfo I've seen."

"Yeah, he kind of likes it, too."

"Is he singing with San Francisco? I'd love to hear his Rodolfo again."

"He's semi-retired and teaching at Cal. He's also the Assistant Director at the Opera House. Once in a while, he takes a lead role if pushed to it."

"What a loss," Dennis moaned. I frowned, nudging him and giving him a look that warned of dire consequences if he didn't stop.

"Some think so," Quinn answered, shrugging.

"Well, you're not here to talk about your father," my brother sighed and nudged me.

We three sat in silence, watching the activity on the ice. A girl who had been practicing *salchows* now attempted a triple and took a sudden spill. A collective gasp went up from the spectators in the stands.

"That rink is tough, isn't it?" Quinn said. "I stopped skating when my mother said I looked like a baby giraffe on ice skates or Bambi on the ice with Thumper."

"Olympic skater?" I asked.

"Ice hockey. Didn't help when I took a puck to the head."

"Poor you!" I gasped. "Is that why you went into music?"

"No, I've always wanted to be a musician. My father was against ice hockey. I wanted it."

"My mother wants me to be a doctor, but I don't know."

"Well," Quinn said, glancing in my direction and then

back at the ice, "if you did go into medicine and became a doctor, the next time I took a puck to the head, you could stitch me up."

I gave Quinn a sideways glance, and he did the same. We started to laugh—I didn't know why, but it was probably because we connected and felt a kindred spirit then. Dennis winked at me and offered the rest of the ice cream, which I shared with Quinn. He didn't miss a thing and reminded me of that day while we sat in The Curiosity Shop after the blink of an eye.

"What makes you think I ever forgot?" I asked him, walking up to the counter where The Proprietress held my book in her hands. She snatched it away just as I was ready to open it and reached on the topmost shelf behind her for my cask, setting it carefully on a square of velvet on the glass top of the display case.

"Well?" she hissed. "Your moment has come. The hour is now!"

I opened the box slowly as if snakes on springs would leap out at me. If not snakes, a bright light would blind me, or a cartoon mouse would pop up and squirt some disgusting liquid in my face.

I lifted the satin-finished brass latch, ran my fingers along the parquetry edges and the velvet linings, and discovered…

Nothing.

"I'm sorry," I sighed. "Is this where I don't see what's in the box because I haven't figured out what I'm doing here and why two wrongs make a right?"

"Well, aren't you silly!" The Proprietress sniffed. "There's nothing in the box, Alice Rose."

"Then why did you give it to me?"

"Darling child, you have to put something in it! Honestly, do you ever pay attention?" She tapped her perfectly manicured nail on the box lid and frowned, waiting.

I spun about, looking at Athena, Joan of Arc, and Richard the Third for a clue. Marie Antoinette shook her finger at me while she shook her head.

"What did we talk about before, Alice?" The Proprietress sighed. I stared back, no doubt a blank look on my face.

"Broken hearts have pieces, Alice! They have pieces!"

"That's what I'm supposed to put in the box? Of course! But how do I get them?"

"That's for you to figure out as you struggle with two wrongs making a right!"

The Proprietress nodded at the box, and I snatched it off the counter before she could take it away. The box now in my possession, I closed the lid and found myself sitting on the front porch steps of our house in Berkeley, holding a package of Hostess Donuts in my lap. Quinn sat on the porch with me, a plate of fruit and two glasses of milk between us. The day wasn't too cold for February, so sitting outside with the boy I thought was the kindest and most handsome junior at Berkeley High was no hardship. Well, I wouldn't have minded even if it had been Chicago in the dead of winter.

"I'm sorry we have to sit here," I lied to Quinn. "It's just that the nurse is over from the hospital to give Mom her medicine and look in on her. She gets self-conscious about the house, her appearance, you know."

"I'm sorry about your mother," he answered. "What's the problem?"

"Ovarian cancer. That's what it is this time. She's had so many things go wrong in the last year."

"Shit! That's so unfair," Quinn whispered. He glanced at me and saw that I was staring back. We both looked away. "I guess that's why your brother's home from school?" he asked.

"Pretty much."

I opened the package of donuts, and he chose one of

the plain, while I decided on the powdered. "I hear the kids at school talking, but I never guessed your mother was so sick," he mentioned.

"If it's the popular clique whispering, it's about me."

We took sips of milk, shared an orange, and went through the box of donuts silently, watching the foot traffic on Rose Street and listening to the sounds coming from the house.

"It was great to run into you at the rink today," Quinn said suddenly.

"It was fun just to sit and talk," I replied, hiding my blushes with the hair spilling around my face as I turned. "There's one last donut," I offered, holding up the package.

Quinn took it and smiled, saying, "You've got powdered sugar all over your face."

I turned away, brushed the powder off my face, and turned back, grinning like a fool. We laughed together and then sat quietly again, for it seemed we didn't need to say a word and still be in perfect agreement and harmony.

"Did you see that new movie, *Romeo and Juliet*?" Quinn asked after a time.

"My English class went to see it last week. I didn't go. My mom…"

"My class went. I thought of you since you like medieval stuff and history."

"You did? How did you know?" I shot a look of surprise at him. Until now, Quinn was a boy I watched from afar, never said a word to for fear of rejection.

"Winter play—the drama club did *Becket,* and you designed the costumes and sets."

"You went?"

"With my mom," he answered sheepishly.

"Wow, I didn't…"

"Those costumes and the scenery looked great, like a movie. Are you doing anything else?"

"The drama coach wants to meet with me next week to plan some things, so I've started a book and some storyboards—those are little sketches that show each scene."

"I've heard of that. When I perform at some theaters, I've seen people working on them."

"Do you do a lot of concerts?"

"A couple a year. My dad wants me to be a concert cellist or a Conductor."

"Wow."

"But I like rock n' roll, especially Hendrix, The Airplane, the Beatles. Are your designs supposed to be a secret?"

"No. D'you want to see them?"

"Sure!"

We scrambled to our feet, and I led the way through the garden gate to the yard. A path led the way past rose bushes and gladiolus, pansies, and petunias to a stairwell up to the laundry room and kitchen. We entered the house through the back door, skirted through the dining room to the second-floor stairs, and up to my room before Dennis, my mother, and her nurse could see us.

"My mother's bed and all of her stuff are in the living room," I explained as we entered the bedroom. "It would embarrass her, I think, to see anyone new."

"Understandable," Quinn said, sitting on one of the window seats while I took a portfolio from the other. He glanced around and said, "This place is much neater and cleaner than mine."

I quickly surveyed the room; the bed was almost made up, and fortunately, I didn't leave any bras and underwear laying around. My art supplies and sketching pads were everywhere, as were my history book and notebooks, my typewriter on its stand with a page draped over the carriage, the menagerie of stuffed animals shoved to the foot of the bed and on top of my mother's hope chest that was draped with a sad little afghan I'd knitted up the summer before when I was bored and needed something new to spark my creativity. The room was decorated in shades of blue, beige, and peach. Very simple and utilitarian, with chests in the window seats to store my treasures—except for the four-poster bed with lace curtains.

"Here we are," I said, throwing myself at Quinn's feet. I untied the laces that held the portfolio together and opened them to costumes for a fantasy piece I'd been working on.

"Are those Hobbits?" Quinn wanted to know, preventing me from moving the sketch aside.

"Yes, I'm working on a *Lord of the Rings* project. Here's Aragorn, and Arwen, Frodo, oh, and here's The Witch King and Galadriel. Legolas is in here somewhere…."

"These are amazing! This is pretty much how I imagined the characters. You're good, Alice."

"Do you think so? Thanks." I looked up and smiled. "No one's seen my work at this stage."

"Well, I guess that means this was an honor," Quinn said gently, his hand resting on mine.

"Do you like Tolkien, too?"

"It's okay. Some of it is hard to get through."

"Oh, no! If you think of it as theology—like the story of Jesus- you can get some of it. At least, that's what I've figured out."

I was nervous and trembling; Quinn was still smiling gently at me, and it wasn't one of those grins meant to impress, but it looked as if he was really paying attention and cared. As much as I wanted to kiss him, I could not.

Not now. Now was not the time…

Quinn started to lean in when we heard the shout.

"Alice! Mom needs you right now!" Dennis called. The screen door to the front porch slammed. "Alice? Quinn? Where the hell did you…?" We went to the landing as soon as we heard the footsteps on the stairs. Dennis stopped halfway up and frowned.

"Tell me you're behaving yourselves?" he demanded, shooting a look at Quinn that meant trouble.

"Strictly honorable," Quinn said, coming down to shake his hand.

"Oh, back off, Prince Charming," Dennis teased. He glanced at me and said in an apologetic tone, "Sorry, Faery Princess, today's a really bad day."

"We'll clean up the porch, and I'll be right there," I said as we brushed passed him. We retraced our path to the porch and took time cleaning up our picnic. Once everything was in the basket, Quinn opened the front door and waited as I entered.

"Well, it was fun, Alice. Just to sit and talk. I like the yard, with the roses and the Canterbury bells. It reminds me of my grandmother's place in Northern England. God, I'm rambling. Sorry."

"No worries."

He waited, hoping.

Not now, not yet!

"Well, see you at school?"

"Sure, maybe we can have lunch now and then."

The look on his face was hopeless dejection.

"Alice! Come on, dammit!" Dennis called.

I touched Quinn's cheek gently and smiled. "How about Monday?"

"Monday?" Quinn asked brightly.

"Sure. See you."

I watched him go up the street, and at the corner, he looked back. I went down to the street and waved. He raised a hand tentatively, then smiled, and went on his way. I watched until his tall figure disappeared around a corner. Once more, the lightness was overwhelming, the sense of peace and contentment, of harmony.

As I turned to go into the house, the light in the sky

started to change, and I looked up, watching for storm clouds and wondering if Quinn would arrive home before the rain started.

Something extraordinary happened then: rain did not fall from the sky, but light. Pastel light in shades of blue and beige, peach and apricot, opalescent and warm. It came down like a shower and enveloped me so that I felt warm and loved. I hugged myself and closed my eyes and when I opened them, I was back in The Curiosity Shop, holding my box. Joan of Arc looked up from her reading of *The New York Times Book Review* and I noted the smile— and tears.

The Proprietress said nothing of the change over me when I walked up to the counter with the box and set it on the velvet square. Snapping her fingers, she pointed to the box, and I dutifully opened it. To my surprise, on the velvet cushion was a curious jewel, opalescent and bright, one that changed color as you turned it in the light. It was the size of an apricot.

"Hmm, just as I expected," The Proprietress nodded. She said nothing more, took the box, and set it up on the topmost shelf. "Two more will be needed, Alice. Oh, don't look at me like that!" she sighed, glaring at me from over her glasses. "It will be easier."

She snapped her fingers and pointed behind me to the brochure rack. As Eleanor of Aquitaine walked in, she took a pamphlet from the rack and handed it to me in passing.

"Unfinished business, Alice," she said over her shoulder.

The pamphlet in my hands was a map of the Yorkshire coast with the city of Scarborough figuring prominently. Hildegard von Bingen entered with a bouquet of—what else?—parsley, sage, rosemary, and thyme. "Remember me to one who lives there," she said, winking, and turned to the flower boxes on the sill. The herbs started to glow and transformed with the light until they were a mixed bouquet of bright spring flowers that I arranged in my office at York St. John's.

"All settled then, Professor Martin?" a secretary asked as she passed my door.

I turned and smiled. "Yes, thank you, and thank you for the vase. My only other choice when I bought them was to use a milk bottle. I didn't see any vases at home."

"Oh, I thought they were from that young man waiting in the hallway!" The secretary was pointing behind her.

I followed her out and saw Quinn in one of the chairs outside the faculty advisor's office. He smiled sheepishly and rose as I approached, ignoring the appreciative stares and look-backs of female students passing by.

"I owe you an apology for the night before," he opened and looking around, added, "Can we go somewhere to talk?"

"I'm finished for the day. Carry my books? We can have dinner at home if you want."

"Sure. Can we make a stop on the way to your place?"

The stop was his grandmother's store in The Shambles.

The scents of lavender and spice filled my nostrils when Quinn unlocked the door and switched on the lights. Carefully setting down my things, he reached for the sheets protecting the goods for sale on the tables and counters and drew them off, going around to the cash register on the counter in the furthest corner of the little Victorian shop that looked like it belonged in my village.

"I meet with the solicitors tomorrow and need to make an account. I don't think Ellie took care of the receipts the day she went into the hospital."

"Is that us?" I exclaimed, looking at a framed photograph above the register.

He turned and looked behind him, smiling. "February

of 1970, right before I came here to spend Easter Vacation with Ellie."

"Is that when you bought the musical globe and the silver rose?"

"She gave them to me. I told her all about you. We went for tea, and she wanted to know what made me happy, so I told her."

Quinn sorted change and pound notes, taking a ledger from a drawer below the register and making entries. While he did this, I explored Eloise Radcliffe's Antiques and Curiosities, a place I knew from his descriptions and anecdotes.

Porcelain dolls dressed in period costumes stood on shelves beside music boxes and sachet pillows, bundles of dried flowers and strands of beads, packages of handmade notepaper, and snow globes. Boxes of toy knights made of pewter and lead were lined up beside painted wooden castles with working drawbridges. Metal cars painted in bright colors filled spaces beside cricket bats and balls. Books had places of honor in the windows with tea sets and souvenir items displaying the white rose of York.

"I understand why you love this place," I commented, running my hand over the cashmere scarves folded neatly on a counter, taking stoppers out of the perfume bottles, and sniffing the natural floral scents. "It's welcoming, comforting."

"That was Ellie," he said, finishing his work at the register and putting the money and ledger in a large envelope he placed with my things. "When she found the silver rose, she put it in the window, and it wasn't there a day before I asked about it, so she gave it to me and said, 'This belongs to your Alice.' I wonder if you still have it."

I unbuttoned the top buttons of my cardigan and pulled the rose out. Quinn held it in his hand for a moment and then laid it against my camisole, keeping a finger on the silver petals a little longer.

"I know what this means," he whispered. "At least, I hope I do. Maybe you'll tell me what I don't want to hear?"

Nodding, I drew a breath, summoning courage, and said, "He wants to marry me, Quinn. He pushed for a wedding in August—this August. Dennis and Harry say it's a bad idea."

Quinn was ready to say something and then shook his head as if to dispel the thought. He looked stunned. A lump was starting in my throat, and as much as I wanted to run away, I stayed.

"I was pregnant, and he insisted we get married, do the right thing, then I lost the baby—but there wasn't one, it was a cyst—and so I thought, but he didn't, and we decided to just go through with it…."

"You don't sound happy about it," Quinn said after a time.

"I was at first, but I'm having second thoughts."

Another first! I told the truth!

"Is that the reason you're in England? Running away?"

"No, I'm here to lecture in medieval studies at College of Ripon York St. John's for the summer term. It's part of my contract with Brown University. I'm joining the faculty there in September."

"Really."

I glanced up and saw his skeptical glance. "Really."

The perfume bottles with their Victorian labels and illustrations held my interest longer than they should have, and I picked up the freesia and studied it carefully. The label had no instruction: two dabs and uncomfortable moments disappear.

"Here," Quinn said, taking the bottle from me. He reached over the counter, placed it in a bag with lavender stripes and Eloise Radcliffe's label, and handed it to me. "I want you to have it. Ellie would want you to have it. It's your scent."

"We're not talking about perfumes, Quinn."

"I know. C'mon, Woman. Make my supper."

It was out in the open.

Strangely, he seemed to take it in stride. The old Quinn had surfaced and kept me company that evening. We talked about everything, laughed, and shared memories, but we avoided that elephant sleeping in the parlor until Quinn offered an evening stroll along the city walls.

"When in August?" he said all of a sudden.

"The twenty-sixth."

"Well," he sighed, taking my hand as we climbed the stairs from Bootham Bar, "You're not married yet."

"Is that an offer of infidelity, Maestro?" I jested, but I wasn't joking.

"No, I think that would make us both miserable. It's an offer of friendship for life, for those times when you have no one to turn to. Or when the loneliness gets unbearable, because, Faery Princess, I get a feeling that despite everything, despite your wealthy archeologist with a building, you're lonely," Quinn said. Then after a time, "I know I am. Friends are a precious commodity."

The pain was unbearable, but I smiled and said, "I thought after all of your travel, your fame, that by now you'd be married."

"Who'd want me?" he laughed sadly.

I would!

"What do you mean?" I demanded gently. "I mean, look at you. You were gorgeous nine years ago, but now...."

"There was only one girl I ever loved."

"Your cello Petula. I still can't believe you named your cello," I teased.

"Before I loved you, I loved Petula Clark."

"Justin Hayward of the Moody Blues."

"That was never a secret. Why do you think I used

their music for my light shows?"

"Ah, you were trying to impress me?"

"It worked, didn't it?"

"Pretty much. I had to wear a turtleneck for two weeks to hide the hickeys. It didn't fool anyone."

I started to laugh, and happily, he joined in, raised my hand to his lips, and kissed it. "The girl of my dreams does have the curves of my cello, a bit thinner, though, and my mother would call her scrawny even. She's got mellow sounds, but she isn't predictable or static. She's got a heart and a soul. A sense of humor. She's smart, beautiful, with a smile that takes your breath away and eyes that are so incredible. And she's still all that."

"Well, I know what happened to her. What happened to you?"

"I was stupid. I was given choices. No. I was forced into ultimatums."

"Why didn't you fight?" I asked, my voice tremulous and wondering, hoping for an answer.

"I wish I could tell you why," Quinn said. "It came around to ultimatums."

"I was in the next room."

"Pardon?"

"When you told your parents we wanted to marry. I heard your argument with them—it was hard not to."

"I wanted to forget that day…"

"And I waited at the library," I added quietly and unemotionally. "When you didn't show up, I assumed you didn't want me, and when we got together later, we never talked about it. I guessed it was too painful a subject to broach. An old wound that didn't need opening."

"I wanted to tell you what was happening—it's still too hard to talk about. And it was painful enough without making you feel any worse," Quinn said.

"You might have said something. It would have explained a lot. I don't know what I could have done, but at least knowing,"

"Now you're a bride-to-be, a month away from her wedding, in a foreign country with a former lover. And I've got a soulless, heartless bitch for a girlfriend."

"Sounds like a bad Jane Austen novel," I quipped.

"Sounds like life. I can break it off and risk a seventy percent salary or job cut, but I think you love your archeologist."

"In a way," I began. "But I love you—always have, always will."

"Alice,"

"Say the word, Quinn."

He stopped and leaned against the ramparts facing the city. "Not yet," Quinn muttered to himself. "It's not time, and I've only got a week."

I couldn't believe I'd heard him right, and when I joined him at the ramparts, clouds began forming as if a late spring storm was coming in. The shadow became shade under an oak tree in The Village, where I sat in a park on the high street across from the church.

"I don't suppose you'd hazard a game of Risk with me?"

I looked up and saw Anne Boleyn smiling down. She had the game in her arms and now pushed it toward me.

"Risk takes a while, a couple of hours," I said, opening the box and setting up the board.

"You and I know we have all the time in the world. Ah! Here come King Richard and Queen Eleanor."

"Join us?" I invited.

"I'm not very good at these games," Richard the Third confessed.

"One of England's best strategists and defender of the Commons not good at a board game?" Eleanor of Aquitaine scoffed.

"Pardon me for saying so, but look what happened to him," I interjected.

"A challenge is a challenge, Alice," Anne said.

The playing pieces were sorted and distributed, and the cards were dealt. Eleanor handed me the dice, and I rolled, starting the game. I moved several armies facing the English Channel from the European continent to the French coast. Eleanor guffawed in a most unladylike manner.

"That is precisely what I was going to do!" she laughed.

"It figures," Richard sighed.

"Roll the dice," I commanded.

We rolled. Richard came up with a three and a seven; I rolled two sixes.

"It isn't the first time I've lost England!" he grumbled.

"Alice needs to conquer England, Your Grace," Anne Boleyn said as she studied the playing board map and moved armies. "That is where her heart lies, and love resides. Your Grace! Roll the dice."

Richard glared at Anne and tossed the dice so that one of them fell into the grass.

"Game over!" I declared and walked across the street to the church.

Today no one sat at the organ and played Tallis, but The Proprietress was laying out fair linen, and Hildegard von Bingen was changing the flowers.

"What are you doing here, Alice?" Hildegard asked kindly. "Shouldn't you be on the way to New York for your wedding anniversary celebration?"

"I have a question," I said, approaching them. Only Hildegard stopped what she was doing to pay attention. The Proprietress fussed with the fair linen, making a great to-do of getting the hems even along the sides of the altar. "When I was in York, I heard Quinn say, 'Not yet. It's not time. I've only got a week.' I don't remember him saying that in 1978. I don't remember it all, and as soon as I arrive somewhere, it seems that I do remember what it's all about, what I'm supposed to say and do, and it's all like the first time around. But not what Quinn said. Why is it different?"

"Why do you think, silly girl?" The Proprietress demanded as she peered through cat's eye eyeglasses on a level with the altar. It wasn't the fair linen she was sizing up.

"I don't know what to think!"

"Dear me, she is still clueless!" sighed The Proprietress at Hildegard. "Well, that can be remedied. Hildegard, if you would?"

"Looks like you're going to New York for a concert whether you want to or not."

Hildegard held out a perfect white rose from her arrangement.

I looked over at The Proprietress, who now snapped and turned the fair linen, ignoring me. "Isn't there something I don't have to change? Something painful I don't have to relive?" I pleaded.

"It's random, Alice," The Proprietress said, turning her attention to purificators and chalices, lining them up on the credence table. "How long have you been with us? You should know all from advice and experience. If it comes up, you don't have a choice—you just have to make the best of it and hope that what you say and do will make a change for good or ill."

"I'm sorry, but game over," I stated.

"No reset button, Alice," Hildegard said, pushing the rose toward me.

"You're going to New York. Now deal with it!" The Proprietress hissed, snapping her fingers.

"You can go to Hell!" I muttered as I grabbed the rose.

"How do you know we're not already there?" asked Hildegard as I did a magnificent storm-out.

Slamming the church door felt good; it certainly gave

me a sense of power and control. Something I'd not experienced in a while, but when I found myself at Lincoln Center in New York, walking out of the elevator on Donovan's arm as we followed a group of concertgoers to the luxury boxes,

Oh God....

CHAPTER 16

"YOU LOOK MAGNIFICENT tonight," Donovan murmured as we strolled towards a bar that had not yet been discovered.

"Thank you. I feel like a celebrity—dressing up, limousine service, on a handsome man's arm. You should have warned me about the paparazzi!" I said happily, though I was trembling, worried that Quinn would come around the corner or someone would know about our past together and blurt it out in front of Donovan, who knew about the friend who broke my heart but didn't know that the friend was the Conductor of the Royal Philharmonic.

"Happy first anniversary," Donovan whispered, planting a kiss on my brow. "I confess I didn't know this would be such a media event. It's something about the Conductor. He's supposed to be the new *wunderkind* and prodigy in the world of classical music. My mother would know." He winked at me and then smiled at the pretty bartender who asked for his pleasure. "Let's see, two Perriers with lemon."

With drinks in hand, we continued to the boxes, and I smiled demurely as a local news celebrity blocked our path when he recognized Donovan and wanted his thoughts on the concert we were about to enjoy.

"It's our wedding anniversary, and so we'd just like to enjoy the concert," Donovan said, turning on all the charm as television cameras burned brightly on us. The crew moved on, and I kissed Donovan's cheek as the usher greeted us and pulled back the velvet curtain so we could enter our box.

"What was that for?" Donovan chuckled, unused to my public display of affection.

"For mentioning that it was our anniversary. Do you know how many women in the United States are envious of me right now? To have a husband that didn't need a browbeating to remember and to announce it on national TV?"

"Eight weeks."

"Pardon?"

"My other gift to you is eight weeks of sobriety."

We kissed passionately from the sight of others, and his arm stayed around me as we found our seats, front row, stage right. We were the only occupants, as this was my mother-in-law's box, and these were her season tickets for the concert series.

I nestled up against him as he flipped through the program. "This might interest you," Donovan was saying. "Here." He leaned close so that I could see what he was pointing at.

My heart leaped into my throat.

A photograph of Quinn was all that I saw.

"Tarquin Radcliffe was born in England and raised in Berkeley, California, yadda, yadda, when the Orchestra isn't touring, spends most of his time at his home in the hills of Marin County, and he went to Oxford. What musician goes to Oxford? Don't they go to the Conservatory or the Royal Academy? Anyway, it's the Berkeley connection I knew would interest you, but I guess Berkeley High was so large you wouldn't have run into him."

"Quite a bit, actually. He's the friend," I said matter-of-factly, taking a sip of my Perrier and wishing my hands would stop trembling.

"The friend...oh. *Oh!*"

The house lights dimmed, and after a moment, the concertmaster tuned the orchestra, each instrument answering the request.

There was silence; then he appeared.

Dressed in an impeccable tuxedo and the silver cummerbund Dennis made, he was dashing, and more than one woman in the boxes on either side of us made racy comments about how handsome he was. I tried not to smile; I fought tears. I would not allow Donovan to see how affected I was. Out of the corner of my eye, I saw that he observed me as if taking mental notes to be stored away for a quarrel later or used as an excuse to open that bottle of scotch I knew he so desperately needed. I even managed to contain myself when the Orchestra performed the *Fantasia on a Theme by Thomas Tallis* after *Greensleeves, Lark Ascending*, and *Five Variants on Dives and Lazarus*.

It was the surprise finale that made me lose my composure.

Quinn turned towards the audience and, in the glare of a spotlight, said, "I've invited a friend to join us this evening. Jordan Gregson."

The audience erupted in applause and squeals. Jordan Gregson was a heartthrob tenor whose crossover work from classical to pop gave him several Grammys the year before. When he came out on the stage and shook hands with Quinn, I thought several women below us in the orchestra seats would faint; one lady shouted, "I LOVE YOU!" which brought laughter and applause. It took a moment for the house to settle, and as soon as that happened, Quinn stepped off the podium and handed his baton to the concertmaster. This brought whispers and murmurs of speculation. One stagehand brought Quinn's cello, and another brought a chair and placed it on stage right where Jordan sat at the piano, almost directly in front of our box. Quinn set himself to play and then smiled wistfully at the audience.

"You may recognize this song. It's a special one for a special friend from home."

Donovan shot me a look.

Jordan began on the piano—measures from Nino Rota's music from *Romeo and Juliet*, which Quinn picked up on the cello. After an introduction that gave me chills, Jordan sang *A Time for Us* in Italian: *Un Giorno Per Noi*, accompanied by the Royal Philharmonic Orchestra with Quinn's passionate and breathtaking solo at the chorus.

He closed his eyes, and his concentration on perfecting every note, like that day in the school auditorium, altered his features slightly so that there was a sadness, a hardness to them, but beautiful all the same. His hair fell across his brow and moved with every bow stroke. On and on, with every note more perfect than the last, he played scales, arpeggios, and runs until the audience began cheering and applauding when he finished, and Jordan and Quinn smiled as Jordan picked up the tune for the last verse. They were not expecting this response!

Nor had Donovan expected mine.

"Hey, are you okay?" Donovan asked, noting that I was the only person in the house not on their feet for the curtain calls and cheering.

I shook my head and, choking back a sob, asked, "Did you know?"

He winced and nodded. "I didn't think it would blow up in my face. I called Harry and asked what would be a special present for you since I never seem to get it right, and he suggested the concert when I told him some ideas I had. He said the *Fantasia on a Theme by Thomas Tallis* was your favorite classical piece. That much I knew, and when I heard that the Orchestra was beginning a U.S. tour here and saw the program, I thought it would please you. I didn't know about you and Radcliffe—at least I didn't know he was the friend who broke your heart. I'm sorry, Angel. I wanted to please you for once."

"No, it's okay." I reached for his hand and smiled. "It was a thoughtful gift. Thanks."

"It comes with a second half. We've been invited backstage and to the reception for Radcliffe. Mother's art foundation put it together," Donovan explained, and I took the handkerchief offered and dabbed my eyes with it.

"Well, if she put this together," I said, gesturing towards the stage," then how can you say you didn't know?"

'I just said it was Mother's idea. Would it bother you to go?"

The voice had that argumentative edge. If I said yes, I'd be subjected to hours of interrogation over what I had long ago decided was private. Donovan would ask again, demand answers, and hope I'd slip up or admit something to give him license for neglecting me or, worse, to drink.

I waited a moment, perhaps too long, and shook my head. It was a moment before Donovan smiled— perhaps disappointed —and held a hand out as I stood. "Hopefully, Radcliffe will get you to smile," he said.

We were escorted backstage by a security guard once Donovan showed his credentials and, more importantly, was recognized as the son of Senator and Arielle Trist. Society mavens stopped pushing toward the dressing room when we entered the corridor and stared at Donovan, then at me, whispering behind their hands and programs.

The door to the dressing room was open, and I could see Quinn towering over adoring patronesses of the arts and their single daughters. He'd been profiled in the *Times* entertainment page that morning, revealing nothing new to me; he was talented, dashing, handsome, and available.

"Wait here," Donovan murmured, leaving me in a corner. He pushed forward to use his clout for a private audience.

I watched as Quinn turned when he heard his name and moved as best he could toward Donovan to shake his hand. From what I could hear, Quinn thanked Donovan for the welcome to Lincoln Center and then bent forward to better listen to Donovan. Quinn's head shot up, and he glanced in my direction.

It was a theatrical moment: Quinn stared at me while Donovan kept talking about his family, particularly his mother, and it seemed we were the only ones in the crowded dressing room. He looked at Donovan and then at me and listened intently, finally nodding as Donovan extended a hand in my direction. They were both coming towards me, and I felt my knees would buckle. My heart was pounding, and I knew I would be sick. Quinn was a few feet away when the Director of the Center suddenly appeared with photographers, and he was lured back on stage for a photo op. Quinn stared at me again for a painfully yet wonderfully long time, and I stared right back. He offered a loving, tender smile that wasn't lost on Donovan, who, failing to secure his private audience with classical music's latest *Wunderkind,* was agitated and annoyed. And why wouldn't he be if he could read all the signals?

"I suppose it'll be the same at the reception," Donovan grumbled as we walked towards the exit.

"We don't have to go," I said as cheerfully as I could.

"But he's a friend and seemed really interested in seeing you again."

"Well, if you think it's that important, we can call his manager and set up a lunch or dinner while he's in town," I said dismissively.

"Why don't you do that? We could invite Mother to join us."

"Don't have his number."

We were on Broadway and 65th Street at the foot of the Grand Stairs, waiting for our car to be brought around when we heard the shout.

"Alice!"

Donovan tightened his hold on my waist, and we turned as one to watch Quinn sprint toward us.

Concertgoers paused to whisper and stare at the Conductor of the Royal Philharmonic as he took the steps two at a time and landed almost at our feet. It didn't help that photographers were following him.

"Maestro," Donovan greeted, smiling for the press corps starting to circle.

"Alice," Quinn said, trying to catch his breath, "Alice, my mother told me about Denny—I'm so sorry."

"Thanks. He did ask about you in the last weeks," I murmured.

"I was home a month after, and Harry said you'd gone, so,"

"Donovan had to get back to the dig at Petra, and I had lectures, so we couldn't stay in Berkeley for very long."

"Do you want to come to the reception?" Quinn asked me. "I know Doctor Trist spent a fortune on food and drink and wouldn't want it to go to waste."

"Angel?" Donovan asked, turning to look at me.

Again, I took too long to decide, looking at their similar faces, one anxious and one smug. No matter what I did, it would be the wrong move, and I would suffer for it. Finally, I shook my head and smiled, extending my hand to Quinn.

"It's been a long night, Quinn, and I haven't been feeling well," I said. "But Donovan, you should go. I can take the car back to the hotel." I looked up at Quinn. "You do understand? It's nothing personal."

"No worries," he whispered, smiling.

"I am sorry—it's been a while, hasn't it?"

Quinn looked as if he were going to speak and then merely nodded. Donovan beamed with what I thought was a victorious smile and invited Quinn to show him the way. As they departed, two photographers hovered and took my picture as I waited for the car, which, when it came, was a godsend. I hoped it would take me back to The

Curiosity Shop, but it brought me to The Plaza.

I finally drifted off to sleep hours later when the telephone rang, and I rolled over to look at the alarm clock. One-thirty in the morning; most likely Donovan calling to say he'd be at the hotel soon, just waiting for a taxi.

"Hello, Faery Princess."

"Quinn? How did you—?"

"You can hang up if you want, and I'll understand completely. Your husband told me where you were staying…Hello. . .Alice?"

"I'm still here. Where is he?"

The last I saw of him was with the Opera Company Director having drinks."

"He *what?!* Oh, never mind…I thought as much…"

"Look, I don't want to cause any trouble. I just wanted to talk to you."

"I'm listening."

"Y'know, we almost didn't come to New York. I wanted to skip it altogether, but it's been good."

He paused, and I could hear a pencil in the background. The familiar *tappa-tap-ta-tappa*.

"Did he tell you why we came to New York?" I asked.

"Yeah, a wedding anniversary. Has it been a year?"

"Almost to the day."

"I didn't mean the wedding," Quinn said.

"Neither did I."

"You don't sound happy, Alice. If I'm bothering you…"

"It's not that. As soon as I knew we were coming here, I started dreaming about that summer."

"I can't stop thinking about Scarborough and York and *Here Comes the Sun*," Quinn sighed and laughed. "And *Un Giorno Per Noi*." He sighed again, this time more seriously. "So. What do we do?"

"We stick to our promise, our plan—all I know is that

I haven't forgotten, and I doubt I will, no matter what."

"You're so beautiful, Alice."

"Thank you," I whispered, swallowing my tears.

The familiar *tappa-tap-ta-tappa* filled the void. He was on the other end of the line, and that was all that mattered.

He started to sing *Here Comes the Sun,* and I joined in. Quinn laughed after he finished the verse. "Wait a minute! Do you know that's the first time you've said 'thank you' after I told you you're beautiful? Usually, you change the subject."

Maybe it's because I hear it so seldom now…

"I'll take every compliment I can get these days!" I laughed.

"You're beautiful!"

"Thank you again!"

"Alice, it was great to see you tonight. I wish I'd known you were coming."

"Didn't you? I thought *Un Giorno Per Noi…*."

"Oh, it was for you, most definitely. I added it to the repertoire at the last minute. Like tonight. Maybe I was hoping I'd find you if I sang it enough times."

Tappa-tap-ta-tappa….tappa-tap-ta-tappa.

"Well," Quinn said, "I have a nine o'clock rehearsal tomorrow."

"I have to get back to Providence."

A long, painful pause. "Alice, you will hear from me, I promise."

"I know."

"I love you!"

"Always. I love you. Good night."

I replaced the receiver and stared at the phone, willing it to ring again as in the old days when Quinn had one more thing to share and wanted to tell me again that he loved me. When nothing happened, and I closed my eyes, opened them again, and wasn't in The Curiosity Shop, I plumped up the pillow and burrowed deep under the blankets, falling asleep towards dawn.

CHAPTER 17

IT WAS PAST ten o'clock when I woke. The Manhattan skyline was a silhouette on the drawn curtains, and the August morning sun burning through the damask threatened a sweltering day. I heard the shower running and wondered when Donovan finally got in. I ordered his favorite things for breakfast. When he came out of the bathroom and entered our sitting room, I was at the table with The New York Times, digging into waffles and sausages.

"Hello!" Donovan greeted happily. He leaned down to kiss me and then sat, dragging his chair to be opposite me, as always. I offered a part of the newspaper and poured a cup of coffee.

Suddenly he laughed and took a bite of eggs, pointing with his fork at the page. Photos of Donovan, Quinn, and me were splashed above the fold in the Entertainment section: the one of me was from the mob scene backstage, while Quinn's picture had been taken at the reception. Donovan was beside him with his arm around Quinn's shoulders.

"Well, we knew *this* was going to happen!" Donovan chuckled. He read aloud, "'Radcliffe's mysterious love interest revealed! A year of speculation ends.' Hah! There were rumors about his being a homosexual," was Donovan's aside over the newspaper. Then he added, "Looks like every debutante is cursing the day you were born. Sorry Angel, you wanted to be remembered for your work as a history professor and author of serious work. Looks like you're getting a different legacy!"

"I will be taken seriously for my work," I said defensively. "And I'm surprised you find it so amusing, since," here I took the paper and out of his hands and read, "'the talented and young Conductor of the Royal Philharmonic Orchestra made no secret for whom his haunting rendition of *A Time for Us* was intended: a demure and beautiful young and married woman, Doctor Alice Martin formerly of Berkeley, California and now on the faculty of Brown University in Providence, Rhode Island, who happens to be the daughter-in-law of Presidential contender Senator Trist of Rhode Island.' Your mother isn't going to like this at all—and here she went to all that trouble for the reception."

"I find it funny, that's all. Radcliffe gets to dream about you all night, and I've got you in my bed."

I folded up the newspaper and tossed it on the floor. "This isn't a competition, Donovan."

"Isn't it? He couldn't take his eyes off you as soon as he knew you were in the room."

"We were high school and college sweethearts. That's the way it always is with first loves. You see them again, and you wonder what might have been."

"Not with mine."

I winked at him. "Maybe that's because you cut a swath through the New England social registry, and they're still trying to finish the count—or dig up the bodies!"

Donovan leaned in and gave me a warm kiss that I returned in kind. "You're funny," he murmured, then fed me a strip of bacon.

It didn't end there. We decided to have dinner that evening at Le Cirque in the Mayfair Hotel and enjoyed a quiet meal and mundane conversation. It seemed our First Anniversary weekend would be without high drama.

I was running a bath when I heard the phone ring and came out to answer it, but Donovan had the receiver in hand, saying, "I told Andrews to call me if there was anything new about the excavations at Petra—reporters have been calling for a story…Hello? Hi, Mother. Yes, it's been a great weekend." He winked at me and puckered up, blowing a kiss in my direction, and I started back to the bathroom. "We did. He seems like a nice guy. Taller than expected, but you're right; we look like brothers!"

I retraced my steps to the sitting room, pretending to find toiletries in my luggage to eavesdrop.

"No, Alice came back here—she's been under the weather. I stayed, though…What? Hold on, you're sure? You're kidding, right? Where'd that come from?"

Donovan frowned and glanced at me, then turned his back.

"Was it on the news? What about the *Journal?* Mother, calm down. It's nothing. Why anyone would care is beyond me—yes, I know, but I don't think Dad's career would be jeopardized. No, no, *no! Not* the building, Mother! C'mon, what does the building have to do with a story that's probably a rumor anyway…well, as to that, they better get their facts straight. That's no one's damn business!"

I slipped back into the bathroom, and upon closing the door, I was in The Shop and went over to my table without anyone noticing except The Proprietress.

"Aren't you forgetting something, Miss Alice?"

Wincing, I rose slowly and shuffled over to the counter where she had placed my book. A minuscule star was stuck onto the page.

"I guess you've run out of the large ones, huh?" I queried.

"You'd like to think that, wouldn't you?"

"It was an accident that we met in York, Quinn and me, Quinn and I, I mean."

"You'd like to think that."

"Wait 'til you see what she does for an encore," Sigmund Freud snickered at Marie Antoinette, who frowned and wagged a finger at him.

I wanted to snap at them but decided it wasn't worth the breath and went out into the high street. "Mind where you go," said Hildegard von Bingen as she paused in tending the flower boxes. "Change is in the air, Alice."

I shot a look of surprise at her, and she smiled and held up a hand to bless me. Looking up, I didn't see a single cloud in the sky nor felt a breeze, but the light had grown softer, perhaps dimmer. Even more curious were the lights starting to shine in shop windows and the church's stained glass.

"The week is almost up, mind you," Anne Boleyn commented as she left the apothecary's shop. "Oh!" She whirled about, her skirts spinning like a top, and held up her wrist in the universal position of trying a scent. "What do you think of this?"

The perfume had musk undertones, with top notes of freesia and rose. I pointed to The Shop, and she nodded 'yes' happily before crossing the street.

It was yet another Victorian shop out of a Hardy novel. Behind the smooth oak counters were shelves upon which sat jars labeled not with medicines or herbs, flowers, or perfumes but with emotions. Each jar was of Italian *majolica,* with a medieval lady's profile portrait gracing the round bowl of the container.

The Shopkeeper wasn't The Proprietress, but my mother.

I stepped cautiously up to the counter and whispered hello. Mother turned and had a look of surprise on her face.

She looked as she had before disappointment and illness set in, etched lines into her face, and made her lips purse. It was me at the same age. I was sure of it. She had always been strikingly pretty, perhaps beautiful. At least men thought so by the appreciative stares and look-backs she got when we were out together.

"There isn't much time, Alice Rose," Mother chirped. How many times had she said that whenever I procrastinated and waited until the last minute to finish homework or anything else?

"A week, I was told. It's almost up."

Mother glanced over her reading glasses and put down her copy of *The Bell Jar* to smile at me as she used to before I came in to say goodnight.

"One thing about you, you always listen! And you're clever, too. So my dear girl, what will you have? A bit of fun?"

She took down a bright pink jar, and when she opened it, it smelled like a bakery—that sweet smell of frosting and cake.

"What about determination?" Mother asked now, reaching for a jar with purple and yellow stripes chasing around like a barber's pole. The scent that wafted out was of a fresh spring morning, of damp earth, sharp and biting, how the world smells just at dawn. As tempting as that was, I pointed to a sky-blue jar with gold stars decorating it.

"What about this one?"

Mother nodded and winked. "Ah, love! Well, it makes sense."

The jar was placed before me, and Mother nodded, coaxing me. I drew the stopper, and the scents of the ocean overwhelmed me: salt tang and earthy aroma that filled the nostrils and made one take giant breaths because it gladdened the heart and soul.

"I thought it might smell like baby powder or lotion, ivory snowflakes, or—"

"—Or Donovan's aftershave? Please!" Mother shook her head and dabbed the scent behind my ears and on my wrists. "This will get you through what's to come, darling. Now, hurry! I'll see you in a bit!"

She gently pushed me towards the door, and before I

could protest or at least ask her about my father, Mother blew a kiss that sent butterflies and rainbows my way, bright shocks and bits of color that distracted me momentarily. When I tried to grab a purple butterfly and succeeded, I opened my hand to find nothing. Glancing up for an explanation, I saw that Mother had gone, and The Proprietress stood in her place, in her clothes, smiling at me.

"I don't have time to go over what's expected, Alice. Put things right, would you?"

She waved me away, and The Shop and The Village dissolved as if they were tablets in water, the bubbles rising to the ceiling of the hotel bathroom where I now stood.

I could hear Donovan still arguing with his mother and could only guess what it was about. Once the tub was top-heavy with bubbles, I slid into the warm water and closed my eyes, anticipating the worst that was yet to come.

The knock on the door didn't surprise or startle me.

"Yeah!" I called.

He poked his head around the door and forced a smile. "That looks like fun," he greeted.

"Want to join me?"

"Thanks for the invitation. I just might," he said, dropping his bathrobe and climbing in behind me. He kissed the top of my head and picked up a wash mitt and the soap. "Here, let me scrub your back."

Donovan's hands, not the mitt, smoothed the creamy soap across my back and around to my breasts, where they lingered, slowly working us into a lather.

"So," he said between kisses, "my mother says there's a story in the *Providence Journal* and on the local stations about a certain young and dynamic Conductor of the Royal Philharmonic and his mysterious lover being seen around a northern English city last year about this time. July maybe? There are pictures of them walking hand-in-hand, some with their arms around each other. They're smiling at one another and look like they're laughing."

I pulled away gently, angry at Donovan for using seduction to get to me. I shouldn't have been surprised: sex was his best weapon and defense.

"Why does Arielle care?" I asked, careful not to sound defensive.

"You and I were engaged at the time. Need I remind you?" Donovan asked, reaching for me.

"We had dinner a few times, went up to Scarborough to the castle, and talked about old times. We were two friends from home meeting up by accident in a foreign country." I said, grabbing a towel and climbing out.

"Mother seems to think it's a scandal, of epic moment, in her words, and it will ruin my chances at getting the new building and damage my father's presidential bid."

"Compared to what? What your father's done? Not to mention your track record."

A few moments passed before Donovan followed me into the bedroom. He found his pajamas and made a great to-do of slipping them on, buttoning each button on the jacket—something he rarely did, as he never wore pajamas. It was a means to collect his thoughts and plan his attack, which came swiftly and quietly once we were in bed. I had turned out the light and leaned over to kiss him goodnight when Donovan said, "I think there's something you're not telling me, Alice."

"What do you want to hear?" I demanded just as quietly.

"That it's me you love and not him."

"I told you. How many times need I say it?"

"Maybe you just need to forget about him!"

I kissed his forehead. "I'm here with you. Didn't you say this morning that Quinn got to dream of me all night, but you had me in your bed?"

"I did. And we had Florence."

"I loved you in Florence. I fell in love with you in Florence."

That led to a night of sex. Not love, not passion, but sex. It made no difference. The battle wasn't won or decided. Donovan kept demanding that I admit loving Quinn and confess my sin of infidelity.

"What you're really saying is that you married me without love being part of the equation," Donovan said the following day. "You married me because we thought you were pregnant, and you felt pushed into it. Why don't you admit it?"

"When you came to Berkeley last year, I told you it would take time. I wanted to take things slow and postpone the wedding."

The argument continued when we returned to Providence two days of angry sex later.

"So why did you marry me, Alice?"

I paused and took a breath before answering. Putting my toothbrush back into the holder next to his, picking up my hairbrush, and running it through my hair, I saw his reflection in the mirror. He looked like a little boy, hurt and unhappy.

"I liked being with you, your intellect, and your passion for your work."

"What about my passion for you?"

"Yes, that too. And I know you wanted to keep your mother from being embarrassed when I tried postponing the wedding. But I wonder, for you at least, if it wasn't just having someone your mother disapproved of and winning a fight with your parents."

"I told you I fell in love with you in Florence — hell, I fell in love with you on that first date in Verona!"

"And then you stopped trying once you thought I was won. What mattered to me no longer mattered to you, except that I work on the east coast instead of the west, so it doesn't inconvenience you. Everything that matters to me isn't important." I climbed into bed and pounded the pillows into the shape I wanted while Donovan took off his watch and glasses and wound the alarm clock so tightly I thought it would explode. After the lights went out, he finally got into bed and stared at the ceiling for a long while.

"I've tried so many times to make you happy, to figure out what you want, Alice. Can't you at least admit that you have some affection for me? That you love me?"

I said in the darkness, "I do have affection for you," and it was the truth. "But if you want to know how deep that affection runs, I can't tell you. When you came to California to pick up where we left off, I was skeptical, but at the same time, I wanted to recreate what we had in Florence. Your eyes followed my every move. Your smile was warm and tender. I wanted you to be beguiled again, romantic. I wanted to love you like I did, not the comfortable everyday love, the love of familiarity and security. I wanted the excitement and passionate love, our breathless love. We came close in those days in December last year, and I guess once we decided to get married, it died."

He turned to look at me, and I could see his eyes, two dark moons in the reflected light of the streetlamp outside the window. "We did have that, Angel."

"Why can't we have that again? Lord knows I've been trying. I've been trying to the point of exhaustion. I don't know what else to do."

"Yes, you do," Donovan whispered, coming closer and putting an arm around me. "We're both frozen by fear."

"What is there to be afraid of?" I laughed bitterly.

"Losing one another. Of making the same mistakes that keep pulling us apart. We just need to think about and decide what we want. If we put our hearts and minds to it, I'm sure we'll discover that we have the same goal and future in mind."

"Or," I sighed, "we rush into yet another decision that has unfortunate consequences or results. You know, I should go out to California and see how Harry's doing. He's been asking me to visit, to help him sell the house, and going through Denny's things." I paused here and added, "And the time away will give us time to think about all this."

"Do you love me?" he asked.

"Stop asking."

It was surprising how well Donovan accepted my decision.

That evening we recreated something of Florence. As usual, we used sex to heal wounds and find intimacy. It was a night of anger and passion, of nothing said and nothing explained or asked, and I was glad when Donovan left earlier than usual for work.

I was already on a plane to California when he returned home that night.

CHAPTER 18

THE CORRIDOR FROM the airplane to the terminal gate led me into The Curiosity Shop, and I was not surprised. In truth, I was relieved. I was glad to see Joan of Arc with her copy of *The New York Times Book Review*, Richard the Third still struggling with the crossword, Athena trying to talk philosophy with Marie Antoinette, and Sigmund Freud arguing with Eleanor of Aquitaine about a mother's role in history. I knew Dr. Freud was in for a nasty surprise on that one. I was expecting to find my brother Dennis, and there he was, drawing in one of my old sketchbooks from school. A plate of cheesecake was suspiciously absent from his table beside mine, and I pointed that out when I sat down and took up my bottle of Diet Pepsi.

"No cake?" I queried.

"Nothing to celebrate yet," Dennis said as he continued to draw. I leaned in, hoping to make eye contact, but he moved away, saying, "It's not ready yet."

"Alice…"

The Proprietress was crooking her finger at me. The box was taken down from its place on the shelf, and she opened it.

Tap-tappa-tap-tap.

Her finger clicked on the box lid, and she raised her brows at me.

Tap-tappa-ta-tap, Ta-tap-tap-tappa.

"Well?" she hissed.

I raised my brows, crooked my head to the left, and frowned.

"In your pocket, Miss Alice, in…your…*pocket!*" She

said.

I felt around in my sweater pocket and caught what I thought was a piece of smooth glass between my fingers. Drawing it out, it looked like a giant ruby teardrop. When The Proprietress snapped her fingers, I gave it up and watched it go into the box.

"You never said what made you return, " Dennis said.

"I thought it was quite evident," Eleanor of Aquitaine said as she got up from her argument with Freud and came to where I stood. She reached out and stroked my cheek with a perfect hand, the great wedding band on her finger cold on my skin. I was about to speak when Eleanor's cool, patrician beauty started to morph like gelatin into the face of Donovan, and suddenly I was back in Providence. It was Donovan's hand on my cheek.

"I know why you left," he whispered. "I just want to know why you came back and if you're going to stay."

"I'm pregnant," I said with very little emotion.

His eyes nearly popped, and it was a moment before he smiled. "Really?" he asked. "Really!"

"Count back to our trip to New York."

I walked past him and went up the stairs to our bedroom, where I dumped the carry-on and suitcase, glancing about to see if anything had changed in the four months I'd been in California. Nothing. Proof of that was the film of dust on my vanity, the laundry still folded on top of the dresser, waiting to be tucked into the proper drawers or onto the correct shelf in the closet.

He was standing in the doorway of the bedroom, glass in hand. "It's mine, I hope?"

"Donovan, please. Endearing comments like that make me want to get back on a plane to California," I said as I threw open the suitcase and started unpacking. "Are you so unsure of yourself, so intent on shooting a torpedo into this marriage, that you keep opening your mouth and letting anything idiotic come out?"

"I wasn't the one who went to California. Maybe you ran into that high school flame that hasn't died out."

"That would have been impossible. From what his mother told me, he lives in England for most of the year." I looked at him and saw the most painful expression I'd ever seen on his face. "Oh, for God's sake, Donovan! Of course it's yours! There hasn't been anyone else since I met you in Verona, and that was what, two years ago?"

"Well, that was a lie." Richard the Third sighed. He was seated at my table in The Shop, leaning his chin in the palm of his hand, frowning at me. I had been propelled back to The Shop and felt like I'd gone down a roller coaster. My stomach was queasy, and I avoided the looks that came from everyone, from The Proprietress to Sigmund Freud.

"Why didn't you tell him the truth?" Richard the Third asked.

"You can't lie to us," Marie Antoinette purred.

"I didn't want to raise a child without the father. Remember most of my childhood?"

A half-dozen heads turned toward me, and now I faced them down. Only my brother looked sympathetic.

Freud came to my table with hot chocolate and made himself at home. "No one here believes that. Even you don't believe it, Alice." He said. "Drink your cocoa."

"You know I hate hot chocolate."

"You do not. You think you don't."

"But…!"

"Drink your hot chocolate like a good girl and catch your train to Scarborough. It's time at last, and you know it."

I held the mug to my lips.

"Go on,"

After taking a sip and trying not to gag, I returned to York in May 1978 at The Bitter End in The Shambles. My hot chocolate was now a glass of foamy beer, and I was seated in a corner booth facing the door. The publican brought a pitcher and a second glass and nodded thanks when I gave him a substantial tip. No sooner had he gone than the door opened, and Quinn entered with the sunset on his shoulders and shining in his tousled hair like a rosy halo.

"Sorry I'm late! Last-minute meetings about the recording session in London," Quinn said breathlessly as he slid into the booth and sat close. He turned and smiled. "How is the faery princess today?"

"Hopefully ruler of all that I survey," I quipped as I poured a glass for him and topped off my own.

"Well, you know the answer to that," he responded with a wink. He took a drink and dug into the fish and chips just presented to us in paper baskets lined with newspaper. "Did you give any thought to my invitation?"

"Yes, and I think I deserve a real weekend off. I haven't had one in a long while."

"Excellent! I've got tickets on the sleeper over to Scarborough."

"You were that sure I'd want to come?" I laughed.

"I was prepared to do some pretty serious convincing. Maybe some groveling. I do both well."

"And how would you have done that?"

Quinn leaned in, his eyes bright and clear, his smile captivating. He was leaning in further still. I closed my eyes and hoped for a kiss. I held my breath, waiting…

"*Are you going to Scarborough Fair, parsley sage, rosemary, and thyme? Remember me to one who lives there. She once was a true love of mine…*" he softly sang, with lips tantalizingly close. "Convinced?" Quinn murmured in a sexy, husky voice.

"When do we leave?" I asked breathlessly.

"Two hours. We can meet at the station, or I can pick you up."

Back at the flat, I put together a bag stuffed with a change of clothes, toiletries, and lingerie. There would be no books or papers except maybe the Sunday *Times*. I hoped signals from Quinn weren't crossed, mixed, or wrong.

As I passed the nightstand, I noticed the letter I'd started to Donovan and picked it up. In three pages, I summarized all the reasons I could think of why postponing the wedding was a good idea, or even better, calling it off altogether and going our separate ways. Donovan had not tried to call in the three months I'd been in York, even though I knew he was back in Providence. My messages were never returned, and my calls were never answered. If actions spoke louder than words, as he was wont to preach, then Donovan had also made up his mind. Turning the letter over and re-reading it for the third time, I put it in the nightstand drawer with the photograph and closed it slowly as if giving myself time to reconsider.

I was slipping the silver rose around my neck when I heard the doorbell. Skipping down the stairs, I panicked, thinking when I opened the door, I would find Donovan on the stoop and have to explain myself, and I hesitated on the landing. When the bell rang again, and then a third time, I took a deep breath and told myself I was silly.

I opened the door and was greeted by an enormous bouquet of pale silver roses, white lilies, and white roses. Quinn peeked out from behind them and smiled.

"Freesias were out of season. Ready?"

"Ready!"

The bouquet took up half of the back seat in the taxi and was placed on the bench across from where I'd thrown myself down when we found our compartment on the Flying Scotsman. Quinn shut the door, and rather than sit beside me, he sat on the bench next to the flowers. "I love looking at your eyes when we talk," he explained.

"You always know the right thing to say," I murmured. "You're teasing me, right?"

"No, just speaking the truth. And you've always been

truthful with me, Alice Rose."

I suddenly felt a shock, a surge of electricity going through every artery and vein in my body. I wanted to speak but couldn't and was grateful the Conductor entered our compartment to take our tickets. With a rich northern accent, he smiled at me and said, "Something you need, Miss?"

"Oh no, nothing. Sorry! I was expecting the guy who usually works this route. We became friends the last time I took the Scotsman."

No, this Conductor wasn't Jack Lemmon, and I was a little disappointed when he left without humming a song.

Reality started sinking in; what I was doing I'd never allow from Donovan, or Quinn, for that matter. And yet, here I was…

I fumbled in my bag for something to do and pulled out a mirrored compact, opening it to check my lipstick and mascara. The Proprietress winked at me from the mirror. When I shifted to look around the mirror, I was in The Shop.

"Why the long face, little miss?" The Proprietress wanted to know. The smirk spread across her face, from perfectly applied red lips to masterfully arched and tweezed brows.

"I'm having second thoughts," I admitted, glancing at my table where the laptop sat open and ready for me. The coffee mug would still be warm, and the Diet Pepsi cold and fizzy.

"You should have thought about that in 1978, my girl! Once a thing is done, it's done."

"And it's like being on a roller coaster," Dennis said, joining us at the counter. "Once you get into the car, you're in it for the ride. You can't pull over and get out just because it's scary and uncomfortable."

I turned to my brother and pulled him outside to the high street. "I will be no better than Donovan!"

"Spending time with a friend? Taking walks along the shore or climbing castle ruins? Having a sympathetic ear or shoulder to cry upon and know that the affection and concern are real? Why is that so bad, Alice?"

"I'll be with Quinn. You know!"

"I know you'll be doing Quinn a world of good," Dennis laughed. He took my hand as we strolled towards the park where Richard the Third and Anne Boleyn were still locked in a game of Risk. "And how do you know that's what he has in mind?"

"He's a guy!"

"Oh, thank you very much, Faery Princess!" my brother chuckled. "Glad to know you think all guys are rutting dogs and just want one thing. What happened to the girl who used to say the love between two people wasn't just about sex, but about the soul and the mind, the spirit, and all combining to make a tie that cannot be unbound?"

"I said that?" I asked, incredulous.

"I can recite chapter, verse, date, and time."

"The Trist Effect, dammit!"

"Pardon?"

"I fell prey to the effect of Donovan Trist. I got used to his idea of love. The love between two people is all about hormones and physical sensation. He uses it to trap and capture, to keep you bound to him."

We sat on a bench across from the Risk game. Dennis leaned forward, his elbows on his knees, and watched a quarrel starting between Anne and Richard. "I think, Alice, you're strong enough to break that rope. I think that's what you had in mind all along. You just need to let go of the fear."

"I'm not afraid!"

"Of rejection, of society's disapproval? Yes, you are. And think about this. To whom did you first make a promise?"

I pondered this with brows knit together and was ready to speak when Dennis got up to referee the game, which was getting out of hand. Richard was throwing little wooden army pieces at Anne, who was cursing him in medieval French. Dennis snapped his fingers, and I was back on the train, staring out the window.

"What's wrong?" Quinn asked now, leaning forward to take my hands.

I shrugged. "Some of my Catholic guilt has resurfaced."

"Meaning…?"

"We're both in relationships, and yet here we are."

"Two longtime friends spending time together, not legally bound to others…maybe bound to each other by a promise made not long ago."

"Yet we broke it and may break it again."

He leaned back and exhaled a sigh. "Well, we can turn around at Scarborough if that's what you want."

"No. The trouble is I don't know what I want. I thought I did."

"You're not alone there. Let's use this time to figure things out."

"Maybe I want, or I'm expecting, something more than you're willing or able to give," I confessed.

"You don't know what's being offered," he jested lightly.

Quinn slid across the compartment and held me in his arms as he had on our first date. Leaning back against the armrest, he stretched out over the seat and brought me with him so that I was snuggled in his arms. "My beautiful Alice," he whispered, "one thing you must know is that you will always have my love."

I wanted to respond, but I was warm and contented in those arms that I'd dreamt of so many times, inhaling the clean sweetness of his aftershave and his natural scent. I became deliciously drowsy and finally fell asleep.

When I woke, The Proprietress stood over me, Joan of Arc and Richard the Third flanking her. My brother had an arm around me protectively. No one else was in The Shop, and though I was exhausted and could barely open my eyes, I noted that the light had changed and the sun was setting over The Village. My head was cradled on my forearms, my mother's cashmere sweater used for a pillow. I could barely hear my brother's voice, but he was angry.

"Didn't I say this was a bad idea? Send her back!" he growled at The Proprietress. "What's a year or two?"

"Didn't I say?" The Proprietress mimicked. "Matters must be set in play, and decisions must be made! It's the same for everyone, even your precious little sister!"

"There are only a few years between—"

Dennis' protest was drowned in the whistle of the Flying Scotsman, and I felt a soothing movement of rocking back and forth as if I were in my mother's arms. I drifted into a comfortable, warm sleep and was awakened by a kiss.

"Alice, we're here," Quinn whispered.

I sat up and immediately fussed with my hair, swiping my fingers under my eyes to remove the mascara smudges. It was around midnight, and we had arrived at Scarborough.

"Are we staying in a railway hotel?" I asked as we disembarked and walked from the platform to the station waiting room for our bags, the night air both shocking and delicious.

"Nope, somewhere better. My house."

"Your house?"

Quinn fell in love with Scarborough when the orchestra appeared there at a summer festival. He said on the taxi ride that when he'd made enough money, he purchased a house facing the south bay in the shadow of the massive keep of Scarborough Castle. One could see the castle and the sea from the balcony off the master bedroom, and tonight lit by a full moon, it was spectacular. I couldn't wait until morning to see it in daylight.

A thump behind me confirmed that Quinn had come up the stairs and dropped my suitcase on the floor. "Wait 'til you see it tomorrow," he said.

"I was just thinking that."

"Tired?" Quinn stood behind me now and drew me close, kissing my hair.

"I didn't realize how hard I've been driving myself until we got off the train," I admitted with a yawn.

"You have two choices. You can sleep in here, and I can take the bed in the study, or we can share this bed, and we both promise to behave ourselves."

We shook on it. After a quick shower, I slipped into bed and listened as Quinn washed up and brushed his teeth, was drifting off in the cloud of featherbeds and comforters when he slipped in beside me, pulling me close.

"This is the way it's supposed to be," he whispered after a long, passionate kiss goodnight.

And so we slept until the sun rose on a wet summer morning. Quinn offered a quick kiss and slipped out of bed, tossing on a robe. I stayed under the covers for a while, hoping he would return and we could snuggle and talk. When he didn't, I threw back the covers and reluctantly got up.

Quinn was downstairs in the kitchen, staring into the refrigerator.

"Ever close the door and then open it again, hoping something new will appear or you missed something on the first pass?" I teased.

"Funny. I'll ring the grocer and see about putting in some food for the rest of the weekend—I had them bring some milk, eggs, and the basic stuff when I decided to come over. Unless you want to eat out," he answered.

"Why don't you let me worry about this while you take

a shower?" I offered, playfully shoving him in the direction of the stairs. For once, I didn't mind hearing the taps go on or the white noise of the shower while I worked in the kitchen. By the time Quinn came back downstairs, I'd managed to brew a pot of coffee and made omelets and French toast.

"I thought I was wrung out, but you must be exhausted from the touring," I mentioned, taking the cup of coffee he offered. "You fell asleep the moment your head hit the pillow."

"I've got a lot on my mind right now," Quinn answered, tapping my nose in his playful way. "And you should know that's the first restful sleep I've had in ages. Thank you."

"For what?"

"For saying yes and coming with me to Scarborough. Just knowing you were beside me, Faery Princess. It meant a lot."

A lump formed in my throat, and I looked down at the food he brought to the table to avoid looking at him. Now he sat beside me in the little nook and nudged me playfully. "Forgot you were left-handed. Elbow wars at the table, just like the good old days!"

"We can't play catch with the toast, though. We need dinner rolls for that."

"Who cleaned up after that Thanksgiving dinner, I wonder?"

"I think it was Harry," I said, trying to keep my voice even though I wanted to sob.

"Poor Harry! He always drew the short straw except when he met Denny. I'd like something of what they had," Quinn said softly into his coffee mug.

"Lightning doesn't strike twice, they say," I murmured.

He glanced out the window, his attention drawn to something. Just as suddenly, he looked away and said, "Maybe?"

"That's optimistic."

Quinn reached for a slice of French toast and applied butter and syrup to it, saying, "We should visit the castle today. You don't mind going in the rain to see it? I want you to see it and the view. It's incredible," he said as he helped himself to more eggs, and poured another round of coffee.

"Sure, why not?"

The tone of my voice betrayed my feelings, and Quinn turned to look at me. When our eyes met, he leaned over for a hug. "Oh God, I've upset you, haven't I?"

"No, no, it isn't you. It's knowing I can't stay here forever and that things will change between us." I sobbed into his shoulder.

Outside, a clap of thunder rolled for the longest time, and the sky grew darker. I peeked out, frowning, expecting to see The Proprietress standing in the rain and dripping wet.

And there she was, scowling, with the rain sliding off her nose and pillbox hat, looking very much like the quintessential wet rat. She tapped the wristwatch on her left hand and then walked away, muttering to herself.

"Maybe things will change for the better. Of course, no one knows, but I'm hoping," Quinn said. Again, a clap of thunder rumbled and shook the house, and the sky lit up with the bluish tinge of lightning. Quinn hugged me tighter. "Please don't cry! You know how I feel about you. And right now, I just want to spend a few days with you, showing you this place I love, reacquainting ourselves."

"Sorry," I sniffed.

"Don't be! Remember, we're here to figure things out. It's bound to be bumpy. The path to that place is pretty steep and rocky."

I couldn't believe what I heard.

Hadn't Dennis said that to me?

He had!

Now I glanced at Quinn suspiciously and watched as he finished his breakfast. He looked over with brows raised in amused question.

"What?" he laughed.

"Nothing. Are you sure we can see the castle in this?" I gestured towards the buckets of rain pouring down and splashing on the windows, lightning ripping through dark clouds.

"This? It'll clear up soon."

I sniffed back the last tears and looked up at him from under my lashes. "Wouldn't happen to have a Risk game handy, would you?"

"Left it at my London flat, but I have something better in mind."

"What could be better than my losing another game of Risk to you?" I teased, taking the last bit of French toast from his plate and popping it into my mouth.

"You'll find out. I'll clear this away and do the dishes while you settle in. Then you'll get your surprise, and hopefully, the weather will cooperate with my plans."

Gulping down the last of the coffee in his cup, Quinn pushed me gently towards the stairs.

It was difficult not to study the photographs on the dresser, the artwork on the walls, and the personal touches to his vacation home. I did notice a framed snapshot of us taken the Christmas of 1972, right before the breakup. There we were, Quinn, Dennis, Harry, and me, sitting on the backyard steps, and we each wore a scarf that Dennis knitted. I noticed the absence of photographs of his parents, though there were quite a few of Quinn with Ellie. There were none of other women or friends. I wondered about that.

I was lacing up my boots when Quinn knocked on the door. "Whenever you're ready," he said.

I shoved myself off the bed and placed my brush on the dresser. "Do you still have that scarf?" I asked, pointing to the snapshot.

"Yes, it's in London. Still have yours?"

"Everything Denny's made for me I wear—mostly because he'd comment if I didn't," I said. "It's nice to see that photo again. That was a happy time."

"I think of it as my family portrait," he murmured, dusting off the frame with a gentle finger.

"So! What's this surprise?" I asked, wanting to change the subject and the mood.

"Follow me, milady."

We raced downstairs to the little study off the living room, where an upright piano and Quinn's cello nearly filled the space. Quinn led me to the overstuffed loveseat and sat me down, kissing the top of my head, and then he sat with the cello.

"This is a special song for a very special friend," he said and began to play.

My breath caught when I heard it: Nino Rota's love theme from *Romeo and Juliet*—the popular version known as *A Time for Us*. He began to sing in his bari-tenor voice, and the familiar verses were not in English, but Italian. After the chorus, he played the theme and added incredible arpeggios and lush and spine-tingling chords. When he finished, Quinn leaned back in the chair and closed his eyes, exhausted. Moments passed before he opened his eyes and saw me staring.

"I hope you liked it," he said, smiling and eyes glistening with tears. He reached for me, and I melted into his arms, listening to the heart pound in his chest. "That was for you, Alice!"

I started to weep from the emotions roiling in me. Just the idea that someone would do something as romantic as Quinn had just done was too much.

But it was Quinn, wasn't it?

He laughed gently, holding me tighter. He started singing *Here Comes the Sun,* and I joined in. "Hey!" Quinn exclaimed in mid-verse, pointing at the window. "Here comes the sun!"

We went on the outing that would change, yet bind, everything.

CHAPTER 19

THE STRAINS OF the Rota song and Quinn's interpretation were still spinning around in my head and making me drunk with love as we climbed to the ruins of Scarborough Castle that afternoon.

"Here, this is what I want to show you."

Quinn led me to the eastern tip of the promontory, where the castle stood facing the North Sea. Below us was the shore, and to the north, the flat darkness of the moors. Patches of green were speckled with whitewashed towns and villages along the horizon. I turned slowly to take it all in: the waves rolling and crashing on the beach, the vast, empty horizon to the east where France and the Netherlands lay, to the fishing boats and touring yachts bobbing in the harbor as waves slapped against them, the daffodils and gillyflowers, white roses in clumps near the foot of the donjon, the cliffs of Scarborough and the town nestled above, around, and upon them, the clusters of houses along the quay and around the approach to the castle itself. The wind picked up as we walked higher still, turned to face the sea, and let the breeze gently buffet us. It swirled about in my hair and around us, making the georgette crepe of my dress dance. I pulled my sweater closer for warmth and smiled at all this beauty. Waves crashed below, and gulls cried as they soared and dove, circled, and lit on the traceries of the castle donjon. The air was crisp and sharp with the tang of the sea, the damp earth after a rain.

I had been here many times in my dreams.

"Remember what you said?" Quinn asked as he came

up and wrapped me in an embrace. "'A meadow, or a moor at sunrise, or walking across the moors, standing on a cliff, looking out to sea….' Every time I come here, and that's a lot, I think of what you said and of you, especially you."

"You said I'd be part of the picture," I whispered.

"You are. You always are."

I closed my eyes and, took a breath, swallowed hard. "Then tell me about this shadow hanging over us and what it is that you're holding back, dying to tell me, but can't."

He leaned in and put his chin on my shoulder, holding me tighter now to prevent me from escaping or keep me from falling. I could have gone either way.

His sigh brought goosebumps to my neck. "I've been dreading this," Quinn said. "But I'm not ready to watch you walk away forever."

"Oh God, you're married or engaged to that princess!" I blurted out and made ready to run, but Quinn held me firmly.

"No! It's not that."

"Then what? Are you dying of cancer or something? Is it guys? Do you prefer men?"

"Not that, either. And I don't have cancer or something. First confession. I lied to you, Alice. We aren't dating. Briony Atwell and I, it was a political thing for the orchestra. I broke it off. It was a sham, anyway."

"Were you trying to make me jealous?"

"Pretty much. No, I don't know what I was doing. I was jealous of your archeologist."

"Would you please stop calling him my archeologist? I don't own him, and he certainly doesn't have rights to me."

"But you're getting married in a few weeks, right?"

"Haven't made up my mind."

"Well, think about going through with it."

I was ready to argue, but his expression as he turned

me to face him convinced me silence was best.

"Second confession," he sighed. Quinn looked around, motioned towards a park bench near the Visitors Center and the castle precincts' outer curtain, and led me there.

"Alice, I haven't been telling you the truth about a lot of things."

His voice was serious, as were his dark eyes now catching the late afternoon sun. I felt a heaviness I'd not felt before, as if something or someone was pulling out my heart. The pressure seemed unbearable at first, and as the sky above me started to darken, I felt faint.

"Let's sit here," Quinn was saying. He sat close, took my hand, and was silent for the longest time. Finally, he turned and lifted my chin as if to kiss me. I would never forget that look.

The sun suddenly appeared from behind the clouds and shone brightly on us, glinting off the windows of the Visitor's Center so that it was annoying and blinding. I squinted as the light grew brighter and brighter, and then I sensed myself screaming, though no words or sound came from my throat. When I opened my eyes, I was in The Curiosity Shop.

"*NO!*" I screamed at The Proprietress. "It isn't fair!"

"Who said anything about life being fair—am I right, Your Grace?" The Proprietress sniped, tossing a look at Richard the Third.

"Don't bring me into your silly argument," Richard grumbled as he put aside his crossword puzzle and made for the espresso machine.

"Silly, is it?" Joan groused, joining me at the table.

"Of all emotions, love is the silliest," he countered. "And I think you would agree." His pencil was directed at The Proprietress.

"Indeed," she sniffed. "It makes us do foolish things, as your brother once said, Alice. It forces us to make decisions and promises that can't be kept. Or that we want to keep."

"Here's a thought," said Tyrone Power as he looked up from his poker game with Sigmund Freud. "It makes us happy."

"Can't argue with that," Freud sighed, throwing in his hand.

I ran to the literature rack and spun it, hoping a train ticket or anything like it would take me back to Scarborough. There was nothing to help, and I looked around The Shop desperately. Tears started welling in my eyes, and I swallowed the lump in my throat as I choked back a sob.

I reached into my pocket for a tissue and pulled out a marvelous, beautiful, perfectly oval stone instead.

It was the color of my book, which The Proprietress removed from the case and placed on the velvet cushion. She fished about in her handbag, pulling out a transfer sheet upon which there was a single gold star. It was placed carefully in the middle of the next to the last page. The star suddenly became iridescent and sparkling as if alive.

"Alice, if you please?" The Proprietress took my box from the shelf and opened it, looking at me from over her glasses. She jerked her chin towards the box, and I set this new object with the other two. "Now it's done—or will be soon enough. Two wrongs definitely make a right!"

The stones began to glow, and the light became a blinding, painful flash. When I was able to see again, I was back at Scarborough. The sun was setting and had stopped glinting off the windows. I glanced at Quinn and waited.

"The stories about me, well, some of them were true," he began. "I won't get into the whole story now because they're in the past, and the only person I hurt was myself. But I wanted you to know. I ruined every chance I had with the orchestra to get back at my parents. I wanted to show them I was a regular guy with regular interests, not some damn musical prodigy. More than anything, I wanted to ruin my father's career because that was my life. My life, my accomplishments, and my talent were my father's career. I atoned for those sins and am where I am because, fortunately, someone had faith in me."

He paused a moment, wiping a tear from his cheek. Then, "You know what my life was like growing up—what with my parents, everything. My father controlled everything, from when I got up and what breakfast I ate, to who my friends were. I was pretty much forced into everything I did except the attempt at ice hockey. Everything I wanted was taken away until I only loved the music and the cello. I was able to lose myself and get away from everything that hurt."

"I always felt bad because I couldn't help you."

"You did. You weren't so much a faery princess as an angel. My guardian angel."

"Please don't call me an angel. I'm far from that!" I protested.

"You are! Don't you see, Alice? You kept me sane, and when we were together…"

"Why didn't you stand up to him? If you had, we'd be married today."

"You've got every right to resent me for that," Quinn sighed as he let go of my hands and moved away just a bit, looking at his hands, which were trembling.

"I'm sorry! I've been holding that in for years," I murmured and wiped away fresh tears.

"And I blew some pretty good opportunities to set things right with you," Quinn said now, turning to face me.

Here it comes. . .

"Well, that goes both ways, doesn't it? I did some things,"

"Even so, I'm one fucked up guy. You must know

that. If we had gotten married, God knows what might have happened. It might not have lasted a year. And it's all because of my father. I know that now."

"Quinn,"

"Alice, he was a monster. He did things to me..."

"Don't tell me, please. I can guess. It will only make me sick to my stomach!"

Quinn kept going, however. "It went as far as my mother, too. This wasn't something we shared with our friends and neighbors. We didn't talk about it then—we don't today. If I had courage! Look what I've done!"

He broke down. I embraced him as hard as possible and felt his tears on my shoulders and didn't mind that he was squeezing the air out of me. He was safe with me, and he knew it.

"Quinn, no matter what, no matter . . . I love you! I always will!" I whispered. "I just wish I could have helped."

Quinn nodded and moved away, wiping his eyes. "It broke me, destroyed me. Now I'm so confused about who and what I am, Alice. My father taught me that what he did was normal. I was confused and ashamed. I saw how other parents acted with their kids, and there were Dennis and you. The love was so obvious, and it was there. I wanted that kind of family, a place where I felt safe. Ever since I can remember, my father used me."

He paused, and I drew Quinn into my arms. He leaned against me, and again, I felt his tears, how he desperately tried to stay composed. I kissed him gently and touched his cheek.

Drawing a breath, he continued. "That Christmas when I proposed, and my parents and I argued was the worst. When I got home from your place, I unlocked the gun my mother kept in her study and thought about killing myself. Then I found my father and threatened him. He turned it around and threatened you, said he knew people who could ruin you and Dennis, said he'd send someone to your place—never mind. This is probably shocking you, isn't it?"

I shook my head.

Not what I had done before.

"I got the worst beating of my life when he followed me to the library and asked what I was doing. So I got on that plane as my parents demanded and regretted it. I soon started to forget and got lost in my studies and work, but there wasn't a day I didn't think about you. I wanted to pick up the phone, but I thought you wouldn't care by then. Or you'd hate me."

The sky was darkening as if the sun was being extinguished. The shadows were lengthening. The wind became bitterly cold, and I needed to be away from Quinn despite this. I was going to be sick. Whispering an apology, I locked myself in the women's room and knelt over the ancient toilet as waves of nausea made me vomit for what seemed forever. And then I wept.

I don't know how long I knelt in that stall, but The Proprietress was there and handed me paper towels and a glass of water when I came out.

"You weren't supposed to know all of it." Her voice lacked its sarcasm and bite. It was a quiet statement and one made with concern.

"It's not something people talked about then," I said, wiping my mouth and then rinsing, taking a drink of water. "He needs me, and I won't be able to help."

"He needs time, and you can give him that."

"But that would mean…no."

"Which Hell is worse, Alice Rose?" The Proprietress asked quietly. "His or yours?"

It dawned on me, then. "Two wrongs make a right," I whispered.

"Get back out there. Quinn needs you. You need him."

Obedient to her will as always, I nodded and left the women's room. Quinn was still sitting on the bench, not, as I imagined, standing at the cliff and ready to throw himself off. He looked up and smiled as I approached and held out his hand.

"Thank you. I've been holding that in for so long. You are the only person I've told."

"Haven't you told your mother?"

"No. I'm almost ready for that. You know, I've always felt so ashamed, so different. And then I met you. I've always been attracted to you since we came from England. I was ten. I never knew what to say to you or how to act, but you had such a beautiful smile, large eyes, and gentleness. I could lose myself and my shame just being around you. All I had to do was say, 'Hey! Alice.'"

"And I waited for you outside my locker, hoping you'd come by and say hello."

"Here's another confession. At first, I wanted to be with you to annoy my father. Oh, it did—he didn't like it one bit! Then after we started meeting in the music room for lunch, and when we went on our first date, I knew that wasn't the real reason. It was because I loved you. I couldn't wait to see you every day, and when we made love…."

My heart was pounding, and I was breathless when he took my face in his hands and kissed me, perhaps one of the most intimate and passionate we shared.

"I need your forgiveness, Alice!"

I smiled up into his eyes, which were brighter now. "No, you don't," I whispered. "I've forgiven you a hundred times."

"I'm afraid I'm going to hurt you again." He cradled my head on his breast and said, "I want to be with you for the rest of our lives. I've never given up hope, but I must figure myself out. I need to handle my anger and pain, and I can't expect you to take on the burden. I need time."

"How much do you want, Quinn?"

"I don't know," he repeated himself. "That's why you should go ahead and marry him if that's what you want. I can deal with it."

"And if I don't?"

"The time isn't right. Not yet. One last confession. When I go home next month, I'm going to the Berkeley Police and tell them all that happened. It's going to kill my mother, I know it. I hate doing this, but I can't go on. And I'm going to get some help."

"You know that I will always be there for you no matter what. When you've sorted out things, give me a sign, and I'll come to you, and we'll take it from there. If it turns out that we cannot be lovers, at least we will be friends. I know that much," I whispered as I kissed him.

"I'm asking so much of you!"

"It's something I'm not afraid to take on."

He stood and pulled me up with him, and we walked down Castle Hill with the sun barely a pink ribbon on the horizon. Back at the house, I curled up on the rug at his feet while he played the cello. Before we went to bed that night, he played his rendition of *A Time for Us* again, singing the lyrics in Italian in his clear, bari-tenor voice.

Going up, he turned me gently on the stairwell and whispered, "You're not married yet, Alice!" before he kissed me.

Our two nights together were nothing like those I had with Donovan. They were full of tenderness and love, a passion born of love and respect that made his revelation easier. It made our parting less painful—and full of hope.

I took the Ralph Vaughan Williams album from a cupboard in my living room in Gillygate and handed it to Quinn when he came to say goodbye after our return to York.

"Here's the sign. Return it, and I'll know we'll both have a lot to talk about."

Quinn's eyes widened at the sight of the album. "I gave this to you…are you sure about this? Everything?"

"It gives me, us, hope."

That hope, which had faded and died several times in my life, was reborn in me the day the record album arrived.

CHAPTER 20

THE RECORD ALBUM sat on a shelf for weeks while I made plans.

"Why are you keeping it?" Donovan wanted to know when he found it and blew off the dust. "We don't have a turntable."

"Donovan, it's a memento from a simpler time," I remarked, looking up from my monograph editing. "Leave it, would you?"

Donovan's face screwed up in a frown. "Dear God in heaven! It's that Vaughan Williams piece, the one you played over and over. Didn't you ever get tired of listening to it?"

"Leave it!" There was too much emphasis on the word 'leave.' I grabbed the album from him and tucked it into a cupboard beneath the stereo.

"As you wish," he said sarcastically and walked across the living room to the liquor cabinet, pulling out his bottle of scotch and a glass.

Three, I counted to myself. Three drinks, and it was only eleven in the morning.

"How'd the meeting go?" I asked, listening to the crackle of liquid hitting ice.

"Wish you could've been there, Angel. The dig at Ephesus looks like it's the next big thing. National Geographic is coming along. They're also going to fund the exploration and dig of a nearby Crusader castle, and I thought of you immediately for a historical authority in determining provenance. My department head agrees."

"Not that." I scratched out a sentence so violently that

my movement tore the page. "The Al-Anon meeting—oh, sorry! You skipped it."

"Well, if you knew I skipped it, why'd you ask?" Donovan laughed.

I tossed down the red pen so that it clattered on the tabletop. "It hasn't been that long since the hearing, and you promised the judge and your probation officer that you'd show up!"

"This dig is bigger and better than Petra, Angel, and will make me in the community."

I leaned back in the chair and folded my arms across my breasts. "Won't mean a thing if you get thrown into jail, Donovan."

"So I'll ask my father to talk to his friends at the courthouse! Besides, I don't think Turkey has an extradition agreement with the United States."

"Thought of everything, have you?" I asked quietly. "Donovan, I'm sick and tired of your using the family name and wealth to get what you want and get you out of trouble. This isn't a traffic ticket that can be fixed!"

"Calm down!" Donovan snickered. He knocked back the drink and poured another, bigger than the last. "Want to come? We can use your expertise on the period."

"You've never asked me before. Why start now?"

"I'll be gone for several months. It's been rough, what with the accident and losing the baby. We haven't spent much time together and talked about things. We could use the trip for that if you want."

"I'll think about it."

"Don't take too long, Angel. We leave at the end of the week."

He picked up the drink, took a pull, and raised the glass to me, winking, as he left the room, whistling *A Time for Us*.

"Do you love me, Alice?" he whispered as we said goodbye three days later. He was going to Turkey alone.

"Yes," I said.

I waved from the stoop as the airport van pulled away from the curb, then closed the door quietly.

"I lied," I said to the empty room. I had decided my fate.

While Donovan dug in ancient ruins and made more money for his building, I packed up everything I owned and shipped it to California. I turned in my resignation from the university and sent Harry word that I was coming home. Late that night, before my flight back to California, I felt more alive than I'd ever been.

I fell into a blissful and comforting sleep and woke on the park bench across the street from the church in The Village. Strangely, the sky was dusky, and lights were going on the entire length of the high street. The Proprietress was closing the blinds and locking up for the night—something I'd never seen before. One by one, Joan of Arc, Sigmund Freud, Richard the Third, Marie Antoinette, and Anne Boleyn, the other historical personalities and luminaries, left The Shop and dissolved as if into vapor as they walked down the lane, replaced in turn by fireflies. Even the train went through The Village without stopping, becoming a flickering light on the horizon.

Only Dennis, my brother, remained in The Village. Standing at the window in The Curiosity Shop, he turned and smiled as I gathered my things.

"You broke a few rules. It doesn't surprise me," he commented.

I spun around; my brows knit together in puzzlement. "I did exactly what you told me I could do. As I thought of them, I relived moments."

"And you changed the ending to the story—several times. It's been interesting."

"That's an understatement, Denny!" I laughed.

"How do you feel?"

I paused, carefully slipping the garnet cross around my

neck. "I feel like—I want to go home."

"Soon."

"But I feel like I am home."

"You get that way. It gets to you eventually, and you want to scream. And then you just settle."

"What about you?" I asked.

"Oh, I've done this already. This was for you. I've stopped wondering, stopped worrying. You will, too, in time," he said, joining me at the table. He picked up one of my sketchbooks, pausing at the sketches of the prom dress, the fabric swatches taped to the drawings. "One last question."

"Not a question, but an answer. The two wrongs that made a right—Donovan and everything he did, and the Professor," I said as I shut down the laptop and loaded the messenger bag. "The right was us. Quinn and me."

"I knew you'd eventually get it."

"See you around, Dennis," I said, kissing his cheek. I wasn't surprised that it felt cold and that he started to lose his robust color and age before me. Nor was I surprised when I glanced at my reflection in the window as I went out the door that I was a middle-aged woman. Turning back, I looked closely. I looked the same, but there was a difference. There was tranquility, a softness. The hair was now a white-silver that shimmered in the dusky light; the face was surprisingly unlined—there were a few lines around the mouth and eyes, what people call laugh lines; the eyes were still large and luminous despite the eyelids gently folding over them.

"Mighty fine, Alice!"

Dennis winked and was transformed by soft showers of color and finally into a speck of light, a firefly, but that light dissolved slowly.

Peace continued to settle on me as I watched him leave. I breathed and sucked in the early night air out in the street.

I didn't know where I was going, but I started to walk up the street towards the church. With each step, I felt like someone was pulling on me, shaking me. Then I felt as if I was floating and falling; I began to effortlessly glide until I was flying through the iridescent lapis stone, overwhelmed by the beauty of the color and warmth. I never wanted to leave this place.

The voices came to me slowly, gibberish at first, then as if they were underwater—or was I underwater? I couldn't tell.

I opened my eyes and looked at the doctor staring down at me. "Doctor Martin, can you hear me?"

Of course I could! Why was he shouting?

Other faces peered down at me; their expressions were all the same: disbelief and shock. The desire to sleep was overwhelming, and as I closed my eyes, I drifted back to The Village and found it empty. I walked up the high street and looked for my friends, who were gone. A hundred fireflies seemed to light up the night sky. It had never been night before in The Village. Again, I was floating, bathed in glorious light that changed brightness and hue, so beautiful I wanted to weep with joy.

The voices came out of nowhere, and I felt something cold on my forehead. When I opened my eyes, a nurse was checking my vital signs. "Don't exert yourself, Doctor Martin," she said kindly and patted my hand. "That tube is a bother, isn't it?"

I tried to nod, but a tube going down my throat made it impossible to move without pain. Very weakly and with great effort, I tried to point to the tube, trying to make a sign that I wanted it out. The doctor was at the bedside again and seemed to understand. He took the hand not running IV lines. "When I draw out the tube, Doctor, I want you to cough."

The pain was terrible, but I sucked in great breaths and tried to smile. The doctor and nurses surrounding me nodded and looked at each other, smiling as if I had done something remarkable.

"Amazing," one nurse said quietly to another. "I counted fifteen minutes—it's impossible."

"She's here with us, isn't she?" Harry was at the bedside; his face blotched with tears. He took my hand and leaned closer, whispering, "He arrived a few minutes ago. I'll go get him…"

No!!

The last person I wanted at my deathbed was Donovan Trist.

"How…can you …do this . . . to me?" I croaked with ragged gasps for breath. "Haven't I been through enough?"

Harry looked above me and to my left at a cardiac monitor. "It's jumping around again, Doctor! Can we get something for her?"

Harry, Dennis was right! Please, no more! Why are you doing this?

The words were there but wouldn't come out of my throat. I looked at everyone in the room desperately, pleading. They just kept smiling.

"There's my faery princess!"

Quinn's voice was like an electric shock.

I turned and succumbed to his awkward embrace necessitated by the tubes and IV units, the machines that had and were keeping me alive.

How good of him to come, I thought. Donovan hadn't made an effort. But then, he had never been one to deal with others' pain.

Quinn brushed the hair out of my eyes, and I noticed the white gold wedding band on his ring finger. So he had married, after all, I thought mournfully. Then I saw the matching band on my left ring finger and gasped and laughed.

"What's so funny?" Quinn wiped my face gently with

a rosemary-scented washcloth. "You look like a faery princess with a secret, Missus Radcliffe."

"Then I've done it," I murmured, smiling and feeling like I would sleep again.

"Done what?" Quinn laughed gently.

"Dennis said I could do what I wanted—it wasn't about angels getting wings or Buffalo Gals. I could do what I wanted. It was all about what I wanted," I murmured as sleep overwhelmed me. "I got what I wanted after all."

The world between consciousness and sleep had now taken over entirely. I willingly gave myself up to its deliciousness; the bed was Quinn's in Scarborough; I was covered in the fluffiest eiderdown and the softest wool. Everything held his scent. I closed my eyes for a moment and then opened them, quite sure that Quinn would be gone and part of a lovely dream was finally over. Donovan would enter the hospital room and begin disapproving of everything and everyone.

No, there was Quinn.

I heard his voice softly singing to me as if he could read my thoughts. I started to laugh, though the pain was shooting through me.

"One pill makes you larger, and one pill makes you small…"

"…I honestly didn't think you would have the nerve to do it," said The Proprietress a very long time after my release from the hospital.

She brought me a cup of coffee in my favorite mug, the travel mug with the strawberries on it, and set it before my laptop on the table—my usual table by the window looking out onto the high street of The Village. It had come back to life when I returned. Fortunately, I was one of the sages this time, helping lost souls figure out what they wanted to do. Joan of Arc was with me, as were Richard the Third, Anne Boleyn, and Eleanor of Aquitaine. Marie Antoinette stopped by now and then when she wasn't in a snit over something Richard or Joan had said or done. The others came and went as they pleased. Dennis spent most of his time now correcting, or what he thought was correcting, the costume sketches in my notebooks or proofreading my writing. Once in a while, he commented on something.

The Proprietress pasted stars in books and stamped inside covers. Once in a while, she took a box to be opened by a novice guest down from the shelf and placed it reverently on the velvet cushion. The light that shot out of the box when the lid was thrown back was always spectacular.

"It couldn't have happened any other way," Joan of Arc said.

"I'd like to think that I mended a broken heart," I chirped as I settled in for that day's work. "I put the pieces back together, didn't I?"

"Yes, you did!" Joan exclaimed and clicked her coffee cup to my travel mug.

My new life began.

Well, it didn't truly begin for another day, or what might have been a day in The Village where the sun rarely set, a village that looked like it was taken from the pages of a Thomas Hardy novel—or one of mine.

That day began like any other.

The Proprietress stood behind the counter stamping books, and my brother Dennis was whipping up a cheesecake at the café bar. Joan of Arc and Richard the Third shared a crossword puzzle, and Joan managed to keep her temper and her hand off her sword. Eleanor of Aquitaine had taken up a pencil and sought to improve my costume sketches. No one looked up when the bell over the door tinkled.

I heard the footsteps and looked up from my writing and felt a familiar blush rising in my cheeks as Quinn, looking lost, glanced around and saw me. He smiled and joined me at my table, suddenly comfortable and aware of his new home, looking perfectly happy.

In that knee-weakening smile, the same smile that had stolen my heart so many, many years before, I knew I would be loved for all eternity.

Not Quite the End ....

Books by Ellen L. Ekstrom

The Legacy
What She Wished For . . . a Cautionary Tale
Armor of Light
Tallis' Third Tune – Midwinter Sonata, Book 1
Scarborough: Quinn's Story – Midwinter Sonata, Book 2
St. Edmund Wood
Ascalon
The Shop Girl of Flowergate

Forthcoming Titles

George of Grasmere
The Shambles – Midwinter Sonata, Book 3
Swannsaeld
The Sometime Queen – A Cheshire Tale
In Fair Verona
Ladysword

❀WRV❀

About the Author

Ellen L. Ekström is a native of the San Francisco Bay Area and was educated locally. She received a bachelor's degree in theological studies with her concentration in Christian Mythos, also known as church history, and a sub-specialty in Christian Social Ethics. She took honors for both. Ordained to the vocational diaconate in 2002, she is a clergywoman in the Episcopal Church and is retired from parish ministry but still active in social justice issues and pastoral care.

Ellen has been fascinated by all things medieval since childhood. Her preferred genres are fantasy and historical. Just as a painter has many subjects to bring to a canvas, Ellen believes that there are many stories to tell, and to limit oneself to a niche isn't the way she lives or thinks.